CURRENTS OF POWER

CURRENTS OF POWER

▼

A Modern Political Novel

Claude Walker

Writers Club Press

San Jose New York Lincoln Shanghai

Currents of Power
A Modern Political Novel

Writers Club Press
an imprint of iUniverse.com, Inc.

For information address:
iUniverse.com, Inc.
5220 S 16th, Ste. 200
Lincoln, NE 68512
www.iuniverse.com

ISBN: 0-595-18518-5

Printed in the United States of America

Dedicated to my wife, Ngoan Lê,
my mom, Nancy Ferraro,
the memory of my pal, Kevin Sullivan,
and
anyone who has ever worked on a political campaign.

Acknowledgements

Humble acknowledgements are extended to the following authors:

Joseph Conrad, *"Heart of Darkness"*
Ralph Waldo Emerson, *"Two Rivers"*
Herman Hesse, *"Siddhartha"*
Langston Hughes, *"The Negro Speaks of Rivers"* and *"The Negro"*
Mark Twain, *"The Adventures of Huckleberry Finn"*
Walt Whitman, *"O Captain, My Captain"*
Photo: R. Shapiro

"Springs, streams, creeks. They all eventually flow into that river," Billy said, gazing out from their perch. *"Same as politics. Different forces surge and then subside. Some dry up, like Abernathy Creek over there. Some coalesce into floods…"*

Billy A. Miller, Democratic Party Chairman, Sauk County

Contents

Cast: *The Forces of Nature*

The Candidates

Philip Royce Blasingame III, 31, Vice-President of Blasingame Steel & Coil Company

Thelma Burnett, 57, *"Amen Now!"* State Action Coordinator

Professor Dan Clark, 34, instructor of History and Political Science at Flagstaff Community College

Alderman George "Butchie" Kaminski, 36, Jackson City Council member representing the 6th Ward

Commissioner Mary Moore, 56, Acting Chairperson of the State Public Utilities Commission

Alderman Shawn Petacque, 45, Jackson City Council member representing the 15th Ward

State Senator Paul Podesta, 64, (D-Mohawk Valley)

Commissioner Graciela Torres, 38, Jackson County Board member

The Deceased

Commissioner Calvin Reynolds, 52, Chairman of the State Public Utilities Commission

Eva Vargas, 27; Felicity Vargas, 5; Bree Vargas, 3, and the other 15 victims at River's Edge

Bosses & Pols, Hired Guns & Rented Strangers, Advisors, Lovers, Players, Betrayers

Michelle Baldini, 25, secretary
Tina Bishop, 41, Political Director for Royce Blasingame campaign
Jimmy Blake, 49, operative-at-large for Gov. Langley
Tug Blaney, 71, Republican Chairman of Fox County
Anna Bloom, 34, Democratic fundraiser
Piney Blue Bluford, 78, retired musician
Peggy Briscoe, 43, Communications Director, Mary Moore campaign
Pudge Carson, 66, fishing buddy and confidante to Sen. Paul Podesta
Liz Chinn, 30, Dresden Foundation staffer on loan to run Dan Clark's campaign
Rev. B.J. Crandall, 59, Christian Marchers state director, possible U.S. Senate candidate
Johnny "Boss Chizz" Czyz, 72, Democratic Committeeman of Jackson City's 6th Ward
Jim Davis, 22, recent college grad working at *ProAction*
Petra Dresden, 57, philanthropist, President of the *Dresden Foundation for Democracy's Future*
Deanna Drew, 34, Deputy Campaign Manager, Shane for Governor
Seamus Dunne, 67, Democratic Committeeman of Jackson City's 3rd Ward
Chemuyil Gardner, 33, Chief-of-Staff to Ald. Shawn Petacque
Stan Flanders, 54, Vice-President for Legislative Affairs, Eaton Gas Company
Niles Flint, 49, Chairman of the State Democratic Party
Gretchen Hanson, 50, Chairman of the State Republican Party
Amy Harris, 21, spy
Jimmy Juarez, 61, Democratic Committeeman of the 33rd Ward
Mike Kula, 32, Aide to Ald. Butchie Kaminski
Governor Tom Langley, 62, three-term Governor, soon to retire
James LeMans, 63, entrepreneur, philanthropist
State Sen. Beatrice Madison, 66, legislator, Democratic Party leader

Damen Maxwell, 27, Moore Campaign Manager
Consuelo Milagro, 42, wife of Ald. Shawn Petacque
Billy A. Miller, 41, Democratic Chairman of rural Sauk County
Tony Moore, 24, son of Randall and Mary Moore
Wally Mraz, 45, political operative and dirty trickster hired by Podesta
Kevin O'Malley, 52, lobbyist
Steven Page, 36, Special Advisor to Gov. Langley
Nicky Pulver, 33, Vice-President of *ProAction*, a political consulting firm
Sam Roth, 22, Political Director for the Torres campaign
Manny Ruiz, 35, Director of *Flagstaff Friends & Neighbors*, college buddy of Dan Clark
Sandra Siquieros, 38, Torres Campaign Manager
State Rep. Laura Southampton (R-Jackson City), 48, Jackson City Coordinator for Blasingame
Timmy Sullivan, 35, labor operative assigned to Sen. Podesta's campaign
Mayor Bob Townshend, 62, Jackson City Mayor for 13 years
Arnold Wiser, 39, whistleblower at Eaton Gas Company
Lupe Zarate, 27, Chief-of-Staff to Comm. Graciela Torres
Del Zink, 46, Issues Advisor, Moore Campaign

Candidates for other offices

Lawrence Burl, 59, publisher and a Democratic candidate for Governor
Jackson County prosecutor Aviva Benson, 48, a Republican candidate for Attorney General
Attorney General Lou Calcagno, 62, Democrat seeking reelection
State Rep. Tom Cummings, 36, Democratic nominee for State Treasurer
Secretary of State Richard Dobbs, 64, a Republican seeking reelection
Philip Driscoll, 52, a Republican candidate for Attorney General
Karen Hogan, 44, state Arts Council member and Republican nominee for State Treasurer
Mayor Bill Karmejian, 56, Democratic nominee for Secretary of State
Congressman Paul Prentice, 61, a Republican candidate for Governor

State Senator Esther Ruelbach, 70, a Republican candidate for Governor
State Senator Debra Shane, 49, a Democratic candidate for Governor

The Media

Peter "Pequeno" Barragan, 65, Editor of *"Hoy!"*
Darlene Dawes, 24, street reporter for Channel 14 TV
JJ Springfield, 53, Editor of *"JJ Springfield's Daily Bulletin"*, a political gossip fax service

Chapter One

Wellsprings, Part I

"Going up that river was like traveling back to the earliest beginnings of the world, when vegetation rioted and big trees were kings."

-Mark Twain *("The Adventures of Huckleberry Finn")*

Commissioner Reynolds never saw the truck that hit him.

He had just spent two uneventful days and one hot night in Cancun, Mexico. The two days were courtesy of the state's taxpayers, who had graciously sent him to the Caribbean Mecca for the 18th Annual Conference of State Public Utilities Regulators. His one eventful night was courtesy of Ana Villasenor, a 34-year old teacher from Chetumal, who was in town visiting friends.

After the final, painful seminar on the "Future of Digital", Reynolds changed clothes at his hotel and strolled the beach in Cancun's glitzy hotel zone. It was early Friday evening; he had two nights and a day of free time and was ready to relax. The turquoise blue water, powdery white sand and several Corona's helped Reynolds disengage from the arcane world of utility regulation.

As he approached one noisy beachfront cantina, Reynolds immediately spotted Ana Villasenor and her bikini-clad girlfriends. Reynolds, a tan and trim Vietnam vet, lost no time in striking up a conversation with the trio, in particular Ana, whose English was flawless and smile dazzling.

No stranger to the Cancun late night discoteca scene, Ana was quick-witted and flirtatious. She traced her fingernails around Reynolds' "Saigon" tattoo and he flirted back, mocking his inability to pronounce her name and brushing against her. Within hours, after countless margaritas, the two of them were in passionate embrace in his beachfront hotel room.

After a sumptuous room service breakfast and jacuzzi romp the next morning, Ana explained she had missed her ride back to Chetumal, the state capital. The chivalrous Public Utilities Commissioner quickly offered to escort Ana home, a four-hour drive.

Heading south from Cancun to Chetumal, the flat, dry limestone and hennequin of Yucatan's east coast gradually gives way to hilly, misty forests where jaguars roam. Tarantulas creep slowly across the highway. The Spirit of Maya pervades.

Chetumal, a raw bustling port city of a quarter-million people, became the state capital of Quintana Roo in 1974. Ships dock there to export timber products. The highway from the north is usually desolate except for hardworking lumber rigs.

Zipping down that highway, Reynolds was still basking in the sweat and bliss of his night and day with Ana when the front left tire blew on his rented Volkswagen. After ten frustrating minutes of figuring out the jack, Reynolds crouched next to the wounded Bug, which was parked on a shoulderless winding road with jungle walls encroaching on the potholed asphalt.

Guillermo Chavez had been driving trucks since he was 14. He could handle any kind of rig under any conditions. This morning, Chavez had a full load of freshly hewn timber destined for Galveston via the docks in Chetumal and he was running late. He glanced at the clock in his dashboard. The dash was decorated with pictures of his wife, a plastic statue of Our Lady of Guadalupe and a Florida Marlins sticker. A Madonna cassette blared from tinny speakers.

A mile south, Ana watched Reynolds changing the tire. He seemed like a really nice guy. Probably married she thought, and kind of old for her taste, but a sweet lover. She drew on a cigarette and vaguely noticed the echoes of the downshifting truck gears, but they seemed remote. Several trucks belching smoke and commotion had passed them since the tire blew.

As he rounded the curve, Chavez heard the ping of the snapped cable and felt the load of logs shift on his truck's rusty flatbed. He tapped the brakes and the rusty rig weaved. The load shifted again. He caught a fleeting glimpse of the slim woman and the red VW. The veteran trucker did not, however, see Reynolds crouched next to the vehicle, nor did he hear the truck's front fended severing Reynolds' spine, killing him instantly.

So Commissioner Reynolds, who adeptly maneuvered in the jungles of Vietnam and the corridors of power in his state Capitol, ended a distinguished career of public service on a desolate Mexican highway. Changing a tire.

*   *   *

Steven Page had been an aide to Governor Tom Langley for nearly twelve years and was looking forward to the end of this term. Langley recently announced his plans to retire after three terms in the Governor's Mansion, and Page, who had put his life on hold when Langley recruited him as a scheduler in his first campaign, was ready for a break.

Twelve years ago, Page had been humbled by Langley's job offer. Precise and diligent, Page brought efficiency to the candidate's chaotic scheduling operation, and mastered the art and science of advance work. He worked 16-hour days for months, never griping. While not known as an "issues man", Page did his job well and rose through the ranks of the campaign hierarchy. After the victory, Page was rewarded with a $79,000 "Special Advisor to the Governor" post. Pleasant and methodical, he was a frequent traveling companion of the Governor and Mrs. Langley.

Page was in the front set of the Governor's black limousine along with Slim Hodges, gubernatorial driver, bodyguard and bartender. In the plush back seat sat the Governor, Mrs. Langley and "Tug" Blaney, the longtime Republican boss of Fox County. Blaney was briefing the Governor on the need for more state highway jobs to be given to worthy Fox County Republican precinct workers.

Blaney didn't miss a beat in extolling the splendid work ethic of Fox County Republicans when the car phone chirped. Page grabbed it and was surprised to hear Elinor Rollins, the Governor's personal secretary, say the U.S. State Department needed to speak with the Governor about an "emergency situation".

Page dialed the State Department regional chief and handed the phone back to Langley. The State Department regretfully informed the Governor that Commissioner Reynolds had suffered a close encounter with a fender in Mexico.

*   *   *

For decades, the state Public Utilities Commission had been a sleepy little bureaucracy, a patronage dumping ground for whichever party occupied the Governor's Mansion. Two previous PUC Chairmen had gone onto higher office—one U.S. Senator and one state Attorney General—but most PUC Chairmen went into private sector work (often with one of the electric, gas, phone or cable companies) following their tenure.

The PUC Chairman had been appointed by the Governor since 1913. Then, about ten years ago, the Democratic House Speaker and Democratic Senate President conspired to ram a bill through changing the Commission Chairmanship to an elective post. The maneuver took Langley by surprise and put him square in the hot seat. The clamor by the state's editorial boards and good government types compelled him to sign the bill. He then pushed hard in the special election that followed for his old Army pal and chief fundraiser Calvin Reynolds, who easily became the state's first popularly-elected PUC Chair.

Reynolds had no public utility experience. He had no experience in government regulation or public administration. His sole qualification for the job was serving in the Army with Langley during the fall of Saigon in 1975 and a knack for raising campaign funds in huge sums.

Active in his local Chamber of Commerce, Reynolds was an unabashed supporter of the business establishment. As Public Utilities Commission Chairman, he wielded a tough gavel at public hearings on utility rates and service issues. He opened the door for the big electric companies to build nuclear power plants across the state and winked at the gas companies when some consumer groups howled about pipeline safety. And the utilities were appreciative of the Governor and his "PUCK Czar", as Reynolds' called himself. Various loopholes in the state's antiquated campaign finance laws allowed utility companies to express that appreciation in large fashion.

Reynolds, an energetic campaigner who had been elected by wide margins, was an odds-on favorite to win another term next year. The rumor mill was aquiver with the word that Reynolds had a cool million in his campaign war chest, enough to discourage serious challengers from either party. A million will buy plenty of TV airtime and Reynolds cut a dashing figure: War Vet. Businessman. Loving Father and Husband. Public Servant. And thisclose to the Governor.

During Reynolds' last race (which turned out to really be his last race), the number of Reynolds ads TV was surpassed only by the number of "Langley for Governor" spots. And with Langley's recent decision to retire, the pundits were already proclaiming Reynolds the next Governor. Until that fender in Yucatan.

$$* \qquad * \qquad *$$

"Uh, Tug, we got a situation here, gimme a moment," Langley said as the sun set over the cornfields.

"Wha, sure 'nough, Governor! Now Miz Langley, lemme tellya, the Republican Women's Auxiliary of Fox County have put together a little, uh, a little recipe book as sort of a fundraisin' gimmick, ya know, and

some of these recipes lemme tellya are out of this world, in fact ahm proud
to report to ya that my little niece Jessie, ah believe you 'n the Governor
met little Jessie at the State Fair last summer, well anyhow, Jessie has her
own recipe for a pumpkin cream pie that'll just knock yer damn socks off,
Miz Langley, no offense intended, ma'am." Blaney took a breath.

"None taken, Tug, it sounds delicious. Pumpkin cream pie," Betty
Langley said, smiling and feigning interest just as her husband had only
moments before. Her primary concerns were to avoid having Tug's unlit
saliva-coated cigar brush against her dress and to find out what big news
flash had just been relayed to their car.

Langley leaned toward the front seat. "Steven, get through to Mary
Moore right away, and whoever the PUC flack is."

"Peggy Briscoe?"

"Yeah, Briscoe. Have Moore come down to the Capitol to meet first
thing tomorrow morning. Call Blake and have him call the Speaker,
Podesta, O'Malley. Dammit. Have Elinor send Moira flowers; I'll call her
later. And call that State Department guy and find out what the hell our
boy was doing in the goddamned Mexican jungle."

Page took it all down and took the carphone back from the Governor.

Betty Langley knew that moments like this—moments of crisis—were
those when her husband was at his finest, when he truly defined himself.
He was getting bored and impatient with all the small talk, gossip and
innuendo of politics, and was getting less enthused about spending hours
riding through endless cornfields with guys named Tug. Maybe it was his
military training or his zeal to get things done, but when it was crunch
time, Tom Langley was a rational man of action. He was a galloping gladiator when the clock was running.

The Governor settled back into the leather seat and looked ashen.

"Calvin's dead. Car crash in Mexico."

Betty gasped. There was silence in the limo except for the wind
whistling through a vent window Slim had cracked opened. Everyone,
even Tug Blaney, knew how far back Langley and Reynolds went.

"He was a good man, Tug, a good friend," Langley whispered. Betty squeezed his hand.

"Yessir, Governor, a very good man," Tug replied, knowing the Governor didn't hear him and was already deep in thought and memories as the black gubernatorial limo hurtled through the dusk.

*   *   *

Mary Moore, Vice-Chair of the state Public Utilities Commission, was, of course, among the first to hear of Reynolds' accident. As his first-in-command, Mary Moore ran the Commission's day-to-day operations, managed the 230-person staff and became a self-taught expert in utility rate-setting.

As a blond, teenaged cheerleader, Moore had volunteered for the Barry Goldwater campaign, caught the political bug and worked her way up to head the Republican Party in Zane Township, a rural area just beginning to suburbanize some 50 miles east of metropolitan Jackson City. In those days, Zane Township was home to about 10,000 residents, mostly the Republican sons and daughters of farmers.

Farms soon gave way to strip malls. Mobile-home Bible-thumpers gave way to SUV-driving, pro-choice soccer moms. Zane Township grew to more than 50,000 residents, including former city dwellers fed up with grime, crime and corruption.

The one-time Goldwater Girl became more moderate as did ZaneTownship. Moore expanded her political power base in suburban township GOP politics and discovered her vocational niche at the Commission. She went back to school and earned an MBA, specializing in the politics of utility deregulation. Their last child, Tony, had just moved out, so Mary and her husband Randall were thinking about remodeling the house, maybe traveling in Europe.

When her phone rang at home that Saturday evening, Mary was somewhat surprised to hear the voice of gubernatorial aide Steven Page. She had always liked Steven, remembering his youthful Ken-doll looks during Tom Langley's first race.

"Well, Steven, how's our favorite Governor tonight?" Moore could tell Page was calling from a car phone and rightly guessed that Langley was within earshot.

"Well, Commissioner, I'm afraid we have some very distressing news," Page spoke slowly. He understood that part of his job entailed being the occasional bearer of bad news, sometimes being the hatchet man. Steven never enjoyed these roles (though he suspected that aides like Jimmy Blake relished them) and this one was particularly tough.

"What is it, Steven?"

"Well, apparently Commissioner Reynolds has been in an accident of some kind in Mexico."

"A car accident?"

"Yes, ma'am."

"Is he okay?" Moore asked, but a lump was already forming in her throat, cutting off her breath.

"No, I'm sorry, we're told it was a fatal crash and he was killed," Page paused. "We don't really have too many details. It was in Mexico. He was a good man, Commissioner Reynolds was," Steven struggled to keep his composure.

Mary felt a cold shudder tremble across her body. She had worked closely with Reynolds for nearly a decade. She was his teacher on matters of utility economics and he taught her about fundraising and campaigning. Their spouses and children had socialized together.

"So, Steven, you're quite sure about this? Couldn't there be some mistake?" Moore knew Reynolds was in Cancun for the conference.

"Our information is from the U.S. State Department."

"How's Moira?

"We're trying to reach her now."

Mary was still in shock and breathless. "We'll all miss him."

"Yes we will, Commissioner," Steven sympathized, wondering how to broach the next order of business. "Uh, Commissioner, the Governor would like you to get down to the Capitol tomorrow morning to discuss the situation, the arrangements and so forth. Is that possible for you?"

As her thoughts began to jumble, she drew a breath and agreed to see the Governor the next morning at 10:00 a.m.

*   *   *

State Senator Paul Podesta got the news a few minutes later.

As Chairman of the powerful Senate Public Works & Utilities Committee, Podesta (D-Mohawk Valley) had toyed with running for PUC Chair if Calvin Reynolds did indeed show gubernatorial aspirations. At age 64, Podesta had gradually and reluctantly given up his youthful ambitions of being Governor or U.S. Senator, but the PUC Chair was still do-able.

Podesta had methodically worked his way up through the leadership ranks of first the state House and then the Senate. As a Democrat from a small, rural town, he learned the art of accommodation and earned a reputation as a skilled, though acerbic, legislator.

Podesta's name had circulated in past years as a "ticket balancer" whenever the Big City Dems had too many of their own on the slate, but things never quite clicked. Now in his 35th year in the legislature, he was starting to daydream about his pension and a long, never-ending fishing trip. His wife of 40 years, Emily, wholeheartedly endorsed that notion.

As Chairman of the Public Works & Utilities Committee, Senator Podesta had always seemed more interested in public works than public utilities. To Podesta, public works meant contracts, jobs, ribbon-cuttings, easy campaign cash. In Podesta's hometown—Mohawk Valley—small utility coops provided gas and light, and the local phone company was literally a "mom-and-pop" operation. "These are my neighbors, hard-working people," Podesta would often say. "Where else you gonna get your light and heat from?"

The utility company lobbyists who testified before Podesta's Committee knew they had a friend with the gavel. They were well-prepared and brief, which suited Podesta just fine. Too many of the Big City do-gooders who testified were neither prepared nor brief, and Podesta enjoyed giving them a hard time.

Podesta rankled some colleagues in the Senate Democratic Caucus for his unabashed defense of the industry, but he could care less. He hadn't faced a serious primary opponent in 17 years and the Republican candidates he faced were usually ignored by the State GOP. Besides, he enjoyed strong labor support, and was a revered Senate elder, a member of the State Democratic Central Committee and a vengeful in-fighter.

So when he got the call from gubernatorial hatchet-man Jimmy Blake about Reynolds' accident, he expressed his shock and sadness, asked about Moira Reynolds, inquired about funeral arrangements and thanked Blake for the call. Podesta hung up and immediately dialed Pudge Carson, his confidante, fishing buddy and alter ego.

*   *   *

Jackson City Alderman Shawn Petacque was working late in his inner city ward service office on a Saturday night.

Petacque, 45, was a workhorse—always had been—which made it all the more perplexing that some folks rapped him for being elected on his father's name. His dad—the legendary Larry Petacque—had been a Democratic Party loyalist, city forestry worker, precinct captain, ward boss, State Senator, rising star in Jackson City African-American political circles and a shoo-in for a Congressional seat until his heart gave way just before Election Day.

That was more than a quarter-century ago. At the time, Shawn was a student at Berkeley and was caught up in the civil rights, anti-war, Black Power, End Apartheid and mescaline movements. He was immersed in Marcuse and Malcolm X, and found his father's establishment politics to be reprehensible. After a Thanksgiving Dinner shouting match between the two, Shawn stormed out and never spoke to his father again, which he since regretted mightily.

Upon graduation, Shawn needed a change. He sought refuge from the turmoil of Berkeley, his dad's sudden passing and his own growing heroin habit by heading to Paris. There he worked as a cabbie, taught himself French and lived in a rooming house with a group of political expatriates, writers and artists. As an African-American with Creole heritage living in France, Shawn Petacque gained profound perspective on his roots, the world and his place in it. After three years, he returned to the USA, ending up in a studio apartment in Brooklyn and grad school at Columbia. There, he met Consuelo Milagro, a philosophy student from Venezuela. She was his first real love and they soon wed. They explored New York City, became active in a neighborhood organization, and made love loudly and often. Their first child, Monique, was born a few years later.

The sudden death a few years earlier of Boss Larry Petacque had caused upheaval in his 15th Ward. A series of nondescript aldermen and ward committeemen came and went for nearly two decades. When Shawn Petacque decided to move back to Jackson City with Consuelo and Monique, he felt like he was returning from a self-imposed exile to the old 'hood. He arrived with a charming wife, a beautiful daughter, a graduate degree in history and a decade of community organizing. He even spoke French!

Plus, he had a terrific name which people still regarded with fondness and pride.

So when his dad's old aldermanic seat opened up, Shawn Petacque ran hard in a crowded field and won handily. He made peace with his rivals (some of whom had been his father's rivals in ancient times) and was quickly recognized as a rising star.

A skilled organizer and articulate orator, Petacque tackled tough issues, forged unlikely coalitions and made sure the trash was picked up in the 15th Ward. He was witty and glib in media interviews, and not shy about fundraising. Two years after his aldermanic victory, he was elected

Democratic Ward Committeeman, further tightening his reins on his dad's old Ward.

But organizers are, by their core nature, restless spirits, never truly content. Shawn's daddy had told him, "Power is tough to get and tougher to hold onto, so use it when you got it." Shawn was getting itchy and had flipped on his radar screen. So when Consuelo called him at the ward office and urged him to be with his kids and lover on a Saturday night, she mentioned that she had just heard on the radio that the Governor's friend, Calvin Reynolds, had been killed in Mexico.

"The PUC Czar," Shawn said. "They say what happened?"

"Car accident, I think. Come home, baby."

"In awhile, *cher*." But Shawn's radar screen had lit up big time and he brought up some voting data on his computer just as soon as he hung up.

*   *   *

Across town, Petacque's City Council colleague, balding and burly 6th Ward Alderman George "Butchie" Kaminski, was sitting in the living room of the unpretentious brick bungalow he shared with his mom.

Lounging in his favorite red vinyl recliner, Butchie was watching a hockey game on his new big-screen TV and working on a twelve-pack. Butchie had played some hockey as a kid and was still a big fan. Few things gave him such pleasure as a perfect slap shot or a clean check into the boards. Butchie had delivered a few shots, first as a high school All-City linebacker, later as a regular brawler at local bowling alleys, bars and softball diamonds.

His mom—Helen Kaminski—was a no-nonsense precinct captain in the sprawling empire of Democratic chieftain Johnny Czyz, known simply as "Boss Chizz". The tough, wiry Czyz had run the 6th Ward Democratic Organization with an iron fist for 30 years, just as his father had for 20 years before him. Czyz had no aspirations beyond being at the table for the slating of aldermen, legislators and mayors.

And plenty of jobs for "his people".

Czyz had hundreds of precinct captains, assistant captains and their relatives on various payrolls. Boss Chizz had people at the City Water Department, Park District, Port Authority, Liquor Commission and Library. A few dozen more were at the Jackson County Highway Authority, Mosquito Abatement District and County Hospital. His state patronage included positions at the Tollway Agency, Department of Corrections, Racing Board and a state Supreme Court clerk. Plus the FBI, INS, U.S. Labor Department and somebody at the U.S. Embassy in Warsaw. If that wasn't enough, he squeezed a couple hundred more jobs out of major corporations and local merchants alike.

Czyz was not greedy. Oh, he spread it around. He got jobs for neighboring ward bosses to dispense, the only condition being that these new hires belong to Johnny on Election Day. Every Election Day. As long as they're alive.

With a vast Get-Out-The-Vote operation, Czyz delivered. A candidate's name on a Czyz election day "palm card" guarantees 85-90 percent of the vote in the 6ᵗʰ Ward, which enjoys huge voter turnout, always among Jackson City's top five or six wards.

The 6ᵗʰ Ward is home to blue-collar workin' stiffs and a disproportionate number of Jackson City's finest. A Democratic "bungalow belt" bastion for a century, the 6ᵗʰ Ward strayed for Reagan in '80 and an occasional Republican for statewide office, but for the most part it is a Democratic powerhouse of a ward and the envy of other ward bosses across the City.

Once an entry point for Polish, German, and Dutch immigrants, it was now attracting newly-arrived Koreans, Bosnians and Palestinians. Czyz saw it coming a mile away and quickly recruited from the new residents. His ward meetings were beginning to resemble the United Nations, but there was something tribal about the 6ᵗʰ Ward Democratic Organization and Boss Chizz was undisputed chieftain.

Among those loyalists were Helen Kaminski, a widow, and her happy-go-lucky son, Butchie.

When the 6ᵗʰ Ward's previous figurehead alderman unceremoniously resigned after Boss Chizz discovered the guy had used City workers and ward political funds to install a backyard pool, Butchie was anointed the new 6ᵗʰ Ward figurehead alderman. Czyz knew Butchie wouldn't get out of line or Helen would smack hell out of him. Since Butchie and Helen were both on the payroll of the City Electrical Department (along with Butchie's Aunt Violet), he was seen but not heard.

Occasionally, Alderman Kaminski would slip up and revert to his old barroom brawler self, or would get himself arrested for tearing down campaign posters or would introduce off-the-wall resolutions in City Council like having the state National Guard go to Chechnya or banning rollerblades. But for the most part, Kaminski voted however the Mayor (and Czyz) wanted and kept his lip zipped with City Hall press corps. Ward services were delivered quickly, thanks to his efficient Chief of Staff, Mike Kula, and to the fact that about half the ward worked on a public payroll.

The ringing of the phone that Saturday night jarred Butchie from the hockey game.

"Butchie!" barked the cranky, gravelly voice.

Shit, it's the Boss, Butchie realized, wondering why he picked up the phone, wondering why the Boss is working on a Saturday night.

"Butchie! Who we got over at the PUC?"

Hazy from his brew-soaked hockey reverie, Kaminski was not clear on Czyz' meaning. "Over the puck, Boss?"

"The Public Utility Commission, ya moron! How many people we got over there?"

OK, OK. The Boss was either testing Butchie's grasp of their vast patronage network or he had finally gone senile.

"The PUC. Well, there's Diane Radikovic, uh, Sal Lopez, uh, Bernice Plucharski's kid's a lawyer there, uh, uh, the wife of that new Korean assistant captain in precinct 49, ain't she over there?" Butchie's toasted brain cells worked faster as he tried to recall which of the hundreds of his constituents who were on public payrolls were on that particular public payroll.

"Yeah, Mrs. Cho, bookkeeping or accounting or something," Czyz said, his own ancient brain cells also puffing along. "I think Romano's kid's there, uh…"

"What's up, Boss?"

"Ahh, the top dog there—Reynolds—killed in Mexico, car crash or somethin'. We gotta protect our people." Czyz knew that patronage was a fragile and ever-shifting web of jobs and favors and forces and histories and vengeances.

By "our people", Kaminski knew the Boss meant not only their 6th Ward constituents, but people from neighboring wards who were at the Commission because of Czyz, whose ability to open doors and keep them open was the reason he was the *de facto* Democratic Party leader throughout the City's northeast side.

"Butchie! Figure out who we got there. Breakfast tomorrow. The Danzig."

That last part went without saying. Every morning, seven days a week, Boss Chizz held court at the back table of the dingy Danzig Cafe. A man of modest means who preferred power to wealth, Boss Chizz moved instinctively to protect what power he had.

*   *   *

Dan Clark, 34, didn't so much as hear the news of Reynolds death as unknowingly view it on a TV suspended from the ceiling in a smoky bar crowded with Saturday night revelers in Jackson City's bustling Flagstaff neighborhood.

Nirvana's *"Smells Like Teen Spirit"* was cranked to several hundred decibels on the juke, as it should be, Dan thought. He had been drinking shots of tequila all night, and just returned to the bar after smoking a joint in the alley with Manny Ruiz.

Fifteen years earlier, Clark and Ruiz had been college roomies, both later earning master's degrees in public administration, a calling in which both had since lost interest. Ruiz now headed Flagstaff Friends &

Neighbors, a block club network in their rapidly-gentrifying artist/yuppie neighborhood. Manny always joked that Flagstaff had started out as Bohemian and had now, a century later, turned bohemian!

For the past ten years, Clark had been teaching political science and history at Flagstaff Community College, was occasionally active in the environmental movement and dabbled in local progressive politics. At age 24, he even ran for the City Council as a "Green" candidate, garnering seven percent of the vote and was in debt for several years as a result.

In the past, Clark and Ruiz had shared apartments, girlfriends and a love of hard rock. Now, they still loved rock-and-roll. And they shared an affection for their Flagstaff neighborhood and a grass-roots approach to politics.

Buzzed from their trip to the alley, Manny pointed to the TV screen hanging above the bar. "Hey, Danny, isn't that your old buddy from the utility commission?" Manny yelled.

Clark squinted at the headshot of Reynolds up on the TV screen. "What's that asshole doing now," Dan mumbled to himself, mindlessly stroking his neatly-trimmed beard. He had neither forgiven nor forgotten the rough treatment he'd received from Reynolds a few years back. Clark had appeared at a PUC public hearing on the potential health hazards of power lines. He was testifying on behalf of a group of parents concerned about the planned construction of high-tension power lines across a playground.

Months of solid research, done by volunteers, had been crafted into convincing testimony. After sitting through hours of testimony submitted by the electric company's hired guns, the PUC Czar wearily invited public comment. As Clark made his way to the witness stand, Reynolds stage-whispered to his number-two, Mary Moore, "This better be quick."

Well, Clark's testimony was not quick. Reynolds interrupted Clark repeatedly, asking him who funds his group, what were his credentials, what was his fee for testifying (no fee, Clark smugly replied). Clark held his own, but Reynolds clearly had the upper hand. He later ruled, predictably, for the power line construction.

"Hey, Danny, I remember how that asshole treated you on that electric line thing," Ruiz yelled over Nirvana's rage. "You oughta run against him and take that sucker out!"

"Yeah, Manny, right," Clark scoffed, his attention already drifting to the sight of two young lovelies who had been eyeing Manny and him ever since they'd returned from their smoking break in the alley.

*   *   *

Alderman Shawn Petacque always felt comfortable with computers. His ward service office was well-equipped with five computers, high-speed modems, a scanner, Jackson City's first aldermanic web site, DSL and a great Bidwhist program.

Petacque and his staff were all well trained, too. He sent his new staff members to computer classes, and tried to keep up-to-date himself. His computer system had a complete data base of every registered voter in the ward, their ages, their frequency of voting, "D" or "R" (90 percent "D"), if they've ever requested ward services or expressed a view on any issue, homeowner or renter, occupation and what magazines they subscribe to. He never realized how many people read "People Magazine" in the 15th Ward.

On another database, Petacque had lists of donors and scanned-in news articles about him. He couldn't understand most politicians' intimidation by computers. Man's Best Friend, he thought as he perused election totals from the last statewide race.

Hmm, four million registered voters in the state, with about half voting in primaries and half of them—about a million—voting Democratic.

Shawn noticed a sharp drop-off from numbers for Governor to those of the lesser-known races. A half-million Democrats voted in the last primary for PUC Chairman. A lackluster field failed to excite Dem voters, Shawn recalled. This time should be different. With the Czar out of the picture, and an open Governor's seat, turnout for both the Democrat and Republican primaries should be much higher.

Petacque's fingers danced over the computer keys.

650,000 registered African-American voters statewide. If 45 percent go to the polls on primary election day, and 90 percent of those vote Dem and 90 percent of those will vote for an African-American candidate, that's 236,925 votes.

Assuming the African-American vote isn't split, 236,925 is a nice chunk of change in a crowded primary race. Hell, 200 thou may be all a candidate needs. Add another quarter million Hispanic registered voters with 80 percent of them going "D", that's another maybe 75,000 votes up for grabs. And not to mention the lefties…

An African-American had never run for Chair of the State Public Utilities Commission. It's do-able, Shawn thought. He exited the data base, began a web search for the state budget and called home.

*   *   *

Chapter One

Wellsprings, Part II

The obit was pretty much the same in all of the state's Sunday morning papers. For example, the *Harbor Heights Beacon-News* had it on the front page:

"PUC CZAR" REYNOLDS DIES IN MEXICAN TRAFFIC MISHAP

Calvin Reynolds, 52, Chairman of the state Public Utility Commission and long-time confidante to Governor Tom Langley, was killed Saturday in a freak truck-car collision on a desolate highway north of the Mexican city of Chetumal. Mr. Reynolds was in Mexico on state business, attending a conference of state utility regulators in Cancun.

Ten years ago, Mr. Reynolds became the state's first popularly-elected Public Utility Commission Chairman, a post previously appointive. Mr. Reynolds won reelection twice since then with large margins. As Chairman, Mr. Reynolds presided over the computerization of the office and a doubling of its staff, but raised the ire of consumer groups with his pro-nuclear stance.

Mr. Reynolds served four years in the U.S. Army and was awarded a Bronze Star for a stint in Saigon during the final days of U.S. involvement in Vietnam. There he met Tom Langley, who became a lifelong friend. Mr. Reynolds was a

*prolific fundraiser for Langley and was widely-believed to be the frontrunner to
replace Gov. Langley, who recently announced his retirement.*

*Gov. Langley issued a written statement saying, "The state has lost a dedi-
cated public servant—a Vietnam veteran, a businessman, a father—and my
family has lost a true friend."*

*Upon his return from military service, Mr. Reynolds went to work for his
future father-in-law's furniture manufacturing company in downstate
Belmont Park and in 1985 was named President of the firm. Mr. Reynolds
held a variety of posts with the State Chamber of Commerce and his local
Rotary Club. An avid hunter, Mr. Reynolds was also active in his church and
a licensed pilot.*

*Mexican authorities have charged the driver of the timber hauling truck
that struck Mr. Reynolds with reckless homicide and driving an unsafe
vehicle. Mr. Reynolds was killed instantly by the truck as he changed a tire
on a rental car near Chetumal. Survivors include his wife, Moira, and
children Michael and Maria. Visitation and funeral arrangements are
pending. Burial will be private.*

*   *   *

The sun peeked over the eastern horizon, igniting the Capitol Dome
into a shimmering beacon. Mary Moore had taken the first flight down
and told the cabdriver to bring her directly to the Capitol. She'd taken this
ride a thousand times, and seen the Capitol Dome almost as many times,
but it had never glowed like this, with a luminescent vitality, Mary
thought, or maybe it was her emotional state, lack of sleep and anxiety
about seeing Reynolds' empty office at the Capitol.

The Capitol halls were empty and gray, except for sharp slits of sunlight
piercing through the narrow panes encircling the Dome over the rotunda.
A typical dawn in the state's political epicenter. Moore walked down the
hall, past the murals of long-forgotten battles between pioneers and
Indians. She unlocked the Commission's executive office entrance and

walked into Reynolds' inner office, half expecting to see him sitting there in his favorite leather chair, working the phones, doing ten things at once.

The office trophies were a biography of the man. The stuffed swordfish he snagged off Fort Lauderdale, a fading photograph of Reynolds and Langley in a Saigon bar, framed headlines from his first victory, a "1992 Man of the Year" from the Boy Scouts, silver cups and dusty plaques. Photos of the kids. Photos of the staff. Photos of celebrities. Photos.

Mary slumped in the chair she usually occupied at senior staff meetings and, for the first time since hearing the news the night before, had a good cry.

She pounded the arm of the chair and the tears flowed. So utterly senseless. A totally decent man, she thought. He survived Vietnam, for godsakes. Worked so hard, always made time for his kids. A man on the rise. So senseless. Mary gazed around this office that had provided her with ten years worth of great memories. She had experienced so much in this space, learned so much, laughed so much.

A true military man, she thought. The order and absence of clutter reflected his style and priorities. He believed in hierarchy, structure, precision. Methods.

Moore opened the curtains to give the early morning sun full access to Reynolds' inner sanctum. She shuffled around the office, poking into a few cabinets, before she finally sat at his desk, which she had been resisting. More photos of the kids, a gold elephant from the '96 Republican National Convention, a Swiss music box Moira had given him. An in-box awaiting his return from Cancun.

She aimlessly rifled through the in-box. Reynolds' schedule for the upcoming week, newsclips, weekly updates from department heads, a brochure for a conference in New Orleans next month at which Reynolds was to be a featured speaker. She gingerly opened the large desk drawer. Binoculars, a roll of antacids, duck hunting season information, his rolodex of phone numbers (he would never leave it on his desk), a box of raisins. She noticed a metal container, smaller than a phone book, that was locked. She'd deal with it later, Mary thought.

At 9:35 a.m., the phone on Reynolds' desk buzzed, startling Moore. It was Steven Page, who was upstairs in the Governor's office, saying that the Governor was ready to meet now if she was. The morning sun was now drenching the Capitol rotunda and the murals of long-forgotten battles as Moore walked through the empty halls to the Office of the Governor.

*   *   *

The Very Right Reverend B.J. Crandall had finished his early morning prayers and breakfast in the old frame farmhouse he called home and headquarters, and was preparing for church services. His wife had the local TV news on in the living room and he heard about the reported death of Public Utilities Commission Chairman Reynolds.

Crandall watched the report of the freak truck mishap in Mexico, which included file footage of Governor Langley at Reynolds' campaign kickoff a few years before, the official Reynolds family photo and a statement from the local Mexican consul regarding the charges filed against the truck driver.

"God rest his soul," Reverend Crandall murmured half-aloud, immediately wondering who would replace Reynolds.

Crandall had recently become an avid student of state politics. His statewide organization, the Crusade of Christian Marchers, had just reached an all-time membership high of 40,000 dues-paying, God-fearing good people all across the state. The coffers were full.

Crandall, 59, knew that if properly funded and organized, the Crusade could be a potent force in state politics. Crandall himself had lobbied the legislature on school prayer, abortion and the flag-burning amendment. "I have witnessed the power of the players under the Capitol Dome," he delighted in telling his supporters. "But I have also witnessed the power of the 'pray-ers' out there in the small towns and tiny churches all across our state."

Crandall was riding high. His recent lively appearance on *ABC's Nightline* regarding lesbian grade school teachers had established him as a player in the state's right-wing political/religious circles, and he was planning a statewide tour to visit with local Crusade chapters and local media.

A U.S. Senate race in three years was beckoning. The U.S. Senate would be the ultimate arena to debate the great issues, B.J. thought. Even if he loses, he could shift the discussion to issues some Republicans prefer to tippy-toe around. Besides, he's 59 and what's he got to lose. He had begun exploring it in earnest. How effective a voting force would the Crusade be? Can 40,000 members translate into a quarter million votes? What would it cost?

Since he was so closely identified with the Crusade, Crandall had decided to test the real electoral strength of the group with a test run for a lower level statewide office in the upcoming statewides by someone other than himself. This Reynolds thing offers possibilities, he thought, as he knotted his necktie, combed his thinning brown hair and headed for church.

Real possibilities.

*   *   *

Shawn Petacque awoke in an empty bed to the smell of bacon and sound of Sunday mornings.

The night before around 1:30 a.m., Shawn e-mailed the databases he had been working on to his home computer and locked up the ward office. The Jackson City downtown skyline shimmered a few miles away, looking magnificent—almost Oz-like—under a full moon. He leaned his six-foot frame against his car and smiled, feeling exhilarated and exhausted. He had done some serious number-crunching, gained an understanding of the state Public Utilities Commission and asked himself some tough questions.

It wouldn't be an easy race. Could he raise the money? (Probably, he thought, but what candidate doesn't think so?) Was he ready to give up the City Council to be a state regulator? (Yes, and the serious increase in pay and staff would help.) Could he stand being on the trail away from Consuelo and the munchkins? (Ouch.)

He had grabbed a pound of fried shrimp and a six-pack, drove home and worked for another few hours. He would need to be the only African-American candidate and would need to score big in the liberal wards and with Hispanics. He fell asleep thinking about the excitement and challenge of a statewide race.

When he straggled into the kitchen the next morning, Consuelo and the kids were sitting at the breakfast table, already on seconds of bacon and waffles, the standard Sunday morning fare in the Petacque-Milagro household.

"Well, at least somebody had a good time on a Saturday night," Consuelo said, pointing to five empty beer bottles on the kitchen counter as Shawn slowly walked into the kitchen.

"Sorry, baby, was on a roll," Shawn said, grabbing her and planting a kiss on her smirking lips. She could never stay mad at this guy, she thought. He grabbed her wonderful butt, so firm under her robe.

"Mommy, Mommy, Daddy's grabbin' ass!" Monique shrieked, as she and her younger brother, Lawrence, began jumping and squealing in delight. Their dog, a collie named Napolean, started yapping. The TV was blasting.

"Now, what do you know about grabbin' ass, little girl?" Shawn was grinning. What a great family. Do I really want to give this up for a year? Consuelo grabbed his ass back.

                    *   *   *

The Danzig Cafe offered grease-caked neon and fluorescent lighting, chairs held together with duct tape and high-cholesterol cuisine. It was noisy, smoky and always crowded. The waitresses—all gum-cracking smart-asses—knew everyone's name and usual order.

John Czyz loved it like it was his own home.

The Danzig served as Czyz' office for two or three hours every single morning, when it was the political center of the 6th Ward. Boss Chizz would hold court, be greeted by patrons, scheme and bark orders to underlings, like Alderman Butchie Kaminski. Sunday mornings are standing room only at the Danzig, but Czyz, Kaminski and aldermanic aide Mike Kula had their usual booth in the back.

"Well, Butchie, I count 14 people we got at the Public Utility Commission," Czyz growled. "That sound right to you?"

Actually Kaminski only came up with ten names, but knew the Boss always had a few folks planted here and there. "Sounds 'bout right, Boss," Butchie said, still hung over from last night's beer and hockey.

Czyz reached into his jacket pocket and pulled out a list, slowly, with clear dramatic effect, and slid it across the table to Kaminski. "Read it."

"Stanley Plucharski, Legal Division, $91,000. Salvador Lopez, Public Outreach Officer, $52,800. William Romano, Jr., PUC Archives Division, $46,000. Diane Radikovic, Administrative Assistant, $45,700. Mustafa Hadda, Security, $44,800. Ann Cho, Bookkeeping, $38,500. Tammy Bliss, Receptionist, $34,500…"

The list went on. "Some good people here, Boss," Kaminski commented between bites of potato pancake.

"Yeah, and most of 'em ain't protected. New guy comes in and BOOM!" Czyz slammed his spindly fist on the formica table for emphasis, prompting young Kula to spew his oatmeal.

"So what happened to the top dog?"

"Aw, c'mon, Butchie, dontcha read the papers other'n the funny pages? Car crash in Mexico."

"So, who's gonna be in charge there?"

"This Mary Moore, I figure. Real straight arrow. We gotta keep on top of this."

"Gotcha, Boss," Butchie pledged. "On top of it." Kula nodded in agreement.

The loss of a single job at the PUC might jeopardize his relations with other chieftains and threaten his precarious claim to being Big Dog on the northeast side, Czyz knew. He wished he had somebody besides these two—a moron and an innocent—to carry on the tradition in the 6th Ward, the unbroken continuum of power enjoyed by the same organization his father grew up in. Maybe this PUC lawyer, Stanley Plucharski, is aldermanic material.

"Hey Boss, could you pass the maple syrup?"

*   *   *

Two hundred miles away in another greasy breakfast diner with an overflow Sunday morning crowd, Senator Paul Podesta tore into a stack of buttermilk pancakes. His pal of 35 years, Pudge Carson, squeezed his 300-pound girth into their favorite booth and ordered a fruit salad. "Doctor's orders," he said to a disbelieving Podesta. "Anything new on the accident?"

"Nah, Langley's people are duckin' behind the State Department, some investigation, I guess," Podesta said. "Mexican cops charged the truck driver. Reckless homicide. Mighta been a dame with Reynolds when he bit it."

"Ooh, messy."

"Yeah, sounds like ole Calvin went out in style," Podesta chuckled.

"So, we're assuming Mary Moore takes over? Knows the business. Local Party activist. Articulate. Plus, she's a good-lookin' blonde."

"Yeah, but only as caretaker, I'd say, until Langley can find somebody strong enough to make the race next year." Simultaneously, the radar screens of these two old war-horses began scanning the field, looking for the blips of potential candidacies.

"Well, on the Republican side ya got that fellah from Valdosta, Fitzgibbons, makin' noises about statewide. Your pal Esther, too.

"Naw. She'd never leave the Senate for this."

"Maybe. Lemme see, the Dems could put up Debbie Shane, she'd be attractive. Maybe Flint himself," Carson said, referring to Democratic State Party Chairman Niles Flint.

"I dunno, Langley may want to keep Moore in there, even though she's got an independent streak," Podesta said. "Woman on the ticket, an established suburban base of her own, no skeletons…"

"That we know of," Carson jumped in.

"Hey, who doesn't have a few. Let's see, who else?"

"Figure a black, maybe a woman. Your City Cousins'll have somebody; nobody comes to mind, though," Carson leaned across the table and lowered his voice. "Paul, if you announced next week, you'd be the frontrunner. You know that don't you?"

"Emmy and I were up all night talkin' about it. You think it's a good fit, Pudge?"

"Chairman of Senate Public Works & Utilities Committee. Experienced lawmaker. Party leader. Can bring together labor and the utility companies. Shit, man, it's a perfect fit!"

"Be nice to avoid a primary fight," Podesta said.

"Whoa, daddy, this ain't no local yokel senate district. This here's big-time, statewide. Major air wars. Could be a crowded party," Pudge said, finishing his fruit salad in record time. He scanned the diner for their waitress.

"Well, I'm gonna call Flint, O'Malley, a few others today, to get the lay of the land," Podesta said, already compiling a mental list of the hundred or so calls he needed to make today.

"The race is to the quick on this one," Pudge drawled. "If you want it, get your name out fast and freeze the field. I think I'm gonna need another fruit plate."

*   *   *

Governor Langley sat behind his huge, hand-carved oak desk, the same one used by the state's chief executives since 1920. He was dressed Sunday morning casual: knit sport shirt, khaki pants, canvas shoes. Dark bags draped under his bloodshot eyes.

Langley and top aide Jimmy Blake were deep in conversation when
Mary Moore walked in. She was relieved to see Steven Page in the meeting. As much as she was fond of Page for his sincerity, nice appearance and
pleasant demeanor, she loathed Blake for his sneakiness, greasy obesity
and arrogant condescension.

Blake had not been with Langley as long as Page, but as Campaign
Manager of Langley's last race, Blake had the Man's Ear. A shrewd strategist
who, like Langley, was a student of military history, Blake often referred to
obscure battles in conversation. Langley loved it and the two of them would
engage in cryptic discussions about the need to "Inchon" somebody or to
beware of a "Pickett's Charge" on that bill. Others wouldn't know what the
hell the two of them were talking about, which suited Blake fine.

As soon as the Governor spotted Moore, he jumped up and embraced
her. "Mary, how are you doing," he asked with genuine concern in his
voice.

"Our good friend is gone," she whispered, somewhat surprised to be
hugging the Governor. He seemed to be getting a little choked up, too,
reminding Mary that Langley had known Reynolds far longer than she.

They sat on the leather couch, composing themselves. "Coffee, Mary?"
The Governor reached for the pitcher.

"Thanks, Governor. How's Moira holding up?"

"I just spoke with her. Sounds better than last night," Langley said,
refilling his own cup. "Still not clear what happened. Changing a tire on a
jungle highway. The Mexican authorities have charged the truck driver
who hit him."

"It's so unbelievable, so unfair." Mary could feel the emotion rise again
and fought it. "He worked so hard, had such a future."

"I'm still in shock myself, Mary." Langley turned to Page. "Steven,
what's the latest on the arrangements?"

"Mrs. Reynolds is flying to Cancun today to bring him back. Closed
casket visitation in the Capitol Rotunda on Tuesday, funeral back home in

Belmont Park on Wednesday. Flags at all state facilities at half-mast for one week, beginning today."

"The visitation in the Capitol is a very gracious gesture, Governor," Moore said.

"Well, he was one of a kind."

They shared reminiscences about Reynolds. Campaign moments, travels, funny episodes. Langley even talked about the last days in Saigon, a topic he rarely brought up. They refilled their coffee mugs.

Finally, Blake, silent until now, leaned over to Moore.

"Commissioner, have you had a chance to go through Calvin's things?"

She was taken aback by the directness of the question. "Well, Jimmy, I've poked around a little. The usual stuff in the in-box. Governor, he was so proud of that Saigon photo."

"Oh, could you save that one for me, Mary, unless Moira or the kids want it, of course," Langley said, munching on a donut. "By the way, Moira said she would come by a few days after the funeral to go through some of Calvin's personal effects, so do you think you and Jimmy and Steven here could take a little time this morning to y'know, go through his things some?"

Moore turned to Blake and Page who both sat solemnly with folded hands, totally nonidentical twins, almost cherubic, Mary thought, nearly laughing for the first time since hearing about Reynolds' death.

"Certainly, Governor," Mary said.

"And Mary, we'd like you to continue to run the show on a day-to-day basis, just keep on doing what you've been doing so well," Langley said as he put his arm around her shoulder and began walking her to the door. "Calvin would certainly want it that way."

"Why, thank you for your confidence, Governor," Moore said, turning to the Odd Couple. "Ready, gentlemen?"

*　　　　*　　　　*

Nicky Pulver was the only one in the ProAction office that morning which was fine with him. He could monitor the Sunday morning talk shows, use the video production facilities without interruption, maybe chip away at his growing in-box.

The hottest political consulting firm in the state, ProAction was launched nine years earlier as a PR firm by a group of grizzled young veterans of Jackson City's political wars. At first, few clients, little income. They worked out of a dusty loftspace that at least offered great views of the sunset from its rooftop. They worked hard and played hard. And things started happening.

ProAction offered political candidates a diversified package. They had hired specialists in direct mail, fundraising, polling and opposition research. A client could select cafeteria-style from various ProAction services such as scheduling, radio spots, press conferences, debate prep or Election Day operations.

ProAction won a few out-of-state congressional campaigns, including one upset that the *Washington Post* called the year's "biggest shocker". They lured a few commercial and not-for-profit clients, and grew to a 30-person staff, most of whom put in 70-80 hour work weeks, including the Veeps like Nicky Pulver, who had been there from the beginning.

He heard the fax beep. Incoming. Gotta be JJ, surmised Nicky, as he trotted to the fax machine. Sure enough, JJ's working on Sunday morning, just like Nicky, he chuckled as he read the blaring headline on *"JJ Springfield's Daily Bulletin"*, the daily fax and e-mail communique which was must-reading for public officials, reporters, lobbyists, grapevine shakers and political junkies across the state, despite its pricey subscription. Everybody read JJ.

"PUC CZAR'S MEXICO TRAGEDY POSES QUESTIONS"
"DATELINE JJ: The entire state is mourning the sudden and tragic death of Commissioner Calvin Reynolds in the jungles of Mexico. The gregarious Reynolds will be remembered fondly by all who knew him, including this reporter.

"Questions remain. What was Reynolds doing so far away from the conference he was attending on the taxpayers' dime?

Question: Who is this Ana Villasenor, the only witness to the fatal incident, who was questioned by Mexican police and State Department investigators, but refused to return this reporter's long-distance phonecalls?

Question: How will this affect pending and upcoming utility rate hike requests before the Public Utilities Commission?

Question: Will #2 Mary Moore be designated Acting Chairman? Will the Governor push for a more seasoned campaigner come election time, someone perhaps like veteran State Senator Esther Ruelbach? Are the Dems salivating at the thought?

"Sources tell JJ that a Tuesday visitation in the Capitol Rotunda is planned. Stay tuned to JJ Springfield's Daily Bulletin."

Man, that's cold, Nicky thought. Body ain't even in the ground and already JJ's handicapping the succession. Esther'd be tough, Nicky thought, flipping on his political radar screen.

*　　　*　　　*

Petra Dresden noticed the Reynolds' obit over breakfast in the Japanese-style garden she had put into her 40-acre homestead.

Multimillionaire heiress. Philanthropist. Stylish. A gracious socialite interested in social change. Founder and Director of the "Dresden Foundation for Democracy's Future". After her husband died in 1988, Petra Dresden, a young and charismatic widow, took a flair for charity fundraising and the Dresden name, and turned her sights on politics.

She aided candidates with reputations as mavericks, iconoclasts, boat-rockers. She was an early supporter of Jesse Ventura in his upset win for Minnesota's Governorship. She funded referenda for term limits and abolition of the death penalty. She endowed the "Dresden Foundation for Democracy's Future" (also known as "Double DF" or "DF-Squared") to push for campaign finance reform and foster independent and third-party candidates.

As she scanned the Reynolds' obituary, Dresden thought about the Public Utilities Commission, how Reynolds had been a Langley fundraiser, his coziness to the gas and electric companies. Wonder what the signature requirements are for this job? She made a note to call Liz Chinn, the Dresden Foundation's energetic point person on political matters, and then turned her attention to the koi goldfish in the lily pond.

*   *   *

Paul Podesta waved as Pudge's black Cadillac barreled out of the restaurant parking lot and headed down Main Street, Mohawk Valley. Pudge lived in a wooded area some ten miles out of town, while Podesta lived right in town, less than a mile away. Seemed like a perfect day to walk. Podesta had spent his whole life in this town, not counting his time in the service. As he strolled down Main, he was greeted by other Sunday morning strollers.

Podesta had been the classic Hometown-Boy-Made-Good. As an industrious lad with an extensive paper route, young Paul became well-known throughout the Valley. A popular football star at Mohawk High, he earned a reputation for tenacity and an occasional low-blow. Son of a dry goods storeowner, Paul had an eye for a deal, which would serve him well later in the Capitol. After touring Europe with the Army, Podesta returned to Mohawk Valley and took over management of his dad's popular dry goods store.

Soon, he and his high school sweetheart, Emily Westin, wed. That was 40 years ago and they were still just as in love now as then. Life partners in every regard, Emily was involved in all of Paul's major political decisions. Like so many political spouses, she'd been through the cycle of decision-making every candidate faces when contemplating a run for higher office, or even whether to seek re-election. Emily knew Paul's thought process and ambitions. She could spot him rationalizing something a mile away and was the only person (besides Pudge) who would call him on it. They had been discussing retirement. The Florida condo was empty most of the year. His pension and their good investments would make for a comfortable life.

But as they listed out the pros and cons of a Podesta for PUC Chairman Campaign, Emily sensed the glint in his eye, the tone in his voice, the adrenaline in his heart. He was going for it, she figured, and maybe he deserved one last great shot in the career for which he had sacrificed so much, so she voiced no objections.

The more he ruminated on it, the more Paul liked it. But Pudge was right. Whoa, Daddy, this ain't no State Senate district here; this is statewide and this is one big state. Podesta walked slowly through the majestic oaks and maples of the town square, with the soaring, romanesque Mohawk County Courthouse on one side staring at the low-slung glass-and-steel municipal center on the other.

The park bench in the center of the square had been the center of Paul's universe since birth. He could recall playing here with his parents as a toddler, smoking his first cigarette here at twelve, holding campaign rallies here as a young politician. Hell, I'll probably end up playing checkers here with a bunch of old men in another ten years or so, he chuckled.

Podesta sat on the bench and lit a cigarette, the sun illuminating his silver hair. It was so peaceful here at his sacred, special spot.

A chorus of crows dueled with the Sunday morning chorus at St. Paul's Lutheran, two blocks away. The Civil War cannons stood defiant, immobile. A young mother pushing a baby carriage happened by.

"Morning, Senator! Beautiful day!"

"Hiya, Joanie!" Podesta waved, struggling to remember the baby's name. There was a time he knew the name of every baby in the Valley. "How's the little one?"

"Keepin' us up late." She smiled and waved. "Say hello to Mrs. Podesta for us."

It struck Paul that he had been sitting on this very bench 35 years ago when he made the decision to challenge the incumbent state representative, a Republican who had been in a little too long. Podesta had been back from the Army for a few years, had made some money and friends in the dry goods business, and was still remembered for his paper route and gridiron heroics.

That first race was a doozy. With no primary opponent, Podesta ran hard against the incumbent and a sluggish economy. His farmer-labor coalition just plain out-hustled the Republican, who never saw it coming. On Election Night at 4:00 a.m.—in this Courthouse—Podesta was declared the winner by an 8,052 to 7,967 vote.

In his first term in the State House, Podesta's hustle propelled him to the front of the freshman class. He quickly befriended labor leaders and agriculture lobbyists, as well as many from the other side of the aisle. He counted many Republicans as friends, partly because he genuinely enjoyed their friendship and partly because he knew it could be useful. And when Podesta first stood for re-election, the Republicans fielded a weak candidate. Podesta won easily and became the undisputed top dog in the Mohawk Valley area.

His gaze swept the square.

He had organized colorful, beer-fueled rallies here in his early days, complete with red-white-and-blue bunting, brass bands and dancing girls. He announced his first bid for the State Senate here 18 years ago. A very special place. The sun was getting high in the sky. He leaned back on the bench, lit another cigarette and stretched. Retirement sounded good, no doubt. He knew Emily was eager to spend more time at the Florida condo. The fishing would be great.

A statewide run would be physically and emotionally grueling, he knew. Different than a state legislative race, which is sweaty and fleshy, up-close and personal, church bingos, high school football games, county fairs. After decades of being a ground warrior, Paul would need a crash course in aerial combat and go from retail to wholesale. Not easy for the son of a dry goods man.

The up-and-coming crop of the state's political leaders left Podesta unimpressed. The new generation was born of focus groups and poll-driven direct mail, not precinct work and doing what you can to help your neighbors. Most of 'em couldn't give a spontaneous stump speech in the town square even if they were arguing for their own lives. Slick, shallow, unseasoned. Just like some of the names likely to be floated in the next week as the next PUC Czar, Paul snorted.

As a young man, Paul had dreamed of being Governor or U.S. Senate. He had mulled a statewide race his entire career. This is it, he thought, the last call, the Last Hurrah. A storm of black crows swirled overhead, shrieking, *"Paul! Paul! Paul!"*

Pudge was right. Damn good fit.

At that moment, Paul decided to go for it. First, get a better lay of the land, the old gladiator thought. He flicked the cigarette butt, walked home and began eight hours of long-distance phonecalls.

*   *   *

Professor Dan Clark woke with a killer headache.

Tequila, rum, reefer and cocaine made for a unique pain the morning after, compounded by regaining consciousness in the bedroom of a woman whose name he couldn't recall. Sherry? Clark tried to sort out the previous night's events. Manny had initiated conversation with the other woman—Madonna? Next thing he knew the quartet was in the alley smoking a joint.

Dan and Manny had always been pretty discrete about smoking dope with strangers, but these two seemed okay. And both were hotties. As he drew on the joint in the alley, Manny agreed with Donna that rum and reefer are a great blend. "Well, you know what else goes with rum and reefer," Donna giggled and put her index finger next to her nose and sniffed.

"Ah, the happy snowstorm," Manny grinned. "But, sorry girls, we can't help you with that stuff."

"Well, we can," said Shelly (who turned out to be Ms. Michelle Baldini.) "So, why don't you guys get us a couple of bottles at the liquor store and we can walk to our apartment. It's only a few blocks over." The two men glanced at each other, as if to say 'we should discuss this', but there was no way. After the mission to the liquor store, they hastily beat a path to the ladies' apartment, a modest two-bedroom in a courtyard building. Within moments, Manny was in the kitchen slicing limes for the Cuba Libre's. In the living room, Michelle pulled out several small wax paper triangles, a razor blade, a mirror and a straw and began the ritualistic preparation of the narcotic.

As she chopped the cocaine with the razor blade and arranged it into eight healthy six-inch lines, she chatted speedily with Clark. She was a 25-year old secretary at a small factory, had just moved to the Flagstaff neighborhood from the eastern suburbs and really thought it was cool living here. She said she liked the rock band Nirvana, ensuring Dan that he and she had at least one thing in common. They could hear Manny and Donna making out in the kitchen. Michelle bent her head over the mirror and quickly snorted two of the huge lines.

"Whoo! Have some."

Clark wasn't as adept at snorting, but he too did two toots. It burned his throat, but the rush was immediate. "Yow. Nice," he said, grinning ear-to-ear. "Hey, Manny, bring out those Libres! Party time!" Clark was feeling great and Michelle, maybe ten years his junior, was looking great in a tight T-shirt and tighter blue jeans.

The four of them did a few more lines. The stuff was pure, with no additives or speed. "This is great stuff," Manny said. "You ladies are too generous."

"Well, I've got a few extra packets here. $150 each." Michelle said. "Want to buy a few?"

"Sure, why not, we'll take a couple," Manny replied without hesitation. Between Dan and Manny, they had about $220. "Can we owe you the rest?"

"Sure, honey, why not," Michelle said, watching as Manny, his hands shaking a little, opened the tiny packet and began the ritual, although not as expertly or stylishly as Michelle.

One organ affected quickly by cocaine is the tongue and soon all four tongues were getting active. Dan and Michelle headed to one bedroom and Manny paired off with Donna in the other. For hours, the ecstatic cycle of coke, rum and frantic sex pervaded the apartment. Michelle was a hungry lover and coke made her voracious. She wept when she orgasmed and the two finally drifted into a semi-dream state.

After dawn, Dan heard Michelle get up and do another line. She climbed back into bed with Dan and began rubbing against his lean torso. He peered at her through the tiny slits that were once his eyeballs. She still looked terrific.

"So, Danny Boy, I never asked you what you do for a living anyhow. Lawyer?"

One effect of cocaine is paranoia and Dan had it.

"Well, I write about history," he said evasively.

"Ooh, a historian. I didn't know historians were allowed to move like you did last night," she said, rubbing her naked breast across his back. "Another line?"

"Sure, why not," Dan said, realizing he was in for a royal hangover, but already getting aroused again.

*　　　　*　　　　*

Jimmy Blake and Steven Page followed Mary Moore down the empty Capitol halls to Reynolds' office. All three stood for a moment and gazed at the plaques and trophies. Blake opened the closet. "New golf clubs."

"He was such an active man," Moore said. "Loved fishing, duck hunting. Took the kids whitewater rafting last summer. Learned to fly."

Blake was not the sentimental sort. "OK, let's put the purely personal stuff on the conference table, PUC business can stay where it's at for Mary and any political stuff, uh, let's put it on the couch for now." General Blake was clearly asserting himself as head of this search-and-recover mission.

The three retreated into their own thoughts and began rummaging through cabinets and drawers. Blake seemed to be looking for something in particular, Mary thought. Page tackled a credenza, finding thousands of *"Reynolds is My Man"* emery boards. Calvin's staff would pass these out at the State Fair, 4th of July parades and party functions. Steven noticed the nail files didn't specify what office Reynolds was their man for. Could've used these in a gubernatorial race.

Reynolds would have had the inside track to the Mansion, Steven thought. He had built up an overflowing war chest, developed a statewide political network and hired sharp staffers like Moore. Ever since Langley announced his retirement, other contenders' names had floated. Congressman Paul Prentice, a photogenic and moderate Republican barely known outside of his suburban district, would be well-funded. State Senator Esther Ruelbach, who never missed a parade, told JJ Springfield that it's time for a woman to be governor and maybe she's the one!

A gaggle of Democrats were lining up for the top spot, too. Often mentioned in the gossip columns and Capital bars were the state's ranking-Democrat Attorney General Lou Calcagno, millionaire publisher Lawrence Burl, Congressman Zigmund Prybyl (Boss Chizz' man in Washington), State Senator Debra Shane and perennial candidate Wendell (Cut Taxes Now) Wardell, who legally changed his middle name to make it more ballot-friendly.

Reynolds' could have taken any of them, Steven thought, staring at the box of nail files. So many campaign events, smiles, hands shaken, fast food meals, endless miles of asphalt. Steven had done it for the past 12 years and was burnt out. How many of those nail files did Reynolds himself hand out during his decade in office? How many State Fair-goers thought to themselves, "Ya know, Reynolds is my man" every time they did their nails?

Blake found a carton of campaign finance reports and started rifling through. Mary remembered the metal box in Reynolds' desk drawer she noticed earlier. She found a tiny key in Reynolds hidden compartment and quietly opened the container. Inside was a sheaf of papers, maybe 20 pages. Looked like a list of names, Mary thought. She read the top page.

"5K. Edmund Jensen, Ann Jensen, Ed Jensen, Jr., Peter Fortunato, Simone Fortunato, William Fortunato…" The "5K" list went on for a few more pages, followed by several "3K" pages. Some sort of race, Mary thought, swimming or running?

"Steven, does this make any sense to you?"

Page put down the Playboys he found in the credenza and walked over. "Whatcha got?" Blake barked.

"Some list of names," Page said blankly.

Blake motored over and after a quick glance at the list, folded the whole thing and put it in his pocket. "This is political. I'll take care of it," Blake said in a tone discouraging debate.

*   *   *

At that moment, Lobbyist Extraordinaire Kevin O'Malley finally tracked down Eaton Gas Company Vice-President Stan Flanders at Flanders' out-of-state vacation condo and delivered the bad news about Calvin.

Every morning during the legislative session, a dozen lobbyists and operatives for the state's various utility companies met over breakfast in the restaurant of the plush Parker Hotel, just walking distance from the Capitol Building. Over the decades, many a deal was cut—and many a throat, too—in the legendary Parker Hotel. The breakfast club of utility powers–known informally as the "Consortium"–was doing its best to live up to the Parker Hotel's storied reputation. They would review the day's legislative calendar, help each other with testimony, swap gossip, caffeinate hangovers and sometimes actually strategize, though not nearly as often as opponents would suggest.

One of these lobbyists, Kevin O'Malley, was a highly-regarded and highly-paid freelance lobbyist. He represented Eaton Gas, the state's largest natural gas supplier. He represented the state's fast-growing casino industry, the Newspaper Publishers Association, the state Dental Association and countless municipal bodies. A charming, solicitous bear of a man with a full shock of jet-back hair and an uncontrollable beard, Kevin O'Malley always came to battle prepared.

Chairman Podesta liked that. Over the past three decades, Podesta and O'Malley had grown from being raw rookies to grizzled aces, and had developed a warm friendship. Podesta and his wife had even accompanied O'Malley, PUC Czar Calvin Reynolds and Eaton Gas Veep Stan Flanders, and their wives on a golfing trip to Maui a few years ago. These friendships were at the core of an unspoken alliance on most issues between Sen. Podesta, PUC Czar Reynolds and the utility industry.

Flanders and O'Malley went way back. They had once worked for the same lobbying firm, but quickly outgrew it. When O'Malley decided to fly solo, a decision that made him a millionaire, Flanders took a $150,000-year post with Eaton Gas, working his way up to Vice-President for Government Affairs. As the Capitol's two leading voices for utility interests, they became the nucleus of the Consortium.

The Consortium had already decided that Calvin Reynolds was their guy for Governor when Langley retires. This accident was a stunner. O'Malley described what details he knew about the incident—rumors of Ana Villasenor's presence at the crash site were deafening—and Flanders let out a long, low whistle.

"Man, I just talked with Calvin last week. Hear from Moira?" Flanders asked O'Malley.

"Left a message. Guess she's heading to Mexico today."

"Gotta figure Mary Moore takes over, at least for now," Flanders offered.

"Makes sense to me. Question is whether Langley'll call a special election or just tough it out with her 'til next year," O'Malley said, referring to next year's regularly-scheduled statewide elections. "Probably name Moore as 'Acting' or 'Interim' for the rest of Calvin's term. Then slate somebody like Esther Ruelbach."

"Question is, Kevin, whether Mary will be as kind to us as Calvin." Flanders paused. "So did Calvin get our, uh, package before he left?"

O'Malley knew that question was coming.

"Yeah, I gave it to him the day before he left. Too late to retrieve it. I already talked to Blake."

"Shit. Well, at least the Reynolds kids can go to Harvard now."

*   *   *

Chapter One

Wellsprings, Part III

Calvin Reynolds wasn't the only public official from his state in Mexico that week.

A thousand miles away in a Monterrey hospital, Jackson County Board Commissioner Graciela Perez Torres had just visited with her grandmother who had checked in with chest pains. The family in Monterrey thought it serious enough that la familia en Estados Unidos should come and say their goodbyes to the ancient matriarch. It was, of course, another false alarm, thankfully! Dios Mio! But everyone enjoyed the unplanned Torres family reunion.

"You know that Abuela will outlive us all," Graciela said to her cousin Freddie, who had just flown in with Graciela's uncle from San Diego. She hadn't seen Freddy in eight years and was amused at how he had gone from being a gawky seven-year old with brown eyes bulging out to a gawky 15-year old with brown eyes bulging out. He grinned shyly. He hadn't seen Graciela since before puberty and, like many men, had immediately fallen madly in love with her in the hospital waiting room.

Torres had left Monterrey—called by some the "Pittsburgh of Mexico"—as a teenager some 20 years before. Her father loaded up the station wagon with the four kids, some basic clothing, a photo album and a great-grandfather's precious stirrup once worn by Pancho Villa, and trekked off to realize the American Dream. The car made it to Houston. Staying with cousins for two months, they saved up for another station wagon and completed their emigration to the industrial heartland where jobs grew on trees in the snow.

Upon arriving in Jackson City, the Torres family settled in "El Puente", a bustling Hispanic neighborhood with residents from Mexico, Puerto Rico, Cuba, Columbia and Honduras to name just a few motherlands in this dynamic enclave. They were packed into a cockroach-infested, two-bedroom dive at first, but Ernesto, Sr. found an apartment large enough for four teenagers.

Her mother had died in Monterrey when Graciela was twelve, so, as the eldest, Graciela increasingly assumed the duties of running the household in the New Land. She dealt with the landlord, paid the utility bills, taught the little ones how to read in English and espanol, cooked and counseled. Her dad, Ernesto, Sr., worked long, hard hours in a garment factory, so Graciela ran the show.

The Torres kids were all good students and popular in the neighborhood. Vivacious and big-hearted, Graciela was elected Student Council Treasurer in her senior year. Ernesto, Jr., was the starting shortstop on the varsity baseball team and the youngest, Dolores, won a citywide poster contest on fire prevention.

But the crime, grime and winters began to take their toll on the Torres family. Younger sister Soledad dropped out of school, had a miscarriage and was deep into the rave/Ecstacy scene. Ernesto, Sr., was drinking heavily again and Ernesto, Jr., took up with a group of menacing-looking thugs who were not really a gang, he explained, just his "social unit".

The unofficial leader of this "social unit" was Bobby Perez, a dashing 20-year old from Michoacan, Mexico. He was charismatic, quick-witted and drove a Firebird. Graciela fell hard and they soon tied the knot and had two children, Roberto, Jr., and Raisa. Graciela worked part-time at the grocery and Bobby drove a cab.

Bobby and Ernesto's "social unit" grew and became more entrepreneurial. Moving small quantities of marijuana and fake ID's led to crack and a modest fencing operation. As the unit expanded, it moved onto a collision course with another social unit, one that carried more serious firepower.

One sunny morning, as Bobby Perez, Sr., and Ernesto Torres, Jr., stood outside a panaderia in their El Puente neighborhood, a shotgun blast from a slow-moving carful of Insane Purple Royals ended both of their lives and changed Graciela's forever.

A young widow with two children, especially one who is attractive and articulate, does not go unnoticed. The Democratic Boss of the 33rd Ward—Jimmy Juarez, whose sons knew Bobby and Ernesto—arranged for a secretarial job for Graciela in the City Water Department.

Thanks to her instinctive management skills, bilingual fluency, breezy charm and, possibly, her dazzling smile, she rose quickly in the bureaucracy to the rank of Deputy Water Commissioner. She taught herself about water, and how bringing it to residents and then flushing it all away is the lifeblood of a city. She was a frugal administrator, understood the budget process and caught the eye of the Mayor.

Following a reapportionment that created two new "Hispanic" districts on the Jackson County Board, Jimmy Juarez muscled Torres into the seat that included El Puente. At first she was stunned that she had been given such an opportunity. A girl from a modest Monterrey home, still struggling with English. But she also felt supremely confident about her new role as a public official. And Juarez' confidence in her was boosted after she assured him that he would be the doler of whatever county patronage she could rustle up.

Her first few months on the County Board were action-packed. With a budget to open an office and hire a staffer, she began stretching her wings. She hired Lupe Zarate, a popular young reporter for the local Spanish TV station, as her administrative aide. Torres relied heavily on Zarate and the two became inseparable.

Torres didn't exactly rock the boat, but she was able to get some things done, such as increase the number of Spanish-speaking staff at county health clinics and replace sewer pipes in many older—primarily low-income and minority—communities. Her experience in the City Water Department gave Graciela a natural niche on the County Board. She spoke out on the safety of drinking water, flood prevention and dredging the harbor, and became a self-taught expert on the County's huge public works budget.

Thanks to Zarate's media savvy, Torres became well known in the Jackson City's Hispanic community and beyond. She was becoming a regular "guest analyst" on a local Sunday morning public affairs radio show. And last year, *La Latina*, a national magazine, cited her as one of "100 Latinas to Watch" in the upcoming year. Graciela had the page laminated and framed for her office.

Thanks to Torres' hard work (and the media's recognition of it) and Jimmy Juarez' clout with other Hispanic ward leaders, Graciela ran for re-election unopposed. Now in her second term, she was looking at new issues to expand her repertoire, maybe health or housing. But the County's water reclamation and delivery system was still her top priority.

As she sat in the hospital waiting room in Monterrey, she leafed through the *USAToday* that Freddy picked up on his flight. In the state-by-state capsules, she noticed the item about Commissioner Reynolds' freak accident in Mexico. Graciela recalled meeting him once; he didn't seem like the kind of guy who would explore the jungles of the Yucatan, but who knows? She made a mental to note to call Lupe later.

"Graciela, este es Tia Juanita," exclaimed one of Graciela's many cousins, introducing her to an octagenarian aunt whose face was unfamiliar and whose location on the family tree she couldn't quite place. "Ah, Tia Juanita!" Graciela bubbled and hugged the aging woman. Freddy gawked at her with his bulging brown eyes.

It was great being back in Monterrey.

*   *   *

The response Paul Podesta had gotten Sunday from his marathon phone attack surpassed even his own expectations.

First he called his base, about twenty fellow rural Democratic county leaders. Nearly every one encouraged him to run and either agreed to endorse him or agreed to think about it. Then he called some of the older labor leaders, particularly from the building trades. Again, great reactions, even some unsolicited pledges of troops and money. The President of the Steelworkers even offered Podesta the services of Timmy Sullivan, one of labor's best young political organizers. Paul was somewhat surprised—even a little moved—by the unquestioning support from old friends, some of whom had been rivals or foes at one time.

The intelligence Paul was getting was useful, too. Nobody out there making noises except him. The buzz from his pals on the other side was that Langley would appoint Mary Moore as Acting, but would then push for Esther Ruelbach later. Podesta had served in the Senate with Ruelbach for years and liked her, but knew he could take her, too.

Why hadn't he tried this before, he joked to Emily, who could tell Paul was sky high. The two of them had martinis on the back deck as darkness fell. He slept well, awoke early Monday and started another marathon day of phonecalls.

*   *   *

Thousands of fax machines across the state chirped simultaneously Monday morning with the latest scoops *from "JJ Springfield's Daily Bulletin."*

"MOORE TABBED TO REPLACE REYNOLDS; PODESTA POLLS POLS"
    DATELINE JJ: As reported exclusively here yesterday, visitation for the late Public Utilities Commission Chair Calvin Reynolds is set for Tuesday, 2:00 to 8:00 p.m. in the Capitol Rotunda. A Wednesday burial is planned in Belmont Park, Reynolds' hometown. Flags at all state facilities will remain at half-mast for one week.

Item: JJ's snoops say Mary Moore—#2 at PUC and long-time Zane Township GOP leader—will be named by Governor Tom Langley to replace Reynolds…expect a formal announcement in a week or so.

Item: Many Democratic pols (a few elephants, too) got a Sunday phonecall from Sen. Paul Podesta (D-Mohawk Valley), and it wasn't to talk football. The powerful Chairman of the Senate Public Works & Utilities Committee may toss his hat into the ring in next year's election for PUC Chair. Podesta's dipped his toes into statewide waters before—fell a few votes short of State Treasurer slating in '92—but never pulled the trigger. Most labor fakirs and rural Dems would line up for Old Paul, but Jackson City ward bosses have never been fond of him and the feeling's mutual. Question: Last call for Paul?

Item: PUC Flack Peggy Briscoe called JJ at home on a Sunday night! She wanted to respond to JJ's Question about the impact of Reynolds' death on pending cable and electric rate hike cases. No impact, she insists. Any responses to JJ's Questions about possible improprieties in Reynolds' South-of-the-Border behavior? No comment, she insists!

*   *   *

Goddamn leaks, Steven Page thought. How does JJ get this stuff? The Governor's press office was already besieged with inquiries about the circumstances of Reynolds' death and Moore's likely appointment as his successor. Langley will be pissed, Steven thought. He assumed (correctly) that Jimmy Blake was the source of the leak. Either Blake called JJ himself or planted it in midnight conversations at one of the many bars near the Capitol patronized by reporters, lobbyists, lawmakers, bureaucrats and spin-doctors. The currency is gossip, the fuel is alcohol, and the goal is prestige and maybe a one-nighter.

Jimmy Blake was known in the Capital for his rumor-mongering, sometimes devilishly clever, sometimes totally unfounded, always rare and spicy. But, why would Blake leak this, Steven wondered, maybe to project an image that things are fine and under control at the PUC, or to nip in the bud any potential primary rivals for Mary? Maybe with the Governor's tacit aproval. Or maybe Blake was just sitting at some bar being the big man.

Steven took pride in his discretion, his ability to keep a secret. In twelve years of being Langley's main body person, he never once blabbed to a reporter (or a potential lover) about things he had seen or heard in the presence of Governor Langley. One more year to go, he thought.

*   *   *

The futuristic-looking office of the Dresden Foundation for Democracy's Future was also located on Petra Dresden's manor, a ten-minute walk from Petra's Frank Lloyd Wright residence on the other side of the lagoon.

Petra herself tried to stay out of the staff's hair, trusting the 10-person team to promote the mission—and Petra's vision—of DF-Squared: part think tank, part guerrilla political shock force, part intellectual playground. A fun place to work where dedicated people can make a difference and a living.

Liz Chinn, 30, the Foundation's Director of Community Action, had started at the DFDF ten years earlier as a college intern. A skilled and versatile organizer, she coordinated the petition drive on term limits and became Petra's point person with the campaigns and causes Petra funded. Liz and Petra became friends, playing tennis, traveling to New York and Washington, D.C. together, and even, despite their age difference, swapping man stories.

Petra had called Liz on Sunday evening about the Reynolds obituary. They discussed the signature requirements to get on the ballot for PUC Chairman and agreed to have brunch Monday at the gazebo, also on the Dresden Estate. The gazebo, surrounded by sunflowers and ferns, was Petra's favorite spot, with a stage about four feet off the ground, magnificent ironwork and screens if got too buggy. Petra saw Liz strolling from the Foundation office, her long hair gleaming in the sunlight.

"'Morning!" Chinn carried a file folder and laptop computer. "The fruit salad looks great. I haven't eaten yet."

"Dig in. Have a muffin, too. How are things across the lagoon?" As always, Petra's blond hair was tied in a severe bun and she used little make-up, but still radiated with her energy, her zeal.

"It's Monday morning. Kind of quiet. A couple staffers drove up to Duluth for that City Council race."

"Oh, the Reform guy, Norgard, Norden?"

"Right, Bud Norden. He's got a shot, so we have the troops there until Election Day, a week from tomorrow. Mostly Election Day volunteer recruitment, some door-to-door. Still, it's a long-shot." Liz pulled out a file. "Okay, you'll love this."

She handed Petra a chart listing the nominating signature requirements in all 27 states with elected PUC Chairs. Their state was at the very top: 40,000 signatures required for independent and third party candidates, and, adding insult to injury, only 25,000 signatures required to get on the ballot for the two major party candidates.

Dresden and Chinn shared a grin; they both knew they had a new issue and maybe a new campaign.

*   *   *

Philip Royce Blasingame the Third had never heard of Reynolds the PUC Czar, or the Mexican fender bender. Didn't matter.

Royce or "The Third", as friends and family called him, was living La Dolce Vida. One of the nation's wealthiest 31-year olds, Royce had been "working" as a "vice-president" at the corporate headquarters of Blasingame Steel & Coil ever since his days at the state university. His dad, P.R. Junior, was under the impression that The Third was happily being groomed to take over the company started by P.R. Senior, in 1956. Wrong impression.

Royce had been bitten by the bug. The political bug. A very serious bite.

A few years ago, Royce was bored and had gotten involved in the Mayor's re-election effort, agreeing to serve on a Fundraising Dinner Committee. He loved it, the action, the people. And the people treated Royce like a prince. Public service called; Steel & Coil stood no chance.

The Blasingame family should not have been surprised. Royce didn't have a head for business, but was the life of any party. He was well bred, well-read and had seen the world. Royce had carefully built and nurtured an extensive network of acquaintances, classmates from his prestigious prep school, college frat pals, business contacts established for him by his father and grandfather, people he met at parties. He understood the importance of socializing.

One drunken night last year, Royce had decided to run for office, some office, he wasn't sure which yet. His parents weren't crazy about the idea, but knew his resolve.

Royce began courting elected officials of both parties by setting up courtesy calls with the state's entire congressional delegation. While some of these politicians weren't sure why they were meeting with this earnest, well-groomed scion of industry, but you just don't refuse courtesy calls from millionaires. Royce's purpose in these meetings was to evaluate the terrain, possibly decide who would be a weak opponent. He subscribed to P.R. Senior's maxim: "Always look 'em in the eye."

Unlike his father and grandfather who were virulent conservative Republicans, The Third considered himself a moderate—sometimes liberal—Republican with a libertarian streak. He was still formulating his political ethos. Like his dad and grandfather, Royce believed government should keep its nose out of the business of business. Unlike dad and gramps, Royce was a globalist, pro-choice, in favor of gun control, and for decriminalizing and taxing marijuana. He sometimes felt uneasy at Republican functions, but knew that seeking office as a moderate Republican made the most sense for him.

As he sat in his favorite Starbucks Monday morning, he read about this Reynolds fellow. Tough break, Blasingame thought. He pulled out his cellphone and dialed up Nicky Pulver, his old college fraternity pal who was now a mucky-muck political consultant at ProAction. How 'bout lunch?

*   *   *

Like Royce Blasingame, Thelma Barnett had never heard of PUC Czar Reynolds. Until she got a call from The Very Right Reverend B.J. Crandall.

Thelma Barnett had been on the frontlines for years with Rev. Crandall and the Crusade of Christian Marchers. She was a regular outside of abortion clinics where she obtained frostbite, an arrest record and a reputation as an in-your-face agitator for Christ and Crandall.

A few years ago, Thelma had her 15 minutes in the national consciousness when, appearing on a local public access cable TV program, she attempted to burn a copy of *"Romeo and Juliet"* which she found "provocative." The stunt backfired, so to speak, when the book became too hot to handle, giving Thelma second-degree burns on her zealous hands and frying her eyebrows. Thelma's recklessness caused smoke and water damage to the tiny cable studio as well.

But the videotape, played repeatedly on TV stations across the nation and on a network broadcast of "America's Goofiest Moments", showed Thelma's stunned look as the Bard flared up in her hands. Her fortitude caught the eye of Rev. Crandall.

The Barnett kids, Mary and Peter, were in grade school when the United States Supreme Court ruled that mandatory school prayer violated the constitutional separation of church and state. Watching the news coverage on the tiny black-and-white Zenith in her house trailer, she knew this was another example of the godless creeping communism threatening our very core! First JFK and flouridation, and now this!

Thelma Barnett considered herself a patriot.

Years passed, Thelma worked as a cashier at Woolworth's, Mr. Barnett died and Thelma's eyebrows grew back. The kids had moved out and were both making good money as computer something-or-others. Thelma's first grand-child was on the way and she was cutting back on her hours at Woolworth's, where she had recently been honored for her 30 years of service.

So when Reverend B.J. Crandall and his Crusade launched a drive two years ago called "Amen Now!" to restore school prayer, he named Thelma Barnett to spearhead the drive, which she did with passion and missionary commitment. She soon became a household name in the homes of Godfearing Good People all across the state. Her leadership skills were evident and dedication beyond question. The legislature refused to even consider the issue, but not without feeling some heat generated by Crandall and Barnett.

Reverend Crandall called Barnett first thing Monday morning.

"Thelma, have you ever heard of Commissioner Calvin Reynolds?"

"No, Reverend, that name is not familiar to me."

"Well, Thelma, he was elected to serve the people of this state, and he was, uh, caught fooling around down there in Mexico and the Good Lord struck him down," Crandall intoned.

"The Lord giveth and taketh," Thelma responded.

"Well, Thelma, that is so true, so very true. Anyhow, this Commissioner Reynolds is now paying his penance in the hands of the Lord."

"Amen, Reverend. Bless his soul."

"Uh, Thelma, the reason I'm bringing all this up, is to suggest that the people and the Lord might be best served if the Crusade of Christian Marchers rallied together and elected some of our own, don't you think, to elected office?"

"We have seen it too often, Reverend: heathen and sinners in the highest levels of public service," Thelma said, not sure where BJ was going with this.

"Thelma, you have shown us time and time again that you are prepared to take a giant step in the service of the Lord," Crandall said. "Please come out to the farm some time this week so we can pray and explore this challenge together."

Thelma mumbled her appreciation, not realizing how her life was about to change.

*   *   *

Mary Moore's life had changed too, but she was keenly aware.

Monday at the Public Utilities Commission was rough. The flag hung at half-mast out by the parking lot, staffers spoke in hushed or shocked tones, a few just finding out about the boss's demise. Mary could sense people talking about her in the hallways. Actually, more of them were discussing Ana Villasenor.

Moore convened a meeting first thing Monday of all department heads and briefed them on the situation. Mexican authorities had charged the truck driver. Moira Reynolds was in Cancun now to bring back the remains. In respect to Reynolds' visitation in the Rotunda Tuesday and funeral Wednesday, the PUC would be closed until Thursday, except for emergency services. Governor Langley had asked her to carry on. This wouldn't affect any of the cases being considered by the PUC. Life as usual, stiff upper lip, Calvin would've wanted it that way, he was a decent man and will be missed.

Mary said she would address the entire staff in the Auditorium at noon and tell them likewise, which she did with poise and dignity, and earned an emotional and cathartic standing ovation from the 230 staff there.

Her life had been changing in recent months on the home front, too. The last of her brood had just flown from the nest. Her son, Tony, had gotten his first apartment, a studio with a view of a brick wall, in Jackson City. She and her husband, Randall, were eager for some quiet time. Don't need four bedrooms anymore; maybe rehab the old house. Turn one bedroom into a home office for her.

Randall Moore had maintained a hands-off attitude about Mary's political activities. He was only casually interested in politics, though he enjoyed exploring the economic questions posed in Mary's profession. When Mary went back to grad school, he took some courses with her and became a self-taught expert on phone deregulation. He was excited for Mary's new opportunity, though saddened at the circumstances.

As she went into a lunch meeting with PUC Communications Director Peggy Briscoe, Mary wondered about her Sunday morning conversation in the Governor's Office. He didn't come straight out and say he was appointing her Acting Chair or that he would recommend her to the Senate to fully succeed Reynolds as Chair. He was so adroit at ambiguities, at shades of gray, so smooth, she marveled. And that Jimmy Blake fishing expedition in Calvin's office, when he snatched the list of donors or swimmers or whatever. What a roller coaster. She barely had time to grieve. Only spoke with Moira once.

*   *   *

Nicky Pulver left ProAction's loft office, grabbed a cab and headed to *"Harbor"*, the hottest new seafood eatery in town. Royce's suggestion. It had been a while since Pulver had last seen Blasingame and even longer since their fraternity house days at state university. In those days, Nicky Pulver had no idea of the career path ahead, had never heard of "oppo" or "GOTV". And, Nicky mused, brother Royce sure as hell never demonstrated any inkling towards the noblest profession: Politics.

After graduation, Pulver had volunteered and occasionally earned minimum wage for a string of losing candidates. Candidates for Congress, for city council, state senate. Once he drove Michael Dukakis to the airport. When some fellow campaign junkies invited him to join their new firm, Pulver didn't hesitate. He joined ProAction on the ground floor and they grew together.

The early emphasis for ProAction was opposition research and Nicky became "Doctor Oppo". He claimed he would never "peek through a motel window", but he'd come close, like that one night he camped out for hours in the snow disguised as a shrub. He got the photos.

He was adept at not only digging up dirt, but knowing how best to use it. Sometimes best to use it on TV or with JJ Springfield or in last-minute mail or by word-of-mouth in bars. Sometimes you use it early to put your foe on the defensive, distract him, prevent traction. Sometimes it's an "October Surprise" or a "Hail Mary Pass", coming too late for effective rebuttal. Or sometimes—Nicky's favorite—you show it to no one except your opponent, if you learn he's got some goods on you.

On top of oppo, Pulver had become adroit at getting out the vote on election days. His GOTV operations were crisp, disciplined and usually successful. He could tap into local organizations or build from scratch. His highly-targeted use of election day "walkin' around money" was legendary.

By specializing in oppo and GOTV, Pulver was guaranteed a role in the beginning and endgame of every campaign. Nicky loved it.

Seven years ago, hearing a crying plea from the world's emerging democracies for good political consultants, ProAction launched a "global strategy". Pulver was dispatched to Bolivia, the Philippines and Poland to show candidates how to research an opponent, do radio spots and run pluses on election day. Candidates were also shown how expensive U.S. consultants were.

There was that little patch of bad PR when it was revealed that one ProAction client, a parliamentary candidate in a small Caribbean island, had been a ruthless torturer during his country's "dirty war" in 1979. ProAction lost that one. But, as fame is fleeting, so too is bad press. ProAction had since opened three offices and boasted of clients in nine countries.

And whether the client was running for President of Mali or Mayor of Mayberry, ProAction's formula was the same: good oppo, raise a ton of early money, go on the air first, go negative first and have the most troops on Election Day. Last year, their batting average was .700.

As the cab pulled up, Nicky saw Royce in the lobby of *"Harbor"*.

"Brother, my, Brother!" Blasingame called out and waved. Royce had put on a few pounds, Nicky thought, probably pushing 250.

"Third! You're looking good! How long's it been?"

"Oh, man, must have been Remo's wedding?"

"Shit, my head still hurts from that one!"

The frat brothers got caught up on the latest they had heard about some of their old housemates. Some personal chitchat. Steel & Coil. Oppo. Neither had spouses or children, but both had seen the world.

"So Nicky, I saw the coverage of the Puck Czar's funeral," Royce said, chomping on grilled calamari. "Just what were his qualifications for that post besides knowing the Governor in Saigon and being his money man, tell me please?"

"You need more reasons?" Nicky asked, still working on the shrimp satay. "Far less qualified candidates have been elected to much higher positions."

"Yeah, Ronald Reagan."

"Hey, give Bonz a break. So, you're thinking of a career change? Steel and Coil ain't doin' it for you anymore?"

"Shoot, Nicky, I hate it. I'm making more money than I can spend, but I just dread going to the office. You know I worked on Mayor Townshend's Fundraising Committee, did a huge event right here at 'Harbor', raised $90,000." He popped a deep-fried conch nugget into his toothy mouth.

Old Blass was still pretty clueless, Pulver sensed, but he had that earnest, sincere Royce style of talking. And talking and eating.

"So one night last summer I'm sitting at our beach house in South Carolina, drinking ouzo with my cousins, looking at the stars, getting buzzed and it hits me that I should run for office."

"Right there on the beach? Hits you, eh?" Nicky asked, dipping a shrimp into the tangerine ginger sauce. "Drinking ouzo?"

"Yep. And, Nicky, I think I'm ready for this."

"Man, you got no name recognition, no base, no organization," Nicky said. "But, we could fix all that. Any office in particular?"

"You tell me, Bro, you're the expert."

"Well, Langley's retiring from the Governor's seat," Pulver joked.

"I'm not sure I'm quite ready for that," Blasingame replied, only half-jokingly.

"You thinking statewide?"

"I'm no small-time Charlie, you know that, my Brother," Royce said, beaming that big Blass smile. "So tell me about this Public Utilities Commission."

Nicky smiled. He knew it.

"Well, it regulates utilities."

"Well, that sounds exciting."

"Royce, you may not realize it, but some people in this fine state actually pay phone, gas, cable and electric bills."

"No!"

"There's a staff of about two hundred, maybe more. Chairman's paid about $95,000. Offices in both Jackson City and the Capitol. Sometimes it's a springboard. Old Senator Colgan got his start there. "

"How much would a campaign cost?"

"Maybe a mil."

"Any strong candidates besides this Mary Moore?"

"Just you Brother," Nicky knew he had hooked a big one. Each candidate brought in as a ProAction client yields a bonus to the entrepreneurial staffer, plus the firm gets 15% of the cost of the TV ads, which in the case of "Royce Blasingame for Whatever", would be substantial.

"ProAction would handle it?"

"With pleasure."

"Let's do it." Blasingame crossed into a New World.

Many of ProAction's clients required a total makeover. Royce needs some work, Nicky thought. He's 50 pounds overweight, dresses like a preppy millionaire and likes to play just a little too much.

On the other hand, he's likeable, quick and rich. ProAction had done more with less.

"I'll send over some background on the PUC, and draw up a proposal and an initial planning memo," Nicky said as they wrapped up lunch. "Meanwhile, you get your personal affairs in order, start jogging, bone up on state government and make a list of everyone you've ever met who will give you $1,000."

"Awright Nicky! Let's win one just like the old days," Blasingame bubbled as he downed his second glass of champagne. Pulver couldn't recall specifically ever winning one in the old days with Royce, but he bubbled back.

*   *   *

"So?"

When Consuelo had that tone of voice, no one, even Alderman Petacque could resist.

"Sew buttons!" Shawn replied, grinning.

"So? Is it do-able?" Of course Consuelo knew what had obsessed Shawn for several days. He had been crunching numbers, looking at maps and websites, stroking his salt-and-pepper goatee. Everything but consult a crystal ball. Or talk to anyone about it.

"Oh, *cher*, I dunno, it's a toughie. I think the numbers are there, if there's only one Black candidate in a crowded field."

"And African-American voters all vote for you", Consuelo said, skeptically.

"Right. Well, like 95 percent."

"And they turn out."

"Right, which should happen with an open gubernatorial."

"Yeah, well don't count on it."

Consuelo's political acumen and moxie sometimes surprised Shawn. She had always been the grassroots organizer type, sometimes the sage political philosopher, but never a political nose-counter. But she regularly jolted him with insights into the shifting political winds and the human condition. One more reason to be so crazy in love with this woman, Petacque thought. One more reason not to be out on the road in this sprawling state, going to pig auctions or whatever they do on campaign trails outside of Jackson City, instead of having Sunday mornings with the kids eating waffles.

Petacque hadn't discussed his interest in the PUC race with a soul outside the Petacque-Milagro household. That was his way. His political and personal network was extensive, but he had only a handful of trusted counselors, of which Consuelo was Number One. She had encouraged him to run for the City Council and campaigned hard for him. She had been an enthusiastic political spouse, putting up with his crazy schedule and the socializing that went with the job.

But a statewide race? On the road for months and months?

Consuelo reached across the dining room table for Monique's calculator. "Let's go to the abacus. Okay, how many African-American registered voters?"

"Census says 650,000. Real number's lower, maybe 630," Shawn said wistfully.

"Maybe six hundred." Consuelo, Voice of Reason. "What was turnout last election?"

"For the whole state, I think around 48 percent. Maybe 45 percent for African-American precincts, which generally go 90 percent Dem."

"Okay, six hundred thou times 45 percent times 90," Consuelo's fingers punched the keys. "Two forty-three. Maybe half are for Petacque," she said playfully.

"No way. 99 percent, at least!" Shawn was amazed how she cut right to the nub of the numbers.

"I'll give you 90 if you give me a massage later. Okay, you get 218,700 votes just for being such a fine brother. Figure 50,000 from the white libs, another what, 40,000 Hispanic votes and another 10,000 from people who think 'Podesta' is too damned ethnic. Shoot, these numbers…you should just run for Governor!" Consuelo smiled impishly, her dark eyes flashing. "Just kiss the kids and the wife and this lovely body goodbye and hit the campaign trail for a year. Adios! Good luck on the open road!"

Shawn wrestled with her and kissed her urgently. She was so great. Their tongues mingled and she undid his belt. "Time for that massage, Governor."

*   *   *

The public visitation for Reynolds was held under the rain-soaked Capitol dome in the statued Rotunda.

For nearly seven hours, thousands of state employees, Republican Party leaders and people who used a *"Reynolds is My Man!"* nail file passed by the closed coffin, paying last respects to Calvin and offering condolences to Moira and the Reynolds kids. Governor Langley stood next to Moira in the receiving line the whole time.

The outpouring of tributes from all sectors demonstrated the wide number of people touched by this man, Mary Moore thought as she sat in one of the hundreds of folding chairs set up in the Rotunda. Cabinet members, state legislators, wheelchair-bound Vietnam vets, Chamber of Commerce leaders, Boy Scouts. Mary wept a little, thinking about all the unselfish things this man had done, so many accomplishments, such a great future.

The rumors of his fling in Cancun with Ana Villasenor could no longer be ignored, but that kind of thing wasn't discussed during the visitation. Nor was there open speculation on the horse race that had aready begun for his successor.

*   *   *

Like Thelma Barnett and Royce Blasingame the Third, Eva Vargas, 27, had never heard of Commissioner Reynolds or the Public Utilities Commission.

Eva had come to the United States from Puerto Rico a few years ago and had lived on the edge ever since. With little formal education, Eva and her husband, Mariano, lived and struggled in the River's Edge public housing complex with daughters Felicity, 5, and Bree, 3. Mariano had just landed his first job in months as a night watchman at a factory out in the suburbs.

An aging, battle-scarred facility, River's Edge was in the heart of the El Puente barrio, next to a sewage creek and not far from the much nicer residence of Jackson County Board member Graciela Torres. In fact, Torres had campaigned several times in River's Edge and always came away feeling sad, angry and helpless. Despite a running war against gangs, graffiti, litter and despair, the tenants' association had recently organized a community garden and were planning on setting up a day care center, so there was hope.

The night after Reynolds' funeral, Eva Vargas was awakened by little Felicity.

"Mommy, my tummy hurts."

Eva squinted at the clock. 3:00 a.m. Some asshole in the courtyard was blaring a radio. Mariano wouldn't be home from work for another four hours.

"C'mere, sweetie."

Eva sat up in bed, reached out to Felicity and immediately noticed an unusual smell. The last sound Eva heard resembled the scream of an incoming bomb.

The explosion tore through the Vargas unit first, instantly disintegrating Eva, Felicity and Bree. Shock waves, followed by sheets of flame, ripped through the thin walls and ceiling, sending pieces of the Vargas household like shrapnel in all directions.

Directly upstairs, Rosa and Julio Delgado, both in their 80's, were sound asleep and never knew what destroyed their apartment and lives in seconds. In fact, a wooden dresser from the Vargas unit had shot upward through the floor and demolished the Delgados' bed.

The Vargas' next door neighbor, Juan Melendez, 39, was an unemployed carpenter from Brazil. He was engulfed in a white-hot ribbon of fire and suffocated instantly, as did the never-to-be-identified woman in bed with him, just before the ceiling crushed them.

Fire raced through the River's Edge complex with blowtorch ferocity. The horrific screams of pain, terror and panic quickly alerted other tenants.

The conflagration immediately engulfed all twelve units on the first floor. Second-and third-floor units were collapsing downward, victims still in their beds telescoping into hell. Toxic black smoke thundered, the smell of burnt flesh and gas wafted. The blast blew down an overhead electrical line, illuminating the insane sight with snapping electric bolts.

The sprinkler system was working only in isolated areas, but Engine Unit 17 of the Jackson City Fire Department was on the scene within four minutes. They immediately detected gas and notified the Eaton Gas Company.

Within hours, 19 bodies had been pulled from the smoldering ruins of River's Edge. All Hispanic, many kids. Some 60 others hospitalized with burns, smoke inhalation and broken bones. Nearly 100 left homeless. Electric and gas service knocked out in several neighborhoods, leading to sporadic looting. The City's worst fire in decades, a tearful Mayor Townshend would proclaim at the scene, promising a complete and thorough probe.

*   *   *

Chapter Two

A Stream Becomes a River, Part I

"The offing was barred by a blank bank of clouds and the tranquil waterway leading to the utmost ends of the earth flowed sombre to lead into the heart of an immense darkness."

-Joseph Conrad (*"Heart of Darkness"*)

The Big Boards at the Jackson City Emergency Dispatch Center lit up in a flash. Hundreds of "911" calls reporting the blast and power outage overwhelmed operators. The City's "red lines" to Eaton Gas and the Union Megawatt Electric Company were activated. The Mayor's Chief-of-Staff and the Deputy Fire Commissioner were both phoned at home; both promptly contacted their bosses.

Fire equipment, police squads, utility emergency vehicles, TV trucks, neighbors and gawkers quickly descended on the grisly scene. A smoldering, ground-zero cavern in the center of the complex gaped where the Vargas, Delgado and Melendez households were only minutes before.

Flames churned through windows, doors and rooftops throughout the complex. Burning debris fluttered overhead in a pre-dawn sky rendered surreal by billowing smoke, crackling power lines and a growing intensity of floodlights.

Bloody victims were everywhere. Stunned and soot-coated, night-clothes blown off. Limbs blown off. People screaming in pain or confusion, some in a shocked daze, not sure if their slumber had resulted in this dark, Dali dream. A delirious, shrieking cacaphony of English and Spanish.

Frantic Fire Department rescue teams were joined by heroic neighbors in pulling out those trapped in flaming rubble. The confirmed death toll began rising. A makeshift triage center and morgue were set up in St. Elizabeth's Catholic Church basement across the street, where the 80-year old stained glass window had blown instantly into the heavens. Paramedics struggled to save those on the edge as Medical Examiner's staffers struggled to match body parts.

*   *   *

Roberto Perez Torres, Jr., 16, was sitting in the back yard at 3:00 a.m., sneaking a smoke. He figured his mom knew he'd taken up cigarettes lately, and she warned him about it, but he liked the feel of the smoke in his lungs. Plus, he felt cool lighting it up. He had taken a few puffs off a joint at the playground and liked that, too.

Graciela, Roberto and Raisa lived in a recently-rehabbed century-old brownstone in El Puente. One of Jackson City's highest-density neighborhoods, El Puente was lively and colorful and dynamic. Graciela loved it. But, she also loved getting away to her urban oasis. When she needed a respite from crime and grime, she could always relax in her modest backyard garden. She installed a winding brick path and a tiled patio, and the kids gave her a wooden bench on Mother's Day. She planted cilantro and strawberries, and Raisa planted some flowers that smelled like Mexico.

Roberto was sitting on the Mother's Day bench when he felt the blast six blocks away. He first felt the shock wave echo through his stomach, and then, a micro-second later, the crashing thunderclap of the explosion itself. Within five seconds, the electric power went out.

Windows flung open immediately. Sleepy, wary faces peered out. Graciela opened her bedroom window and saw her son down in the darkened yard.

"Que paso, 'Berto?"

"Big explosion, Mami," replied a shaken Roberto, who had just stubbed out his Marlboro.

Simultaneously, they both heard sirens and smelled gas.

Raisa came into Graciela's bedroom, rubbing her eyes. "Hija, it's okay," Graciela said as she picked up the phone and called the local police district. She identified herself as Commissioner Torres and was told there were reports of an explosion at River's Edge and that help was on the way. Graciela reported the power outage.

"I'm going over to River's Edge," Graciela told Roberto, who was back in the kitchen. "Me, too, Mami," Roberto said, pulling two flashlights from the junk drawer. "No! Stay with your sister. Go to the yard. I'll be right back." Graciela took one of the flashlights, her cell phone and a handkerchief to filter the thick odor of gas, and set out on the six-block walk to Hell.

As Graciela approached River's Edge amid a growing crowd, scores of fire engines, ambulances and police squads raced by furiously. With the streetlights dark, the only illumination came from other flashlights and the snarling sparks shooting from downed power lines. Graciela arrived on the scene to witness a carnage like she had never experienced.

*　　　*　　　*

The slogan of "Action News 14" was "We're Your Eyes on Our City's Streets". Channel 14 News had made its reputation by having a fleet of small, speedy TV vans, handheld cameras and reporters with street smarts. Their coverage was gritty and raw.

Darlene Dawes didn't mind working the overnight shift at the station, where she had been a street reporter since graduating from journalism school two years earlier. A willowy African-American woman with piercing hazel eyes and a dozen rings piercing her ears, Dawes, 24, had covered fires, murders and mayhem and always kept her cool in hot situations.

Darlene was the first reporter on the scene at River's Edge. When she arrived at 3:20 a.m., her initial reaction was the surreal hellishness of it all. Noxious gas, fire alarms and car alarms, anguished screams, smoking phosphorus wreckage. The blast's initial fireball fried the electric power line running overheard and knocked down two utility poles, igniting a current-fed crackling of broken wires and a nightmarish high-voltage lightshow. Red and blue flashing light from fire and police vehicles pulsated. Incredible lighting, Darlene thought as she flicked on her super-lightweight video camera and dove in.

She slowly panned the inferno, taking in the blazing rubble, zooming in on the gnarled crater that once housed the Vargas family. As she moved through the crowd, Darlene interviewed survivors, witnesses, neighbors, cops. Only the emergency personnel from Eaton Gas Company seemed unwilling to talk, but Darlene could see they were in a panic.

Action News 14 went live with Darlene's reports almost immediately. The smoky and surreal atmosphere, the raw footage and Darlene's determination made for a stunning live broadcast. She wished she had studied Spanish more.

As the scope of the tragedy became apparent, Darlene's live broadcast from the scene was picked up first by Channel 21 ("El Mundo"—the city's Spanish TV station), and then by CNN. Within minutes, the global village was aware of River's Edge and El Puente and Darlene Dawes.

The crowd was growing. Darlene looked around, deciding which direction was next, when she recognized a woman in the crowd who was a politician.

"Excuse me. Darlene Dawes. Channel 14. Aren't you on the County Board?" Darlene asked.

"Right, Graciela Torres. I live just a few blocks away. This is so incredible."

"I hear the death toll is nine and rising," Darlene said. "A morgue's been set up over at St. Elizabeth's."

"How awful for these people. And that smell of gas is still so strong. Wonder what happened." As Graciela spoke a scuffle broke out nearby, in Spanish, between a bloodied, disheveled resident and a City emergency services worker.

"Do you speak Spanish?" Darlene asked Graciela. "What's happening there?"

"The resident claims he smelled gas at 2:00 a.m. and called the gas company, but nobody came."

"Would you mind translating if we can interview him?" Darlene said, turning the camera on the victim before Graciela could reply.

With the camera running, Graciela calmed and comforted the man, whose arms were burned raw. "His name is Paco Rivera," Graciela said into the camera. "He lives on the first floor over there," pointing to a burning two-bedroom unit. "He doesn't know where his sister is. He says he called the gas company at 2:00 a.m., but they didn't understand him. They laughed at him, he says."

"Ask him did he call the policia?" Darlene said in a low key to Graciela.

Graciela whispered to the man.

"He said he did call the police, just before the explosion."

Paco became agitated again and began weeping. Graciela, who had been sleeping in her bed less than an hour before, put her arm around Paco and consoled him softly in Spanish, unaware that her words and actions were being viewed live by millions around the world on CNN.

Within minutes, a dozen other TV crews descended on the scene and helicopters churned overhead, but Darlene Dawes' poignant footage of Graciela and Paco was the most-remembered, defining image of the tragedy.

*　　　*　　　*

Arnold Wiser, 39, was fairly new to his job with Eaton Gas Company, having just relocated his wife and infant daughter hundreds of miles to start a new life in a new state. The one-time "Vermont Prep Fullback of the Year", Wiser was a college football star until a knee injury ended his game. After graduation, he worked at the water department in his Vermont town and married late. Now a bit paunchy and balding, Arnold still had quick hands and a fearless attitude.

As an overnight "emergency inspector", Wiser was one of the first on the scene and knew there was almighty trouble. The stench of gas—Eaton Gas—was palpable. He joined in with Jackson City Bomb & Arson personnel in the first wave of investigators to comb through the still-smoldering ruins around 3:40 a.m.

Wiser had a schematic diagram of all gas lines and meters in the River's Edge facility and neighborhood. He had already ordered a cut-off of all gas to the area and taken a call from Stan Flanders, an Eaton Veep who was the company's point man in crisis management. Flanders told Wiser to hang in there and that help was on its way; the Eaton "Go-Team" was en route.

Donning a helmet and gas mask, Arnold picked through the rubble and found the main gas line, which was now a mangled, charred mess of cast iron and cement. He slid down into the maintenance shaft, now partially exposed, and into a crumbling, six-foot concrete cube. His flashlight beam cut through the smoke and revealed remnants of a what seemed to be a master valve and meter. As he leaned over to get a closer look, a small explosion a few yards away shifted the ground and debris began falling in around him.

"Yo, Gas Man! Get the hell out of there! Right now," a firefighter yelled down, grabbing Arnold by the arm and pulling him out just as a wall of the shaft collapsed. Cascading debris briefly trapped Arnold's leg, breaking his ankle and big toe.

"Whoa. Thanks, chief." Arnold had been in life-threatening spots before, but this was a little too close for comfort. His leg hurt. The old college knee?

No, something was definitely broken, he thought. He took off the gas mask and saw the Eaton Gas "Go-Team" running toward him.

"Inspector Wiser, you okay?"

Wiser recognized one of the men, but had never actually seen Eaton's "Go-Team" before. They looked sharp, efficient. Armed with diagrams, flashlights, pickaxes, gas masks, gauges, walkie-talkies, tools and cameras, one of them helped Wiser limp over to a newly-arrived Eaton Gas emergency service vehicle, where a nurse was ready to minister to him. The others jumped promptly into the same shaft Arnold had just emerged from.

*   *   *

At 4:20 a.m., night watchman Mariano Vargas, 29, had just completed his final rounds at Roth & Sons Tool & Die. He wasn't crazy about the commute or the hours at his new assignment, but the pay was decent and the folks at the factory treated him well. He had even met old man Roth, who was actually the "Son" in Roth and Sons.

As Mariano returned to the guard's desk at the entrance to the suburban factory, he was told of an emergency at home. Mariano wasn't aware of the River's Edge blast, but his supervisor told him to punch out and go home early. He tried calling Eva, but the phone was dead. He rushed home to River's Edge.

*   *   *

The grim scene at St. Elizabeth's kept getting grimmer.

Just across the street from the main entrance to River's Edge, the old church suffered some damage from the blast, but was now being utilized as an emergency ER on the first floor and a temporary morgue in the basement. By 5:00 a.m., 14 bodies were shrouded, all in a row. The sounds of sirens were gradually supplanted by the sounds of grief.

The electricity was still out as Graciela Torres headed back to her home to check on the kids. Smoke filled El Puente's pre-dawn streets.

As she neared her house, she heard the smashing of glass and saw a six or seven teenagers break into a small liquor store down the street. She moved into a doorway and dialed 911 on her cell phone, but got no answer. A police squadrol suddenly careened toward the would-be looters, who scattered in all directions.

Graciela practically sprinted the remaining few blocks to her home, where all was safe and sound. What she had witnessed on the street, though, was the first stage of a looting and arson binge that would rage throughout El Puente for the next two days.

*   *   *

Acting PUC Chairperson Mary Moore was awakened at 5:15 a.m. by a call from the State Police Commander informing her of a deadly incident at a public housing facility in Jackson City. Confirmed death toll at 15. Many injured and missing. Gas leak likely. Power outage in the area, a Hispanic neighborhood known as "El Puente". Arson investigators already on site, but, the top cop told a groggy Moore, the PUC's own "go-team" should be mobilized ASAP.

As she brewed a pot of coffee, Mary thought about what a week it had been. Last Sunday, she was cleaning out Calvin Reynolds' desk. The visitation Tuesday. Now this. Yikes. Gas leak and power outage. Damn. Why did it have to be Eaton, she thought, as she began making wake-up calls to her senior staff.

*   *   *

The Eaton Gas Company's Go-Team worked quickly at the site. Two of the Go-Teamers, wearing gas masks and asbestos suits, spent a few minutes in the smoking shaft and then rushed back to Eaton's Headquarters. Other gas mains in the area were checked. Arnold Wiser, meanwhile, was brought to a nearby hospital for treatment of his broken toes and bruises.

*   *   *

This dawn was a smoky dawn, thick and nasty, bending the sunshine through El Puente. The sounds and smells of looting dishonored those who feel asleep at River's Edge and never awoke.

Darlene Dawes continued her live coverage until the death toll reached 18, when her station sent reinforcements and ordered her to go home for a nap. The first newspaper images of the tragedy hit the streets by Noon in a "special edition" of *"Hoy!"*, the region's largest Spanish daily paper. The Internet and CNN propelled the dramatic scene across the planet.

Mayor Bob Townshend spent all morning on the phones with his emergency services people, his spin doctors, the media, Eaton Gas, the Housing Authority and Hispanic politicians. This was the deadliest crisis in all his years as Mayor and he wanted to leave no stone unturned. He was still ticked off at Eaton Gas for their hardball tactics in renegotiating the City's franchise agreement when Townshend first took office, and he wasn't going to let them embarrass him again.

At his impromptu press conference at River's Edge that morning, the stunned Townshend promised a full investigation and full accounting. He already had some names in mind for a blue-ribbon panel, and after a chat with El Puente's Democratic power-broker Jimmy Juarez, agreed to appoint Graciela Torres to the panel. After all, he had already seen Graciela's poignant comforting of Paco Rivera a few dozen times on TV. Plus, he knew that Torres' career was a pet project for Juarez, that maybe Jimmy was thinking statewide office for his project. He would wait, of course, until after the funerals to announce the appointees.

*　　　*　　　*

The Public Utilities Commission had an emergency meeting that lasted all afternoon. Mary Moore had dispatched a team of investigators to the scene, which was still a smoldering mess. They reported a less-than-cordial reception from both the Eaton Gas "Go-Team" and the Jackson City Bomb & Arson Unit. Tempers had flared.

"Chairmadam Moore, the fact is that our own investigators are having a difficult enough time on the site, without getting stonewalled by these Eaton Gas boys," intoned Reverend Commissioner Felix Porteus, the only African-American on the PUC. "The fact is that unless we push for more straightforward cooperation and less jive from these boys, the people of this great state will not be served."

"Commissioner Porteus, you are so right, as always. We have every PUC staffer on the case and have been in constant touch with the State Police and Attorney General," Moore said.

"Well, gentle Chairmadam, the fact is that this particularly incident looks hinky and that this particular gas company has a reputation for hinky. This Commission must go above-and-beyond, yea, above-and-beyond in it's vigilance to protect the consumers and the taxpayers are the good people from all that is…hinky." Porteus took a breath.

Mary knew exactly what the Reverend Commissioner was driving at. Her predecessor/mentor was known to be more than chummy with Eaton Gas. I'm being tested in more ways than meets the eye here, she thought. The Governor had spoken with her earlier and offered to help with the investigation and spin.

"Commissioners, I have ordered the staff—with the full backing of Governor Langley—to proceed full-speed ahead on our investigation. We must go," Moore said, smiling at Porteus, "above-and-beyond." She then received a unanimous vote-of-confidence from the entire Public Utilities Commission.

Moore then held another, more in-depth meeting with her senior staff, and urged them to go "above-and-beyond". Communications Director Peggy Briscoe would issue a press statement expressing sadness, vowing a thorough Commission investigation and reporting the expressions of confidence in Mary Moore made by the Governor and the full PUC.

*   *   *

The looting had ceased by mid-morning, but flared again after the schools let out. A Jackson City police officer was in serious condition after being hit by a brick. City bus drivers refused to go into El Puente. The paroxysm of burning and pillaging spilled out of El Puente and into adjacent communities. Governor Langley offered and Mayor Townshend accepted several National Guard units. The sounds of helicopters buzzed over the city all day.

By mid-afternoon, Mariano Vargas was still in shock. He had arrived home that morning to find his life shattered. His wife Eva—the light of his life—at Ground Zero of the blast. His beloved, innocent daughters blown to bits. His modest home and meager belongings vaporized.

In a zombie state, Mariano went to the Jackson City Human Services Agency shelter for the survivors, almost all of whom had lost everything. Mariano had the difficult task of calling Eva's mother in Puerto Rico to deliver the gut-wrenching news. Life in the United States was supposed to be a dream, not this.

*   *   *

Eaton Gas Go-team leader Ken Lee met with Eaton Vice-President Stan Flanders back at the gas company's palatial headquarters. They stared at the charred ruins of the valve assembly on a conference room table.

"Keep in mind this is very preliminary and instinctive, Stan. But, I think the valve and connector worked fine," Lee said reluctantly. "The problem was an inspection that took place two or three days ago. Our guy must have been asleep at the switch. Probably left it open just a tad. Pressure built in the shaft and then it just blew, I figure."

"Any chance it was tampered with? Rough neighborhood there. Maybe vandals?"

"Nope. That shaft was secure."

Flanders knew the implications of this initial analysis. Couldn't blame the Swiss manufacturer that made the valve. It was our employee's fault, pure and simple.

"Damn. Okay, we'll get the records of the inspection and yank the employee's personnel file," Flanders said. "How's Wiser?"

"Broken toes. A JC firefighter yanked him out just before the shaft wall collapsed. Not sure how long he was down in the shaft."

Meaning, Stan understood, how much Wiser saw when he was down in the shaft.

*   *   *

Alderman Shawn Petacque wasted no time in blasting the negligence of the gas company. His first order of business was to brainstorm with his Chief-of-Staff, Chemuyil Gardner.

At 33, Gardner was coming into her own politically. The daughter of a Jamaican diplomat and a Honduran teacher, Chem hit it off immediately with Petacque and his wife when she first interviewed for a staff assistant job four years ago. Bilingual, bicultural—and, she once told Consuelo, bisexual—Chemuyil Gardner was well-read and well-organized. Her gorgeous dreads and knock-your-socks-off smile became a familiar feature in the 15th Ward. She truly had a knack for addressing the needs of Shawn's constituents and became Chief-of-Staff last year.

Chemuyil drafted a press statement saying the pipeline disaster was a tragedy waiting to happen. The safety standards for gas pipelines had declined and the company was more interested in profits than in maintaining pipes in older, inner city neighborhoods. Do you ever see this kind of negligence in affluent white neighborhoods? Petacque was interviewed on several radio talk shows during afternoon drive time, and indicated his availability to serve on the Mayor's blue-ribbon panel.

*   *   *

Sen. Paul Podesta had been following the disaster's coverage since 6:00 a.m., when he awoke for his morning exercises and flipped on the radio. He saw the endless images of Graciela Torres and the burn victim, and the Mayor's vow to name a blue-ribbon panel. He saw Eaton Gas flacks speaking in spin-babble, expressing sadness, vowing a full investigation. As Chairman of the Senate Public Works & Utilities Committee, he had the power to announce a probe of his own.

"The only problem with that, honey, is that you could be viewed as an opportunist, just jumping on the investigation bandwagon on the backs of those poor victims," his wife Emily advised him over breakfast. He had always valued her common sense analysis of all things political. He knew he had his own separate problem with a legislative inquiry: his own long-time relationship with Eaton Gas and Stan Flanders and Kevin O'Malley.

In chewing it over with his pal Pudge Carson, it dawned on him that one advantage of his holding hearings is the bottleneck it could pose on other pending legislation, including the approval of Mary Moore's likely confirmation. "Plus it'd be fun to stick it to Moore some. Watch Mary dance, y'know?," Pudge chortled. "But, I'd wait 'til everybody's in the ground, then come out swingin'."

Podesta knew that the first horse out of the gate gets the most scrutiny. This one is sticky, he thought. But that's why I love this game.

*   *   *

Hubert Qualls, the Eaton Gas Company inspector who had been out to River's Edge just two days earlier had been with the company for 11 years, his personnel file revealed, but had accrued a spotty record.

Qualls had been reprimanded several times over the years for chronic tardiness. He had enrolled in the company's substance abuse program for a codeine dependency problem two years ago, but had never totally kicked the stuff. His culpability in another explosion—one that resulted from a similar valve being similarly not properly closed—was never proven, but his supervisors always suspected Hubert's role. Fortunately, that incident destroyed only some construction equipment and no one was hurt.

When Hubert was questioned by the Go-Team and Eaton's lawyers about River's Edge, he was evasive and uncooperative. He swore the valve was properly closed when he left the site. Usage records showed differently, though. Internal records established a slow leak beginning 36 hours ago.

And a phonecall from a unit at River's Edge just before the blast.

Eaton's top lawyer called Stan Flanders and informed him that the company better gird itself for lawsuits. And Inspector Qualls needs to pee in the cup. This would be ugly.

                    *   *   *

That night, a press conference was held in the City Hall Pressroom to call for an end to the looting that had raged all day in El Puente. Every prominent Hispanic leader was there: ministers, sports celebrities, musicians, restaurateurs and politicians, including Jimmy Juarez and Graciela Torres. From the crowded stage, the speakers addressed a blinding array of TV crews, microphones and newspaper photographers.

When invited to the podium by "Miguelito", the one-named, one-armed soccer star who had captivated the city, Graciela was taken aback by the applause from the crowd and the interest in her from the media. She was received as a celebrity, the local hero. All I did was some translating, she thought to herself, as she looked into the cameras. It had been a very long day since she had seen Roberto sneaking a smoke in the garden at 3:00 a.m., and she was running on adrenaline and caffeine. She had a few talking points offered by Lupe, but no real speech. Yet the words began to flow, back and forth in Spanish and English.

"Mis hermanas y hermanos. Our community has suffered greatly on this day. The flames at River's Edge scorch our hearts, todos, all of us. To the victims, we honor you. To the survivors, we embrace and comfort you."

As she said these words, Graciela immediately thought of Paco Rivera, as did every TV news director in town, most of whom used that bite on the 10:00 p.m. broadcast.

"To those in our community who smash windows and burn and steal from our own people, we urge you to stop this madness now! Please do not further disgrace the people—our people—of El Puente! Do not dishonor those who perished in this horrible accident!"

She looked into the gaggle of cameras and wagged her finger.

"Little brothers and little sisters! Do not disrespect yourselves! Alto! Stop the looting!" Graciela was near tears, but held on to salute the brave firefighters and cops and ambulance drivers, especially those who worked in County government. The crowd of VIP's on stage applauded her heartfelt appeal.

Still, the looting flared up again that night, with more than a hundred arrests, another 15 buildings torched, countless windows smashed, several sexual assaults and one riot-related fatal heart attack, all compounding the smoldering misery of El Puente.

*　　　*　　　*

Chapter Two

A Stream Becomes a River, Part II

The morning edition of *"Hoy!"*, the state's largest Spanish-language newspaper, devoted front-page coverage to a color photo of Graciela Torres comforting River's Edge victim Paco Rivera and an stern editorial by Peter "Pequeno" Barragan, Editor-and-Publisher. The Elder Statesman of Jackson City's Hispanic media, Barragan, at 65, still considered himself a classic muckraker, constantly suspecting—and even occasionally proving—corporate greed, public corruption, racism and societal injustices.

In two languages, Barragan eloquently expressed sympathy for the families of the victims, blasted the Housing Authority for the inhumane conditions and in particular, tore into Eaton Gas.

"The arrogance of this company! To the hundreds of thousands of Spanish-speaking customers of Eaton Gas, they are saying: You don't count. Pay your bill on time and call us if you have a problem with your gas, but bring your own translator, they are saying to us.

"And this is not the first time low-income people have fatally suffered due to substandard service from Eaton Gas. Remember the explosion just four years ago at the Monroe School that killed two little girls? Not to mention

the criminally-high number of heat shut-offs in the dead of winter last year. This company has only gotten more unresponsive.

"The readership of 'Hoy!' can be assured that we will be journalistic watch- dogs—bulldogs!—to find out what really happened at River's Edge and what caused the brutal, humiliating rioting which has inflamed our community in the aftermath."

*　　　*　　　*

Graciela Torres had tried to sleep after the late-night press conference; after all, she was running on empty. Been awhile since she'd been up for 24 hours straight. But the disturbing images of the day and the sounds of looting in El Puente kept her up.

As the dawn neared, she downed a shot of tequila, went out to her backyard oasis and sat on her Mother's Day bench. The autumn scents of the garden were refreshing, cilantro and spearmint. She shed a few tears, but was too tired to mourn further. She closed her eyes and drifted off, not realizing the photograph of her comforting Paco Rivera had made the *New York Times.*

The phones that morning at her County Board office never stopped ringing. Her aide, Lupe Zarate, handled hundreds of press inquiries from across the nation and even from Mexico and Puerto Rico. It's amazing, Lupe thought, how Graciela had worked so hard and long on issues like the harbor dredging and health clinics, and a tragic chance occurrence puts her in the *New York Times.* What a business.

*　　　*　　　*

"Stan, we just need a little more cooperation here. The PUC Team and your Go-Team had some problems out there on-site that we don't want to extend into the investigation. Anyone's investigation," an exasperated and tired Mary Moore told Eaton Veep Stan Flanders.

This is not Calvin Reynolds, Flanders thought to himself.

"Commissioner, we are doing everything we can here, every available resource. I am sorry about the on-site friction this morning. We will get to the bottom of that. You have my word."

Years of lobbying had given Stan the Voice. The ability to modulate ever so slightly to fix any situation with a politician. Some, like Calvin, could see through it and tell him to cut the crap and cut to the chase. But Flanders didn't quite have a read on this Mary Moore yet.

*　　　　*　　　　*

JJ Springfield's Daily Bulletin got the Blue Ribbon scoop. Chemuyil Gardner saw it first, called Ald. Petacque on his cell phone and read it to him.

"DATELINE JJ: Watch for Jackson City Mayor Townshend to tab County Board Commish Graciela Torres for his Blue-Ribbon Truth Squad on the Eaton disaster. Torres was sponsored by Hispanic power broker Jimmy Juarez, who also engineered Torres into the County post a few years back. While no automatic rubberstamp for the Mayor, Torres—who resides just a few blocks from the explosion—will take a tough stand towards Eaton.

"Question: Between Juarez' clout and the now-famous image of Torres on CNN, in the New York Times and everywhere else, how could the Mayor not appoint her?

"Question: Is it true that State Rep. Seth Dickerson, Jr., son of legendary Ward Boss Seth Senior, has the inside track for a slot on the panel?

"Question: How many probes? Mayor Townshend's Blue Ribbon Panel will be one of several, looks like. The state Public Utilities Commission has already launched a probe, the City's Bomb & Arson Unit is investigating, maybe the Feds, Attorney General Lou Calcagno and a state legislative committee. Stay tuned to JJ…"

"Dickerson. Damn," Petacque said.

"He seems to be the Mayor's pet lately," Gardner offered.

"Yeah, just like his Pop."

Shawn was vaguely aware of an ancient animosity between his own late-father and old man Dickerson. He had researched it a few years ago and found its genesis in a squabble over the slating of a judge. Thirty years earlier, Dickerson, Sr., had apparently insulted a judicial supplicant who had kicked in $500 for "election day expenses" to Petacque, Sr., but not to Dickerson, Sr. A fistfight broke out, with some of the Petacque forces pummeling Dickerson, Sr., and knocking out his two front teeth. Shawn had never mentioned it to Dickerson, Sr., who was by now somewhat senile, but the animosity echoed through the generations.

Young Seth Dickerson was a dead-ringer for his dad—220 pounds with a silvery Afro—and even more overtly ambitious. Junior had been rewarded for his years of service in a ghost payroller job with a real job in the State House. Some of Mayor Townshend's operatives had taken a liking to the young lad and had been gingerly pushing him onto a faster track.

The same track as Shawn, a fact known and left unspoken by both Chemuyil and Shawn.

Shawn had used back channels to reinforce his radio statements about his availability for service on the Blue Ribbon Panel. He called the Mayor's key African-American operative and met with several religious leaders who had the Mayor's ear. He knew, as Graciela Torres must have, the vehicle this thing could be.

"Well, if it's Dickerson, it's Dickerson," Gardner said. "Then you bang on it from the outside. Keep hitting on Eaton, the 'you-never-see-this-in-the-white-burbs' rap. And maybe tweak Dickerson and Torres while you're at it. Could even be a blessing in disguise."

"Chem, you're the best. A spin doctor in dreads."

"Oh, yah, Frenchy," Gardner said, her playful nickname for Petacque when they were alone.

*　　　*　　　*

The media release issued from the Mayor Townshend's office after the final River's Edge funeral was succinct.

Rep. Seth Dickerson was indeed named to the ten-member Blue
Ribbon Commission, along with Comm. Graciela Torres. The investigation would be chaired by former Jackson City Mayor Pinkerton "Pinky"
Banks and would leave no stone unturned. The Banks Commission would
have a budget to hire staff and would convene immediately.

*   *   *

The front page of *"Hoy!"* featured, for the second time, a color photo of
Commissioner Graciela Torres, flanked by a complete bio and flattering
interview. She spoke movingly about the River's Edge "moment" and her
own path from Monterrey to Houston to Jackson City. She thanked the
Mayor and Jimmy Juarez for their confidence.

On Page 3, her appointment to the Banks Commission was hailed by
Editor-and-Publisher Pequeno Barragan. *"Finally! Someone from Our
Community who we can rely on to get to the truth and see that justice is done!"*

*   *   *

The various investigations commenced at varying speeds.

The state Public Utilities Commission probe seemed to focus initially
on the gas company's inexcusable response to Paco Rivera's frantic call in
Spanish. A second-by-second account of the disaster put Eaton in a very
bad light. The call from Paco Rivera's unit was confirmed, as were three
other calls from River's Edge residents.

Investigators from the Jackson City Bomb & Arson squad ruled out
foul play, but hinted at negligence on Eaton's part.

The Blue Ribbon "Banks Commission" hired three investigators and two
support staff, and announced public hearings. Early indications were that its
Chair, former Mayor Pinky Banks, was primarily concerned about the lack of
smoke detectors and overcrowding at River's Edge. Of the various investigations, the Banks Commission had the greatest resources, was most organized
and enjoyed the most media attention. Commission members met almost
daily to sketch out their plan of attack. Some members, including Graciela

Torres, had tried to move the panel's focus away from smoke detectors and response times to the actual cause of the blast. They hired engineers and heard lengthy testimony from Bomb & Arson and forensics experts.

Pinky Banks thought it would be a great idea to organize a field trip to the site, a terrific photo opp if there ever was one. It became an especially tough outing for Graciela, though, as she ducked under the "Police Line" ribbon and was immediately confronted with the cavity that was once the home of Eva, Felicity and Bree Vargas.

Led by Pinky, the Commission members and staff trekked through the boarded-up complex, with the media held at a respectful distance. The whole place had been evacuated. Most of it was a total loss. The Mayor had confidently vowed to "Rebuild River's Edge!" Anyone walking through the charred ruins would wonder why bother. This tiny speck on the planet had experienced such extreme horror and pain. Ghosts would occupy this space forever.

As they gingerly walked amid the burned-out residences, the smell of flames and gas still pervaded the air, probably soaked into the ground and trees. Graciela was recalling so vividly the moment she first saw the disaster sight, with the macabre snapping of electric wires and auto alarms and screaming in Spanish…

"And over here is the shaft leading down to a concrete chamber where Eaton housed the valve assembly," said the Jackson City Housing Authority Chief Engineer, who was conducting the hellish tour. The Commission members craned their necks to see down the narrow shaft, which was lined with jagged metal and concrete chunks. "This is where that fellow broke his toes…"

"Wiser," intoned Banks.

"So, Mister Engineer, what happened to the valve?" Rep. Seth Dickerson asked.

"That is the Question, Representative Dickerson. As you all know, Wiser said he might have seen the valve when he went down, but a small explosion over there at the electric substation forced him to leave the shaft.

He was pulled out by a Jackson City firefighter. Where's the valve? All we know is it ain't down there now."

The Commission staffers were stonewalled and befuddled on this point by Eaton, whose lawyers and administrators basically said, "No subpoena, no discussion." They refused to allow the members of their "Go-Team" to be interviewed by the Banks Commission. After an energetic start, the Banks Commission was going nowhere fast. Torres was getting frustrated.

*   *   *

The Shawn Petacque Aldermanic Website became a popular clearing-house of information, gossip, maps and conspiracy theories about River's Edge.

The Kiddie Corps—high school and college interns recruited and lorded over by Chemuyil Gardner—would monitor every newspaper article about River's Edge and pore over every page of testimony in the various investigations, much of which they posted on the website. Diagrams of the Swiss valve assembly, schematics of the pipeline system, even a history of gas pipeline disasters were eagerly viewed by website visitors.

Reporters covering the investigations came to rely on Shawn's website, which itself made news, revealing discrepancies between the second-by-second disaster timetables prepared by Eaton Gas and the Public Utilities Commission. The chat rooms were always active and Shawn responded to every e-mail, no matter how wacky. Special e-mail updates were transmitted every few days. Hundreds of concerned citizens asked to be placed on Shawn's mailing list. Sometimes, Chemuyil assured him, an outsider with a website has more clout than an insider.

*   *   *

Over at the Public Utilities Commission, Mary Moore worked closely with Steven Page, the Governor's designated point man on the investigation. PUC attorneys had grilled Arnold Wiser, who had broken his ankle and toe during his initial inspection of the disaster. Eaton Gas lawyers persisted in denying any liability, pending the outcome of their own probe.

"Well, Steven, where are we at?" Moore asked every morning, hoping that something clear and distinct had materialized. Usually Page had nothing earth-shattering to report. But after a sleepless night, he confessed his concerns to Moore.

"Commissioner Moore, one of our investigators thinks there may have been a problem with a valve."

"Which investigator?"

"One of the guys from Boone Engineering, Biff Fahey." The PUC had contracted Boone for the investigation.

"And what does Mr. Biff Fahey think?"

"The missing valve, the logs of the inspectors, the origin of the blast, the very rapid response by Eaton, the on-site run-ins with other investigators. Smells bad," Page said, his blond hair hanging across his forehead. "He does not believe a valve can vaporize."

"Good work. Encourage Mr. Fahey. Keep at it," Moore said, admiring Page for his candor. The distance she had imposed between herself and Eaton must be widened, she knew. This would probably put her in conflict with Jimmy Blake, who she knew had close ties to Stan Flanders and Kevin O'Malley.

But Governor Langley had urged her to do the right thing and she would.

*   *   *

Sen. Paul Podesta continued playing his quiet, inside game, as if the River's Edge disaster had not happened.

He decided that convening hearings on the matter was a minefield he didn't need. Plus, he had gotten very negative signals from both his wife Emily, and his favorite lobbyist, Kevin O'Malley. Besides, Pinky Banks' probe and the PUC probe and the Bomb & Arson probe and Eaton's internal probe and who knows what other probes would probably cover all the same ground.

Paul figured he'd keep his powder dry for awhile. He knew that if the Governor nominated Mary Moore to fill out Reynolds' term, there was a chance—a better than even chance—that the confirmation process would have to march through the Senate Committee on Public Works & Utilities. Paul Podesta, Chairman.

Meanwhile, he lined up broad institutional support for his PUC Chair ambitions: local Democratic Party leaders, elected officials, the trade unions, lobbyists. Money began to roll into his campaign fund, even though he was not even close to a formal announcement. His pitch was: the Eaton mess makes Mary Moore extremely beatable. Maybe wily ole Calvin Reynolds the PUC Czar could weather something like this, but not a naïve rookie like her. Plus, it's time to return those 200 jobs to us Dems!

The Steelworkers had known Podesta for years and wanted another friend in statewide office. They signed on early and offered Paul the services of Timothy Sullivan, a battle-tested political organizer. Wiry and balding, Sullivan was the son of a frequently-unemployed steelworker. Fourteen years earlier, Timmy made waves fresh out of college by engineering the defeat of a prominent anti-labor state legislator. Since then, he had worked in a dozen legislative and Congressional races, usually in the role of labor coordinator or field director. He was particularly adept at targeting and Get-Out-The-Vote operations.

Like Podesta, though, this would be Timmy Sullivan's first statewide race. Unlike others in the Podesta War Council, however, Sullivan had done politics in every corner of the state and had built extensive connections. He was responsible for lining up much of the institutional support so crucial to Podesta's strategy.

One call made by Sullivan did not go well. He knew that Podesta was not well-liked by some of the old-time party bosses in Jackson City. Those calls were very tough. If a Ward Boss actually took his call, they would grunt or just say nothing, speaking with empty space.

The worst was John Czyz.

Czyz had heard on the grapevine that Podesta was already running hard, that he had brought in this Steelworkers' whiz kid and that he expected a clear field. But what really got Johnny's goat was not so much that Podesta had this kid call him, but more so the gossip that Podesta was about to hire Wally Mraz to run his petition drive in Jackson City.

Few people irked Johnny Chizz like Wally Mraz.

He had gotten Wally his first patronage job 19 years earlier, and Wally's brother, too. Then the two Mraz brothers stabbed him in the back by actively supporting a Mayoral candidate not endorsed by Johnny. Stabbed in the friggin' back. Johnny stewed over that for about a decade. Plus, Czyz was still fuming that his man in Washington, DC—Congressman Ziggy Prybyl—was being strongly discouraged from seeking any statewide office by State Party Chairman Niles Flint and other Party Higher-Ups.

"So, Committeeman Czyz, I'd like to buy ya lunch and maybe talk some turkey about this PUC race," Timmy gamely started. "We can bring back plenty jobs with this Commission, ya know."

"Hey, kid, I already got plenty jobs there. What's this I hear about you guys bringin' in Mraz?" Boss Chizz was crabby and direct.

Sullivan was caught off-guard. "Well, y'know, there's been rumors, but I…"

"I don't give a shit about your goddamn rumors. All I know is Mraz is a termite, a little squirmin' vermin, maybe lower than that. Wally the Weasel stabbed me in the back and he'll do it to your guy, too. You got Mraz, you ain't got Chizz." He slammed the phone down.

At that moment, Sullivan realized the City Cousins would be a tougher nut than he thought, and Johnny Chizz realized he'd have to run somebody for this PUC thing, maybe this PUC lawyer Plucharski or even Butchie Kaminski. Screw Mraz, Podesta, Flint, the Steelworkers. Screw the whole sorry lot, Czyz thought. I'm 72, I got nothin' to lose.

*　　　*　　　*

Governor Langley had convened a Kitchen Cabinet brainstorming session in the "rec room". This dungeon-like hideaway deep in the bowels of the Governor's Mansion was equipped with an old Space Invaders video game (probably from the Kirkland administration, Langley figured), a battered ping-pong table and a well-stocked wet bar.

Langley's favorite feature was a bizarre photo wall of fame featuring previous Governors posing in unlikely shots. Gov. Kirkland with Mick and Bianca Jagger at the State Fair's "Hall of Goats"…Old Gov. Champ O'Leary in a tuxedo and Uncle Sam hat riding a donkey into the 1952 National Convention…Gov. Billy Byrne dressed in a Charleston flapper outfit tripping the light fantastic with actress Kim Novak…

Soft track lighting had long-since supplanted the Dungeon's kerosene lamps. Tony Bennett on the stereo. A circle of couches and recliners. Drinks flowing, as usual.

The Governor's Boy Wonders were there, Jimmy Blake and Steven Page. So was Langley's hand-picked State Party Chair, Gretchen Hanson. His hammer in the legislature, Sen. Bruce Cavaretta (R-Mary's Rock), puffed on a cigar to Gretchen's obvious discomfort. Congresswoman Violet O'Hara (R-East Jackson), a Langley confidante for 20 years and a colleague of Congressman Paul Prentice, chatted with the First Lady.

At times like this, Langley really noticed Calvin Reynolds' absence, missed his military discipline clad in a breezy, casual style. The Governor opened the discussion. "So, any chance Esther might back off from the top spot, maybe settle for something winnable, say State Treasurer? Bruce? Violet? 'Cuz I'm sorta likin' Prentice."

"She's a tough ole bat. Served with her on Senate Budget Committee. Gutsy lady," Cavaretta drew on his cigar. "She's got a little of the sainthood thing goin'. I think she'd rather end her illustrious career crashing in a blaze of glory for the top spot than play it safe with something further down."

"Prentice could aid and abet on that aspiration," Blake tossed in. "Our numbers show he'd be strong."

Congresswoman O'Hara and Gretchen Hanson then took turns warning of dire consequences for the ticket if there are no big-name women, especially if Langley openly backs Prentice over the venerable Esther Ruelbach.

"She's got a real following out there," Gretchen said.

"Every League of Women Voters member in every corner of this state loves Esther," O'Hara reported. "She can help really with some legislative races in swing districts, especially in the suburbs."

"Okay, okay. Look, Esther's not the only qualified Republican woman who could run a credible race statewide," Langley said. "How about Aviva Benson or Judge Parrish or, uh, Karen Hogan, uh, or that commissioner in Sayles County…"

"Linda Whitman," Page murmured.

"Yeah, Whitman. Or maybe a couple of your Senate colleagues, Bruce…"

Clearly to everyone, the Langley farm system was not deep with female candidates.

Cavaretta framed the question. "Okay, who's where here? We got Prentice and Esther for Guv, Dobbs again for SOS…"

"One last trip for the Boy Mayor," Langley chuckled.

"Maybe Aviva Benson for Attorney General…"

"Driscoll's been makin' noises about AG," Steven Page slipped in, referring to anti-abortion activist and millionaire gadfly, Phillip Driscoll, a long-time thorn in Langley's moderate side.

"That'd be a disaster," Langley grimaced. "Aviva's sharp, could run up some numbers in the City, has fundraising potential…"

"That leaves State Treasurer open," O'Hare concluded.

"Well, and the PUC," Blake shot in. "How 'bout Esther for that?"

"Jimmy, we have an incumbent PUC Chair, in case you forgot," Violet O'Hara quietly replied.

What a jerk, Steven thought. Here we are trying to renovate Mary Moore from a well-informed party loyalist into a credible statewide campaigner, and Blake's trying to zap her. Down here in the Dungeon.

"My hunch is that Mary will do quite well. The River's Edge smoke is clearing. No one can blame her for that," Langley said, dismissing Blake's direction, but not totally endorsing Moore, either. "How are the numbers, Jimmy?"

"On the Governor's race, Esther's name is better-known, 43 percent, a few points higher with women," Blake said. "But very few voters can associate her with any single issue, education mostly. Prentice has lower name ID—around 31 percent—but has great favorables in the suburbs, like 5-1."

"The military base-closing issue," O'Hara offered.

Blake sipped from his scotch on the rocks and went on. "Dobbs is through the roof. 81 percent name ID. A whopping nine out of ten drivers license facility users say efficiency is greater under Dobbs. Plus, the Boy Mayor's sitting on nearly a mill. He should crush Karmejian or anyone else in the fall."

"Have we polled for Mary?" Gretchen Hanson asked.

"Name ID mid-teens. Decent numbers in her home base, nowhere else. More importantly, though, people blame Eaton Gas for River's Edge, not the Governor or the Housing Authority or the PUC. And Calvin still polls well from the grave," Blake blithely noted. "Ah, sorry Governor."

"Well, it's still early," Langley said, signaling support for Mary. "We'll get her up there."

By the end of the boozy evening, the Governor's slate was set.

Congressman Prentice would replace him in the Governor's Mansion. The ticket would include the articulate Jackson County prosecutor Aviva Benson for Attorney General against incumbent Lou Calcagno (assuming Calcagno stayed put there), incumbent Secretary of State Dobbs for a last hurrah and Mary Moore for PUC Chair. Bruce Cavaretta would feel out his Senate colleague Esther Ruelbach; if she turns down the Treasurer's spot, that would go to Karen Hogan, a member of the State Arts Council and daughter of Charlie Hogan, a veteran Capitol lobbyist/fixer.

Hanson and Page started playing ping-pong, and the Governor cracked open another bottle of Southern Comfort for Cavaretta. Congresswoman O'Hara and Mrs. Langley chortled at the photo of a dripping Langley perched over a dunk-tank at the State Fair. Blake viciously whacked the side of the well-worn Space Invaders to re-start.

The Langley Farewell Tour Ticket was set.

*   *   *

ProAction's numbers were similar to Blake's.

Nicky Pulver had already done preliminary polling on the PUC race for Royce Blasingame and the results were to be expected. Mary Moore's name ID was at 17 percent—a little higher in the suburbs—and only a handful of respondents had an unfavorable impression of her. Nicky noticed that a rapidly-increasing percentage of Republican female voters would vote for a qualified woman over a qualified male candidate in a blind horse race.

While 13 percent had heard of Blasingame Steel & Coil, only 5 percent thought they had heard of Royce Blasingame, a statistical black hole. Most consumers thought it was very important for their utility service to be safe (95 percent), affordable (90 percent) and reliable (82 percent). Among likely Republican voters, a PUC Chairman with close ties to the utility companies was viewed unfavorably by 27 percent, with 55 percent saying it didn't matter.

And Calvin Reynolds polled well, for a dead guy, Nicky Pulver told Royce.

Nicky put Royce on a tough physical regimen, working out with him daily from 6:30—8:00 a.m., at Jackson City's prestigious Old Hickory Bath & Tennis Club. Royce was a decent swimmer and swung a mean tennis racquet, but hated the treadmill and exercycle. So pointless, he protested. Still, he took a few pounds off and the two of them spent some quality time in the sauna, whirlpool and tanning booth. Nicky even lost a few pounds himself.

To Nicky's pleasant surprise, Royce became a self-taught expert on the Public Utilities Commission. He devoured the last few PUC budgets, analyzed key rulings and became familiar with everything from electromagnetic fields to water treatment. Royce also cut a personal check for $100,000 to his newly-formed campaign fund and in just a few weeks shook another $175,000 loose from family and a few close friends.

For the first time, Nicky was not just spinning Royce when he said this was winnable. He needed to boost Moore's unfavorables, though. And the quick-and-dirty opposition research he'd done on his own candidate had turned up a few embarrassing nuggets.

*   *   *

Out of respect for the victims of River's Edge (and a keen sense of timing), Governor Langley quietly notified the legislative leaders that he was formally nominating Mary Moore as Chairperson of the PUC to fill out the balance of Reynolds' term, signalling his desire to see her elected next year. She would continue to serve as "Acting Chair" until the State Senate confirmed the nomination.

*   *   *

Sen. Paul Podesta sat on his favorite bench in the Mohawk Valley town square.

The Senate had 90 days to confirm or reject Langley's nomination of Moore to serve out Reynolds' term. Podesta had intimidated members of the Senate Democratic Leadership into assigning the confirmation process to his turf, the Committee on Public Works & Utilities. Since Paul was not yet an announced candidate for the PUC Chair, there would be no conflict-of-interest, he explained to a young Capitol reporter who called him about his plans for the confirmation process.

"Hey, Missus Moore deserves her day in court. We'll play it fair-and-square…or you guys'll fry me!" Paul had laughed.

It was a sweet opportunity, Podesta knew. The real issue was how best to play it. There were two basic routes, he figured. He could put the confirmation on a fast track, leaving Moore less time to prepare for hearings, with River's Edge and all, and cast her as inexperienced and in way over her head.

Or he could drag the confirmation out for the full 90 days and then some, keeping her in limbo. The stalling maneuver would distract and annoy her, and keep the focus on Paul's Committee.

A brisk October wind whipped through the square, blowing leaves into tiny tornados. The usual cloud of crows circled over Paul, declaring, *"Stall! Stall! Stall!"*

Paul grinned.

*   *   *

The Shawn Petacque website received thousands of visits to its "Eaton Gas Disaster" page and Shawn tried to keep up with the hundreds of e-mails. One curious e-mail was caught by one of the Kiddie Corps.

"Obviously valve was leaking and is Exhibit #1. Company is saying valve was destroyed in the aftershocks; blown to high heavens. Vaporized! Bomb & Arson found no valve remnants when they investigated that night. Valve probably stashed in some closet at Eaton HQ right now.–Mountain Referee"

"What the heck is 'Mountain Referee'?" the intern asked Chemuyil.

"Some crazy screen name," Gardner said, typing a response.

"Mountain Referee. How do we even know there was a valve there in the first place?"

Instantly, a response flashed on the screen.

"Because I know. Who's talking please?"

Whew, Chemuyil thought. Somebody on the inside?

"Chemuyil Gardner. Ald. Petacque's Chief-of-Staff."

"Chemuyil. A nice name. Check Eaton inspection records at Riv Edge from two days earlier. An inspector named Qualls. Royal screw-up. May have not properly closed valve after inspection. Would take pressure a few days to build and blow."

"These are excellent leads if they are true, Mountain Ref."

After a pause, Mountain Ref replied.

"They are, Chemuyil. More later. MR"

*   *   *

The full-page ad featuring a pointing Uncle Sam was placed in every daily newspaper in the state.

"WANTED!" A Candidate for Public Utilities Commission Chairman who is independent, fair and willing to work long hours! BOUNTY! $50,000 now, $50,000 later! Contact the Dresden Campaign PAC."

The ad went on to explain the role of the PUC, make the case for reducing the signature requirement and vow $100,000 for a credible candidate. Petra Dresden called JJ Springfield herself and outlined her stake of $50,000 for a candidate's petition drive and another 50K once that candidate was on the ballot.

The placement of the ad generated great media coverage, thanks to Liz Chinn's tireless working of the state's political reporters. Most observers missed Petra's main argument, that the signature requirements for independent candidates were extraordinarily high, focusing instead on the size of the "bounty". But the word was on the street.

Manny Ruiz hadn't talked to Dan Clark since the coke-and-rum party. The residual hangover and embarrassment had lingered longer than usual. As soon as he saw Petra's ad, though, Ruiz e-mailed Clark. *"You know this stuff, man. 50-Kay ain't chickenfeed. Sure beats standing in a classroom with a bunch of slack-jawed 19-year olds! Go for it,"* Manny urged Clark.

Then Ruiz e-mailed Liz Chinn at Dresden, who he had worked with on a senior citizens transit project a few years ago. *"Yo, Chinn, I've got the perfect candidate. Send me the Bounty so you and I can elope in Tahiti! Call me.—Manny Ruiz"*

*   *   *

"*DATELINE JJ: The recent nomination by Gov. Langley of Acting Chair Mary Moore to fill out the late-Calvin Reynolds term may face rough sledding. Senate confirmation duties have been handed to Sen. Paul Podesta (D-Mohawk Valley). A possible candidate himself, Ole Paul's in no rush to coronate Moore. Podesta, a wily veteran of parliamentary in-fighting, has flexed his muscle before in stalling confirmations of Langley's people.*

"*TODAY'S BONUS QUESTION: How long did Podesta drag out the confirmation of Luke Blaise, the Governor's pick for Highway Commissioner four years ago? ANSWER: 14 months. Good luck, Acting Commish Moore!"*

*   *   *

The Mayor's River's Edge probe had stalled. Pinky Banks didn't have the zip he once enjoyed and the Blue Ribbon staff's focus was diffused. The Mayor's more loyal appointees were primarily interested in protecting the City and the Jackson County Housing Authority from blame and lawsuits.

At one hearing which addressed the response time, Graciela Torres went after the Eaton Gas explanation that their Spanish-speaking emergency operators were "away from the desk" when Paco Rivera called. Torres produced Equal Employment Opportunity data showing that of 122 employees considered "emergency operators", only six spoke Spanish, a percentage far below other utility companies serving large numbers of Hispanic customers, Torres noted.

"In fact, isn't it true that only one Spanish-speaking operator was on duty that night and that she was in the company infirmary most of that night?"

"Well, Commissioner Torres, that data is inconclusive and…"

"So how many Spanish-speaking emergency operators do you have now, sir?"

"I really couldn't say…"

"Humor me with a guesstimate," Torres shot back.

"Maybe we're up to 12 or 13."

"Wow. And doesn't this suggest a larger pattern of arrogant neglect towards the tens of thousands of customers of Eaton who speak only Spanish…"

"Madam, I would not characterize it as arrogant or neg-"

"And doesn't this suggest that if you had hired just a few more Spanish-speaking operators, then quite possibly this fatal, horrible disaster could have been avoided?"

"The cause of the blast has not yet been ascertained," the Eaton mouthpiece said defensively.

"You and I both know that if Eaton had visited the site at 2:00 or 2:30 a.m., then the leak may have been noticed and an evacuation could have been implemented. Right? Maybe little Felicity Vargas or Rosa Delgado would be alive today. Your arrogance and insensitivity may have been the biggest cause of this tragedy. No further questions, Chairman Banks."

Of course, Torres' inquisition made TV news and the front page of *Hoy!*. But Graciela felt like she had fallen short, that the real source of the explosion had still not been delved into yet. The Spanish-speaking operator angle was important, to be sure, but Graciela knew it was not at the core of the problem.

*　　　　*　　　　*

Chemuyil Gardner saw the e-mail addressed to her from "Mountain Referee".

"Chemuyil. Attached are records showing steady leaking of valve for 36 hours prior to blast. Qualls must have lied on inspection report. Rumor is he is serious codeine-junkie…MR"

Gardner opened the attachment. The documents showed the detection of gas in the valve chamber almost immediately upon the completion of Qualls' inspection. The pressure in the sealed chamber also was measured and it too spiked upward after Qualls was there.

"Referee. This is hot stuff. Can we go public with this without implicating Mountain Ref? Do you think Eaton may dump Mr. Qualls overboard on this? And where the heck is that missing valve? Chem Gardner. P.S. thanx!"

*　　　　*　　　　*

"Aw, c'mon, Paul," griped Sen. Betsy Gitz, the Republican minority spokesman on the Senate Committee on Public Works & Utilities. "Your motives here aren't pure, but they sure are transparent."

A grinning Podesta had just provided her with the hearing schedule for the Mary Moore PUC confirmation: 30 days for research and investigation. 30 days for public hearings across the state. 30 days for Committee hearings. Then they would consider it.

"The People deserve a thorough examination of all nominees and they are depending on our Committee to…"

"Aw, bullshit, Podesta. You're pulling another Luke Blaise here," Gitz shot back.

"Betsy, thanks for remembering our bipartisan effort to protect the state's motorists from an incompetent hack."

"Yeah, well, I was new then. Look, Mary Moore is a friend of mine. She's gone through a tragedy with Calvin and the gas explosion."

Paul smiled. He really liked his Republican counterpart on the Committee, but she was a featherweight. She would accept his timetable and like it, he smirked, confident that his 11-8 edge on the Committee would hold.

"I'm a reasonable man. You're a reasonable woman. I'll cut the number of public hearings from five to three."

*　　　　*　　　　*

"We have reason to believe that Eaton Gas was tracking the build-up of gas and of pressure in the valve chamber as many as two days prior to the blast," Ald. Shawn Petacque boomed at his press conference. Every TV crew in town attended the "blockbuster announcement" which had been promoted on his River's Edge website.

"And we have reason to believe that Eaton Gas knew that the employee assigned to inspecting the valve just three days before that blast has had a serious substance abuse problem for some time. Finally, we have reason to believe that Eaton Gas illegally removed evidence from the scene of the blast, impeding the Jackson City Bomb & Arson investigation. It is even possible that this evidence—a valve assembly—may actually be stored as we speak at the Eaton Gas Company Headquarters!"

"Alderman, what are your sources?"

Petacque paused dramatically. "We have a whistleblower on the inside, a courageous Eaton employee. I challenge Eaton to deny the veracity of these allegations."

Eaton Gas issued a statement pledging to "thoroughly look into" all of Petacque's allegations. They conceded the gas and pressure build-up, but denied knowing about it. They called Petacque's characterization of Qualls as a substance abuser a "blatant invasion of privacy" and mocked Petacque's "wild speculations and web-fueled conspiracy theories" about the missing valve assembly, which obviously was destroyed in the blast.

Petacque's press conference was well-covered and confirmed what most observers had suspected. And he was able to shove Torres and Dickerson and Moore and Podesta out of the media spotlight on the issue. His website was getting unprecedented traffic.

*   *   *

Chapter Two

A Stream Becomes a River, Part III

Sen. Paul Podesta was the first to officially announce his candidacy.

Under a golden sun on a clear October noon, with Emily at his side on a stage set up in the same town square where he had announced his candidacy for the legislature about a hundred years earlier, Podesta threw in.

"I am here as a bridge-builder. I am here as one who understands the needs of everyday people," Podesta said to a crowd of about 500 supporters organized by Pudge Carson and Timmy Sullivan. The Civil War cannons flanked the stage, giving Paul the image of being the General, exhorting the troops into battle.

"My 35-year record as your voice in the Capitol speaks for itself. I am ready to bring the values of the good folks of Mohawk Valley to the highest levels of state government," he said as Emily beamed with pride, near tears.

"And that is why today I am throwing my hat in the ring to be your next Public Utilities Commission Chairman!" With that, the balloons burst into the high sky, the band struck up "Happy Days are Here Again" and Emily broke down, despite having vowed not to. Paul hugged her, waved to the crowd and began a new chapter in his already accomplished career.

"He's smooth. Whaddya think?" Sullivan asked Pudge Carson.

"It's our to lose, Timmy, my boy. We're in a good post position with an experienced pony, and we're out of the gate first and fast."

*   *   *

Podesta received good reviews and decent media coverage for his kick-off, which included the mandatory statewide fly-around. It was early enough in the campaign season that it was a novelty; other candidates for statewide offices were still laying low. Every pundit anointed Paul the frontrunner and Mary Moore offered a subdued "welcome to the race" comment. The general election was still thirteen months off.

But within a week, Christian Crusader Thelma Barnett announced her intentions as a Republican candidate, vowing to bring the Power of the Lord into the shamelessly godless Public Utilities Commission. The "Amen, Now!" Coordinator announced plans to hold a prayer vigil at each of the state's nuclear reactors.

*   *   *

"Nick-key! When?"

Blasingame was getting nervous. Mary Moore obviously was running with Gov. Langley's support, now this zealot nutcase Thelma was in and Podesta was acting like he'd already been coronated. Royce thought he should just announce. Right now.

"Keep your powder dry, Third," Pulver assured him. "Remember when we used to play 'Blink' in the frat house?"

A card game of chance and bluff popular when Royce and Nicky were undergrads, "Blink" built nerves of steel. Royce was good at it, Nicky recalled.

"Okay, okay. When?"

"I say keep 'em guessing. The petitions aren't due until December, so let's just keep learning about gas companies and dialing for dollars and swimming every day. Stay cool, bro," Pulver said with utter confidence. "You're fine."

*   *   *

Dan Clark and Manny Ruiz walked into the Dresden Estate in awe. The lagoon, the Frank Lloyd Wright home in the distance and the sculpture garden were impressive, a little intimidating for a community college teacher and a neighborhood organizer. Liz Chinn met them at the front gate and gave Manny a hug.

"Hey, hombre, gained a few pounds, eh?"

"Chinn, not being around you makes me eat to forget," Manny flirted. "You look great. Meet Professor Dan Clark, my old college bud."

"Dan, it's a pleasure. Petra is really excited about meeting you both."

The strolled through the gardens to the gazebo, where Petra sat reading *Architecture Digest.* She beamed radiantly as they approached. "Gentlemen! Welcome! Hope you're hungry!" Liz was always amazed at how svelte Petra remained despite her need to meet over food. Out of nowhere appeared one of Petra's personal staffers with a tray of crepes.

"I love your sculpture garden," Dan gushed. "Was that a John Henry by the lagoon?"

"Very early John Henry," Petra replied. "You have a good eye."

"There's not much that gets past Danny Clark, Ms. Dresden," Manny offered.

"Please. It's Petra. So Manny, Liz tells me you were in the trenches together a few years back?"

"Right. A transportation plan for seniors in Flagstaff which has been very successful. That was my first exposure to the good works of the Dresden Foundation, too."

"Well, then, you're familiar with our mission," Petra said. Over crepes, she described her late husband's idealism, the early days of the Foundation and recent endeavors such as the Ventura upset.

"And Dan, I understand you were a candidate once?"

"Not quite as successful as Jesse, though. Maybe I needed to pump more iron," Dan joshed. He described his long-shot Greens candidacy for the City Council a few years earlier, how it left him cynical, broke and exhausted. "No regrets though, Petra. A campaign is a real learning experience, especially for the candidate. You learn about so many different issues, about your community, about yourself. I recommend it to all my students."

"Well, we're learning new things all the time here," Petra said. "Especially how difficult it is for challengers and for independents to win. Our system needs an overhaul. Like Thomas Jefferson said, a little revolution goes a long way."

"Old TJ would have enjoyed the politics in this state," Manny said, eager to move to the task at hand.

"Now Dan, Liz has done some research on the Public Utilities Commission and, if you'll pardon our snoopiness, some research on you, as well. You have a very impressive background as an academic, an activist, an advocate," Petra said.

"Uh oh. All of my dirty little secrets are known to the world, eh?" Dan glanced at Liz, who smiled sheepishly. "Well, I appreciate your kind words."

"The Dresden Foundation, as you surely know, has fought to make ballot access easier for independent candidates, and we'd like to use this race for the PUC Chairmanship as an example, a test case," Petra paused for effect. "And we'd like to organize that effort around a Dan Clark candidacy. Interested?"

Dan sat there, somewhat stunned by her directness. Agent Ruiz jumped in. "Petra, my old college pal here is too modest. He's already demonstrated that he's a great advocate for utility consumers and, with proper resources, he'd be a terrific candidate. He knows this stuff cold, is no stranger to the campaign trail and isn't afraid of hard work. So you can just tear up your 'Wanted' posters!"

Petra smiled. "Professor? Mister Ruiz has spoken. Now, what say ye?"

Clark recognized this as a watershed moment.

Running as an independent would enable him to skip the primaries and be guaranteed a spot in the Finals. He had never held the two-party system in very high regard, but this would certainly be a final severing. And he would need to take a leave-of-absence from Flagstaff Community College, with little savings in the bank.

"Petra, I am not a wealthy man, just a humble school teacher. Of course, Manny and I have discussed this into the wee hours of the night and the opportunity to speak out on these issues, without hindrance, is extremely appealing."

Liz pulled out a proposal for a research grant to examine the history of utility regulation in the state. "The Dresden Foundation is prepared to offer you this grant for $50,000 to tide you over during your leave-of-absence from the Community College. The Dean at your school is an old friend of the Foundation, so securing a leave is no problem. Further, our political action committee—DresPAC—will front $50,000 to get you on the ballot and another fifty as seed money for the campaign."

"Plus, we'll lend you Liz here," Petra offered. "Our top political organizer."

"Whew. An offer I can't refuse. Okay, let's start running," Dan said. Out of nowhere, a waiter appeared with a chilled bottle of champagne.

*   *   *

The River's Edge investigations by the state Public Utilities Commission and Mayor Townshend's Blue Ribbon Pinky Banks Panel had both run their course. Neither had unearthed any bombshells (Shawn Petacque's website came the closest to that) and both panels had issued final reports attributing some responsibility for the blast to Eaton Gas. Both investigations showed poor responsiveness by Eaton's emergency operators and corporate insensitivity to Hispanic customers.

Mary Moore had walked a delicate line throughout the PUC probe. Eaton seemed hot to pin the entire blame on their codeine-head inspector, Mr. Qualls, but Mary was determined to delve into more fundamental safety issues. The suspicion of Boone Engineering investigator Biff Fahey that the valve had leaked due to human error was supported by Petacque's whistleblower, but never totally proven.

A "Mountain Referee" e-mail later informed Chemuyil Gardner that the charred remains of the deadly valve assembly might be found in a cardboard box in Eaton's 14th floor executive offices. Unfortunately, Petacque couldn't figure out how to prove that one and neither investigation pursued the missing valve.

*   *   *

The Mayor's Blue Ribbon Panel accomplished little other than elevate two young politicians in the public mind: Graciela Torres and Seth Dickerson. Torres had already left her mark with the Paco Rivera image at River's Edge.

State Representative Dickerson, on the other hand, was a relative newcomer to the spotlight. Like his legendary father, he played the inside game, rarely sticking his head out of the gopher hole.

Dickerson held his own, though, during the hearings. Mayor Townshend's operatives had prepped him to go after Eaton Gas on some valve maintenance questions. While he was no Johnnie Cochrane, he mumbled and muddled his way through. His ham-handed grilling of one hapless Eaton bureaucrat made the 10:00 news. His star was on the rise.

Despite his website and the whistleblower scoop, Shawn Petacque never quite got the mileage out of the hearings that he'd hoped. As Chemuyil Gardner had advised, he banged away from the outside and even took a few mild swipes at commission members like Dickerson and Pinky Banks, but the media never picked up on it. Confident of his deeper grasp of the issues, he watched with dismay as Dickerson and Torres grabbed headlines. Then, some even worse news was delivered by Chemuyil.

"Dickerson's looking at the PUC job."

Petacque seemed to take the news calmly, but churned inside. "What have you heard?" he asked, knowing Chem's sources to be extensive and reliable.

"Mayor's people. Liked him in the hearings. Want to stick it to Podesta a little, maybe score points in the 'hood."

The last thing Shawn needed was competition for Black votes. His entire strategy depended on decent turnout in the African-American community and that almost all Black voters voted for him. The thought of splitting that bloc with this silver-haired blockhead was depressing. That their fathers had feuded thirty years earlier made this an ironic challenge, though.

He dispatched Chemuyil to meet quietly with key Black leaders: clergy, community activists, businessmen, elected officials. The general feeling was that Shawn was a more formidable candidate than Seth Dickerson, but that Shawn had pissed off the Mayor's people, whereas Seth was a go-along guy. Nobody wanted a bloody internecine battle though.

An attempt to break the logjam was initiated by funeral director-turned industrialist-turned philanthropist James LeMans, Jackson City's wealthiest African-American. In his meeting with Chemuyil, LeMans suggested that Petacque and Dickerson sit down and "work it out like men" and he offered to facilitate and host the meeting.

"I just know Dickerson Junior is loving this," Shawn told Consuelo the night before the meeting at LeMans Tower. "The publicity from the hearing, the buzz about a state race…"

"You really think he cares? He's a small-timer, maybe just doing it for his dad," Consuelo said. "Maybe you're just doing this for your dad."

Shawn grinned, but she had hit a button. He had always regretted the lack of communication with his dad at the end, almost as much as his regret that Larry Petacque and Consuelo Milagro never had the pleasure of meeting. He knew they would have enjoyed one another.

"Just go in there, think of your dad and try not to knock out anyone's teeth," Consuelo said.

So when Shawn walked into the penthouse inner sanctum at LeMans Tower, past the photos of LeMans with Oprah Winfrey, Hank Aaron and Duke Ellington, the spirit of Larry Petacque was with him. Especially when he saw Seth Dickerson, Sr., sitting in a wheelchair next to LeMans and Seth, Jr. All he could focus on was the smile of Seth, Sr., knowing that those two front teeth had been knocked out thirty years before by his Dad's minions.

"Committeeman Dickerson. Representative Dickerson. Nice to see you both," Shawn said with his usual poise and graciousness. "Thanks for seeing me and thank you, Mr. LeMans, for your hospitality."

LeMans wasted no time.

"Well now, Alderman Petacque, we in the community are just so proud of you both, you and Representative Dickerson, for your many civic accomplishments, and we'd hate to see two such promising careers dashed before they even have a chance to blossom."

LeMans was smooth as silk, Shawn thought. Had the Mayor put him up to this? Will my campaign end here?

"Our community needs all the help it can get, Mr. LeMans," Petacque wasn't sure what direction this was going. "We need to foster new talent in business, the arts, academics, politics."

"Ah, politics," LeMans said dramatically.

So far neither of the Dickersons had said a word. The resemblance was frightening, Shawn thought. Chubby, scowling, a full Afro (Senior's was snowy white); the two seemed like identical twins born 25 years apart. Junior glowered, displeased that this conversation was even occurring. Seth, Sr., though, seemed pleased to be away from the nursing home the kids had plunked him in and to be back in a political arena. After a long awkward lull, Seth, Sr., spoke up.

"You're Larry Petacque's boy, ain'tcha?" Senior beamed. "I knew your Daddy."

Shawn and LeMans were both relieved by the cordial tone.

"My father—may he rest in peace—often spoke of you, sir. Spoke highly of you," Shawn said loudly, glancing at a smiling LeMans and an uncomfortable Seth, Junior.

"Oh, yeah, Larry Petacque and I raised some Holy Hell in those days. Gave old Mayor Schneider lotsa gray hairs. 'Member Schneider?"

"A little before my time, actually," Shawn smiled.

LeMans jumped in. "I recall that, Seth. You fellas went after him on some housing issues, right? Didn't Dr. King come to town?"

"Yep. Oh, man, we forced some major, major changes. Ya know, you look just like your Daddy," he said to Shawn. "Is your Momma still alive?"

"She is, sir, living down in Arizona now, and I'll extend her your best wishes."

This lovefest was unexpected. Seth, Jr., decided to change the dynamic. "Don't forget, Pop, you're two teeth lighter thanks to this Alderman's daddy." He tried to phrase it as a joke, but it fell flat and LeMans glared at Seth, Jr.

"Ah, in the heat of battle, Son, just the heat of battle," Seth, Sr. said quietly.

Shawn saw his opening. "Mr. Committeeman, you are a true gentleman to be of such a forgiving mind. You and my father were genuine trailblazers, making it possible for young fellows like Seth and me to make a difference."

This direction pleased LeMans. He rubbed his hands.

"Gentlemen, let's get down to business. Now, I've heard both of your names floated for higher office, specifically for this Public Utilities position." He looked Seth, Jr. directly in the eyes. "How can we possibly resolve this and promote not one, but two promising careers? In the name of unity, how?"

"Well, Mister LeMans, I served on this Blue Ribbon Commission and ya know, the Mayor's people have been sending me signals about this thing, strong signals," Seth, Jr., said, knowing that it was slipping away.

LeMans chuckled, a long, baritone, rolling-thunder chuckle. "Son, they send lots of signals, infinite numbers of signals. Mixed signals. Silent signals. Hell, I get 'em all the time."

At that moment, LeMans knew Petacque was the guy. Classy, formidable, sharp.

"Look, Representative. You got some nice media on that Blue Ribbon hearing, but Alderman Petacque's a good fit, maybe a great fit for this Public Utility thing. You're on a different path to glory. State Senate for sure, maybe Congress…"

Shawn knew it was done. "Seth, it'd be suicide for us both to run. Kamikaze stuff. How can we work this out and work together, just like our fathers did thirty years ago?"

Junior glowered some more and sat mum.

Senior cleared his throat, leaned forward in his wheelchair and chimed in, "We'll need a few jobs once you're in there, boy."

Petacque and LeMans grinned.

"Can you handle that, Alderman?" LeMans asked. "I'm sure he can," LeMans said to Seth, Sr. "And I have a $5,000 check for each of you to express my unfettered confidence that this can be done." He pulled out his checkbook and wrote a $5,000 contribution to the "Seth Dickerson, Jr., Campaign Committee". As he handed it to Junior, he asked, "We okay here?"

"Yessir."

"Well, okay, and here's something for our next Public Utilities Commissioner, the first Brother to be a Czar!" Chuckling, he wrote the check, folded it and handed it to Shawn. Later, Shawn realized the contribution was for $15,000, not $5,000.

The field was cleared.

*   *   *

"Graciela Perez Torres for State Public Utilities Chairman!" blared the banner headline in *"Hoy!"*.

A front-page Pequeno Barragan editorial praised her work on the Blue Ribbon Panel, and recounted her poignant moment at River's Edge and her passionate speech to halt the El Puente rioting.

"As a member of the Jackson County Board and former administrator in the City Water Department, Graciela Torres has dealt with the same kinds of issues facing a Chairman of the state Public Utilities Commission. Her experience, courage and conviction make her an ideal choice to be the first Hispanic statewide office holder."

As Mariano Vargas read Barragan's editorial, tears filled his eyes. Ever since that nightmarish night when he lost his beloved wife and daughters at Ground Zero of River's Edge, Mariano had been meaning to call Comm. Torres. He was still living in a shelter, still on paid bereavement leave from the Roth & Sons Company.

He picked up a legal pad and penned a heartfelt note to Torres. In Spanish and English, he expressed his appreciation and admiration for her work on the Blue Ribbon Panel. He described his loss and grief. He talked about moving back to Puerto Rico, but was grateful that his boss, Mr. Roth, had been so generous in giving him time off.

After signing the note, he added a postscript. *"P.S. I agree with Sr. Barragan in Hoy that you should run for this public utility job! Sign me up to help your campaign!"*

*   *   *

The Podesta Senate Committee was dutifully researching and investigating Mary Moore's background in preparation for the unprecedented public confirmation hearings around the state. Committee staff perused her finances, her party activities, even read her Master's thesis (well, some of it.)

This taxpayer-funded fishing expedition enabled Paul to develop a serious file on Moore, who he figured would be his General Election opponent next year. She seemed squeaky-clean, but Paul learned that Moore's husband Randall made $400,000 in a questionable insider stock deal. He learned that her son, Tony, was gay and owed $1,300 in parking ticket fines.

Time to get these confirmation hearings on the road, Paul thought.

*   *   *

The candidacy of Ald. Butchie Kaminski was announced quietly. No press conference. No kick-off rally. No flyaround. The "Butchie for PUC Chair" effort wasn't even announced by Butchie.

At the weekly Saturday morning meeting of the 6th Ward precinct captains, Boss Johnny Chizz casually said that nominating petitions for Butchie would be available next week. Further, each captain would be responsible for garnering 200 signatures from his or her home precinct and another 100 signatures from "outsiders", as Czyz put it. A trip to Las Vegas would be among the prizes for whoever turns in the most signatures for the beloved Alderman.

"There are people in this state tryin' to screw us! Disrespectin' us! We're gonna give 'em a little taste of 'Love, Sixth Ward Style'," the ancient warrior croaked out to the 150 patronage workers whose families hailed from Romania, the Philippines, Syria and other far-flung places.

Kaminski petitions would also be circulated by the patronage organizations of 3rd Ward Democratic Boss Seamus Dunne and State Senator Mario Camozzi. Really no need for fancy flyarounds or plastic-covered media kits.

*   *   *

The note from Mariano Vargas moved Graciela deeply. She called Mariano's employer, Sam Roth to express her admiration for his giving Mariano an unlimited bereavement leave.

"Well, Commissioner, you're a big hero to not only Mariano, but also my son, Sam, Junior. He just graduated from college and has been killing time by following the River's Edge disaster. Howzabout I treat you and Mariano and my kid for lunch, maybe tomorrow?" It was an odd offer, but Graciela agreed.

The furor over the disaster and the rioting had never truly subsided. The flames of discontent were fanned by neighborhood organizers and lefty religious leaders. Eaton Gas, the Housing Authority and the Jackson

City Police were all targets of hostility. Newspapers like *"Hoy!"* kept the heat turned high.

The *"Hoy!"* call for a Torres candidacy did not go unnoticed by City Hall. Mayor Townshend had a brief conversation with Jimmy Juarez saying Graciela did a nice job on the Blue Ribbon Panel and that it might be "a good fit" for her to run for PUC Chair. Jimmy read the tea leaves and concluded that Townshend would not be jumping on the rapidly-accelerating Podesta bandwagon. The Butchie Kaminski candidacy was already out of the barn and the rumors that Ald. Shawn Petacque was in the race were deafening.

When Juarez discussed the possibilities with Torres, he was pleasantly surprised to learn that she had actually already given it some thought and was open to it. "We'd need more troops, a ton of cash and no other women or Hispanics in the race," Jimmy told her.

The River's Edge experience had changed Graciela somehow. The brevity of life, the uncertainty, the unfairness. She felt frustrated throughout the Blue Ribbon investigation, angry at herself for not digging deeper. Being PUC Chair would enable her to ensure this never happens again. She had discussed it with her sisters, who both offered lukewarm encouragement, and her kids. Roberto thought it was "way cool", but Raisa cried, saying she would miss Graciela too much.

Since Graciela's County Board post had been wholly engineered by Jimmy Juarez, she had to wrestle for the first time with the decision of whether to launch a candidacy. The state was so huge! She was physically and emotionally drained; this was not really the best time for an all-consuming experience.

The lunch with Mariano Vargas and the two Sam Roth's went better than Graciela could have expected. Mariano shared some bittersweet stories about the courtship of his wife and his daughter's first Christmas. Sam Junior diplomatically avoided discussing the details of the blast or the hearings, even though he was itching to. Sam Senior talked about his factory and how his grandparents once lived in the area now called "El Puente", actually not too far from Graciela's house.

It was an enjoyable luncheon. Graciela charmed the three men, of course. Then Mariano pulled the copy of *"Hoy!"* and showed Sam Senior the editorial urging Graciela to run.

"Commissioner Torres," Sam Junior whispered conspiratorially. "You should run. You can win, I just know it. Especially if you're the only woman in the race. Against Podesta and Kaminski and Petacque? C'mon! You win for sure."

"Sam, you follow the political scene more than most recent college grads."

"You've got the credentials and the backing and the charisma…" Sam Junior stopped, somewhat embarrassed by his rant.

"Well, you know, Sam, somebody else just told me the same scenario," Graciela replied. "Takes a lot of money, though."

"Commissioner Torres, if you decide to do it," Sam Senior said earnestly, "I'll be your first campaign contributor. Who knows, maybe you'd hire a couple of guys like Mariano and Sammy here for your campaign."

"If I had Sammy and Mariano on my campaign team I would win. No doubt," Graciela smiled.

The next morning an envelope was delivered to Commissioner Torres' County office from Roth & Sons. Inside was a check for $10,000 and the resumes of both Sam Roth, Jr., and Mariano Vargas. A yellow post-it note read, *"Do it for Felicity and Bree Vargas. Good luck, Sam Roth, Sr."*

That night, Graciela Torres crossed the Rubicon and became a candidate for PUC Chairman.

*   *   *

The speech Calvin Reynolds was to have delivered in New Orleans sat untouched in the in-box on Mary Moore's new desk for several weeks. She couldn't bear to even look at it.

After his death, Moore was invited to take his place as the keynote speaker. The annual Big Easy seminar hosted by the Braxton Group had become a regular stop on the public utility regulators circuit. A large crowd, including many friends of Calvin, would be there, so Mary gladly accepted the invitation. She was relieved to be getting out of town (spouses were invited, too) and humbled at the $25,000 honorarium, Calvin's usual speaking fee.

Some of her staffers had urged against the trip. Peggy Briscoe was concerned that the media would ding Mary for leaving town so soon after River's Edge. And the pro-utility Braxton Group may not be the best venue for your coming-out party, Peggy argued.

But both Steven Page and Jimmy Blake encouraged to her take the trip. It would enhance her credentials as a public utilities expert, enable her to cash in on some of Reynolds' connections and maybe give her a nice tan before they shoot the TV spots. Plus, since hubby Randall was along for the ride, the couple could have some quality time together before the race really got rolling. A very few final quality moments.

Moore opted to go and convened a working group on staff to plan for it. She had kept most of Reynolds' senior staff. She had always been close to Briscoe, the PUC media spokesman and message master. Since Reynolds' accident, Peggy had really stepped up, Mary thought.

Another rising star at the PUC was Policy Director Del Zink. A skinny former seminarian with a Master's in chemical engineering, the bookish Zink was somewhat stifled during the Reynolds Regime, but blossomed recently under Moore. An expert on the decommissioning of nuclear power plants, Zink knew the issue would only get larger and he was in the right place at the right time with the right knowledge. With most of the state's nuclear fleet showing its age, the cost of tearing down the plants had become a thorny issue.

Mary asked Zink and Briscoe to accompany her in New Orleans and assigned them two of the to re-write Reynolds' keynote address. "Make it sound more me," she suggested. "Tone down the jokes. And he'd probably shoot me, but, Del, throw in some pro-consumer language on the decommissioning issue." She looked heavenward. "We have a campaign to run here, Calvin."

A few days before the trip, Briscoe issued a standard media advisory. *"Acting PUC Chair Mary Moore will deliver the keynote address at the 12th Annual Public Utility Regulators Seminar hosted in New Orleans by the Braxton Group, the highly-regarded utility think-tank. The prestigious event will focus on the role of nuclear power in the future."*

Nicky Pulver saw the item about Moore's trip tucked away in a gossip column and did a little dance.

"Davis!" he yelled down the hallway at ProAction. "Pack your bags, boy. You're goin' to the Big Easy!"

*   *   *

"Obviously, Podesta's strategy is to line up as many endorsements from party institutions as fast as possible," Sam Roth opined over coffee and sweet pan dulce on his first day on the job as Political Director of the Graciela Torres for PUC Chair Campaign.

"Obviously," said Lupe Zarate, not quite sure what to make of the new kid in the mix. Obviously, she thought, fresh out of college, maybe Young Dems or Student Government, probably Poli Sci major. Well, his daddy did kick in 10K and gave the still-grieving security guard, Mariano Vargas, a six-month paid leave-of-absence to volunteer on the campaign.

"We need to figure out who's not jumping on the Podesta bandwagon, figure out why not and go after them," Sam said, in a confident tone. At 22, he was indeed fresh out of the State University with a Poli Sci degree, although he'd taken a pass on student politics to focus on what he called "real politics". Ever since he was 14, Sam had volunteered for candidates for City Council, School Board, State Senate and Congress. He had already become a seasoned field organizer, knew the political lay of the land throughout the suburbs and understood computers. He was earnest and diligent; Graciela thought he was a real find.

"Well, we do have the list of the County Chairs who endorsed him at his press conference, right, Lupita?" Graciela asked, remembering how annoyed she was when Podesta first announced.

Posing as a reporter for the "Hispanic press", Lupe had crashed one of Podesta's many red-white-and-blue press conferences. This one was to announce another round of endorsements by Democratic Party officials. Lupe was welcomed into the event and given a "Paul Podesta: The Quiet Worker" biographical video and a slick press kit, complete with a list of the 52 (out of 80) Democratic Party County Chairmen who had pledged to old Paul, friend and patron of local power brokers.

Sam pulled a state map from his new graduation gift briefcase and began to highlight the counties whose party leaders had not endorsed Podesta. A tiny handful could possibly go with Kaminski or Petacque, but Graciela should be able to line up the rest, he said, including the four or five rural counties with significant local Hispanic voting blocs.

As she scanned the list, Graciela was amazed at how many counties existed and so far away from Jackson City! Counties she had ever heard of named after people she had never heard of. And so many hometowns of Democratic Party leaders she never heard of. But she was pretty sure Shawn Petacque and Butchie Kaminski had never heard of these places either, so she launched her raid.

For the rest of the day, Graciela penned—in her loopy, flowery long-hand—personal notes on Monet-adorned stationery to all 28 Downstate Democratic leaders who hadn't joined the Podesta juggernaut. She introduced herself, saluted them for the sacrifices they'd made for the Party, said she was seriously considering the race for PUC Chair and asked to be informed of local party events.

Candidates who employ that kind of personal appeal are rare, so many of the recipients of Torres' note were appreciative, even a little amazed. None came out and endorsed her, of course, but several sent her a newsletter or notice of their next fundraiser. Some wrote back and invited to stop by any time.

One County Chairman took particular interest.

Billy Miller, the lanky, 41-year old Democratic leader of scenic Sauk County had been in his share of dust-ups with Paul Podesta over the past 12 years.

After leaving the county's public defender's office to take a stab at private practice in Seneca, the Sauk County seat, Miller earned a reputation as a tenacious advocate for his clients. His lively courtroom performances woke up sleepy Seneca and he once argued a land use case before the State Supreme Court.

Twelve years earlier, Podesta, who hailed from nearby Mohawk Valley, had proposed construction of a dam on a tributary of the Sauk River. He rammed the plans and the state funding package for the mega-project through the legislature over the howls of local activists, including Billy Miller. Of course, the contracts would enrich many of Podesta's long-time pals and donors: trade unions, local construction contractors and truckers, local iron and concrete companies.

Though outmaneuvered in the drive to stop Podesta's dam—which, once erected altered the region's watershed forever—the protest movement had a galvanizing effect on the Sauk County Democrats. A group of Young Turks led by Miller took over the sleepy party apparatus and Billy was soon elected as Chairman. He figured it would help distract him from his recent, painful divorce.

Party leadership was a double-edged sword. While it certainly boosted Miller's law practice, it took a lot of time and driving and phoning and attending and fundraising. But Billy familiarized himself with every pocket of Sauk County Democrats and environmentalists outside of Seneca. He was easily re-elected four years later and became a leader on the State Central Committee of the younger, more progressive bloc, where again he found himself opposing Podesta on a range of policy and slating battles.

Miller had mulled over a run for public office, maybe Congress, but he was making over $130,000 as a litigator and enjoyed it. Party activities were enough to satisfy his political sweet-tooth, anyhow.

But when Miller heard that Podesta was considering the PUC Chair post, he cringed. Not only did he disagree with Podesta's politics, but he thought Podesta was a small-time Charlie, lacking any vision.

So after reading the personal note from Commissioner Graciela Torres, whose image he recalled seeing in *Newsweek*, Billy grabbed a legal pad and jotted—in his herky-jerky psycho script—a thank-you note to Torres and invited her to attend the upcoming Sauk County Autumn Fest.

*   *   *

The keynote address Mary Moore delivered in New Orleans was a triumph.

While insisting that a fair balance be reached on the cost of mothballing aging nuclear plants, Moore was firm that consumers pick up some of the tab and framed the issue as a question of public safety. Wearing a navy blue suit and her blond hair in a bun, she wowed the crowd with poise and charm. Old Calvin would've had them rolling in the aisles with off-color wisecracks, followed by his usual melodramatic motivational closing. Mary was more professional, yet warmer.

A crowd of regulators and lobbyists swarmed around her after the first day's session with kudos for her speech and condolences for Reynolds' passing. "Hey, Calvin and I used to go to a little spot on Bourbon Street," said the PUC Chairman from Alaska, whose name Mary had already forgotten. "A bunch of us are headed over there after we freshen up. C'mon, Mary, it's Hurricane Time! Let's hoist one for Calvin!"

So Mary, husband Randall, Peggy Briscoe and Del Zink and a group of twelve headed to "Le Mer", a French Quarter grille. They wined, dined and relaxed, the first time, Mary thought, she had really relaxed since Calvin's accident and River's Edge.

Randall and Del were talking baseball, Peggy was being hit on by a lobbyist from a Wyoming electric company and Mary just sat, feeling awed by the day's events. She was moving in a faster lane, playing with a faster crowd. Players. Those who shape policy with billions of dollars at stake.

Money-makers. Deal-breakers. Earth-shakers. She thought of the ease and facility with which Calvin had dealt with these types. She knew she wasn't quite there yet, still felt a little intimidated.

After the feast, the group took a stroll. The street scene was getting intense. Music blaring from all angles, the waftings of world-class restaurants and the flashing strobe lights from the nightclubs assaulted the senses. A dark sea of humanity swirled around them in the night.

"Is this what Mardi Gras is like?" yelled Peggy, who had her arm around the waist of her new Wyoming friend. Randall yelled to Mary, "Hey, Toto, I guess we're not in Zane Township anymore!" As they passed one strip-club, the sight of a topless blonde grinding against a ten-foot high candy cane in the window caused the group to gasp and gape.

From the roiling crowd strode two amazon drag queens, wearing little more than some tattered Frederick's of Hollywood lingerie and their five-o'clock shadows. The first queen, known on the street as "Crystal", walked right up to Del Zink, gave him a hug and grabbed the seminarian's crotch.

"Hey, Slim," Crystal shrieked. "How about a date tonight? I can make you sooo happy!"

Most of the group thought this was just hilarious, but Del thought it was humiliating and Mary steered him away from Crystal and further into the parade of humanity.

ProAction's Jim Davis, who had been tailing the group since they left their hotel and had paid "Crystal" and her pal $50 each, knew it would be his finest work.

*   *   *

Cassandra Phillips had a knack for politics from the first time her father, Bishop Delphi Phillips, hoisted her above his pulpit at the Oracle African Methodist Episcopal Church as an infant 30 years earlier.

By the time Cassandra was nine, she was an accomplished orator, winning a citywide grade school speech contest for her interpretation of Langston Hughes' *The Negro*. "I've been a worker..." her tiny voice barked. "Under my hand the pyramids arose. I made mortar for the Woolworth Building!"

Cassandra watched her father's rise in the AME Church, thrilled to his sermons before larger and larger audiences, joined him in meetings with mayors and Congressmen. She became a force in the Church and took its ministry to the meaner streets of Jackson City. A tireless and ambitious worker, Cassandra had set her sights on elective office. Two years earlier, she had run for the City Council, coming in third in a six-way race. She vowed to her father she would never lose again.

So when the rumors about Ald. Shawn Petacque having muscled out Rep. Seth Dickerson, Jr., began to reach street level, Cassandra—who viewed Petacque as unreligious and somewhat amoral—dipped her toes into the swirling waters.

The first sign was Bishop Phillips' pronouncement that Oracle AME Church would set up a fund to help senior citizens who were having trouble paying their heating bills from the previous winter, with Cassandra Phillips running the project.

Tens of thousands of brochures—with the Bishop and Cassandra prominently featured—were distributed door-to-door by Oracle volunteers. Then a public service announcement—again featuring Cassandra—began airing non-stop on Black radio. Thousands of folks responded and Cassandra called many of them personally.

Having established herself as a "utility activist", Cassandra began speaking at meetings of community groups, block clubs and senior centers. She cut an impressive figure. Her six-foot stature was enhanced with a mile-high hair-wrap, amplified with a dynamic audio. Quietly, the Bishop began lining up support from other AME clergy.

Of course, Petacque first got wind of it through Chemuyil Gardner, who always had her ear to the ground.

"She's out there promising manna from Heaven to anyone who's behind in their Eaton bill," Chem said. "And she's got her rap down."

"Where's the green manna coming from?" Shawn asked.

"Pastors are ponying up. A couple of foundations have kicked in. The Bishop Himself provided five grand in seed money. I think she's comin' at you."

"Maybe it's time for another pow-wow at LeMans Tower," Shawn said, only half-joking.

"Yeah, well, the Bishop and the Daughter answer to a higher power than Dickerson and Son. March to a different drummer," Chem observed. "We need a different strategy here, Frenchy."

"Call her bluff? Come on in, Baby, water's fine?"

"Yeah, maybe scare her off by flexing your war chest muscle and maybe the specter of a closer look at hers."

"Gardner, how did you get so wise?" Shawn smiled.

"Dunno. Now all you need are some muscles to flex, Frenchy."

*   *   *

At that point, however, Petacque's war chest wasn't real scary.

On top of the $15,000 from James LeMans, Shawn had raised about $25,000 in smaller contributions and had about $20,000 already sitting in his campaign fund, leftovers from his previous aldermanic run. Since he had spent zip thus far, he had $60,000 in the bank. He'd need to build it up quickly to frighten Cassandra Phillips or any other potential African-American candidates.

Shawn knew from the get-go that he'd need at least $100,000, probably more like $200,000. He hadn't cultivated big money like some of his colleagues in the City Council…such as Alderman (and Finance Committee Chairman) Al Garber, who was sitting on $300,000, but nothing to run for.

Consuelo and Chemuyil put together a fundraising plan that included three big events and several smaller ones, but most of the income would be generated by Shawn working the phone. College buddies, sympathetic unions, African-American business owners, fraternities. At first Shawn resented having to do it and was embarrassed to make some of the calls. But after the first $10,000, he became a more confident and effective arm-twister.

That pace would not be enough, though, to scare off Cassandra Phillips or others. He needed a big chunk of change.

"MortPAC," Chemuyil said, ominously.

"Don't say it, please," Petacque winced.

"Ya gotta call DeForrest."

Benjamin DeForrest. Head of MortPAC, short for the African-American Mortuary Sciences Political Action Committee. Every Black undertaker in the state was a dues-paying member. Their endorsement was a double-edged sword. On the one hand, it meant dozens of thousand dollar checks and a great network.

On the other hand, the campaign would have to put up with Benjamin DeForrest, a political wannabe who would latch on to candidates and not let go. Nobody wants to be linked at the hip with an undertaker who won't let go, especially one as creepy as Benjamin. His shaved head and sunken, beady eyes reflected his demeanor. He was the world's oldest-looking 44-year old and smelled faintly of embalming fluid. Or maybe Death.

DeForrest had latched on during Petacque's previous Council race, doggedly "accompanying" the Alderman to campaign events and becoming unshakable. He was smitten, everyone suspected, with Chemuyil, which made his ubiquity worse. The thought of Benjamin's dark persona appearing for the next few months was unappealing. But forcing Cassandra Phillips out was essential to Petacque's strategy and would be worth that kind of sacrifice.

Shawn made the call.

"We're way ahead of you, Alderman," Benjamin droned. "Already heard from Jimmy LeMans; you're our guy. We're scheduling a brunch for you in two weeks. Expecting 50 at $500 each. Plus, I'll cut you a PAC check."

"Benjamin, thank you, thank you, thank you. I couldn't do this without you," Shawn smoothly and sincerely replied.

"Yeah, well, that's bullshit man, but I love ya. So, is Chemuyil Gardner still in your shop?"

I knew that was coming, Shawn thought. "Yeah, she's running my campaign as a matter of fact. Took a leave from my Ward Office. Just talking about you recently."

"Give that lovely lady my love and make sure she comes to our brunch. Hey, ya got any events coming up? How's your schedule? I'm ready to hit the trail."

"Great, Benjamin, lemme check at my office and we'll give you a buzz. Got some county fairs in the boonies. That could be fun, eh? Baby goats, quilting bees, sweet potato pie."

"Run hard and run long," Benjamin exhorted, his favorite catch-phrase from the previous campaign.

The MortPAC brunch was a huge success. Joined by both Chemuyil and Consuelo, Shawn gave a stirring speech that even got a rise out of the 75 undertakers present and $42,000 was raised. And DeForrest didn't even ask when the next event was.

Most importantly, Chemuyil planted an item in the Jackson City Review that Petacque had exceeded $100,000 in campaign fundraising. Then she asked a friend in the City Law Department to discreetly request all fundraising and tax records from the Oracle AME Church heating fund, headed by Cassandra Phillips. Plus, philanthropist James LeMans offered to donate a dozen new cribs to the Oracle Day Care Center.

Cassandra Phillips ended her bid for statewide office shortly thereafter. Shawn Petacque would be the only African-American in a crowded field. His strategy was working, so far.

*   *   *

The Torres campaign was ratcheting into high gear.

The insider savvy of Jimmy Juarez, media skills of Lupe Zarate, energy of Sam Roth and determination of Mariano Vargas made a great team. Jimmy had lined up every Hispanic leader for Graciela and Lupe kept fanning the flames in the Hispanic community over River's Edge. Graciela was raising some money, but was still far short of the $250,000 Jimmy had advised. She was, however, capturing free media attention just as much as Petacque and Podesta, and much more than Kaminski. And, most crucially, she had heard no rumblings of any other Hispanic or female candidate in the Democratic primary.

The first downstate campaign swing was planned, with seven stops, including one in rural Sauk County, just a few miles from Podesta's home turf. She would make the three-day trip with Lupe and Sam.

*   *   *

Tina Bishop had earned her stripes in Jackson City's political wars, but her route was different than that of a Kaminski, a Petacque or a Torres.

Born and bred in the City's old Greek community, Tina had been an organizer of campus sit-ins, a neighborhood organizer, a field organizer for the textile workers union, the organizer of huge family reunions and an organizer of the condo association in her high-rise building. Plus, she was very organized.

She was surprised when she got the call from Nicky Pulver at ProAction. She had never done electoral politics before…always thought it was kind of pointless. Her years in the trenches had made her harder and more cynical. At 41, Tina had just discovered her first gray hair and was between jobs when Pulver asked her to join the campaign operation for some Republican millionaire guy she never heard of running for some statewide office dealing with utilities.

When Tina met with Nicky and Royce for dinner, she was charmed by them both. And they both fell in love with this dark, mysterious, older woman. After a few drinks, Nicky felt Tina had enough of a handle on the basic principles of campaign organizing and offered her the job of "political director" on the spot. $5,000 a month, plus a car.

Tina pointed out to the boys that she'd never done statewide politics, never done electoral politics and had never worked for a Republican. The manner in which she spoke these doubts was so endearing that Blasingame wanted to double her salary.

"You'll do just fine," Royce told her. "Just work hard and listen to Nicky."

She did both and Nicky soon decided it was time for Royce to announce.

And it was a high-tech announcement.

Videotaped and uplinked to TV stations across the state via satellite, the press conference had been well-rehearsed. Royce practiced his speech in front of a mirror 20 times, at least. Nicky grilled him with tough questions in a mock Q-and-A. When it was showtime, Royce looked great. He had lost 20 pounds, sported a healthy tan and gave a virtuoso performance.

"My grandfather—a pioneer in this state—taught me the need for public service and classic citizenship. He taught me that government should protect people without being intrusive on people. He taught me the beauty of competition and the market economy, something we do not have today in the provision of electric, phone, gas or cable service.

"We have seen the graphic tragedy of River's Edge and the unseen tragedy of big utility companies—who want to maintain the non-competitive status quo—contributing hundreds of thousands of dollars to candidates for Governor, candidates for the legislature and even candidates for the Public Utilities Commission.

"That is why I am running for Chairman of the Public Utilities Commission. To ensure affordable and safe utility service in a more competitive marketplace. That, I believe, is what the Republican Party of the 21st Century must stand for. And I pledge to you today that I will not accept campaign cash from the big utility companies, and I challenge Mary Moore and Thelma Barnett to likewise!"

Immediately following the press conference, Royce walked up to a laptop computer, unveiled the brand new Blasingame website and started chatting with "typical" consumers (recruited by Tina and Nicky). "Instead of a flyaround," Nicky pitched to reporters. "We're doing a 'web-around'."

Every TV station in the state carried his announcement and the stack of positive press clips was formidable.

Nicky was pleased.

*   *   *

The Blasingame announcement stirred things up. None of the higher-ups in the Republican Party or the Moore camp saw it coming. Royce had kept his powder dry.

Tina Bishop was starting to line up some of the few Jackson City Republicans for Blasingame. She immediately recruited State Representative Laura Southampton, a young, up-and-coming Republican who represented the City's silk-stocking neighborhoods. Ultra-liberal on social issues, but a fiscal conservative, she had clashed with others in her Party, including the Governor. Southampton was eyeing a Congressional race somewhere down the pike and saw Royce Blasingame as one vehicle. She readily agreed when Tina asked her to come on as Royce's Jackson City Chairperson.

Tina had a tougher time in the suburbs, where support for Mary Moore was strong, and in the downstate areas, where old-time patronage and affection for Governor Langley ran deep. Nonetheless, she was able to buy the affection of Republican county chairs from 15 small counties and organized a "Royce is My Choice" committee on every college campus.

The well-equipped Blasingame Headquarters in downtown Jackson City began buzzing. Between Tina Bishop's knack for recruiting self-starting volunteers, Southampton's network and ambition, Nicky's plan of attack and the Blasingame fortune, Royce's campaign operation was suddenly the place to be.

*   *   *

As Billy Miller, Graciela, Lupe and Sam trekked up the old Sauk trail to the bluffs overlooking the river, they saw deer, a first for Lupe and Sam. Lush oak and fern forest gave way to moss-covered granite cliffs as they ascended. The leaves had changed colors. Graciela felt the blood rushing through her system and regretted her lack of exercise as of late. Her legs hurt, but she felt great.

Lupe felt the same, but was further exhilarated by the successful Sauk County event practically in Podesta's back yard, and the obvious political bond established between Graciela and Miller.

Sam was also exhilarated, mostly by walking on the trail right behind Lupe, who wore tight jeans. All of those long hours together in the campaign office, all of the cold pizza and warm beer. Sam was seeing Lupe Zarate in a whole new light as they ascended.

Not unlike the attraction Billy was beginning to feel for Graciela. Her performance at the event was genuine, compelling, even luminous. Not only had he not seen a candidate like her for some time, but he had not seen a woman like her in a long time. As they trudged to the crest of the bluffs, Billy's mind wandered to Graciela's form and he was delighted.

"How close are we?" called out a winded Sam.

"Oh, just around the next bend," Billy replied, obviously having made this climb before. A shaft of sunlight at the end of a mossy green wall beckoned. Chipmunks darted across the steep rocky trail.

As the vista gradually opened, all four felt a mix of relief and awe. They were alone on a granite cliff, hundreds of feet above the river, with a vista as far as the eye could see. Hawks drifted in the clouds below them.

"Fantastico!" exhaled Lupe. They all reclined on the stony overhang. No one spoke, the only sounds being their heavy breathing, a distant boat engine, crickets. An owl's call rippled across the valley.

The river snaked for miles. A freight train lumbered along tracks parallel to the river, then veered off in a straight line to the horizon. Graciela had no idea places like this existed, and only a few hours from El Puente. She marveled at her state's diversity.

"The Sauk Nation had a major fishing village right over there," Billy said, pointing to a clump of trees in the river's bend.

"They ruled the river valley for a century. Built the first fish-farms. Traded clams and mussels for seeds, textiles. Blazed a network of trails throughout the area…one went all the way to what's now Jackson City! They developed a regional economy. Until another civilization—the Santee Nation—came along and pushed the Sauk into oblivion."

"Muscle beats mussels. That's politics," Sam offered.

"Yep, politics." Billy knew that politics was brutal, with victorious forces often annihilating or absorbing the losers.

"What's that area over there," Graciela asked, pointing to a distinctive, bright sandy beach in a horseshoe-shaped cove about a mile away.

"Used to be the mouth of a creek. Abernathy Creek. But the river's changed courses so many times, Abernathy just dried up and filled in, except for that cove. Now it's just known as Abernathy Cove," Billy said with some sadness. "And that stream over there didn't even exist just ten years ago."

They all could see were the river had indeed changed course, thanks to geologic forces and Podesta's dam. Tree stumps stood defiantly in ten feet of water where recent flooding had boosted water to new highs.

"So, Mister Chairman, you get up here often?" Lupe asked.

"Oh, yeah, as much as possible. My favorite spot. It's a great place to relax or just think."

"What do you think about way up here?" Graciela asked flirtatiously.

"Politics, of course," Billy grinned.

"What? Man, how can you think of politics up here?" Sam laughed.

"The forces of nature," Billy said.

"Yeah, like how?"

"Springs, streams, creeks. They all eventually flow into the river," Billy said, gazing out from their perch. Same as politics. Different forces surge and then subside. Some just dry up, like Abernathy Creek over there. Some coalesce into floods…"

This description of politics jarred Graciela. Maybe she had been too close, too immersed in the day-to-day of government and politics to see it in such a lyrical light. She turned to Miller. "So, who are these forces that become creeks or floods?"

"Podesta is. Calvin Reynolds was. You are. I am."

Perhaps it was the steep climb or thin air or rapidly-setting sun, but this revelation had an epiphany-like effect on Graciela. "The winners are the floods and the losers are Abernathy Creek," she said.

"Something like that," Billy smiled.

"And where does this flood end up?" Sam asked.

Miller sat up, back erect, staring out over the river valley. The crickets quieted.

"Well, I've always thought all of these forces end up in the State Capitol. They merge with other streams and floods and pick up steam and flow straight into the Capitol Building from all across this state," Billy said, almost dreamily.

"They come crashing and splashing through the big bronze doors, and swirl 'round and 'round, faster 'n faster under that big old dome, with the shafts of sunlight pourin' through, until everything's mixed together in a cosmic milk shake and comes out consensus, laws, dynasties."

That notion, of streams rising to a head in a great social waterspout under the Capitol Dome just hung in the rarified air high above the river. Graciela was learning new things every day about this huge complex state and Billy's vision framed it just right in her mind.

"Just gotta know how to navigate, eh?" Lupe said.

"Just navigation," Billy grinned, pleased with his spontaneous soliloquy which had hit home with Graciela and Lupe.

The four of them sat quietly for awhile, listening to a hawk's cry, watching the sun turn fiery orange as it edged to the horizon. From their perch, the river had become a brilliant copper-hued snake, winding through the lush green valley into the distant haze.

"Well, enough philosophy," Billy said, pulling two bottles of wine and a corkscrew from his backpack. "Here's to the Sauk. Cheers!"

*   *   *

Chapter Three

River Rising, Part I

"The river went on raising and raising for ten or twelve days, till at last it was over the banks."

-Mark Twain *("The Adventures of Huckleberry Finn")*

Back on terra firma, the various petition drives were picking up steam.

Each candidate needed to submit 25,000 signatures of registered voters between December 1 and December 8. The deadline for challenges to any candidate's petitions was December 15, and the lottery for ballot position was December 22. Happy Holidays to one and all.

Each candidate's petition drive was different, depending on organizational base, personality, resources. Ald. Butchie Kaminski's effort, for example, got off to the quickest start. Thanks to the unrivaled Czyz Patronage Army, Kaminski had 6,000 signatures within a week. All the results of door-to-door visits by precinct captains. All valid, clean names.

The Party Apparatus would be most beneficial to Mary Moore and Sen. Paul Podesta, particularly in their respective bases. Republican state employees in the suburbs and old-time Democratic patronage workers Downstate would move slowly, but surely and reliably. Podesta had the added edge of Wally Mraz, who was running Podesta's petition drive in Jackson City, much to Czyz' ire.

The petition drives for Royce Blasingame and Dan Clark were done primarily by hired guns and rented strangers. The Blasingame Campaign paid top dollar: $2 per valid signature. A determined circulator could easily get 15 good names per hour at a commuter train station or shopping mall, so Royce's petitions were flowing in at a decent clip.

And price was no object for Petra Dresden, who was determined to make a point with the Clark candidacy. Clark recruited dozens of kids from Flagstaff Community College, while Liz Chinn was hiring dozens of under-employed environmentalists and petition-passers from previous DF-Squared ventures. The Clark Campaign was paying $5-per hour, plus 75 cents per valid name. After working grocery stores and college campuses, many of the petition-circulators would head back to the Headquarters to verify the signatures and then send handwritten postcards to their petition-signers, thanking them and reminding them to vote for Dan Clark, Independent. This had the added benefit of keeping the Headquarters lively.

The highest-tech, most innovative petition drive, oddly, was Thelma Barnett's. The Crandall's Crusaders website featured a petition you could download and print with just a few clicks of the mouse. Hundreds of Crusaders were doing just that and the Barnett Campaign was receiving dozens of completed petition sheets daily.

Shawn Petacque and Graciela Torres both had fertile fields to till in their respective ethnic bases.

While the state's African-American population was much larger than the Hispanic, Jimmy Juarez knew how to get plenty of names quickly and efficiently. His patronage network was not as concentrated as Czyz' nor as extensive as Podesta's, but he had people in dozens of City and County agencies. And between Juarez' persuasiveness and Graciela's River's Edge notoriety, every Hispanic political wannabe was out there getting signatures for Graciela Torres.

With only lukewarm petition support from the other African-American Ward Bosses, Petacque was relying on community groups, block clubs, a few pastors, the Morticians and a handful of white liberals. And Shawn was by far the most aggressive candidate at personally getting signatures, posting himself on a different subway station platform every morning for two hours. Gripping his clipboard, he enjoyed the brisk sunrise exchanges with hundreds of voters and even recruited a few volunteers while he was out there. In the first two weeks of petition-gathering, Shawn had gotten the autographs of 1,300 subway commuters himself.

"Each signature is meaningful to me," Petacque told a skeptical reporter who accompanied him one chilly November morning. "It's an affirmation, a civic expression. I get so energized out here, listening to folks talk about their phone bills or cable service. I really love doing this."

*   *   *

Being slated by the State Party provides an incalculable edge. Your petition-gathering worries are over, PAC money comes easier, and you acquire a built-in field operation of party loyalists and patronage workers. You can cut costs on polling and direct mail. In an anti-incumbent year it can cut against you, but only a few of the brave and lonely refuse to accept party slating.

The slatemaking process for statewide candidates differed for Republicans and Democrats.

The GOP followed Langley's utterances, held a series of non-binding caucuses and empowered an Executive Committee—controlled by Langley—to choose the ticket. Geographic, gender and philosophic balance usually resulted.

The State Democrats conducted an open—but raw—process.

First, a series of beauty pageants—cattle calls, really—were hosted across the state to give all possible candidates for statewide office a brief podium. Dozens of young, ambitious Democratic candidate wannabes of all stripes would drive two or three hours, wait in line for another hour in order to speak for five minutes before a crowd of maybe 25 local activists and reporters. It gave the pooh-bahs, pundits and handicappers something to talk about, like NBA coaches speculating about not next year's college draft, but the one after that. Rep. Tom Cummings, Ald. Shawn Petacque and Comm. Graciela Torres were all deemed hot prospects for the future.

And then the State Democratic Central Committee's "Gang of 72" would assemble the slate, usually a raucous event.

Podesta had been a member of the "Gang of 72" for 21 years, nearly as long as John Czyz, and much longer than Billy Miller, Jimmy Juarez or Seamus Dunne. Podesta was a leader of the self-proclaimed "Rube Caucus", made up of pols representing rural farm districts. He also carried the torch for labor and, on occasion, the utility companies. But Podesta had squabbled for nearly three decades with the urban bloc and that wasn't going to help him now, he knew.

The weighted vote prevailed in slating, with 50 percent required. The Jackson City votes were more heavily weighted, thanks to their larger turnouts, so while Podesta had already lined up at least 28 of the 72 voters, he only had a quarter of the weighted vote. At that point he wasn't even sure if Petacque, Torres or Kaminski would even stay in the race. Like any politician who feels the Midas Touch, Podesta half-expected them all to buckle and throw in the towel. Next week's slatemaking hearing would tell.

Podesta put another call into Jackson City Mayor Bob Townshend, who hadn't returned his call from this morning. Or yesterday.

*   *   *

Podesta's Rube Caucus within the State Democratic Party kingmakers seemed to be holding, despite efforts by Billy Miller to nibble at the edges. No major cracks in the labor bloc, although Timmy Sullivan heard the Needleworkers were about to endorse Torres and both the Meatpackers and Postal Workers were with Petacque. No real surprises there. Sullivan was more concerned about rumors that Kaminski might pick up a few trade unions that should be with Podesta.

The 72-member Committee was a colorful polyglot, a mosaic of the Democratic Party establishment.

Jimmy Juarez was the undisputed leader of the six-member Hispanic bloc, Sen. Beatrice Madison was the Elder Stateswoman of the nine-member African-American Caucus and Boss Chizz controlled eight of the "etnics". Lesser tribal chieftains like Seamus Dunne, Sen. Mario Camozzi, Sen. Debra Shane and Billy Miller had at least four votes in their pockets. Labor could always count on 15 solid votes; the libs and enviros maybe ten or twelve.

The wild card was the 12-member Townshend bloc.

A mish-mash of the Committee's three furthest-left members, a couple of septuagenarian Jewish ward bosses, four city workers, two professors and the only Asian American on the Committee—Mary Ikeda—Mayor Townshend had quietly forged a serious, cohesive force on the State Committee. He had already endorsed Shane for Governor, but was still maneuvering to be the deciding voice on a lower level spot, either Treasurer or PUC Chair. And he hadn't made up his mind on either spot, yet.

What to do with the PUC race, Townshend wondered.

Years ago, John Czyz had successfully blocked a very young Mayor Townshend from a possible speaking role at the Democratic National Convention. Townshend had been feuding with him ever since, although it had mellowed with age. And Kaminski was, after all, a City employee.

The Mayor's key advisors had stirred the pot with him over Petacque early on, warning that Petacque was too mercurial and could be a potential rival in the next mayoral election. Townshend liked Petacque personally, but accepted his advisors' recommendation that Rep. Seth Dickerson was the best bet for the future in the African-American community.

Of all the old-time ward bosses, Jimmy Juarez had been the most cordial with Townshend right from the beginning. The price of friendship wasn't cheap, Townshend recalled, with Jimmy swallowing up whole City departments for his suddenly-expanding patronage army. But Juarez had always been straight with him, and the Torres candidacy gave Townshend a possible ball to run with. Score points with Juarez, with the whole Hispanic community, maybe women's groups. And Graciela did a nice job on the Blue Ribbon Panel. Former City administrator. Probably doesn't have a chance in this race, though; who knows about the future? And she is sort of charismatic in her own innocent and quirky way. But she had little chance of success, even if she was slated and won the nomination.

Townshend decided not to return Podesta's repeated phone calls.

*   *   *

"DATELINE JJ: On the eve of the Dem slatemaking, it appears Sen. Debra Shane has a decisive lead over millionaire Lawrence Burl for the Party's Guv nod. Suburban Mayor Bill Karmejian has a lock on Secretary of State. Atty. Gen. Lou Calcagno has no primary opposition.

The State Treasurer's race is wide open, though, with Rep. Tom Cummings (D-Hubbs) and Peshtigo County Treasurer Tammy "Peaches" Piechiowski putting together the strongest bids. PUC Chair endorsement should go to veteran "Gang of 72" member Sen. Paul Podesta (D-Mohawk Valley), but Jackson City Ald. Shawn Petacque is sitting on a bloc of votes. And a few other City Cousins can't stand ole Paul.

Question: Will Dem State Party Chair Niles Flint inject his own candidacy into one of these races, for "the good of the Party"?

Question: Will Mayor Townshend's "12 Angry Men and Women" throw their weight around?

Question: With the slated candidates from four years ago all going down in flames (except Calcagno), do the Donkeys REALLY want to continue this quaint tradition?

*   *   *

Chairman Niles Flint banged the gavel and the State Democratic Party slatemaking was underway.

Sited in the magnificent Grand Ballroom of the Capital's oldest hotel, the St. Charles Royale, the "Gang of 72" were seated in a huge square.

About 300 reporters, campaign staffers and party activists sat in the ornate balcony above.

"We will start by hearing from candidates for Governor," Flint announced.

Seven candidates presented five-minute credentials, although only Burl and Shane were considered viable. After the presentations, a motion was taken from the floor to endorse Shane. While Burl had his backers, he could muster only 18 votes and just 12 percent of the weighted vote.

The other candidates awaiting their turn at bat all marveled at both Burl and Shane. Both so polished and relaxed. Graciela watched Shane to see how she handled the purse and skirt issues (handed-off the purse to an aide on her way to the podium; smoothed the skirt in a single, downward sweeping motion).

Petacque noticed how many of the "Gang of 72" seemed palsy-walsy with Podesta. Working the square of pols, Podesta was masterful, whispering in one person's ear, playfully massaging another in the shoulder, constantly touching, constantly moving. He addressed everyone by first name or a nickname. The Ultimate Inside Gamer, Petacque thought.

Kaminski marveled that Burl was even bigger than he was. A behemoth! And how tiny Boss Chizz looked compared to these other guys. And how State Treasurer hopeful Tammy "Peaches" Piechiowski seemed to be flirting with him. Did she like him or was she after Czyz' votes?

What Petacque, Kaminski and Torres did not know of was the brief meeting of minds among their patrons earlier that day. Juarez and Czyz approached Sen. Beatrice Madison and urged her to hold fast against Podesta on the PUC Chair. She informed them she was committed to Petacque on the first vote and promised not to go to Podesta on a second ballot. On top of that, Billy Miller had quietly lined up seven votes for Torres among Downstate Podesta-haters.

"Motion carries," Chairman Flint barked. "State Representative Tom Cummings of the great Village of Hubbs is our endorsed candidate for State Treasurer. And the Chair salutes the classy lady from Peshtigo

County, Tammy Piechioski, for her very gracious withdrawal from the race. Thanks, Peaches, we'll remember this. Okay, next up, the final seat on the ticket, that of Chairperson of the Public Utilities Commission."

With that, a few hundred antennae in the St. Charles Royale Grand Ballroom started to twitch. The first real conflict of the day, reporters thought. My last chance for a candidacy, Flint thought. One last stab at king-making, Townshend's operatives thought. Showtime, Podesta thought, on my turf.

My chance for fame, thought George Chubb, perennial candidate who was the first of the potential PUC candidates to address the Gang of 72. George's main pitch was that, as a TV repairman he understood technology more than the other candidates (quite true), and that he understood people's needs, and isn't that what the Democratic Party is all about?

The genuine candidates soon appeared, with Kaminski reciting his list of Aldermanic accomplishments ("212 miles of new sidewalks in my Ward!"), Petacque invoking his resume and late-father's name, Podesta recalling his "long friendship" with many of the Committee members and years of service to the Party, and Torres coyly playing both gender and ethnic cards.

Chairman Flint asked each candidate the same question: "If this Committee should select someone other than you to be our endorsed slated candidate, would you support that decision?"

Podesta and Kaminski responded similarly, with a long defense of their party credentials and no definitive answer. Petacque flat-out said "no", adding that this is what his Daddy—"who served on this very Committee"—would have done. Torres stole the show by saying, with a beaming smile, "Well, Mister Chairman, I plan to be the slated candidate, so your point is moot."

"Okay, no further questions? Do I hear a motion?" Flint asked.

"Mister Chairman, I move to endorse Senator Paul Podesta for PUC Chair," called out Congresswoman Edna MacIntyre. "Second!" chorused several members.

"Madam Congresswoman, you have the floor," Flint said politely.

"Mister Chairman, I have known Paul Podesta from the earliest days of his political career. I campaigned door-to-door with him in Mohawk Valley and he has returned the favor in my District. He knows utility issues thoroughly from his legislative leadership. He is a builder, someone who gets things done," MacIntyre said with a flourish honed on the floor of the United States House of Representatives. "And, my fellow Democrats, of all the fine candidates we have heard from today, only he can raise the resources necessary to beat the Republicans in November. Mister Chairman, Paul Podesta is clearly our man for this job."

"Opposition to the motion?" Flint scanned the crowd. Billy Miller had his hand raised, as did Sen. Beatrice Madison. Jimmy Juarez hesitantly put his paw in the air.

Flint recognized the venerated Beatrice. "Senator Madison?"

With nearly as much flourish as Congresswoman MacIntyre, Madison slowly rose, turned on the table mike and glared over her bifocals at Niles Flint. The TV camera lights went on.

"Mister Chairman," she said in a frail, musical voice. "Mister Chairman, I see geographic balance on this ticket, I see youth and experience, and I am so very proud that we stood up for my beautiful colleague, Senator Debra Shane, to be our next Governor."

Polite applause from around the huge table. Everyone knew what was coming.

"But Mister Chairman, how can you of all people fail to find at least one qualified African-American for this so-called Dream Ticket?" Tiny Beatrice was instantly hot. "I am offended and disappointed in you, and in many of my colleagues here. After all we have done for the Democratic Party of this state. We produced huge numbers for the entire ticket four years ago, Niles. Huge numbers. Put Lou Calcagno over the top as Attorney General. And now, we can't even find one single, qualified African-American for this ticket you expect us to carry. Out on the streets. Very disappointing, Niles." A voice in the gallery yelled, "Go, Beatrice!"

Flint rapped the gavel. "Aw, c'mon, Senator, don't blame me. Do you want to speak to the motion or not?"

"I do! I am against it!" Madison raspily shouted. Several of the Black Caucus members started clapping, as did the audience in the balcony. Podesta glared at Madison, who glared at Flint, who banged the gavel repeatedly.

"Call to question, Mister Chairman." One of the Podesta floor leaders made the motion to end debate. Czyz and Juarez exchanged glances. Podesta seemed to think that portraying this as a one-on-one with Petacque would give him an edge with this group. Just ignore Kaminski and Torres, Mraz probably told him, focus your fire on Petacque. Black-and-white.

The Podesta forces—a coalition of labor, farmers and older Party activists—saw the vote on the motion to end debate as a litmus test of their strength. One of his floor leaders was actually giving a "thumbs-up" gesture to their bloc.

"Okay, motion to call the question. Show of hands on this, people," Flint announced. "All in favor?"

The 31 arms of the Podesta bloc shut up in unison. As expected, opposition came from the Black Caucus, Jimmy Juarez, Johnny Czyz, Seamus Dunne, Sen. Mario Camozzi and a group of disenfranchised Downstaters led by Billy Miller.

And, sitting firmly on their hands, were the twelve members of the Townshend Bloc. At that moment, Podesta knew his insider game was over.

                    *   *   *

Further debate included Miller chiding Podesta for his anti-environmental and pro-utility stances. Juarez echoed Beatrice Madison's concerns about the lily-white composition of the slate. Camozzi dredged up some ancient instance of "disloyalty" when Podesta backed a non-slated rural candidate for State Treasurer over a slated Jackson City candidate. The motion to endorse Podesta failed, with 31 in favor and 41 against. With the Townshend Bloc voting "no".

Then, in rapid succession, Czyz nominated Kaminski, Juarez nominated Torres and Madison nominated Petacque. No candidate received more than 20 votes, with the Townshend-istas voting no in each case. Jimmy Juarez thought for a few seconds that they would be with him for Graciela, but they sat.

What the hell is Townshend doing, Flint wondered. If this is deadlocked, a Flint candidacy could blossom. The African-American community would be in a snit, though. Townshend may have a candidate of his own waiting in the bushes, too. Maybe Ikeda?

"Mister Chairman," waved Townshend's floor leader, Mary Ikeda.

"Chair recognizes Committeewoman Ikeda," Flint said, relieved that Townshend was finally playing his hand.

"We obviously enjoy a surplus of superb candidates for the PUC job. I move we find candidates Kaminski, Petacque, Podesta and Torres all 'Qualified'. I realize this is unorthodox and not our traditional slatemaking procedure, but it is expressly permitted by our By-Laws."

The compromise motion was seconded by several Townshend-istas and after no debate passed unanimously. Podesta's Old Guard couldn't produce for him. He had run with this "Gang of 72" for decades, and he couldn't even…

"Congratulations to all of our fine candidates!" Flint gaveled the voting closed and the slatemaking complete.

*　　　　*　　　　*

"DATELINE JJ: Big winners in yesterday's Dem slatemaking party: Debra Shane, who stomped Daddy Warbucks for the Guv nod, and Rep. Tom Cummings who edged "Peshtigo Peaches" for State Treasurer. And how 'bout that Mayor Townshend, who killed Paul Podesta's chances for the PUC Chair slating, instead engineering a "qualified" recommendation for the whole field.

Question: How much will gazillionaire Burl spend to rough up Shane, whose popularity numbers are through the roof?

Question: Will the lack of an African-American or Hispanic on the ticket (despite the fancy footwork for Shawn Petacque and Graciela Torres being 'qualified') hurt in November?

Question: How come the Republicans don't have fun like this?

*   *   *

The Moore campaign Brain Trust knew that Royce would buy some love, and that Mary would have a tough time in Jackson City and on campuses. But Mary's numbers looked okay and they felt confident about their field operation and organizational support as they traversed the state. Langley's network of Republican Party officials was vast and he pretty much turned it over to Jimmy Blake for Mary.

The Republican caucuses, while non-binding, are taken into account by the slatemakers. The first one, traditionally, was always held in Fox County, the Grand Old Party's long-time bastion, run efficiently by Tug Blaney for 30 years.

As they drove to the magnificent old Fox County Civic Theater for the first caucus, Mary, Steven Page, Randall Moore and their new college kid/driver discussed the event. Mary was concerned there hadn't been much advance planning, but Page assured her that Tug, an old crony of Gov. Langley, would do well for us.

As they neared the parking lot, the car phone chirped. Steven answered and put it on speakerphone.

"Commissioner Moore? This here's Tug Blaney, uh, we gotta little situation here," the speakerphone drawled. Steven recalled how it was just a few months ago that he was with Tug in Governor Langley's limo when they received the news about Calvin Reynolds' Mexican accident.

"We're just pulling into your parking lot, actually," Moore replied. "What's up, Mister Chairman?"

"Well, uh, then y'all can see for yerselves in just about ten seconds," Tug said tentatively. "We're gonna do the best we can, though."

Just as he said that, Page saw at least 20 bright yellow school buses lined up, proudly proclaiming "Crandall's Crusaders" in bold red letters, disgorging hundreds of Crusaders who were streaming into the Fox County Civic Theater.

*   *   *

"Dammit! Dammit! Read those numbers to me again!" Jimmy Blake was furious. Screaming, probably spitting and throwing things, Page thought.

"402 votes for Barnett, 295 for Moore and 17 for Blasingame," Steven read to him over the din of what had turned into a truly raucous caucus. "Blaney admits he dropped the ball. He feels very bad."

"Bad? He feels bad? He'll feel worse when we yank his DMV jobs! Shit! Asleep at the switch, drunk, what?"

"Dunno. Media's all over it, though."

The media, in fact, had a field day. *"Raucous Caucus Coup by Crandall Ally"* blared the *Jackson City Review.* *"Moore Stunned by Fox Foul-up"* was JJ Springfield's headline. Even Jackson City TV picked it up.

"This demonstrates a positive, new direction in the Republican Party," gloated a Crandall press release issued that night. "This demonstrates how troubled many right-thinking Americans are with the immorality in public life. With her tenacity and honesty, Thelma Barnett will challenge that system and it will crumble under its own weight."

Even Royce Blasingame piled onto the gang-tackle. "Mary Moore's disappointing showing in Fox County shows the slim support she really has among the rank-and-file," Blasingame said in a statement faxed to all media statewide. He didn't mention his own 2 percent caucus showing.

The episode sobered up the Moore camp, and they vowed never again to take Thelma Barnett—or, more precisely, Crandall's Crusaders—lightly. The Governor asked Blake to do whatever it takes to get the local politicos on board and announced a Gala Fundraiser to Elect Mary Moore, with a goal of raising $300,000.

*   *   *

Thanksgiving came and went with most candidates and their staffers running hard.

Kaminski, Barnett, Podesta and Moore had obtained more than enough petition signatures, while Blasingame, Petacque, Clark and Torres were all still hustling to make the deadline.

Petacque kept looking over his shoulder for another African-American candidate. Hopefully the Seth Dickerson and Cassandra Phillips maneuvers had paid off. If anyone else was out there, Chemuyil Gardner would have heard about by now. And Torres kept wondering if she would be the only Hispanic and only female Democratic candidate. Amazingly, no one else was making noises, with just a week to go for filing petitions.

A split in the Moore camp developed over how to deal with Thelma Barnett. Blake felt that for a lower level race, Thelma's gender would hurt Mary. He advocated the need to undermine Barnett wherever possible. Page, though, was confident in Langley's organizational prowess and felt Thelma could take away from Blasingame more. Page was also concerned about angering the Christian Right.

Each campaign opened up the throttle for the final stage of the petition drive.

*   *   *

A quaint tradition for petition-filing is the overnight line that forms outside of the State Elections Board the night before filing.

Hundreds of candidates, campaign staffers and volunteers gather in a fuel-injected Pajama Party for Democracy. Partisan differences are forgotten as people spend the night in chaise lounges and under umbrellas, clinching their binders of signed petitions. Alliances, friendships and romances can develop by 5:00 a.m., and dissolve by the next day.

Moore, Podesta, Torres and Kaminski had their agents do the overnight shift (Del Zink, Timmy Sullivan, Sam Roth & Lupe Zarate, and Mike Kula, respectively). Other PUC Chair candidates showed up to file their petitions in person.

Despite Nicky Pulver's admonitions that he could be spending his time better elsewhere, Royce Blasingame wouldn't miss this ritual. Arriving at midnight dressed in a high-tech cold-weather outfit, Royce regaled those standing in line with him with tales of adventure on the campaign trail. Tina Bishop and Rep. Laura Southampton handed out hot coffee and cocoa. By 2:00 a.m., people in line were ready to elect the charming Royce as Governor.

Thelma Barnett used the overnighter as an opportunity to push for "prayer circles" within the Elections Board. Rev. B.J. Crandall had put the word out and more than 50 Crusaders joined Thelma at 1:00 a.m. for a somber nocturnal vigil. They prayed, cat-napped and read their Bibles, impervious to the lousy weather and bottles of wine being shared up-and-down the candidates' line.

Since Shawn Petacque had gathered the most signatures personally; he saw this Pajama Party as completion of the project. As an aldermanic candidate, Shawn had filed his own petition signatures, so he viewed this as a must. He and Chemuyil Gardner arrived at 3:00 a.m., woefully under-dressed for the chilly mist. Royce and Shawn waved cordially to one another in the line.

Lights from a local TV crew illuminated the parade of hopefuls around 4:30 a.m. The reporter interviewed candidates for judge, for Congress and for everything else. TV lights can jumpstart any situation and this crowd of about 400 was awake and getting turned-on! By 5:15 a.m., a dozen reporters had arrived, including JJ Springfield. They chatted with candidates, spin doctors, political junkies and true believers as the sky turned from black to gray to pastel pink. Frost covered the parking lot as candidates shivered.

"Hey, Candidate Blasingame! How's your witch doctor, I mean, spin doctor, Nicky Pulver?" JJ Springfield called out. JJ always had an edge.

"More than 50,000 sigs, here, JJ," Royce gleefully held up the leather binders containing the thousands of hours of work put in by Blasingame's hired hands. "We're gonna do this thing. You watch."

"Sure thing, kid. Hey, I see Thelma's having an amen-fest or somethin' over there and Petacque's right down the line a bit. How 'bout a joint press conference at dawn?"

"I love it! Duel at Sunrise. Shoot-out at the PUC Corral!" Royce said effusively.

With no other candidates for statewide office actually there at dawn, the PUC contest had media appeal. Petacque readily agreed to a joint appearance and, after consulting Rev. Crandall, Barnett agreed, too. So, as the sun crested over the gilded State Capitol Dome two blocks south, bleary-eyed PUC candidates Barnett, Petacque and Blasingame took questions from the bleary-eyed press.

The first question: "Why are you out here all night instead of having your supporters here?"

"I'm here because I personally have gathered at least 6,000 of the 38,000 signatures I will be filing," Petacque quickly said. "I have looked these folks in the eye myself. I haven't hired people to do my work."

"Well, I'm sure Alderman Petacque did a great job of personally getting signatures, but there's nothing wrong with having a base of supporters helping you," Blasingame shot back. "Still, I'm sure the Alderman is here for the same reason I am. It's a big moment in any candidate's career, and in a democracy, everyone should experience this ritual first-hand."

The sun now gleamed full above the Capitol, illuminating the crystalline frost and ice in the trees framing the impromptu press conference.

"Ms. Barnett, why are you out here all night?" one reporter asked.

Thelma tilted her head skyward as a sunbeam broke through. "Because the Lord Jesus Christ wills it," she said tersely, and looked away. Uncomfortable glances among reporters.

JJ Springfield barked, "Alderman Petacque. Isn't it true you had to get that number of signatures yourself because of the lack of support you're getting in your own community?"

"My own community? Which community is that, Mr. Springfield?" Shawn laughed. "Man, I got support from community groups, college kids, small businessmen, block clubs…"

"But there aren't many Black leaders supporting you, are there?"

"My support is broad, JJ. The people support me, these thousands of people I met in subway stations and bingo halls who are upset about their phone bills and their heating bills…"

"Uh huh. How about you, Mister Blasingame. Any Party leaders for you?"

"Well, we're here with State Representative Laura Southampton, who's been handing out hot chocolate all night. But, y'know, I'm running against an entrenched insider system, a good-ole-boy—or ole-girl—network," Royce replied. "Up against campaign contributions from utility lobbyists. Patronage workers…"

"So, you and Alderman Petacque hope to build an outsider base…"

"Well, he can speak to his own campaign strategy, and I'd sure love to hear it, but my plan to is remove utility money from the rate-making process, increase utility safety and boost competition."

"I second Royce's emotion, there," Shawn jumped in, "At least about removing the influence of campaign cash from the gas company and the phone company and the…"

JJ shot back, "So, how can you guys be outsider candidates and expect to get anything done in the PUC bureaucracy or in the state legislature?"

Thelma awoke and leapt in. "I will get things done in the Public Utilities Commission by raising the standards of morality and honesty among its employees. And the utilities, too. We believe in the power of prayer as a way of getting things done and will institute prayer circles." She stopped suddenly and looked down.

"Ma'am, maybe prayers can get you signatures and even maybe it could get you elected, but the power of prayer is no match for the Demons of Bureaucracy at the PUC," snapped JJ.

Other reporters lobbed softball questions to Royce and Shawn, who seemed to enjoy ribbing each other. Thelma never spoke again, leaving everyone weirded out by her cultish performance. Newsclips of both Royce and Shawn would run on several TV stations around the state that night. The Dawn PUC Shoot-Out ran out of steam just as the doors to the Elections Board opened, and a cold, yet orderly queue of future leaders shook off the overnight chill and presented their wares.

*   *   *

The Elections Board posted the signature filings on its website the next morning.

"Public Utilities Commission Chairman–Republican Party.
Mary Moore (Zane Terrace)–64,387 signatures
P. Royce Blasingame (Jackson City)–50,079 signatures
Thelma Barnett (Walton's Creek)–31,016 signatures.

"Public Utilities Commission Chairman–Democratic Party.
Paul R. Podesta (Mohawk Valley)–52,290 signatures
George "Butchie" Kaminski (Jackson City)–47,203 signatures
Graciela Perez Torres (Jackson City)–38,361 signatures
Shawn L. Petacque (Jackson City)–37,190 signatures
George W. Chubb (Jackson City)–27,011 signatures"

*   *   *

"Who the hell is George W. Chubb?" Czyz barked out from the back room in the 6th Ward Democratic Headquarters.

"That TV repair guy, Boss. 'Member? He spoke at the slating," Butchie offered. "He sez he understands technology better'n the rest of us."

"Aw Christ, just what we need, another George on the ballot. It's gotta be a Mraz trick. Gotta be Mraz, muckin' things up. Christ Almighty. Two Georges on the ballot."

*   *   *

Jimmy Blake saw this as an opportunity to clear the field a little and remove the gender issue. He set up a conference call with Gov. Langley, Steven Page and Mary Moore.

"Governor, Barnett submitted only 31K. She had people downloading this funky web petition, which may not even survive a legal challenge…"

"Well, Jimmy, we'll check, but it probably will survive the legal challenge," Langley said. "The question is how clean are the circulators? Lotta rookies out there getting' names for God and Thelma. Maybe not real clear on the concept of notaries."

Page jumped in. "Governor, not only could this be a costly challenge, but it could polarize and energize the Christian Right in this thing."

Moore seconded that. "The last thing we need is for the Evangelicals to get all stirred up. Wouldn't help me or Aviva."

The Aviva Benson for Attorney General contest was also of concern to the Governor, since long-time irritant Phil Driscoll had filed more than enough petition signatures for that post and would spend millions against Aviva, who was a real quality candidate, thought Langley.

"It'd be costly for us and even more costly for Barnett and Crandall to defend. And we have more missiles to fire here, Governor," Jimmy said. "We get a one-on-one with Royce and we devour him. Barnett is a third force we don't need here."

"Mary, I'm looking to the future, here," the Governor said soberly. "We hear Crandall's looking at a U.S. Senate race in two years. And, frankly, I'm looking at you for a U.S. Senate race in two years. So, I guess I'm with Jimmy on this one. Pin down the Right Reverend now. The church picnic's over. Time for hardball. I say we challenge Thelma's petitions."

*   *   *

The Chubb petition challenge went a lot easier than the Barnett challenge. Old George the TV Repair Man had signed his own name about 2,000 times and the rest were round-tabled, probably in Chubb's basement over beers, Czyz thought as he filed a complaint on Butchie's behalf. The Elections Board ruled immediately and tossed Mr. Chubb off the ballot. Now Kaminski could be the only "George" on the ticket.

The Barnett challenge was tougher. Every one of her petitions was gone over by Moore volunteers. As Langley suspected, some of the petition circulators were not legit, most due to their not being registered voters. But should that invalidate all of those signers, Mary asked. The law is the law, Blake piously retorted.

Crandall had to retain a law firm to defend against the petition challenge that ended up costing the Barnett Campaign $20,000. The Governor's top election attorney, Dickie Kyle, coordinated the attack. Line-by-line, Kyle's associates and Moore's volunteers scrutinized each of Thelma's signers. With just a day left before the deadline for challenges, Kyle thought he had knocked the number of valid signatures below 25,000.

At the end of a contentious three-hour hearing, though, the Elections Board ruled on the final day that Moore's challenge was denied; Thelma Barnett would be on the ballot.

This glorious news was transmitted promptly by the Crandall's Crusaders website, e-mail network and phone tree. The Crusade has been victorious again! The wedge between the Christian Right and GOP Moderates widened, as did the gap between top Moore advisors Jimmy Blake and Steven Page.

*   *   *

A few days before Christmas, the Elections Board certified the petitions of the remaining Republican and Democratic candidates for statewide offices, as well as third-party and Independent candidates like Dan Clark (who ended up submitting more than 41,000 petition signatures that went unchallenged by both parties.)

The lottery for ballot position was ceremoniously held in Secretary of State Dobbs' office, using ping pong balls drawn from a fedora once worn by President Harry Truman. The outcomes were posted on the Elections Board website immediately.

"Public Utilities Commission Chairman—Republican Party (Primary Election)

Punch #	Candidate
111	*Thelma Barnett*
112	*Mary Moore*
113	*P. Royce Blasingame*

"Public Utilities Commission Chairman—Democratic Party (Primary Election)

Punch #	Candidate
111	*Shawn L. Petacque*
112	*George "Butchie" Kaminski*
113	*Paul R. Podesta*
114	*Graciela Perez Torres*

"Public Utilities Commission Chairman—Independent (for General Election Only)
Daniel Clark

*　　　　　*　　　　　*

Petacque beamed when he saw the ballot lotto results. All those frozen mornings at the subway getting signatures. Top spot on a low level race could be worth as much as 5% extra, he told his staff. Jimmy Juarez reassured a depressed Torres that the last spot was almost as good as the top spot, plus with her name "stickin' out like that". She was glad she used "Perez Torres". Podesta stewed, having submitted the largest number of names among the Democratic hopefuls, yet getting the worst ballot position.

Moore didn't like getting sandwiched in the deuce spot, but Steven Page offered that Blasingame's name appeared ostentatious, whereas she had the name of "the girl next door." Reverend Crandall convinced Thelma that getting the top spot was "Divine intervention" and further proof of the righteousness of the cause.

The horses are nearing the post. The horses are at the post.

*   *   *

Chapter Three

River Rising, Part II

Between the petition filings and the holidays, the political tempo down-shifted. There was minimal fundraising (mid-December wasn't a great time to raise money), some internal organizational stuff, fluffy media. Each of the campaigns went their separate ways for a few weeks, playing different riffs in different parts of the state. Testing their messages like a baby bird on a maiden voyage from the nest.

The messages varied. Podesta was "The Quiet Worker". Moore embodied "A Tradition of Public Service", linking her subtly with Gov. Langley and Calvin Reynolds. Petacque was for "Safe and Affordable Utility Service…for Everyone!" Clark was "Your Independent Voice". Torres personified "Commitment. Compassion. Community".

"Community" was a word that floated through Kaminski's material, but he hadn't crafted a message yet. Blasingame hadn't developed a slogan—Nicky wanted to do more polling—but his message was clear: Moore was too cozy with the industry and lower cable rates were a basic right. Barnett stood for Morality.

Each campaign used this calm before the storm to build or re-tool their campaign teams.

Podesta and Moore both turned inward, using the cautious, front-runner gambit: raise institutional money, assemble a large and professional team, line up endorsements from the pols. Timmy Sullivan was in charge of Podesta's day-to-day operations, while Steven Page took a leave from the Governor's office to run Moore's.

The Blasingame Campaign was open for business and now hiring, and soon Tina Bishop and Rep. Laura Southampton were presiding over a dozen young staffers in their bustling Jackson City storefront headquarters. Nicky Pulver kept things on track, including Royce's exercise regimen.

Petacque's Kiddie Corps was the hardest-working group during this holiday season, Crandall's Crusaders built the most truly grass-roots effort on Barnett's behalf, and the Torres team enjoyed the best diversity and synergy.

The Podesta, Moore and Kaminski teams were similar in their organizational nature: somewhat top-heavy, and very reliant on patronage and professionals.

Petacque had a dilemma. He could play the role of the "Black Candidate" or he could reach out to the white liberals who might be for Dan Clark in the General Election in November, but could be Petacque-backers in the September primary. Few African-American candidates could juggle that combination, but Shawn always viewed himself as a "fusion" candidate who could meld together diverse groups. His schedule reflected this dichotomy; he was constantly torn by conflicting demands from the African-American community and the white liberals.

Torres and Kaminski had a particular dilemma; each was a child of regular organization politics and had a powerful insider behind them. Each had a strong ethnic base and a great name for that base. How could either of them ignore that base? How much could either of them really campaign outside of that base? They were both restricted by that which empowered them. But Graciela had gender, Billy Miller and the River's Edge edge.

*   *   *

Thelma Barnett's game was way out on the edge.

A mercurial personality to start with, Thelma could be a timid church mouse or the loosest of cannons. She could show compassion—genuine caring—for humanity, and then display a mean-spirited bigotry. But she took direction well and Rev. B.J. Crandall was quick to give it.

Since Crandall's real agenda with Thelma's candidacy was to get the lay of the land for his own Senate race two years hence, he organized a whirlwind six-week tour. Barnett and Crandall gassed up his huge RV and barnstormed, staying in Crusaders' homes when possible. They visited every evangelical church in the state and every Christian radio studio, some located in basements or garages. As they drove from town to town, Crandall prepped Thelma on a range of issues, with everything coming back to the basic immorality in politics and government.

Crandall's Crusaders in every county were recruited and activated; Thelma was already well-known through her *"Amen, Now!"* campaign, so she was an easy sell to Crandall's faithful. A county-by-county phone-tree pyramid comprised of 20,000 Crusaders and a 9,000-strong e-mail network were built quickly and tested regularly. Crandall's farmhouse/Camapign Headquarters was overrun with dedicated volunteers.

With the least amount of money and political experience, Thelma Barnett had almost effortlessly assembled the first genuine statewide field operation of any candidate in the PUC race.

        *   *   *

But it was the Nuke Vigil that really established Thelma in the public mind.

Thelma had reasoned that since the Public Utilities Commission regulated the nuclear power plants, she, as Chairperson, could require a higher level of morality in the plants. Specifically through plant-sponsored "prayer circles". Five minutes, twice a shift. Everybody breaks for some "voluntary reflection". And the PUC office itself would be an appropriate place for prayer circles, she told Christian radio interviewers.

So, as part of her border-to-border RV trip with Crandall, Thelma would stop at each of the state's many nuclear power plants and stage a "Rally for Power Plant Morality" outside the main entrance at shift change.

The first few events went well. Local Crusaders were notified and showed in droves. Signs and banners had been spontaneously created saying *"Clean up Politics...Amen to That!"* and *"Men Make Nukes...God Makes Man"*. Local TV crews were notified and, in the smaller markets, would show up and air the story. Flyers calling for school prayer would be distributed to workers arriving for work or leaving for home. Many of the flyers would end up on the asphalt walkway, but some were shoved into the pockets of work clothes.

The Vigil at Munich, though, was the best-remembered.

The huge twin-towered nuclear power facility near the tiny town of Munich (pronounced by locals as "Moon Itch") provided a dramatic backdrop for Thelma's Traveling Prayer-a-Thon. Crandall thought this would be a good spot for an all-nighter. Visually dramatic and midway between two larger media markets. Perfect. There was a well-organized contingent of Crusaders in the region and the plant had frequent overlapping shift changes.

So Thelma sipped at a thermos of coffee and sat in a garden chair outside of the Countryway Electric Company's Munich plant for the next 18 hours. She was joined by local media and dozens of Crusaders. The response from Countryway workers was encouraging. Crandall could tell they were making converts.

After 18 hours, Thelma felt so encouraged by the Vigil, she decided to just stay put. With no sleep and little food, Thelma read her Bible while awaiting the next shift change. Then she would swing into gear and shake the hands of Countryway workers, some of whom she remembered from their previous shift. A few said they would organize voluntary prayer circles inside the plant.

By the 27th hour, Thelma was getting a little edgy and incoherent. Her exchanges with workers rambled and she appeared a little wild-eyed, almost deranged. She needed a bath.

More than 300 Crusaders from the area had come out and were praying loudly at the chain-link fence separating them from the looming, steaming Countryway cooling tower. Regional media began arriving.

As the 6:00 p.m. shift arrived, flyers were again distributed and Thelma worked the line. She approached Andy O'Banion, a burly union steward, and shouted at him to "Bring prayer to your power plant, friend," her standard mantra.

O'Banion hadn't slept in two days and was strung out on methedrine. He was having woman problems, money problems and car problems, so Andy was in no mood for this maniac screaming at him.

"Ah, get this voodoo bullshit outta my face," O'Banion grumbled as he crumpled the flyer into a tight ball and threw it at Thelma, clipping her in the eye. She released an unearthly wail and crumpled to the asphalt.

No one knew who threw the first punch, but a dozen Crusaders—mostly beefy farm lads—were suddenly pummeling O'Banion and two of his co-workers. Gate security sped over with batons swinging and several Crusaders went down, only to be replaced in the brawl by another wave. O'Banion was choking one bug-eyed Crusader while two others jabbed at Andy's torso, an image captured by several news photographers standing nearby. The TV crews rolled tape that would be picked up nationwide. The Munich Police arrived, and 21 Crusaders and nuke workers were arrested, while another 150 Crusaders and nuke workers knelt in prayer around Thelma. Eyes closed, tears streaming, leading a prayer of peace.

Once again, Thelma Barnett was in the center of it.

*   *   *

"Dateline JJ: The Argo Daily Dispatch has done a somewhat unscientific voter poll of candidates for statewide offices. A small sampling, mind you, but it shows both D & R gubernatorials are up for grabs, incumbents Sec. of State

Dobbs and Atty. Gen. Calcagno are both in fine shape, and nobody has focused on the lower tier races. The PUC contest has the highest number of undecideds. Check it out...

GOP:		Dems:	
	29%-Moore		*19%-Podesta*
	13%-Blasingame		*13%-Kaminski*
	7%-Barnett		*8%-Petacque*
	51%-undecided		*7%-Torres*
			53%-undecided

*   *   *

The snow was still on the ground when all of the candidates began to hit the road in earnest.

Blasingame, Torres and Barnett probably logged the most miles, sometimes bumping into each other at Candidate's Forums and American Legion Pancake Breakfasts and tiny radio stations in far-flung places. Once Blasingame ran into Dan Clark in Pomeranian Springs (pop. 3,021) and the two had a delightful lunch at the Olde Pomerania Diner, followed by an impromptu joint cable TV talk show appearance.

Podesta's public hearings on Moore's nomination had put him on the road for a week, but the hearings were a bust. Mary had flat-out refused to go traipsing around the state as a foil for Podesta's road show, and the media and public for the most part ignored it. Podesta had been able to stall the confirmation process another few months, but his delay offense strategy was starting to backfire, as editorial editors and League of Women Voter types chided Paul's molasses-like tempo.

Moore did plenty of traipsing about the state for her own agenda, though. Governor Langley's scheduling operation was the best in the state and he bequeathed it to the Moore Campaign. Their computerized scheduling system recorded hundreds of civic and party events in every county. Each event had a file on it, with an estimate as to crowd size and estimated drive time from the nearest airport or interstate highway. Points were awarded for political value, media potential and fundraising expectation. Mary Moore's advance operation worked closely with scheduling, so that enthusiastic crowds, ample visibility and limited tardiness would be consistently achieved. It was a well-oiled machine.

Billy Miller knew the political landscape of the Downstate counties as well as anyone working on this race, with the possible exception of Timmy Sullivan. Billy took Graciela under his wing and they criss-crossed the state, watching winter turn to springtime overnight, it seemed. As the geese flew north overhead and the tulips stuck their heads out, the romance also blossomed. Graciela would return from road trips looking energized.

*   *   *

Randall and Mary Moore guessed that son Tony may be gay in his mid-teens.

Tony never had girlfriends in high school, although he had many female friends. He skipped prom. When he moved into a well-known gay/lesbian neighborhood in Jackson City, he had the folks over for a home-cooked meal with his roommate. After Chilean sea bass and white wine, he told them.

Mary was neither surprise nor offended and offered wholehearted support. Randall was a little skittish, but Tony's candor and the brochures he gave them about parents with gay children put him at ease. Tony also assured them he practiced totally safe sex.

The issue had never arisen politically for Mary; the PUC was not the kind of agency that dealt with social issues. Last year, a gay staffer had requested equal benefits for his partner, but Calvin had vetoed the request. Still, Mary thought the environment was very tolerant and quietly vowed to revisit the equal benefits issue once she was reelected.

When she was deliberating on whether to run, Mary mentioned to Tony that his sexual preference could become a public issue.

"Aw, Ma, it's a non-issue," Tony said. "Nobody cares about that stuff anymore. Really. Don't worry about it."

Jimmy Blake had warned her that Blasingame's people would do a thorough job of opposition research on her, Randall and her children, and that she should be prepared for anything. She felt that she was.

*   *   *

Both Nicky Pulver and Jimmy Blake saw the bump in Thelma Barnett's numbers after the Munich brawl. ProAction was already tracking and Gov. Langley's operation hired out the polling to gauge all the races.

In ProAction's poll, Thelma's name identification soared, from five percent to 24 percent, a meteoric overnight rise. Unfortunately for her, more likely voters had an unfavorable perception of Barnett than favorable. Nicky noticed, however, that among voters who considered themselves "independent", Thelma fared better. Some undercurrent of the Christian Right?

Nicky also spotted Thelma edging in on Mary Moore among older, white women. Royce was still in single digits among older women; time for Rep. Laura Southampton to trot out some moderate Republican socialite types, Nicky thought. And keep Royce in the gym and tanning booth.

Blake's polling data wasn't as extensive as ProAction's, but he also could see that Moore had lost ground to Thelma with women over 55. Blake was worried from the outset that unless Mary Moore's name identification was boosted well into the 50's, she'd have a problem splitting the women's vote with Thelma. Mary's numbers weren't great. Name ID in the mid-30's, with slightly less than a 2-1 favorable-unfavorable ratio. And while River's Edge had faded some, it remained a concern for many voters.

Still not sure how to deal with Thelma, Blake thought, and he began reconsidering his original instinct to simply ignore her. His primary focus, though, was Nicky Pulver—an old nemesis—and his frisky thoroughbred, Royce Blasingame.

*   *   *

When the date finally arrived for a vote on Mary Moore's Senate confirmation, it seemed like years ago when Gov. Langley nominated her. She had been "Acting" Chairperson for seven months, during which Sen. Paul Podesta used one maneuver after another to stall and delay. Podesta considered running her through the wringer one last time when she was asked to appear before his Committee on Public Works and Utilities. He thought about using the info about her husband's questionable stock dealings, or maybe grilling her on River's Edge. But the Senate Democratic Assistant Majority Leader was under investigation for her own husband's shady stock deals, so that wouldn't fly.

And bringing up River's Edge was sure to remind voters of Graciela in the smoldering wreckage and Petacque's crazy website, so Paul played the role of gentleman and bipartisan Chairman. Moore's confirmation was approved unanimously in both Paul's Committee and the full Senate. She was "Acting" no more.

*   *   *

The arrival of the e-mail was just as abrupt as the sender's disappearance a few months earlier, Chemuyil Gardner thought as she excitedly opened the message from "Mountain Referee".

"Hello, Chemuyil. I'm still here. Sorry I've been incommunicado and didn't return your notes. Glad your candidate is doing so well; I'm rooting for him. Have new information re: valve. Will be in touch. Mountain Referee."

Gardner's e-response was gracious.

"Been worried about you, MR. Thought somebody at Eaton had choked you with your whistle chain. Very very interested in any new info on valve…Riv Edge has sadly faded from headlines. b-careful…chem.

*   *   *

Billy Miller was amazed at how many Democratic officials were not enthused about Podesta's candidacy, even those who had endorsed him.

Podesta had stepped on thousands of toes dating back 30 years; some of those toes were now aimed at his behind, Miller mused.

Miller kept Graciela on the road throughout the spring and summer, going to county fairs, Democratic Party pig roasts and parades, despite lamentations by Jimmy Juarez and Lupe Zarate to stay closer to their Hispanic Jackson City base.

The community anger over River's Edge and the rioting had cooled over the winter. Pequeno Barragan continued to pen outraged editorials in *"Hoy!"* about the gas company's cover-up and the Housing Authority's negligence and Graciela's heroism, but the dust of public focus was settling just as sure as the charred debris at River's Edge had settled.

Miller figured—and convinced Graciela and Sam Roth—that the Hispanics would come out big time, and unlike Petacque, Graciela needed go outside her base, specifically targeting suburban soccer moms and Downstaters who didn't like Podesta.

Graciela had been endorsed by the National Hispanic Women's Alliance, a nod that came with an agreement to pay for an early 100,000-piece mailing targeted to suburban women who were "heads of their households". A beautiful full-color postcard describing Graciela's tough childhood and the challenges she faced as a single-mom was mailed in July, the first mailing by a PUC candidate. The others would soon follow.

*   *   *

Nicky Pulver and Jim Davis sat in ProAction's cramped video production studio and grinned.

The drag queen photo Davis had set up in New Orleans was perfect. Davis had a right to be proud. It was his finest work. In the black-and-white photo you saw Mary Moore and her husband, both appearing slightly tipsy, making "ooh" sounds as Queen Crystal is grabbing a shocked Del Zink. Nicky cropped the photo just above Del's crotch.

"Man, you can pick 'em," Nicky said. "Crystal looks like a Victoria's Secret model on steroids."

"I need more of these road trips," Davis chortled, as he rolled the video.

"Meet Mary Moore," intoned a serious male voiceover.

"She's the Chairman of our state Public Utilities Commission. Here's Mary Moore enjoying a New Orleans junket with her husband and top aides, while the survivors of the River's Edge tragedy try to fix their broken lives. Mary Moore. Taking a $25,000 honorarium from a pro-nuke think-tank. Mary Moore. She's one reason your utility bills have soared recently. Mary Moore wants to be your full-time PUC Chairman…We can't afford Mary Moore's parties and junkets. Paid for by Citizens for Blasingame."

The images flashed quickly.

Drag Queen in lingerie. Mary looking drunk and stunned. Smoke billowing from River's Edge. A dummy state economic disclosure form with the words "$25,000 Honorarium" stamped over it in bold red letters. Pictures of steaming nuclear power plants and telephone poles. Back to Crystal. Snippets of sound cascade into one another: Mardi Gras jazz, echoes of sirens at River's Edge, a cash register ca-chinging. A brutal symphony.

"Thirty seconds of slam-bam. Actually, it's a little over thirty seconds, but we can trim the nuke and phone part," Davis said.

"A work of art, J.D." Nicky congratulated the young operative and immediately called his client.

"Royce, it's a work of art. A thing of beauty," Nicky gloated. "It'll double her negatives in a week." He played the audio over the phone for the candidate.

"Aw, Nicky, are you sure we want to go this negative?"

Blasingame was showing the reticence common to most rookie candidates about getting upclose and personal. "I mean, geez, to show her spouse and this drag queen…"

"C'mon Bro, don't get all wiggy and skittish on me here. Look, hubby-boy got a free ride to the Big Easy. Moore made the quickest $25K she's ever made. And Crystal brings in a little comic relief and will generate some buzz," Nicky said, unmoved by Blasingame's concerns. "Moore's at

54 percent approval and only 21 percent disapproval. More than 2-1. We either drive up her negs or she waltzes in."

"How big a buy?"

"Massive. Time to draw some blood. This'll make up for your having no field ops, no name and no record in utility regulation. Two hundred thou for each of two weeks. Every station in the state. News time. Ball games. Cop shows. Anything watched by independent-leaning male voters. We'll go up right after the Channel Six Debate."

"Isn't it a little early for this stuff?"

"These last few months are gonna fly by. We can be the first one on TV. People will be talking about this spot and Mary Moore and Royce Blasingame," Nicky said. "Trust me, Third."

Man, this TV can get pricey, Royce thought. "I do. Let's do it."

$$*\qquad *\qquad *$$

While there had been countless forums (Petacque and Torres saw more of each other than they did their families) and joint appearances at endorsement sessions, only one formal debate among all of the candidates for PUC Chair had been agreed to. The Jackson City Women's Civic Action League would sponsor a live, televised one-hour debate for each of the statewide offices.

The expertise of handlers like Nicky Pulver and Timmy Sullivan really paid off in the negotiations. As agents for Blasingame and Podesta, they collaborated across party lines to lock out independent candidate Dan Clark, and to require all candidates to be seated on the stage, unprotected by a desk or table. This would give females Mary Moore, Thelma Barnett and Graciela Torres something to think about.

The Great Debate was held in the Channel 6 studio, decorated in festive red-white-and-blue bunting. Each candidate arrived early for a sound check, walk-through and make-up. Podesta and Petacque seemed the least intimidated by the spectacle, while Thelma and Butchie looked scared to death. The candidates each were assigned a tiny "green room" with a sink, mirror, four chairs and a limp veggie spread.

Each "green room" had its own mood just before the opening bell. Candidates were joined by handlers, family or significant others.

On the Republican side of the corridor, Steven Page, Peggy Briscoe and Randall Moore put Mary at ease with light banter, a few jokes. Nicky Pulver, Rep. Laura Southampton and Tina Bishop were getting Royce pumped up like Rocky before the Big One. Tina massaged his broad shoulders while Nicky peppered him with questions. After refusing any make-up, Thelma Barnett was joined by Rev. Crandall, who picked at the cauliflower and then knelt with Thelma in prayer.

On the other side, Emily Podesta and Pudge Carson chatted while Tim Sullivan helped Paul shuffle through 3x5 cards. Sam Roth, Lupe Zarate and Billy Miller chatted with Graciela about another campaign trip downstate.

Butchie Kaminski was a nervous wreck. Mikey Kula had slipped him a valium, his mom Helen had made a stew for supper that wasn't sitting well and he had never worn make-up before. Chemuyil Gardner was reading to Shawn Petacque transcripts of the River's Edge Blue Ribbon hearing as Consuelo rubbed his stockinged feet.

"Candidates to the studio. All candidates to the studio!" blared the hidden loudspeaker. Show time. One last look in the mirror, a final glance at the notes, a last kiss or word of encouragement. All of the candidates bumped into each other in the hallway from their "green rooms", except for Mary Moore, who was purposely holding back at Jimmy Blake's insistence. "You're the incumbent. Make 'em wait for you." Finally, a desk assistant stuck her head in Moore's "green room" and said, "Time to go, Commissioner Moore." Mary kissed Randall and walked down the studio hallway.

*   *   *

The candidates were seated in alphabetical order from left to right on a well-lit, blue-carpeted stage. A tiny table with a pitcher of ice water and a glass was set between each chair. In the center, sat Phoebe Jacobsen, Channel 6 morning anchor and Great Debate moderator.

Once everyone was in place, Phoebe announced two minutes until they were on air live. His stomach churning, Butchie worried his make-up was running with sweat. Petacque suddenly couldn't remember a word of his opening statement. Podesta gazed at the scene with relish; this was his turf and he'd eat these punks up. As designed by Pulver and Sullivan, all three female candidates tried to discreetly cover their legs.

Suddenly the lights increased and a recording of a Sousa march blasted.

"Good evening, citizens and voters! I'm Phoebe Jacobsen and welcome to the Candidates' Speak Out hosted by Channel Six and the Jackson City Women's Civic Action League." Sousa softened.

"Tonight's featured office is that of Chairman of the state Public Utilities Commission, an agency with regulatory responsibilities for our phone, gas, electric, water and cable TV services. The Chairperson will serve a four-year term and supervises a staff of two hundred thirty people in two offices.

"We should note that an independent candidate in the race—Dan Clark—has been not allowed to participate tonight, since the upcoming election is only the primary.

"The rules of the game, ladies and gentlemen: each candidate will have two minutes to open and a very brief closing. Our panel of six prominent civic leaders will ask questions, and—time permitting—we may have some give-and-take among these fine candidates. Candidate Thelma Barnett, you have the first word."

Thelma looked stunned at first, as if nobody had explained these rules to her before. But she recovered quickly and gamely went into her stock speech about the need for morality in public office, the pesky constitutional prohibitions on prayer in the schools and workplace, and her past as a devout young girl growing up on a grain farm.

Damn, Nicky thought, I can almost hear tens of thousands of remotes clicking right now. They'll never get to Blasingame. But Royce's turn was next and after a 15-second bio, he immediately went on the attack, ripping Mary Moore for her close association with "the previous Chairman" who was a "pawn of the utility lobbyists". Royce blasted her for River's Edge, soaring cable TV rates, dwindling water supplies and just about everything else.

Petacque took a similar jab at Podesta, noting Paul's "quite unremarkable tenure as Chairman of the Senate Public Works and Utilities Committee. Should we expect any different from Senator Podesta as Chairman of the PUC?" The rest of the openers, though, were mild and quite predictable, with no fireworks.

In the Q-and-A, Moore defended Calvin Reynolds' record and good name, and tweaked Blasingame for being the "wealthy, new kid on the block" in the utility regulation arena. Podesta rhapsodized—too long and too technically, Timmy Sullivan thought—about his proud record of service, his ability to get things done and to "work on both sides of the aisle: Republican and Democrat, Labor and Utilities".

"So let me ask Senator Podesta," Graciela jumped in, "Where does the consumer or the taxpayer fit into that equation? Anywhere?" That line prompted the first genuine, non-scripted applause from the audience made up of Women's Civic Action Leaguers and a rap on the knuckles for interrupting from moderator Jacobsen.

The questions from the distinguished panel elicited nothing new or spectacular, until something snapped in Barnett's Crandall-soaked brain, and she felt compelled to give a last-ditch plea for school prayer.

Thelma recounted her long, righteous battle and said that opponents of school prayer, "…like Mrs. Mary Moore here—who is hiding a homosexual son—and Alderman Petacque" (which she pronounced 'petack-you') were "secular low-lifes" (Crandall's favorite line) and called Governor Langley a "Godless and gutless leader."

Then she abruptly shut up.

For the first time in the evening, you could hear a pin drop in the studio. Thelma's tirade was so unexpected, so biting and personal. The six other candidates looked at each other uncomfortably, no one quite sure how to exploit the situation. Moore's jaw dropped.

Then Kaminski spoke spontaneously for the first time in the debate. Maybe the first time in the entire campaign.

"Mrs. Barnett, my family, and the family of most of my neighbors, my constituents, came to our great country of America to excape religious prosecution, to worship as they see fit, between them and their creator.

"My mother, Helen Kaminski, prays the rosary every day, Mrs. Barnett, and I was an altar boy for five years at St. Thomas Aquinas," Butchie said, as if everyone in the state knew St. Thomas Aquinas Parish. The valium and beef stew percolated in his gut. Beads of sweat glistened on his Baltic brow.

"And I still attend Masses on Sundays and all holy days of obligation!" Butchie the Brawler was getting worked up and glared at Thelma. She looked at him with fear, convinced that her televised martyrdom would be the right thing.

He was back on his mom. "And Mrs. Barnett, my dear mother prays the rosary because she wants to, not because somebody ordered her to like it was Communist Russia!"

With that, Mad Dog slammed his hand on the side table, sending a sweating pitcher of ice water crashing to the floor.

Due to the phenomenon that causes restaurant patrons to clap when a waiter drops a plate, combined with Butchie's sincere indignance, the studio crowd erupted in applause. Butchie, Thelma and the other candidates looked shocked, frozen. Butchie was the first to kick Thelma's holier-than-thou soapbox out from under her and he had done it in a totally honest and uncalculating way. And the crowd loved it. So did the statewide viewing audience.

The few reporters who hadn't drifted off loved it too. Butchie's ham-fisted swipe of Thelma and the water pitcher would be the only debate footage used by TV stations across the state. Coverage begets coverage, so Butchie's face would appear in every major newspaper the next morning.

As the debate concluded without further ruckus, the crowd still buzzing about Butchie's slam-dunk, the candidates headed backstage. Spin Alley was already jammed with reporters, spinners and handlers, candidates' family and half the Women's Civic Action League. It was pandemonium, with mini-press conferences erupting everywhere. Mary Moore was describing a mother's love for her son, "…no matter what his sexual orientation may be." Blasingame was condemning Barnett's "vicious bigotry that has no place in this campaign."

In the backstage crush, Butchie found himself jammed up against his City Council colleague, Shawn Petacque.

Shawn and Butchie were nodding acquaintances in the Council. They generally voted on opposite sides. Butchie had never gone out drinking with Petacque as he had done with other minority aldermen, but there was no animosity between the two. During the course of the campaign, they had seen a lot more of each other, usually at Party functions. They both knew instinctively that each had his own political and ethnic base, and his own potential voter base for this particular race, and there was overlap of their respective bases whatsoever. They were of absolutely no threat to each other in this race.

So when they found themselves jammed next to one another in the deafening backstage area after the Great Debate, there was a brief moment of warm camaraderie felt by the two men. Butchie leaned into Petacque's ear, as he had done so many times to other colleagues at City Council meetings and said, "She's one wicked bitch, eh, Shawn?"

Petacque grinned. He'd thoroughly enjoyed Butchie's tirade. He draped his arm around Kaminski's massive frame and replied, "Yeah, that Thelma is one wicked bitch. Way to go, man." Then the crowd and TV crews and din swirled around them and they began to slowly make their way back to their respective "green rooms".

Alex Olmstead, a college intern recruited by Wally Mraz to do opposition research for the Podesta campaign, was standing right next to Petacque and Kaminski, microcassete tape recorder running during their brief exchange. "Yeah, one wicked bitch," Alex thought as he rewound the tape to make sure he got it. "Wicked."

*   *   *

"Moore, Podesta Cruising in PUC Playoffs"

"DATELINE JJ: The first poll taken following the only scheduled debate among the contenders for the late-Calvin Reynolds' mantle as 'PUC Czar' shows what we all know…debates don't mean much. Despite the prayer flap between Ald. Butchie Kaminski (D-Jackson City) and gay-basher Thelma Barnett, and the squabbling between Acting PUC Chair Mary Moore and chief rival, steel scion Royce Blasingame, numbers just aren't moving in this contest.

According to a state university poll taken the day after the Great Debate, Moore and Sen. Paul Podesta (D-Mohawk Valley) both continue to cruise in their respective bids for their party's nominations. Here's where we're at:

GOP:		Dems:	
37%-Moore		25%-Podesta	
21%-Blasingame		15%-Petacque	
11%-Barnett		13%-Torres	
31%-undecided		13%-Kaminski	
		34%-undecided	

QUESTION: How much will Ald. Shawn Petacque (D-Jackson City) surge once the African-American community realizes there's an election?

QUESTION: Will the Big City Boys rally behind Podesta in the end, or will Kaminski (and his padrone, 6th Ward Dem Boss John Czyz) get the 'etnics'?

QUESTION: Will gender help Moore and Jackson County Board Commissioner Graciela Torres?

QUESTION: Will any voter care about this race after they're done voting for Governor? (Hint: not many)

*   *   *

The tension between Podesta and some of the white ethnic tribal chieftains percolated just beneath the surface. Czyz was still mad about being dissed by Podesta and was actively pushing Butchie with other Jackson City Dems. His allies, Sen. Mario Camozzi and Committeeman Seamus Dunne could guarantee huge numbers.

With Podesta's tacit approval, Wally Mraz had started a street-level smear campaign on Butchie…He's a Mama's Boy, still lives in his parents' home, never had a girlfriend, etc.

Johnny Chizz had never backed off from a brawl, nor had Butchie Kaminski, so when Wally started with the whispering campaign about Butchie's sexual orientation in old neighborhood bowling alleys and bars, they slammed back. Mike Kula faxed copies of Mraz' DUI's and overdue child support payments to the weekly neighborhood papers. The atmosphere in the 6th Ward office grew poisonous toward Mraz and, by association, Podesta.

One source of pride for Czyz had always been the infinite number of window posters and yard signs which would sprout up throughout the 6th Ward at Election time. On some blocks, every single house was bedecked with candidate signs in their windows and yards, up on the roof, in the trees. And each season, the 6th Ward crew got better, using computer precinct lists, detailed maps, pick-up trucks and cherry-pickers. Anyone who had requested a garbage can or had a tree trimmed by the City had a sign plunked down in the front yard. No discussion.

Since he was a teenager, Butchie was one of the best at visibility and "devisibility". In fact, he acquired the nickname "Mad Dog" for his zeal in ripping down opponent's signage. He once made the news following his arrest for using a City tow-truck with a winch to remove an opponent's 18-foot billboard. *"Mad Dog is Bad Dog"* screamed the headline in the Police Blotter section of the *Jackson City Review*.

Mad Dog was in the Dog House with his mom and Boss Chizz for that caper, but his reputation in the Ward soared, and actually helped position him to be Alderman. Once he was sworn in, Johnny instructed him to knock off the funny business.

But, the 6th Ward Mad Dog tradition lived on in the form of guys like Kula and Eddie Czyz, the grandson of Boss Czyz's brother. Eddie, who called Johnny "Uncle", worked at the City Water Department and was no slouch at devisibility. Like Butchie before them, Eddie and Mike would have a few cold ones before hitting the streets on a devisibility mission. On one particular night, after several hours of removing Podesta signs from lightpoles and yards across the County, Eddie got worked up about the Wally Mraz whispering campaign.

"Man, Butchie's good people. And he's got bigger cojones than Wally the Weasel ever would, that's fer sure," Eddie lamented as they cruised the rainy midnight streets in his blue Camaro. "Why they gotta go after him like this?"

"Ah, politics, Edward," Kula said, draining another beer. "A beautiful thing. Now everyone knows about the Weasel's child support payments. For the little Baby Weasels."

"Yeah, well, it's all still BS." Eddie wheeled onto the expressway. "Hey, Mikey, let's head downtown and see if anybody's still up at Podesta's." Within ten minutes, the Mad Dogs were parked out front of Podesta's slick first floor office.

A cavernous prime location, Podesta had, by far, the largest campaign headquarters of any Democratic candidate. Kaminski and Petacque were both using their Ward offices, and Torres had rented a small storefront headquarters in El Puente.

A massive red-white-and-blue 6' x 30' *"Podesta: The Quiet Worker!"* vinyl banner dominated the back wall. Dozens of computer-equipped cubicles were located on one side of the huge room, while long tables littered with empty pizza cartons dominated the other side. Eddie and Mike stared in through huge picture windows.

"Nice digs, fer an asshole," Kula observed.

"Yeah, the ayatollah of ass-a-hola," Eddie was getting agitated. "Go back to Bumfuck and take Wally the Weasel with yahs," he yelled as he whipped an empty beer bottle through the plate glass window, immediately setting off a burglar alarm.

"Mad Dogs!" Mikey screamed. Within 20 seconds, the remaining 10 empty beer bottles in the Camaro had shattered every window and a few computers, too. Then Eddie put it in gear and the two shock troopers were on their way back to the 6th Ward, feeling gratified and supremely confident.

*   *   *

The aging musician awoke suddenly to the sounds of shattering glass.

Dwight Bluford—a.k.a. "Piney Blue"—had just dozed off on a fire escape in the alley after playing his homemade tin guitar in the subway all evening. He had made enough in spare change for two cheeseburgers, onion rings, a quart of milk and a pint of peach brandy, all of which he consumed quickly on his wrought-iron perch.

Years of performing with screeching sound systems and buzzing amps had made Piney Blue hard-of-hearing, years more of playing for change in subway tunnels left him tone-deaf and six decades of hard liquor made him not care. Homeless for about six years, he would hop a freight for Birmingham, Alabama every autumn and return in spring.

Piney was jolted by the sounds of glass shattering, men yelling and alarms going off. He shook the cobwebs and staggered to the front of the building, just as a blue muscle car sped off. Sweet Jesus Mercy," Piney said, as he realized the windows were totally shattered and the front of the room—some sort of computer place, Piney figured—was in shambles.

The blaring of the burglar alarm rattled Piney's tender insides. Time to move, his instincts dully urged. In a moment of weakness he could only attribute to the brandy, Piney reached in through the paneless window, snatched a boom box and casually started back to retrieve his guitar in the alley.

The police spotlight hit him square in the face.

Piney Blue knew spotlights. Spotlights had bathed him in warmth on the stage of the old Moorland Theater. Spotlights had frozen him in his tracks during his impulsive mad-dash escape from the prison farm in Arkansas. Tonight's spotlight neither bathed nor froze. There was no mad-dash left in Piney's 78-year old frame. He dropped the boom box and calmly walked away, as if he could outwit the unblinking eye with a suave, unnoticed exit. Squads screeched to a halt all around him.

"Hold it, hold it right there, old man!" barked Officer Gus Alexandros, who pulled his weapon when Piney kept moving.

In the confusion and glare and noise, Piney wasn't even sure if the cop was yelling at him. He half-stumbled, half-skedaddled between two parked cars. Piney then reached into his coat pocket for his harmonica—"Didn't want to lose it in all that ruckus," he would later say—and turned towards Officer Alexandros. His partner, Officer Fred Moretti shouted, "Weapon!"

Alexandros would later testify that he indeed thought the harmonica was a gun, and that he once again yelled for the old man to drop it. Piney began to raise his arms, clutching the harmonica, when Alexandros popped him. Twice.

*   *   *

Chapter Three

River Rising, Part III

"Brother Bluford!"

Piney was slowly regaining consciousness when he heard the booming baritone. He was in the County Jail's ER, where the two bullets in his leg had been removed and the gash on his forehead from hitting the curb had been closed with 20 stitches.

"Brother Piney Blue Bluford!"

Was it God? Piney tried to focus.

"You are in excellent hands, Brother Blue!" Piney knew that voice. It was either the Deity or Reverend Hosea Greene, founder of the Bethel Valley Evangelical Church, whose motto was "How Greene is Your Valley?" Piney had spent many a drunken night in Rev. Greene's shelter, earning his keep by strumming his guitar for other residents.

"Reverend, somebody shot me!"

"You were gunned down by so-called 'peace officers', Piney. You just relax and the Lord will Heal."

Piney drifted off thanks to the morphine and traces of peach brandy. The Reverend drifted down to the lobby, where several reporters had gathered in reaction to radio reports of a police shooting at Podesta Headquarters.

"Gentlepersons of the press." Greene had been down this road before and was a master. "I have visited with the victim, my Brother Dwight Bluford, also known as the legendary blues guitarist Piney Blue, a member of my flock at the Bethel Valley Evangelical Church Mission. I refer to him as a victim, because he was shot point blank by a so-called peace officer of our municipality." He drew out the word "municipality", placing the accent on the "tee".

"Piney Blue is an accomplished musician, a cultural gem in our beleaguered community and deserves better than to be callously gunned down by some trigger-happy cops!"

The reporters all nodded and wrote. Most had seen his act before.

"Reverend Greene, what about reports that Mr. Blue was heisting a boom box?"

"Totally unfounded, to my knowledge." Greene started snorting and seemed to slowly expand like a blowfish. "And besides, what kind of civilized people shoot a senior citizen for stealing a loaf of bread? What kind?"

He was now inflated to about twice his normal size. "And what about due process? And what about 'Equal Justice Under the Law'? And what about…"

"Reverend, are you suggesting this officer should be disciplined?"

Some thought Greene's cranium would explode. "And what about the Truth? The Truth Shall Set Us Free! Disciplined? Disciplined you ask me? Maybe tried for attempted murder!" Greene finally took a breath and returned to his normal size to announce creation of the "Piney Blue Legal and Hospital Fund". Care of the Bethel Valley Evangelical Church.

*   *   *

Sheesh, thought Timmy Sullivan. What a mess.

Sullivan had just gotten home and was nuking leftovers when he was paged by Podesta. The Jackson City Police had reported a break-in and shooting at Paul's main headquarters.

Sullivan headed back into the City and was amazed at the activity outside his office. Police investigators, media and gawkers clogged the normally-desolate street. Every window was smashed and two of the computers in the front looked like they were totaled when the main plate glass window shattered. Broken beer bottles were strewn around. A pool of blood a few yards away was being filmed by a TV crew.

Sullivan found the Man-in-Charge, a Sgt. Baum.

"I'm with the Podesta campaign, Sarge. What do we have here?"

"Besides busted windows? Not much. Looks like your computers are intact. One of my officers will do a walk-through with you to see if anything's missing."

"What about the blood?"

"Some fellah was shot by one of my men. Grabbed a boom-box out of your office; not sure if he was the window-smasher. Refused to halt. Another cop thought the guy was preparing to fire a weapon."

"Fatal?"

"Nah, he's in County. Can we ask you to do that walk-through now?"

*   *   *

Piney Blue was still dazed when the detective interviewed him. He recalled how he had eaten his cheeseburgers and killed off the peach brandy on the fire escape in the alley. Heard the sounds of glass breaking, then screeching tires. Ran out to take a look.

"I can't remember exactly about that boom-box," Piney wheezed. "But I wasn't goin' for a gun. No way. Needed my harp is all."

"Your harmonica?" Detective Palmieri asked.

"Yessir. I'm an old man. Why would I be shootin' up police?"

"Okay, we're probably not gonna charge you on breaking-and-entering or burglary. We'll get back to you on the boom-box. Get some rest, pal."

*   *   *

After Timmy Sullivan inspected the Podesta Headquarters with the police, he was happy to discover no apparent theft. Two computer monitors were busted, but the hard drives seemed okay. The water cooler had been knocked over, causing a minor flood, but there was no damage beyond that. A window board-up service arrived and started sealing the place up.

Sullivan held an impromptu press conference on the sidewalk. The "Podesta" banner on the back wall could be seen clearly behind Timmy as he called this vandalism "political mischief" and tried to deflect the police shooting as a separate, unrelated incident.

"Any suspicions who may have done this?" asked Ronna Richards of Channel 6.

"Yeah, a bunch of ignorant losers," Tim smiled.

By 3:00 a.m., the place was boarded up, the blood hosed into the sewer and the media had moved on, except for the Channel 6 crew.

After reporter Ronna Richards taped a stand-up, they packed up the gear and cameraman Frank Nguyen walked across the street to use the automatic teller machine in a bank lobby. As usual, Nguyen made funny faces into the unblinking eye mounted on the ATM. Then it hit him.

"Hey, Ronna, c'mere."

"What, you forget your pin number again?"

As Richards strolled up to the ATM, she saw her cameraman tracing an imaginary line with his eye from the ATM camera to the Podesta Headquarters.

"Oh, yeah! Direct angle," Frank grinned.

When the bank across the street opened at 7:00 a.m., Richards and the Channel 6 crew was outside waiting. The bank's Media Relations Director quickly produced two copies of the ATM tape, one for the Jackson City Police and one for Channel 6. Ronna agreed to wait on airing it until the police gave the green light, in exchange for exclusive rights. A few hours later, Sgt. Baum told Ronna it was okay to put it on air.

*   *   *

That afternoon, Reverend Greene held another press conference to blast the trigger-happy police who were "…engaging in an ongoing pattern of genocidal behavior." The Police Department held a press conference defending their officer's actions, but announcing an internal investigation. At another press conference, the County Jail Hospital Director diagnosed a full recovery for Mr. Bluford. Sen. Paul Podesta took dozens of reporters' calls and condemned the "small-minded vandals" who would resort to this kind of thing, "sort of like the window-smashing Gestapo," he indignantly noted.

Thelma Barnett's homophobic attack on Mary Moore and Butchie Kaminski's attack on Thelma's religious intolerance at the previous week's debate quickly faded from the public's very limited attention of the PUC race.

*   *   *

"Okay, the tape proves that Mr. Blue was not the window-smasher. Let's roll it," Ronna said to the news director of the 5:00 p.m. broadcast.

"Okay, these two guys in a dark Camaro pull up and start launching beer bottles like molotov cocktails. Lemme slow it down here. Watch that big window shatter. The boys get back into the car and peel rubber. Then along comes ole Piney. Here he is snatching the boom-box. Let's speed up. Okay. Finally, we have Piney going into his jacket for the harmonica, which, at initial glance, could indeed be a weapon. Piney stumbles…Officer Alexandros fires."

The News Director was impressed. "It's great stuff, Ronna. Tell Frank Nguyen it's a perfect angle. Good work. Gets Piney off the hook on the vandalism and the cops off the hook, sort of, on the perceived weapon. We're leading with it at five. Maybe we can help ID the perps."

"'ID the perps?' You're watching too many copshows," Ronna grinned.

*   *   *

Channel 6 teased all day long about their "exclusive footage" of the Podesta Campaign Headquarters "break-in". "Our own Jackson City Watergate?" screamed the promos. The grapevine was already active, and when Mike Kula heard about the videotape, he knew it was trouble.

"Eddie," Kula whispered into the phone at Kaminski's 6th Ward Alderman Service Office. "Watch Channel 6 at 5:00 p.m. We maybe got some trouble here."

With a capital "T". Boss Chizz had also heard about the exclusive tape and came into the Ward Office a few minutes before the 5:00 news to watch it there with Butchie and Kula. The three men crammed into Kula's cubicle. Czyz seemed cranky, even for him, Kula thought.

Channel 6 made it the lead item. As the anchor introduced the piece and turned it over to reporter Ronna Richards on the scene, Kula could feel his heart sinking.

"Ronna Richards, live at Five on the scene of a late-night episode of political dirty tricks. Vandals destroyed several thousands of dollars in windows, computer gear and other equipment in a late-night attack on the Campaign Headquarters of State Senator Paul Podesta, a Democrat from Downstate Mohawk Valley who is running for Chairman of the state Public Utilities Commission.

"Channel Six has obtained exclusive footage of the vandalism as it was taking place, shot by a stop-action camera mounted on an automated teller machine at the Madison State Bank & Loan just across the street."

Oh, great, Kula thought, now we gotta worry about Big Brother in the ATM's. Czyz squinted at the tiny screen.

The footage was a grainy, herky-jerky black-and-white film showing the Camaro pull up. Two young white males in black leather jackets jump out, bottles are thrown, windows smashed, the getaway. Then Piney Blue's snatch-and-grab and the shooting, all condensed into less than ten seconds.

"Police officials have defended the shooting on grounds of a legitimate, perceived threat to the officers' safety. County Hospital officials say Mr. Piney Blue Bluford, a one-time blues musician from Birmingham,

Alabama, will be fine. No word on the investigation into the vandalism that sparked it all."

Then there was footage of Timmy Sullivan's 2:30 a.m. statement about "political mischief" done by "ignorant losers", Rev. Greene's cry of genocide and back to Ronna Richards for wrap-up at the scene.

Kula was somewhat relieved that you couldn't tell who the vandals were, only that they were a couple of white guys who drove a dark-colored muscle car of some sort. Maybe dodged a bullet here. Unlike old Piney, he mused.

He was still looking at the TV screen when the Jackson City phone book smashed into his head. He saw stars and stumbled out of his chair as Boss Chizz smacked him full-force with the Yellow Pages one more time.

"The hell were ya thinkin'? Somebody get my shit-for-brains nephew in here," the old man barked.

The next morning, the two City employees turned themselves in at the Jackson City Police District Headquarters. The press had a field day, and Podesta and Wally Mraz couldn't stop grinning.

*   *   *

The mug-shot images of Michael Kula—Aldermanic Aide—and Edward J. Czyz—Power Broker's grand-nephew and City ghost payroller—were displayed in the media as if they were on the FBI's Most Wanted. The photo of Eddie with a cocky sneer on his face didn't help matters much, considering he already sported a swollen cheek from his uncle's phone book treatment.

Both stewed in police lock-up for a few hours, then each posted a $250 cash bond and were put on unpaid leave-of-absence "pending a municipal investigation".

The benefit of all this was to compel Mike and Eddie to work longer hours at no pay for Butchie's campaign. The Boss liked that part. And while he hated giving Podesta any sort of free press, he was also concerned about Petacque getting a boost from "…all these Black preachers crazyin' up the blood," a very real possibility.

*   *   *

While most media focus was on this newest caper, one particular newspaper reminded one particular constituency about Thelma Barnett's crack at the Great Debate the week before.

Thelma's brief utterance about Mary Moore "hiding a gay son" was lost in the cacophony of Kaminski striking a blow for religious freedom by cross-checking an innocent water pitcher. Moore was quoted in the *Jackson City Review's* debate coverage defending her son, but few other media picked up on it, perhaps out of concern that Thelma had just made it up.

The front page of the *"InterOcean"*, a gay/lesbian free weekly with a circulation of 40,000, ran a frightening photo of Thelma over the caption, "Accuses foe of 'hiding' gay son", and a captivating photo of Mary with the caption, "Mom defends son's choices".

The front page article explained the circumstances of Barnett's attack and Moore's defense. Most gay/lesbian voters had probably missed the Great Debate, but none missed an issue of *"InterOcean."*

An editorial sidebar blasted narrow-mindedness and reminded the *InterOcean's* readers that *"…some of our parents may have problems dealing with our sexual preferences and lifestyles, but we can only hope they are as loving and understanding as PUC Chairperson Moore."*

Over the previous few years, the gay/lesbian community in Jackson City had started to flex its political muscles. Lobbyists from "Rainbow-PAC" roamed the Capitol and doled out checks at election time. A well-funded voter registration drive last year had added 8,500 new registrants, mostly young, white professionals who had moved from small towns. Endorsements by key gay/lesbian leaders and organizations were now proudly touted, not whispered, by mainstream candidates.

In her gubernatorial bid, Sen. Debra Shane was the first statewide candidate to court the gay/lesbian vote. She hired a prominent lesbian activist as Campaign Issues Director and promised to sign an Executive Order if elected to provide equal benefits for partners of all state employees.

Petacque had been the only candidate in the PUC race to woo the community. He had attended the annual Gay/Lesbian Pride Picnic and his Kiddie Corps distributed thousands of "Back Petacque" fans on that warm and muggy day. He had encouraged Chemuyil Gardner to massage the G&L media and he was the subject of a flattering piece in the *InterOcean*.

Blasingame had placed half-page ads in G&L newspapers when he announced his candidacy, but hadn't followed up. His Jackson City Coordinator, Rep. Laura Southampton, had sponsored some hate crimes legislation strongly backed by the gay/lesbian community; she was planning on organizing some endorsements for Royce, but hadn't got to it yet.

Torres had received the endorsements of some Hispanic gay and lesbian leaders, but had been discouraged by a slightly homophobic Jimmy Juarez from pursuing anything further.

With the September primary election just a few months off, the gay/lesbian community was starting to focus on the lesser races and the PUC was pretty far down the line.

Thelma's incendiary comments, though, energized the gay/lesbian community in a way similar to the effect River's Edge had on the Hispanic community and the string of police shootings culminating with Piney Blue would have on the African-American community. A cascade of e-mail alerts, letters-to-the-editor and call-ins to radio talk shows elevated the issue of bigotry generally and of the role of parents in the life of a gay/lesbian specifically.

As Thelma's villainization festered, Mary Moore became an overnight symbol to many in the community who had no idea where she stood on anything else; the important thing was her attitude about her son.

A group calling itself the "SOB (Stop Oppressive Bigotry) Sisters" rented a bus and made the long journey to Walton's Creek to protest outside of Thelma's house. Once in town, though, they couldn't locate the rural route where Thelma lived, so 25 body-pierced lesbians staged a happening in the Walton's Creek Dairy Queen parking lot, to the bemusement of anxious locals.

Moore wasn't sure what to make of this phenomenon. Tony was keeping her informed about the latest buzz in the G&L community; he had become a *cause celebre* and had done a touchingly funny interview in the *InterOcean* about life with Mom and Dad back in Zane Township.

Moore's Brain Trust wasn't excited about the unplanned developments.

Steven Page was worried about its effect on the Christian Right, which was already ticked about Mary Moore's challenge of Thelma's petitions in December. "They're with Thelma now, but we need them in November," he argued.

Blake just didn't like any unplanned developments, but saw it as a possible firewall against Blasingame in some of the more liberal Republican pockets in Jackson City. "This will neutralize any role Rep. Southampton would have with the gays," he said. Most of the PUC staff like Peggy Briscoe hadn't dealt with gays much and wished the whole thing would go away.

One added bonus, though, was the smokescreen it allowed her to throw out in response to Blasingame's "New Orleans Drag Queen" TV spot that had started airing right after the Great Debate. Maybe the exploitation of a transvestite shows Royce is a little homophobic and bigoted himself, was the line Blake was spinning.

Mary always tried to keep a wall between her public and political life, and her private and family life. This was cutting it close.

*   *   *

Shawn Petacque loved doing parades. He hadn't done as many as Sen. Esther Ruelbach, who would average 35 parades each summer. But he appreciated the spectacle, the democratic outpouring that a good ethnic pride or 4th of July parade could engender.

And as a candidate he was getting very good at it.

A "Back Petacque for PUC" float featuring a "fire-breathing dragon" (it was on sale) would slowly cruise down a parade route, music blasting from huge speakers hidden in the dragon's chicken-wire belly. The Kiddie Corps would throw lollipops to the crowd as Shawn feverishly ran from one side of the street to the other, shaking thousands of hands until his own hand was swollen.

The 27th Annual Jackson City "African American Heroes" Parade was one of the biggest parades in the state. More than 100,000 people would line the long parade route as marching bands, rappers, teen beauty queens, corporations, churches, athletes and politicians would try to outdo one another.

Chemuyil Gardner had organized this parade entry for Petacque in previous years, so she knew the drill. Organize a few dozen volunteers, have an eye-and ear-catching float, throw plenty of candy and keep Shawn moving. This year they would add the use of noisemakers on the float, aggressive distribution of "Back Petacque" fans to the crowd and a high-tech confetti gun.

The Jackson City "African American Heroes" Parade was never too political, although every politician in town participated. There would be the usual jockeying for position at the front of the parade, and dozens of floats promoting specific candidates. But the theme of the parade was always noncontroversial, usually something like, "Don't worry…Be happy."

Thanks to Rev. Greene and other police brutality protestors, community outrage over the Piney Blue shooting intensified into the summer. Protests at the Jackson City Police Headquarters were happening on a daily basis and the release of Piney from the hospital was a media event, as was the trial of Kula and Czyz.

So as the 27th Annual Jackson City "African American Heroes" Parade stepped off, the politicians in the lead line could sense a different mood, an edge. A little hostility, perhaps. And Rev. Greene's forces had distributed thousands of green-and-blue posters saying, "Piney Blue—Blues Legend—Police Shooting Victim" that speckled the entire parade route.

Petacque's Fire-Breathing Dragon stepped off and began its path, a spectacle inspiring awe and jealousy from other politicians. Between the campaign's high-voltage Kiddie Corps and a busload of kids from the 'hood, Chemuyil had organized an awesome force. Even though Shawn was a jazz fan, the dragon's audio belly belched out high-decibel doses of Snoop Dogg and Dr. Dre to the accompaniment of dozens of kazoos, tambourines, cow bells and ear-shattering whistles. Major din. Lollipops flew into the crowd and senior citizens fanned themselves with "Back Petacque" fans.

Dripping with sweat, Shawn breathlessly dashed from voter to voter at curbside. He noticed all of the Piney Blue signs and heard people chanting Piney's name. One elderly woman responded to his handshake with a hug and handed Shawn her Piney Blue poster. He held it up and the crowd roared. He signaled to one of the campaign Kiddie Corps to grab a few more Piney Blue signs. Pretty soon, a dozen volunteers were walking with Shawn—running actually—and waving Piney Blue and "Back Petacque" signs.

The crowds were loving it.

The float neared a narrow bend in the parade route, a tight little turn in which the crowds flowed from the sidewalk onto the street and right up to the parade marchers. Hundreds of folks leaned out of 2nd and 3rd floor windows. Chemuyil had planned this as the location to fire up the confetti-machine to the max.

As the Petacque float slowly moved into this tight and intense stretch, the music rattled store windows and confetti was jettisoned into a roaring, frenzied crowd. Petacque volunteers were waving Piney Blue signs in one hand and "Back Petacque" signs in the other. Chemuyil was playing the role of cheerleader on a bullhorn, exhorting people to "Remember Piney…Back Petacque!" and thousands were taking up the call.

Some sort of skirmish broke out in the crowd and a few uniformed officers quickly defused it and disappeared. Petacque saw the brief incident and considered his dual emotions. He was strongly opposed to police brutality and its racist implications, but he also supported the rule of law and a civil society, and was glad to see cops there to serve and protect the weak or incapable. He kept waving and shaking hands as the chanting of "Remember Piney…Back Petacque" echoed for several blocks up the concrete canyon.

Sounds of mayhem in his brain, Shawn kept moving. Running hard, running long.

*   *   *

By no means did Shawn Petacque have a lock on the African-American vote.

Some of the preachers thought he was not God-Fearing enough and too liberal on abortion; Rev. Del Crandall recruited a few Men of the Cloth for the Barnett campaign. And both Torres and Podesta hoped to pick up a few percentage points in the Black community; Podesta had talked a few old time Ward Bosses into taking a hike on Petacque and Torres planned to play the gender card, maybe the single mom card.

Still, Chemuyil Gardner and the "Kiddie Corps" of high school and college students had kept their focus in the base. Shawn's original projection—a little under half of the state's 650,000 registered African-American voters coming out and 90 percent of those being for him—had only improved after Piney Blue. Noisy, media-driven demonstrations over police brutality continued outside of the Police Main Headquarters. Another police shooting of a man resisting arrest had re-heated the issue on the front pages and the talk show circuit. Preachers were invoking Piney. Editorialists were invoking Piney. Candidates of all stripes were invoking Piney.

Piney's shooting had caused a wave; Petacque caught it and was riding it strong.

To capitalize, Petacque's Kiddie Corps worked day and night doing voter registration at subway stations, post offices, groceries. Philanthropist Jimmy LeMans offered $2 for each valid new registrant the Kiddie Corps brought in, plus a trip for two to Paradise Island for the top voter registrar in the City.

Chemuyil methodically kept in touch with every Black public official and community group leader in the state, working her way through her rolodex from A-Z and then over again. She and Consuelo kept the candidate on a rigid schedule, half of which was dashing from one event to another within the base.

Unlike Torres, Shawn had spent little time outside of his ethnic base, but he enjoyed a much larger base. And he figured that once people saw him, they'd take notice of the race. And once they took notice of the race, they'd come out on E-Day. And he felt increasingly confident about that.

Until he got the call from Ozzie "The Wiz" Altman, a veteran DJ at WDST-AM, the top Black radio station in Jackson City.

"Got your tape today, Alderman." The Wiz had such a great radio voice, Shawn thought.

"What tape's that, Oz?"

"You know. Thelma!" Altman was chuckling. "Guess you haven't heard it. Lemme cue you up."

Shawn's heart pumped as the heavy bass beat and electronic hip-hop set the table for the vocals. "My Thelma's a Bitch, a Wicked Wicked Bitch." His voice from the Great Debate comment to Kaminski, played over and over to a very snappy melody, followed by Butchie saying, "Your Thelma's a Bitch, a Wicked Wicked Bitch". Then some nice echoes, groaning dubs and sexy house mixes.

"Some nice stylings there, Alderman. Didn't know you rapped."

"Any markings on the envelope?"

"Nah, left in our night drop slot. I got a feeling this ain't a W-DUSTY exclusive, though."

Damn, how stupid could I be, Shawn thought. "So, Ozzie, you puttin' it on air?"

"Well, I hear it's already been up on 'NLT," Altman said, referring to the number one morning drive shock-jock rock station. "Since you've always been square with me, I'll sit on it 'til you can figure out who's behind it. No guarantees after that."

"Thanks Oz, I owe ya one."

"I'll send you a copy for your collection. Hey man, who's Thelma?"

*   *   *

As Wally Mraz had hoped, both Kaminski and Petacque would be damaged by the soon-to-be-infamous tape, which became known as "Salty and Peppy Rappin' 'bout Thelma".

The WNLT morning show played it regularly, accompanied by a woman's loud orgasmic moaning, and put it on the WNLT website, where it became a popular download. While most of the listeners of that particular station were white-males-under-25 who thought Butchie was very cool because of the tape, some political pundits and editorialists ripped Petacque and Kaminski for disrespecting a fellow candidate in such a personal and demeaning way.

Wally's fingerprints weren't on the trick, but many surmised he was behind it. It served his purposes by putting the race up on radar screens while throwing an inside fastball at Podesta's two main rivals in Jackson City.

Petacque was never able to prove who did it, so Ozzie never aired it on WDST, but the damage was done, throwing the campaign's rhythm off. It intensified Kaminski and Czyz' hatred of Mraz and Podesta, and energized Crandall's Crusaders more than the nuke prayer vigil ever could.

*   *   *

"Podesta: The Quiet Worker"

"Wow," Pudge Carson said, dryly. "How long it take 'em to dream that up?"

He shoved the video into the VCR in Podesta's war room. Pudge, Paul, Timmy Sullivan and Wally Mraz settled in to view the first of their three TV spots.

"Senator Paul Podesta," an older male voice pronounced over some sort of inspiring, patriotic march tune.

"He gave up a promising athletic career…" (grainy black-and-white photo of a 17-year old Podesta in a droopy football uniform.)

"…to serve his country." (grainy black-and-white, 20-year old Sgt. Podesta in a droopy Army uniform.)

"And unlike other young men, he came back home. To Mohawk Valley. To give back to the community that gave him so much." (25-year old Paul at the counter of the dry goods store)

"And Paul Podesta continued to give back to the community and to serve during his three decades in the State House and Senate. Fighting to keep your taxes low. Standing up for working people." (color photo of Podesta at the Senate podium, speaking into a microphone.)

"Married to his beloved Emily for 40 years…" (Emmy and Paul's wedding photo.)

"…only Paul Podesta has the experience—the battle-tested experience—to ensure safe and affordable utility service." (new headshot) *"Experience. Leadership. Quietly getting things done. Senator Paul Podesta for Chairman of the Public Utilities Commission."*

"I hate that goddamn head shot. Let's re-shoot it," Podesta growled. "And what's with this 'quiet worker' thing, anyhow?"

"Too many photos, no offense, Senator," Wally said. "And this is all nice and sugary-sweet for seniors and your Downstaters, but it ain't gonna move many hearts and minds up in Jackson. And it doesn't even say 'Democrat'."

"How's Emmy gonna feel about having your wedding portrait in there? She does look good, though, Paul. Ha!," Pudge said, elbowing Paul in his ribs.

"I didn't realize you 'gave up a promising athletic career', Senator," Timmy joked.

"Yeah, right. I coulda been a contender. I really hate that head shot."

"I like the 'battle-tested experience' angle," Pudge observed. "Not too much on utilities or the PUC. Think people'll know what the hell you're running for?"

"If you're the first Dem up on TV—which you probably will be—people will remember the spot just 'cuz it's first up. Although that march music sucks," Wally said.

Podesta had been jammed into hiring an out-of-state video firm connected to the Ironworkers Union. Three $25,000 campaign contributions came with the clear understanding that Podesta retain Slattery Communications to do his TV spots. Slattery had a reputation of being overextended and frequently resorting to cookie-cutter spots.

But some of Slattery's spots had a certain folksy, blue-collar and rural appeal, so Podesta handed over the $75,000 to produce a bio spot, an issues-oriented spot and an attack spot—if needed. They had done some shooting already; Paul decided he just didn't like make-up. Even though that cute little make-up artist hired by Slattery gave Paul an eyeful and smelled great.

"So?" Pudge asked, washing a pretzel down with a diet coke.

"Other than the lousy headshot, I like it," Paul was warming up to the spot, his first statewide television commercial. After decades in the state's political trenches. Aerial combat. They would air it first in smaller markets and then roll it out to the larger, more urban markets. Slattery sub-contracted a modest tracking poll to measure the spot's effectiveness.

Paul figured Petacque would be the only other Dem with the resources for TV. No way Kaminski or Torres could afford TV; radio probably. The issue was when to begin airing. Was it too soon to start now? Would voters forget in a few weeks? A few minutes?

"Well, let's do it, then," Pudge said. "So, Paul, how do you like that headshot?"

*   *   *

The phone poll sounded legitimate enough at first. A female "pollster" would call women who were at home during the day, mostly in rural and suburban areas.

After determining that the resident was a registered voter likely to vote Republican, the caller asked a series of innocent questions measuring opinions on issues related to the PUC race, such as "Would you be most likely to vote for a millionaire's grandson, a lifetime politician or a community activist?"

Then the caller would slip in, "Would you be more likely or less likely to vote for the incumbent, Mary Moore, if you knew that her husband had made $400,000 in an illegal stock transaction?"

And, "Would you be more likely or less likely to vote for the incumbent, Mary Moore, if you knew that she used tens of thousands of dollars of your tax money to finance her own graduate school education?"

Finally the caller would ask, "And would you be more likely or less likely to vote for the incumbent, Mary Moore, if you knew that her son was a well-known sexual pervert?"

More than 25,000 of these calls were quietly made during the summer, helping to slowly boost Mary's negatives with white women in rural counties. Anyone who responded "less likely" to any of the questions was mailed a Thelma Barnett brochure.

The "polling firm" was, of course, a front set up by Rev. Crandall. The oppo data was provided, of course, through back-channels by Wally Mraz. One more way for Podesta to dirty up his likely November opponent without any fingerprints.

*   *   *

In August, the State Elections Board made public the latest campaign disclosure reports on its website:

"State Public Utilities Commission Chairperson:

Candidate/Party	Raised/Loans	Spent	Cash-on-Hand (July 15)
Blasingame–R	$909,872	$647,384	$262,488
Moore–R	$573,983	$367,838	$258,190
Podesta–D	$302,090	$261,091	$ 97,087
Clark–I	$192,563	$102,224	$ 90,339
Petacque—D	$165,003	$ 95,317	$ 87,122
Torres–D	$157,976	$ 81,262	$ 86,973
Kaminski–D	$115,227	$ 45,723	$ 85,283
Barnett–R	$ 64,813	$ 42,050	$ 22,763

This filing sent reporters and opposition researchers scurrying. The obvious big news stories were Royce's record spending, Podesta's relatively meager lead over the other Dems and Clark's surprising war chest.

Digging through the campaign disclosure reports was like wandering into a candy store for political junkies.

Kremlin-watchers could see just how much Governor Langley was supporting Moore by the large number of close Langley associates who had given $5,000. Or the large number of prominent gay/lesbian donors to Mary. Or that a cavalier Podesta had accepted large contributions from utility company big-wigs. Or that Sen. Mario Camozzi and Ward Boss Seamus Dunne had obviously put the screws to their people for Butchie.

More than half of Blasingame's cash came from himself or his family; nearly half of Barnett's war chest came from Crandall. Petra Dresden was true to her word, having given the Dan Clark campaign $100,000 in DresPAC cash and another $30,000 in Liz Chinn's services. Torres and Moore had accepted the most from out-of-state groups, primarily women's groups. Torres had obviously done a fundraising trip to California, as well.

The spending patterns were revealing, too.

Wally Mraz was the highest-paid staffer ($57,000 for nine months) and Sam Roth was the lowest-paid ($18,000 for eight months). Blasingame, Moore, Podesta and Clark had the largest staffs; Barnett had no staff.

Kaminski listed no staff, although Aldermanic Aide Mike Kula was pretty much a full-timer on the campaign.

Royce had spent the most on TV and radio; Mary spent the most on direct mail, Podesta the most on jim-jam like nail files, sponges and balloons. All of the Democrats and Blasingame used union printers; Moore, Barnett and Clark did not.

Moore had spent $47,000 on a Wyoming opposition research firm, Kaminski spent $2,387 for "baked goods", Podesta spent $2,965 on "monogrammed golf balls" and Blasingame shelled out $75 to the "East Jackson Massage Emporium" (a legitimate rub-down, he claimed to bemused reporters). Nearly half of Barnett's expenditures were for lawyers defending her petition challenge.

The campaign disclosure documents provided nuggets of insight into each campaign's strategies and priorities. Opposition research specialists from ProAction dug into Moore's report, Jimmy Blake and the Wyoming hired guns tore into Blasingame's and everyone scrutinized Podesta's. There would be one more campaign finance disclosure reporting opportunity just a week before the election. This was the one the oppo guys would have to run with.

*   *   *

The battle of direct mail was much more furious and expensive for the gubernatorial races than for the Public Utilities Commission contest. But Blasingame, Moore, Podesta and Torres were all doing some mail.

Blasingame had the most distinctive mail. Nicky Pulver had aped one direct mail postcard technique used by a Congressional candidate in Oregon. It featured a mirror surrounded by television sets and mock cable TV bills. *"Feeling squeezed by the suffocating cost of cable TV? Fight Back with Royce Blasingame."* Another Blasingame piece mailed to 65,000 alumni of the state university included a tiny audio chip that played alma mater's beloved fight song. And Blasingame was the only candidate to distribute a free video to potential supporters.

Mary Moore's mail was not as technologically innovative, but she had terrific graphics and photos. She looked vibrant, competent, experienced. The New Orleans trip, despite the Drag Queen episode, allowed Mary to relax and get some color in her cheeks.

The Moore campaign had the biggest budget for mail with nine different pieces during the summer. Jimmy Blake's plan was to start with 2-color biographical stuff to Republican households in suburban target areas, and ratchet it up to multi-colored pieces on specific issues going to all statewide Republican and independent households.

The direct mail strategies for Podesta and Torres were more focused.

Podesta had six different pieces stretched out over a three-month period. The first piece went to every single Downstate voting household, regardless of party affiliation. The other pieces went to likely Democratic voters. His "Quiet Worker" slogan was emphasized. A Man of Accomplishment, Not Promises. Tim Sullivan convinced the major unions to pay for mailings to their members.

Torres did the National Hispanic Women's mailing to suburban soccer moms, and Jimmy Juarez had weaseled a good printing deal on bilingual postcards that were mailed to every Hispanic household in the state. The Needleworkers Union paid for a beautiful full-color biographical piece highlighting Graciela's immigrant experience that was mailed to every recently-naturalized citizen in the state.

And while the Torres campaign did not have the luxury of tracking polls, their guts told them that inroads could be made with the white liberals in Jackson City, where Petacque would be the only primary rival for votes. In August, $15,000 was spent on a piece for three lefty wards highlighting Graciela's immigrant experience and her performance on the River's Edge Blue Ribbon Panel "…standing up for consumers and the less fortunate."

The Battle of Websites had only three combatants: Blasingame, Petacque and Barnett. All three were raising money and recruiting troops online.

Blasingame made the best use of his cyber access. His site was lively and irreverent. He let people respond to a survey with hilarious questions. He held an engaging contest asking "What would YOU do as PUC Chair for a Day?" He was recruiting new volunteers every day through the site and frequently went online himself to chat with folks or respond to e-mail.

Petacque still used his site to focus on the River's Edge blast, but he also put his position papers and questionnaire responses up on the site and he, too, would go online after a long day of campaigning to chat and reply to e-mails. His cyber-fundraising was the most effective, with hundreds of new donors electronically giving thousands of dollars.

The Barnett site was really the Crandall site and after showing innovation a few months earlier by offering the successful downloadable nominating petition, their creative juices seemed to go dry. Crandall used it to notify supporters of events, but beyond crowd-building, it was barely utilized. Thelma never went online herself. Didn't trust it.

*   *   *

Ten days before the primary, the Special Election Edition of *"Hoy!"* carried front page photos of every victim of River's Edge. The editorial reminded readers of Graciela Torres' first-hand experience with the tragedy, her role on the Blue Ribbon Panel, her leadership in the community and *Hoy's* early call for her to make the race. Inside, an interview with campaign volunteer/blast victim Mariano Vargas was heartfelt and moving. A flattering profile of Jimmy Juarez highlighted the long struggle of empowerment for the City's Hispanic community.

A list of polling places in Hispanic wards was included and, at no cost to the campaign, one of Graciela's bilingual postcards was inserted into every copy.

*   *   *

For the home stretch, as air wars gave way to ground wars, Royce would gamble on his "Fabulous 400". Rep. Laura Southampton had carefully targeted about 400 precincts in Jackson County where the Blasingame Campaign would invest nearly all of its resources for the Get-Out-The-Vote effort.

Based on previous voting or demographic patterns—such as lower percentages for Gov. Langley four years earlier, a high number of Republicans who viewed themselves as "independent" and a high percentage of voters under 30—Southampton made sure there was ample phonebanking to identify Blasingame-leaning voters in those 400 precincts.

Visibility efforts were concentrated in these areas and the "Fabulous 400" were the highest priority for Election Day volunteer assignments. Some precincts were in "Poodle Canyon", a high-rent, high-rise area of Jackson City. Laura wished they had done more direct mail and coffees into the Canyon.

Tina Bishop was trying to crank up the "Royce is My Choice" campus effort, but discovered many schools still out on summer break. One more problem with a September primary, Tina thought. The other problem is that the winner of the September primary is in a mad sprint to the November General Election.

This final week should be one mad sprint, too, Tina mused.

*   *   *

Chapter Four

Confluence, Part I

"I've known rivers:
I've known rivers ancient as the world and older than the flow of human blood in
human veins.
My soul has grown deep like the rivers…
I've known rivers:
Ancient, dusky rivers."

-Langston Hughes *("The Negro Speaks of Rivers")*

Eight days to go. Paul Podesta and Mary Moore surely smiled over their morning coffee when they saw the editorial page headline in the *Jackson City Review.*

"Experience over Promises: Moore, Podesta for PUC Chair."

As the state's oldest and best-read daily paper, this was the one endorsement everyone sought. And any candidate who got it, had certainly earned it. The paper required every candidate seeking its endorsement to complete a comprehensive 20-page questionnaire dealing with dozens of issues, educational and professional background, values and vision, personal finances. Then a few candidates were invited to submit to a rigorous interview with the editorial board. Finally, piles of testimonial letters on behalf of the various candidates were sorted through.

The *Jackson City Review* rarely took chances. A dark-horse or long-shot special was unheard of. The paper's reporters and columnists may discreetly be for candidates like Torres and Petacque, but their bosses came from the Jackson City Establishment. The newspaper's Board members served on other boards with the City's political and financial elite. Worked out at the same gym. Sat in the same skyboxes at the stadium.

"Experience over Promises: Moore, Podesta for PUC Chair.

*"PUC Chairperson **Mary Moore** (R-Zane Terrace) has distinguished herself under trying circumstances and performed admirably. Her familiarity with utility regulation—academically and administratively—and courageous spirit earn her the JCR's vigorous nod on the Republican side over steel heir Royce Blasingame and school prayer activist Thelma Barnett.*

*"The Democrats also have a candidate with a strong understanding of utility issues, **Sen. Paul Podesta** (D-Mohawk Valley). As Chairman of the state Senate Public Works & Utilities Committee, Podesta has been a coalition-builder. The JCR favors Podesta over Comm. Graciela Torres, Ald. George "Butchie" Kaminski and Ald. Shawn Petacque, all young and well-meaning elected officials, but not quite ready for the majors."*

Both Moore and Podesta had worked hard for the *JCR's* endorsement, spending plenty of time on the laborious questionnaire and lining up a mile-high stack of testimonials. Both campaigns quickly added an "Endorsed by the *Jackson City Review*" plug onto their TV spots, final direct mail piece and Election Day materials. Wally Mraz rented four huge billboards in strategic downtown locations and hired a driving-billboard truck to haul a 25-foot sign with the simple message: PAUL PODESTA—DEMOCRAT FOR PUC—ENDORSED BY

JACKSON CITY REVIEW. Pure, Wally grinned as he watched the mobile billboard leave Paul's headquarters and nose into traffic.

Petacque, Torres and Blasingame all felt they had a shot at the paper's nod, so sounds of disappointment could be heard at their headquarters. The Blasingame and Torres camps both fired off press releases recounting their own endorsements, mostly from insignificant weeklies and community papers (although Graciela and Royce were both endorsed by the *Daily Orbit*, the prestigious State University newspaper.)

Petacque, Kaminski and Barnett simply ignored the *Review's* endorsement and focused on their bases.

Over at Dan Clark's headquarters, Liz Chinn and her youthful band of guerrillas were keeping tabs on every newspaper endorsement in the state (almost all of which were for Podesta and Moore). A letter-to-the-editor would be sent over the signature of a local supporter arguing the need for an independent Public Utilities Commissioner, not a Party Man or Woman. Liz would track which newspaper endorsements were soft—such as the *Belvon City Journal* urging a vote for Podesta as "a political hack, but one who can get things done"—and target them for the General Election.

The Clark Headquarters was busy during the final week before the Primary, but since his name was not on the primary ballot, it was nowhere near as insane as the nerve centers of the Moore, Blasingame, Kaminski, Podesta, Petacque, Torres or even Barnett headquarters.

Everyone felt the rhythm go uptempo and slightly discordant. The final weekend approached. Showtime.

                    *   *   *

A week before E-Day, the State Elections Board made public the latest campaign disclosure reports on its website:

"State Public Utilities Commission Chairperson:

Candidate/Party	Raised/Loans	Spent	Cash-on-Hand (August 15)
Blasingame–R	$2,078,097	$1,627,477	$450,620
Moore–R	$1,273,555	$ 974,122	$351,478
Podesta–D	$ 467,262	$ 395,879	$112,382
Torres–D	$ 237,887	$ 145,737	$102,409
Petacque—D	$ 234,911	$ 150,721	$101,616
Kaminski–D	$ 161,537	$ 96,823	$ 71,493
Clark–I	$ 201,039	$ 129,937	$ 71,102
Barnett–R	$ 81,767	$ 61,901	$ 19,866

Once again, the lead story was the unprecedented sums being spent in the Blasingame-Moore conflagration and, to keener eyes, Podesta's meager lead over the other Dems. Both Torres and Petacque had set a goal of having 100K on hand at reporting deadline, and they achieved the goal, showing they would be competitive in the final weeks. Clark had slipped some, but as an Independent, was not on the Primary ballot.

In addition to showing how expensive a TV-based campaign was, Blasingame's report showed how little he was hitting up donors outside of his own family. Similarly, Clark continued to be heavily dependent on Petra Dresden and Barnett on Rev. Crandall. Torres' biggest donor was still Sam Roth, Sr., and Petacque's was Jimmy LeMans. Podesta relied heavily on unions and was spending like a drunken sailor.

Obviously, the cash-on-hand figure would change dramatically in the final two weeks, with some candidates in a spending frenzy and others seeing a huge influx of cash. And this figure was easy to fudge in the first place by sitting on some bills, and holding off on depositing and reporting certain contributions that could prove embarrassing.

Opposition researchers went into overdrive.

Moore's donor list revealed 72 utility company employees giving a total of $83,000 and another $20,000 from the Braxton Group and other pro-utility interests, a factoid used immediately in Blasingame's radio spots.

Moore's list also revealed the names of about 40 prominent gay/lesbian donors, a tidbit quietly passed on by Nicky Pulver to Thelma Barnett's campaign for whatever mischief they could dream up.

*   *   *

More than 13,000 e-mail messages and 20,000 automated voice mails were sent simultaneously: *"Return to Munich! Join Rev. B.J. Crandall and statewide candidate Thelma Barnett for a pre-election Rally for Power Plant Morality vigil. Outside of the Countryway Electric nuclear power plant, Route 68, just south of Glenwood. This Saturday. Spread the Word."*

Crandall Crusaders in every corner of the state saw the message and knew it was time to saddle up.

*   *   *

"I can't believe you guys did it," an astonished Graciela screamed to Lupe Zarate and Sam Roth, giving them both a hug.

Sam and Lupe had slipped away to Washington D.C., where they met with dozens of lobbyists and honchos for several Hispanic organizations Lupe had contacted in advance. A slick information package on Graciela included a biography adorned with family photos, a reprint of the *"La Latina"* magazine profile, a list of accomplishments at the Water Department and County Board, and the well-known gut-wrenching *Newsweek* photo of her at River's Edge consoling Paco Rivera.

Sam and Lupe's fishing trip was a triumph. They returned the next day with $38,000 in checks and another $25,000 in solid pledges, crucial fuel for a campaign running on fumes. Up until now, Torres had only been on radio; now they could buy TV. A great TV spot had already been shot, but never used.

It was simple and straightforward.

"Hello. I'm Commissioner Graciela Torres.

"When my family left Mexico to find the American Dream, I was just a little girl. I saw how hard my father worked in the garment factory and I was left

to raise my little brother and sisters. I was so fortunate to get a good education and worked my way up through the City Water Department. Now, I'm a Commissioner on the Jackson County Board, with a record of fighting for safe drinking water and health clinics.

"The American Dream—something all our ancestors worked for—enables anyone—even a woman who was once a little girl in a faraway land—to serve as an elected official in our great country.

"That Dream—our Dream—is why I am running to be your next Public Utilities Commissioner. To stand up for safe and affordable utility service. I need your help on Tuesday. I'm Graciela Torres."

The lighting and photography of the 60-second spot was perfect, everyone agreed. A tight shot of Graciela looking straight into a slowly-circling handheld camera. No red-white-and-blue graphics or Sousa marches, no family photos, just the candidate in a simple navy blue dress, hair pulled back, a professional make-up job, masterfully following the circling camera's unblinking eye as she delivers her Dream message. Elegant, but simple.

The Torres inner circle was split on the message.

Jimmy Juarez was worried about reaction outside of the city to the "crossing the Rio Grande bit", as he called it. "Too Mexican." Lupe understood his concerns, but thought the American Dream angle would resonate across gender and demographic lines. Sam just wanted more on the PUC, maybe more on Graciela's water issues, and thought the "safe and affordable" line was being overused. Billy thought the talking head method was a stroke of genius. She looked lovely, sincere, trustworthy. A real straight-talker, some old Yellow Dog Democrat in Sauk County might say, approvingly.

The debate over where to air the spots grew into the biggest squabble in the Torres camp. For the past week, Lupe and Jimmy had argued for a massive buy in Jackson City; Billy and Sam pushed for diversification by putting half into smaller markets around the state, including cable, college TV and smaller ethnic stations.

"I hear the latest numbers show the undecideds are increasing in the suburbs, and decreasing in the city. People here know Graciela. People in the 'burbs don't. That's the advantage of cable," Sam argued.

"What numbers? Hey, kid, you go fishin' where the fish are," Juarez grumbled. "Besides, the suburbans watch the same TV ads as we do."

Sam had to concede that point, that buying time in the expensive Jackson City market would reach all of those suburban voters, but they were already being bombarded with commercials for Shane, Burl, Prentice, Ruelbach, Podesta, Blasingame, Moore, Phil Driscoll, Aviva Benson, judicial candidates and others. Lesser markets might give us more bang for the buck, he reasoned.

The group went back-and-forth for an hour. If these TV spots were going to be seen anywhere, they'd need to do the buy right away.

Miller stared hard at Juarez.

"Admit it, Jimmy. Petacque and Butchie have totally ignored the state outside of Jackson City. Totally. Graciela and Podesta are the only cards in the deck for most voters in the burbs and boonies. And 50 percent of them are women, maybe more. And there's even a fair number of rustics like me who think ole Paul's a skunk," Billy said in a cornpone accent. "And that's why I'm a-fixin' to take this little filly on the road this here weekend."

He turned to Lupe. "And that's why it would be great to take half of this newly-acquired largesse and buy some TV time in the shadowy backwoods and jungles outside of Jackson, since that's where our candidate's goin'."

"Folks, that's a compelling argument," Graciela said, nuzzling Billy for the first time in public. "Let's spend half in the boonies and let's get me on the road for the final stretch. Whaddya think, Jimmy?"

Juarez, who had long suspected the romance, felt a little jealous. He remembered getting Graciela her first City job right after her husband—that crazy gang-banger, Bobby—was shot to death. Juarez was more than 20-years her senior, yet he had clumsily tried to woo her. She obviously had no romantic interest in him—or anyone, it seemed to Jimmy—but had always been gracious to him. A good friend, too. He was so proud that a protégé of his was knocking at the door, moving up. What a great profession, Jimmy mused, politics. When he started out 40 years earlier, nobody talked about TV buys, especially $60,000 TV buys. That could be a big chunk of change for walkin'-around money on E-Day.

"Okay, I'm for it only if we know there's enough to put our people on the street and keep 'em there on Tuesday," Juarez pronounced. "We still need to pay 400 all-day workers at $50 each. That's 20K. Another ten thou, maybe, for palm cards and y'know, walkin' around money."

"Paid phones?" Graciela wistfully asked.

"Another $20,000 at least for paid phones," Sam said. "Aiming at younger women in the suburbs."

"We'll have it," Lupe sternly announced.

"Then it's agreed," Graciela said. "Let's roll the dice."

Sam started making arrangements to spend $60,000 on TV, Lupe began setting up the schedule for an aggressive drive-around and Billy started calling possible Torres supporters in every county. They would leave at 6:00 a.m. Friday, and finish by Sunday night. Fifty-one stops and 1,200 miles in three days.

*   *   *

On Thursday morning, Shawn Petacque could feel it once again.

The Wave. The Mojo. The Surge. He had caught the wave after he had vanquished rivals Cassandra Phillips and Seth Dickerson, Jr., a wave that crested with the Piney Blue shooting. He then lost it after the stupid Wicked Thelma fiasco.

But campaigning in these subway stations, every morning, every evening, left Shawn with an unstoppable feeling. Typically, the crowds would surge into a narrow sluice in the subway station. They would be bombarded with college students waving the distinctive blue-and-yellow "Back Petacque" signs, handing out flyers and buttons.

A leather-lunged, tap-dancing senior known only as "Bijou" who had been recruited by Chemuyil Gardner would repeat, "Meet Alderman Shawn Petacque. Back Petacque. Young lady, say hi to the Alderman. Meet him…greet him…they cannot defeat him. Your voice is your vote. Shawn Petacque. Right Here. Right Now." Part carnival-barker, song-and-dance man and mob hypnotist, Bijou's theatrics lent to the energetic feel of the candidacy.

"Some sweet street heat, here, eh, Frenchy?" Chemuyil yelled into Shawn's ear over the metallic shrieks of the subway. Morning rush was in full swing.

It was their fifth and final visit to the 52nd Street subway station, Jackson City's busiest. The crowds were receptive, having seen Shawn a few times now. He was shaking hundreds of hands, as fast as a human could politely shake another's hand, look that person in the eye, say your name and something like "need your help" or "nice to see ya", and unclasp. In rapid-fire succession. Shawn was always good at it, able to make quick repartee with many commuters quickly. He loved the sociology, the range of humanity he could encounter in the subway stations, especially here at 52nd Street. He was in rope-line groove, handshake heaven.

Since this was one of the last real subway campaigning opportunities, Consuelo came and brought the kids. Monique and Larry could see what their daddy did for his job…shake hands. Millions of hands, it looked like, as Bijou barked "Back Petacque" over and over and over.

"Stand over there by Daddy," Consuelo instructed the kids, as she focused the new videocam.

"Hey! Lookie who's here," a delighted Petacque said, lifting up Monique.

Monique's happy squeals echoed through the grimy station.

"Hey, ain't you that politician guy, running for something?" a whiny, male voice asked behind him.

Petacque turned to look at the questioner just as the cup of steaming hot coffee hit his face. Momentarily blinded and stunned, Shawn instinctively shielded a screaming Monique as the little man calmly walked to the escalator.

"Excuse me, sir, I believe you dropped something," a baritone Bijou boomed as he followed the little man onto the escalator. The coffee-tosser turned and was met squarely by Bijou's ancient, yet potent, fist. The little man would not awake until he was in the police lock-up.

*   *   *

The story was the lead on every radio news broadcast in the state throughout the day. Every Jackson City TV station sent a crew to the scene of the caffeine crime. Details at Five.

"Jackson City Alderman Shawn Petacque and his young daughter were attacked on the campaign trail this morning. A man identified as Nathan Sherman, 40, of East Jackson was charged with 'assault on an elected official' after he threw a 16-ounce cup of hot coffee at Alderman Petacque, causing minor burns on Petacque's neck and face. His daughter was unharmed. No motive for the subway station attack is known. Petacque is running for the Democratic nomination for Public Utilities Chairman in Tuesday's primary."

*   *   *

Timmy Sullivan and Steven Page had the unenviable assignment of informing their candidates—Podesta and Moore, respectively—that the undecideds were not breaking their way, in spite of the *Jackson City Review* endorsement.

Sullivan had just received fresh numbers. Podesta was hemorrhaging in Jackson City, with Butchie Kaminski picking up a surprising number of undecided likely Dems, mostly white ethnics. Maybe the *Jackson City Review* endorsement didn't mean much or maybe it needed to be highlighted more; who knows? Wally kept the mobile-billboard on the streets 18 hours a day.

Kaminski's numbers were also up slightly in blue-collar suburbs. And if Torres had a "suburban strategy" it was working, as soccer moms were flocking to Graciela. She was even picking up some younger female voters in rural areas in addition to getting 89% of the Hispanic vote, according to Sullivan's newest numbers.

Finally, Petacque seemed incredibly strong in the Black community, despite Wally Mraz' best attempts at voter suppression and whispering campaigns. "There may be a few ward guys who sit on their hands for Shawn, but he's lookin' at 91, 93 percent of the Black vote," Sullivan told Podesta and Pudge Carson.

"More visibility. More TV. We got enough in the bank," Pudge sat quietly. "Use it or lose it, my friend."

Podesta knew he didn't quite have it in the bank.

He had raised nearly a half mil and spent almost all of it. He had taken out a $20,000 loan, and that was to be the cushion. But that was gone, too. He needed at least another $100,000 to crawl across the finish line, he figured. Mraz thought 150. Time for more heat on the trade unions, Wally sharply said to Sullivan.

Time to call O'Malley, Pudge thought.

*   *   *

Steve Page had an even better snapshot of the body politic.

With a large sample and a well-designed poll, Steven knew that Royce Blasingame's New Orleans attack had worked. Mary's negatives had soared before she could introduce herself to the public. Royce (Nicky Pulver, actually) had defined her before she knew that the campaign had started. The Thelma Barnett attack on her son's sexual preferences helped more than it hurt, frankly, but the flap had distracted the Moore team.

Steven was alarmed that Royce's numbers in the suburbs—Mary's home turf—had skyrocketed. Mostly younger, college-educated white males. His favorable:unfavorable ratio was more than 2 to 1.

The state's utilities were called "dangerously unsafe" by more than a third of the likely Republican voters polled. River's Edge still resonated and while people blamed Eaton Gas for the tragedy, they were upset with the government for not providing better safety.

Thanks to Crystal the Drag Queen, a jolting 68 percent thought Mary Moore, "…spent too much on junkets at the taxpayers expense." Those who deemed Moore to be "untrustworthy" tripled from 12 percent before Blasingame's ads to 35 percent now.

"So, Steven," Mary said calmly after hearing the news. "Any suggestions?"

"Time for the DUI."

"Uh, oh. You're starting to sound like your friend Blake," Mary teased.

"Royce's surge in the burbs, his favorables, the obvious effectiveness of the New Orleans hit. Time to hit back," Page said, hoping he wasn't turning into a Jimmy Blake, but wanting so strongly for this woman to win, to thoroughly trounce that unqualified, rich creep.

Mary sighed. She knew this moment was coming since the opposition research team reported their findings. "Launch the Big One, Captain."

*　　　*　　　*

Kevin O'Malley had been expecting this call.

Podesta was matter-of-fact with the veteran lobbyist, noting that he was the best friend the utilities had on the whole Dem ticket, and, win-or-lose, he'd still be Chairman of the Senate Public Works & Utilities Committee. O'Malley couldn't bear to tell Podesta that he and most of his PAC Pals had already given heavily to Calvin Reynolds (which should enable Calvin's kids to go to Harvard) and subsequently to Mary Moore.

O'Malley saw the merit in Podesta's points and had always appreciated the merits of his friendship.

"Paul, if you don't mind my saying so, you've spent an awful lot on yard signs and bumper stickers," Kevin said, gingerly. "And, geez, to not have a little TV cushion for the 9th Inning…"

"I know, I know. This fuckin' Mraz is spending me and Emmy to the poorhouse. On junk like nail files."

"That's for ward-level trench warfare, Paul. C'mon. You're in an Air War Royale now with some young top guns."

"Yeah, well Butchie ain't going anywhere outside of Chizz-land. And Torres is makin' a play for the soccer moms, but I think she's got no dinero, ya know?" Paul said.

"What about Petacque?"

"He's got a base, a following, no question. Nothin' doin' outside of Jackson. An old sixties hippie radical type. Hates your type," Podesta reported.

"Hey, I get along with anybody," Kevin cackled. "It's my type of clients he hates. Hell, I do, too, sometimes."

"Well, I need another $150K for TV by Saturday night. Or you get one of those other clowns."

O'Malley whistled softly. "Man. One-fifty. That's a pretty big TV tab there, partner. I'll do what I can, but some of the boys are tapped out."

"Yeah, I'm sure," Paul sarcastically replied. "Anyhow, I really appreciate it, Kevin, whatever you can do. Pudge Carson'll make arrangements for delivery.

*   *   *

Word of the enormity of the Mary Moore final weekend TV buy stunned even Nicky Pulver. Saturation bombing. Every station in the state. Prime time.

"So, what the hell shitstorm is coming down upon us, my brother?" Royce asked.

"My hunch is the DUI. Possibly grandpa's cover-up. Anything else out there? Dope? Insider stock deals?"

"And how did you know about the DUI?" Royce asked, his tone indicating he knew that Nicky knew.

"Little birdie. Hopefully there's so much white noise being injected into the typical TV viewer's veins that nobody pays it any note."

*   *   *

Chemuyil Gardner's e-mails had gotten more desperate. Missives like, *"Hey, Mountain Ref. You alive? What's new in Valve City?"* went unanswered.

River's Edge had crept back into the public mind in recent weeks. Blasingame, Petacque and Torres all played the card. *"Hoy!"* and Spanish TV had played it up and Petacque's website started buzzing with conspiracy theories once again.

A few days before the election, Chemuyil received an e-mail.

"c.g. sorry for blackout…need to be cautious. am being watched at work (eaton)…thought I could put my hands on physical evidence b4 e-day…can't swing it…this info, however, can be placed on petacque's website: 1. eaton internal probe shows inspector failed blood test showing traces of codeine. 2. the model of the valve—a 1994 Swiss-made cast-iron valve—has a 100 percent reliability performance record. 100 percent! dare eaton to disprove it. good luck on e-day…mountain referee."

Shawn did in fact place these tidbits on his website, along with a list of Eaton Gas Company big-wigs who had given campaign contributions to Paul Podesta. Several reporters picked up on Inspector Qualls' codeine use and the Swiss valve's perfect track record. Too little, too late, Shawn worried.

*   *   *

"Where are you guys?" Sam Roth yelled into the speakerphone. Lupe Zarate sat next to him in the Torres Headquarters war room.

"West Wheaton, I think," Graciela yelled back.

By early Friday afternoon, the Torres road trip had already covered 300 miles. Graciela had done three TV and five radio interviews, met an enthusiastic rally of Hispanic farmers in the middle of nowhere and ate two brunches with local Party leaders. They were arriving at a coffee organized by the Wheaton County Democratic Women, who told Lupe they would present the Torres campaign with a few checks.

Billy and Graciela's sister Soledad rode in Billy's pick-up truck, while Mariano Vargas, Alejandro Pizarro (a college kid who helped Lupe with scheduling), and the candidate rode in the van (although she would some-times trade places with Soledad in Billy's truck.)

Both van and truck were festively decorated and sported huge Graciela banners. Billy delivered Torres signs and literature to friendly Democrats along the way. Billy showed Alejandro the art and science of quickly planting signs in choice locations along the highway. They saw a few Moore and Podesta signs posted along the highway, but none from the other candidates.

As much as she wanted them along, Graciela had asked Sam and Lupe to stay behind so they could run the war room, keep an eye on the volun-teers and Jimmy Juarez, and make sure the TV buy goes well.

"Wish you were here!" said Graciela, as the static subsided. "We met these farmers in this corn field, hundreds of them. All from Michoacan, Lupita! And then we had a great brunch with a group of Podesta-haters in Spring Hill organized by our very own Billy Miller…"

Lupe and Sam looked at each other and grinned. They knew this romance would happen ever since the climb to the bluffs.

"…and that radio interviewer at WSHR was great, Lupe, mark them down for a return trip."

"Right before the General Election, how's that?" Lupe responded, happy the trip was going well, since she hadn't slept for two days getting it organized. "And don't forget to congratulate the daughter of the President of the Wheaton Dem Women."

"Right, Rhodes Scholarship. Denise Pepper. Hey Sam, how's the buy?"

"I've never spent so many pesos in three hours," Sam answered. "We'll be on the air tonight in the markets you visited today and up statewide tomorrow."

"Great, I'll try to catch it from my No-tell Motel. I think the TV takes quarters."

"Just trying to keep costs down, boss," Lupe chirped.

"You're not gonna believe this…Mariano, is that for us?" Graciela said as the two-car parade pulled into the gravel parking lot of the West Wheaton VFW.

Nearly a thousand Democratic women from across the region had gathered in a tent. To see this Graciela Torres in person. Billy and Soledad spent yesterday hastily organizing this one event, not telling Graciela that it was anything but a spontaneous eruption of public love.

And of course, Graciela turned on the radiance, wowed the crowd and sent people scurrying for their checkbooks. She could now cover Jimmy Juarez' Election Day budget. All they needed now was another $25,000 for paid phonebanking, Graciela calculated as the jubilant caravan headed back on the open road, with six more stops before ending up at a fish fry in Salem Bay.

*　　　　*　　　　*

All day and all night cars and trucks pulled up to the drab 6ᵗʰ Ward Democratic Headquarters. The crews—mostly young white males—would run in, kiss Boss Chizz' ring, get their signs and assignments, and dash back to their vehicles. This was Johnny's favorite time of a campaign. This was his time. He sat behind his old desk, cluttered with maps and index cards, and each visibility team member would approach for an audience.

"Hey, Boss. I'm Tommy Grachenski. Fifth Ward, precinct 15," one crew-cutted young man said, "You remember my Uncle Billy Grachenski?"

"Ah, Billy G. Sure I remember. Another fine 5ᵗʰ Warder. Worked at the Park District?"

"Right. Retired now, Boss Chizz. Sends his best," the young man said, paying homage by recognizing Czyz' role in keeping Uncle Billy employed in a do-nothing job for decades.

"Extend him my regards. So, Tommy G, what's your assignment tonight?"

"Yard signs over in the 5ᵗʰ Ward. Posters along the Southeast Expressway."

"And if you see any Podesta signs littering our fair city?"

"No one will see them signs again, Boss. This kind of littering is illegal and highly unfortunate."

Czyz cuffed the kid affectionately. "Highly unfortunate. Here's thirty bucks gas money. But listen to me, Tommy G., no booze 'til the work is done, awright?"

"He's almost a nice guy," Mikey Kula whispered to Butchie.

"Yeah. Almost human." Butchie knew the drill as well as anyone. As the one-time leader of the Mad Dogs, Butchie had stapled, wired, taped, wheat-pasted, drilled and hammered tens of thousands of signs on trees, utility poles, abandoned houses, railroad crossing signs and over rivals' signs.

Without TV or radio, the Kaminski message would be delivered the old-fashioned way. Tonight, a sea of Kaminski signs would blossom like ten thousand flowers across Jackson County. Mad Dog as Underdog.

And this weekend, hundreds of precinct captains aligned with a dozen ward chieftains aligned with Czyz would be armed with shopping bags and poll sheets, going door-to-door to provide 200,000 of the party faithful with sample ballots featuring the Czyz-Camozzi-Dunne slate.

And what a slate.

Engineered by Sen. Mario Camozzi and 3rd Ward Boss Seamus Dunne, with the seal of approval stamped by Johnny, the Boys bucked the State Party by endorsing Burl (who kicked in $35,000 for "printing costs") for Governor. They also recommend Bill Karmejian (who pledged an army of jobs in the unlikely event that he won) for Secretary of State. Plus six judicial candidates at $10,000 each. And **George "Butchie" Kaminski for PUC Chair** in bold type next to professionally-done color photo of a big, ursine grinning Butchie.

On Friday after darkness fell, in special tribute to Wally Mraz—the Traitorous Weasel—Johnny Czyz dispatched ten vanloads of City Streets & Sewer workers to the suburbs and an elite crew of Mad Dogs out to Mohawk Valley. He issued the bounty: 25 cents per Podesta sign brought back to the 6th Ward Headquarters.

By 2:00 a.m., Johnny had happily doled out thousands of dollars, including a bonus case of vodka for the crew who pulled a 6-foot wooden billboard from Emily and Paul Podesta's front lawn in Mohawk Valley.

This was his time. The joy.

*   *   *

At dawn on Saturday, the public parking lot outside of the Countryway nuclear power plant was jammed with RV's, SUV's and pickup trucks. "Crandall's Crusader" buses clogged the tiny road to the plant from Route 68.

Thelma Barnett wasn't scheduled to arrive at the site until noon, but Crandall called her at the budget motel in Glenwood and told her to get to the nuke and start the vigil now. At 7:30 a.m. Because there are already 2,000 people waiting. For Power Plant Morality.

*   *   *

"Philip Royce Blasingame. The Third.

"He talks a lot about "standing up for consumers". Was Royce Blasingame standing up when he was arrested for driving his shiny red Mercedes forty miles per hour over the speed limit? While legally drunk?

"Was Royce Blasingame standing up when the judge dismissed the case after accepting a huge campaign contribution from Blasingame's millionaire grandfather, Philip Royce Blasingame. Senior?

"We need a steady hand on the wheel at the Public Utilities Commission. The next time you hear Mister Philip Royce Blasingame the Third blabbing about "standing up"…tell him to please sit down. Paid for Moore for PUC."

The images were devastating.

A high school yearbook photo of a very preppy-looking Royce, followed by a super-slow motion clip of a weaving red Mercedes careening down a residential street, engine revving, tires screeching, horn blasting. The image dissolves into a black screen with bold red letters saying *"Blood Alcohol Content level: .11%…Legally Drunk!"* imposed over Royce's teenaged acned mug. Then a photo of a tuxedoed Royce Senior floating like a puppet-master over the scales of justice, which were overflowing with piles of cash.

"He'll have no time to respond," Blake confidently told Mary. "We drive up his negatives and engage in a little class warfare at the same time. And how often do ya see class warfare in a GOP primary," he chuckled. "It's beautiful."

*   *   *

"Nicky, I'm so sorry I didn't discuss this DUI with you earlier." Royce was practically in tears.

"Hey, Bro, no sweat. I knew anyhow. What was the real deal with Grampa?"

"Ancient history."

"Royce, you're gonna be asked these questions by reporters in the next 24 hours. What was the real deal with Grampa?"

"Grampa—Royce Senior, that is—had given cash payments to this one judge for years. The guy was on the take. Grampa wasn't the only one and this wasn't the first time."

"Did Royce Senior give money to this judge specifically to bail your sorry ass out on the DUI?"

"I don't think so, Nicky, but I can't be sure."

"But, it's possible."

After a long pause, Royce said, yes, possible, maybe probable.

"Okay, no sweat," Nicky said, shifting into damage control mode. "So, we do a press release ripping Mary Moore for this sleazeball stuff. She's calling your grandfather—a pioneer of this town—a briber! She's calling you a drunk! Was it really a red Mercedes?"

"Yeah, that was a sweet car," Royce recalled fondly.

"Awright, forget the sweet car! We need to do another buy!"

"Nicky, you sound like some sort of desperate junkie."

*   *   *

"*DATELINE JJ: Campaigns sprint to Final Weekend! Primary contests to watch…Can Debra Shane hold on to her slim lead (43%–40%) over publisher Lawrence Burl in the Dem gubernatorial? Will anti-abortion activist Phil Driscoll surprise prosecutor Anita Benson for the GOP A.G.?*

We're still handicapping the races for PUC Chair for Paul Podesta and Mary Moore, but both contests have tightened recently due to surges by Shawn Petacque and Royce Blasingame.

Question: The long-range weather forecast says rain on Tuesday…should help incumbents and organization candidates. I'm betting 39 percent turnout. Any takers?

Question: With the TV screens so clogged with attack and response ads, are viewers giving their remotes a workout?

Million Dollar Bonus Question: Who has spent the most out of their own pockets in the key contests? Answer: Driscoll-$2.6 million. Burl-$2.5 million. Blasingame-$1.3 million.

Question: Crandall's Crusaders are really humping (if you'll pardon the imagery) for Driscoll and PUC candidate Thelma Barnett. Will the Crusaders know where the polls are, if the polls aren't in the local church?

*   *   *

Crandall's Crusaders may not know where their polling places are, but they sure know the way to Countryway.

By Saturday afternoon, in the shadow of the mammoth Countryway Electric Company nuke tower, they were 8,000 strong, quietly holding the usual signs and banners, many on their knees in the parking lot. Television crews, anticipating a raucous repeat of Thelma's last brawling visit, arrived around noon, as did extra plant security.

Rev. B.J. Crandall delivered a spirited "Rally for Morality" sermon, followed by a foot-stompin' performance by the Crusader Youth Chorus and a testimonial by a masked Countryway employee about "prayer circles" as a way to limit pilferage and drug use at the plant.

Finally, Thelma Barnett took the makeshift stage.

In her flowered-print dress, red Easter bonnet and sunglasses, Thelma glowed in the noonday sun. She was pooped, having driven thousands of miles in Rev. Crandall's RV during the past month. She realized this would probably be her final Big Event of the campaign, which would probably be her one and only political campaign.

Thelma gazed at the still-growing crowd. "Hello!" her voice echoed over the throngs and ricocheted off the cooling towers. "Hello, there! I'm Thelma Barnett, Reverend Crandall's coordinator for the 'Amen, Now!' Project and a candidate for the Public Utilities Commission."

A thunderous applause erupted, rippling over the acres of families, picnic blankets, RV's, makeshift shrines and tents. "Thelma! Thelma!" the crowd chanted. She appeared stunned by the reaction; this wasn't about her, she thought, it was about power plant morality and the Rev. Crandall and the Lord Jesus Christ. She turned her eyes heavenward as the sun illuminated her.

And then Thelma's Ascension began.

Nobody knows exactly how it was done—it may have been an optical illusion, or radiation from the looming cooling tower or high-decibel feedback from the giant speakers or just plain, old-fashioned faith—but as the adoring din washed over her, Thelma seemed to slowly rise off the ground.

In her rapture, she levitated an inch, her feet awash in an unearthly smoldering miasma, then another inch, then a full six inches above the orange crate. Tiny lightning bolts seemed to explode from her tiny feet. Crandall saw it first and rushed next to her, exhorting her to rise and rise and…

Thelma could feel the white light, the white heat. She was dizzy, the kaleidoscopic swirling of the thousands of Crusaders giving her vertigo. She collapsed in a heap on the stage. The shrieking frenzy of the Crusaders, amplified through the powerful sound system, seemed to lift everyone off their feet for just a second.

The TV cameras showed the frenzy, but couldn't catch the mass levitation. Still, once again, Thelma Barnett was on the front pages. With four days to go.

*   *   *

Chapter Four

Confluence, Part II

The state's skies and highways were thick with campaigns that final weekend.

Not only were the airwaves saturated with ads for Podesta, Moore and Blasingame, but those three were also zigzagging across the state in private planes courtesy of the Plumbers Union, Gov. Langley's Victory Fund and Blasingame Steel & Coil, respectively.

And while Barnett and Torres were out burning up the highways, Aldermen Petacque and Kaminski chose to stay close to the home turf.

Petacque, enlivened following the hot coffee incident, was dashing from bus stop to church to hair salon in every block of Jackson City's African-American community. The street heat was electrifying and Channel 14's Darlene Dawes was almost mobbed on-air by joyous Petacque supporters.

At Consuelo's urging, Shawn had reached out—belatedly, but deliberately—to the City's liberal activists, buying onto palm cards and sample ballots in the liberal wards, and running ads in the lefty and gay/lesbian newspapers. Still, Chemuyil and Consuelo were both concerned that Shawn was emerging as the "Black" candidate, instead of the "consumer advocate" candidate. The crowds surrounding him on TV seemed a little too "street" for that elderly white woman watching from Cul-de-Sac Lane in Outer Suburbia.

"Well, we probably don't have her anyhow," Shawn said dismissively. "Gotta run up the numbers in the base."

*   *   *

The Blasingame and Podesta fly-arounds were disasters.

The jet leased by Blasingame Steel & Coil had engine problems Sunday morning, desperately delaying a planned-to-the-minute schedule. Tina Bishop was going quite insane at the Blasingame Headquarters, trying to re-shuffle the fly-around schedule while worrying about the chaotic Election Day volunteer assignments and resolving a loud spat in the head-quarters lobby over yard signs.

Nicky Pulver seemed cool as a cucumber to Royce and Tina, but was sweating profusely under his collar.

After just one day of the "DUI" TV spot, Royce's negatives had jumped noticeably in his tracking. Royce's response—"Mary Moore's a sleaze for calling my grampa a criminal!"—was falling flat. Nicky expected the fly-around could be a media disaster, but the damn plane getting stalled would exacerbate the antagonism.

By the time Blasingame finally was "wheels up", Tina had unplugged the first hour of the itinerary, a press conference and county Republican picnic in West Fargo. Still, she was able to hold onto a TV crew and a "Royce is My Choice" rally at the state university.

Royce was surly from the delays, and from a lack of sleep, protein and caffeine. The jet zoomed into a tiny airstrip near the university and two frat boy volunteers crammed Royce into their silver Lexus. The crowd of about 150 "Royce" volunteers chanted his name as he climbed onto a chair in the garden of the Student Union. Many hoisted plastic cups filled with beer, which was apparently being distributed free at the back of the crowd.

"My name is Royce...who is your choice?"

The crowd screamed "Royce, Royce" and joyously jumped in the air.

Who are these people and how did they get here, Royce asked himself. Some had been recruited by Tina Bishop, some by a local Republican leader who had feuded with Gov. Langley. Maybe some of these kids were rented by Nicky. Who cares? Royce beamed. The TV crew turned its lights on.

"A few years ago, I graduated from this very fine institution and I am so glad to be back with all of you!" Audience applause, some bystanders join in.

"I would walk across the Quad, explore in the library, hang out in the Union, not sure what I would do with my life, but knowing that, if I applied myself and took advantage of all this great university has to offer, I might be a success," Royce paused. "And despite that, I ended up in politics!" (Good punchline, crowd enjoys it.)

Royce then launched into his stock speech: the need for—nay, the right to—safe utility service, the utility campaign contributions to his opponent, his love of cable TV and so on. As he was speaking, with the words flowing almost on auto-pilot, Royce felt the positive energy from the growing crowd, felt the very real possibility of victory…

Then he noticed the signs being distributed at the back of the crowd.

Fake "Royce for PUC" posters were being handed out with the word "PUC" ostentatiously crossed out and "DUI" written in.

"Excuse me, Mr. Blasingame, excuse me, sir," a persistent voice whispered from the foot of the stage. A university security guard was trying to get Royce's attention, just as he was wrapping up a great speech and saw these DUI posters floating through the crowd.

"What?" Royce said sharply.

"You can't give out beer in the Student Union, and anyhow it's before noon on a Sunday, a Day of Worship."

"Excuse me for just one second, kids," Royce turned to the persistent guard. "But, I'm not giving out beer."

"This is what I just confiscated from an underage student, sir." The guard handed Royce a plastic beer cup with a professionally-designed logo stamped on it, saying "Vote for Royce Blasingame and get a Free Beer", with a caricature of an obese Royce in a careening red Mercedes.

Royce scanned the crowd and noticed a tall, older "student" in the back handing out the phony "Royce for DUI" posters. The fellow saw Royce looking at him, smiled and hoisted a cold beer in silent salute before disappearing into crowd of students moving across the Quad.

The prank, engineered by Jimmy Blake, made the news that night, and a permutation of it followed Royce for the rest of his Sunday flyaround. At nearly every stop, the bogus "Royce for DUI" posters and free beer cups would mysteriously materialize during his speech.

The president of Students Against Drunk Driving was quoted in wire stories as expressing disgust at Royce's past behavior. The drunk driving TV spot was being carpet-bombed in every market. His sweet red Mercedes and grampa's "cover-up" was suddenly the topic of the day on talk radio across the state. His unfavorable rating continued to climb quickly, while his favorables, never great to start with, sagged.

Blasingame's mini-momentum was stopped.

*   *   *

Shortly after take-off early Sunday morning, Podesta's plane, an old single-engine beater courtesy of the Plumbers' Union, developed fuel line problems. They were already too far from the tiny Mohawk Valley airfield, the pilot yelled back to Paul, and would be forced to make an emergency landing in a cornfield.

For a few seconds, Paul thought the Grim Reaper was knocking.

As the six-seater lost altitude and narrowly missed a power line, Paul prayed. His life had been good, he could have no complaints. He had worked hard, married a great woman, served his country in the armed forces, served his community in the legislature. The golden corn stalks began scraping the thin fuselage of the plane, a deadly whapping sound punctuating the engine's futile groans. What a way to go, Paul thought.

"Hold on to yer hats!" yelled the pilot as he skillfully guided them back to earth. The sound of those damn corn stalks were deafening, Paul thought.

As the emergency medical personnel strapped Paul to the stretcher, Paul wondered if he was having a heart attack. Then he wondered if O'Malley had delivered the cash to Pudge for the TV buy. Smell of gas. Then he wondered why he was feeling so light-headed...

*   *   *

As disastrous as Blasingame's and Podesta's fly-arounds had been, Mary Moore's was going like clock-work.

The Governor's jet worked fine, the crowds of poster-waving support-ers and media at each stop were ample, and Mary's stock speech was get-ting even better. She was warm and relaxed, yet professional and confident. Peaking at the right time, she thought.

The news that the DUI counter-attack seemed to be working was a tonic for the campaign staff and candidate. Plus, an added bonus: their numbers revealed trouble for the Democratic frontrunner, with undecid-eds breaking for Petacque, Torres and Kaminski, but not Podesta. Serves him right for stalling the confirmation hearings, Mary smiled as she reviewed the tracking numbers.

By Sunday night, Mary was back in Jackson City, preparing for a cli-mactic Election Eve Republican Rally hosted by Governor Langley. Running on empty, but she knew. This is it. Calvin Reynolds would have been proud, she grinned.

*   *   *

The Petacque Parade was picking up serious steam.

He was now campaigning with a sound-truck featuring Bijou bellow-ing out his hypnotic exhortations, and a high school marching band fol-lowing on a flatbed truck. The mini-parade inched through every commercial strip in the African-American community, past every public housing facility. As he dashed from one side of the busy street to the other,

Shawn was masterfully shaking hundreds of hands per minute, two at a time, frenetically, as if his life depended on the number of human hands and souls he could physically and emotionally touch. His voice was shot.

The Kiddie Corps was handing out thousands of "Back Petacque" stickers. The street heat was electrifying, contagious. Some people weren't even sure who he is, maybe some baseball player or movie star? "Is that Denzel Washington?" one woman asks her friend, before screaming, "I love you, Denzel!" They know he's a celebrity, though, and they come away star-struck.

Mojo's back, he knew. Just in time.

*　　　　　*　　　　　*

"I told you this was an air war, Senator."

Paul slowly gained consciousness. Still woozy. Vision fuzzy. Some sort of chilly hospital room. Mustard-colored tiles. Harsh lighting. Strange echoes.

He remembered the plane surfing across corn stalks and then being pulled from the fuselage into a golden field under a bright sun. Heavy odor of gasoline.

Pudge and Emily were seated at the foot of his cot. No sign of the Grim Reaper or Saint Peter, Paul thought. Emily tearfully hugged him.

"Heart attack?" Podesta rasped.

"Naw," answered the young doctor attending to a cast on his foot. "Oxygen deprivation, maybe a mild case of shock, couple of broken toes. Everyone got out safely, Senator."

Paul looked at Pudge. "O'Malley come through?"

"Yeah, everything's fine, Man. Just relax."

Podesta drifted back into the land of dreamy dreams, content.

*　　　　　*　　　　　*

Chemuyil and Consuelo sat on one side of the conference room table and the two agents for the "Chrysler Crew" sat on the other.

The conference room at the Petacque Headquarters also served as a war room and lunch room. With just three days left, the room was getting a workout. Volunteers buzzed in the outer office amid greasy towers of fast-food cartons and beer cans, making calls for Election Day workers, stapling posters on hundreds of sticks and xeroxing reams of who-knows-what. A lavish, donated cheese and cold-cut spread was keeping the Kiddie Corps well-fueled in the final lap.

Shawn had been avoiding the "Chrysler Crew", but knew he now needed them. A fixture in African-American political circles for 15 years, these experts at signage and visibility had all been recruited and trained by Chris Chrysler, the master. Chrysler's services weren't cheap, but your name would be methodically plastered everywhere. They used roving crews on flatbed trucks, some with cherry-pickers, blitzkrieging through Jackson City's meanest streets.

"Miz Gardner and Missus Petacque…"

"I go by 'Milagro', but please call me Consuelo."

"Well, Consuelo, tonight may be the last chance for our services. Looks like this dude Burl needs 30 four-man crews for Monday night. That's our entire manpower base."

Chrysler's main man—"Jonas"—stood about six-four, with another ten inches of Afro topped by a beret. He wore mirrored sunglasses, a lime green dashiki and snakeskin cowboy boots.

Chemuyil jumped in. "Jonas, c'mon. Didn't we help you with those construction permits? And the summer job for Chrysler's grandson?" Chem had obviously dealt with this character through the Ward Office.

"Miz Gardner, my hands are tied. I can offer you ten crews for a ten-hour blitz tonight—my ten best—for Five Kay."

"Oh, Jonas, you're breaking my heart. We're a modest, grass-roots campaign here. You can see that," Chemuyil begged.

"We gotta pay our people. You know. We got escalating fuel expenses…"

Consuelo leaned over the table directly into Jonas' face.

"Jonas, my husband has worked so hard, so damned hard on this campaign. Our kids hardly ever see their Daddy. He gets hot coffee thrown in his face by psychos. He's just trying to do good for the people in the community."

She gently placed her tiny hand on Jonas' muscular arm.

"Please give us a little break here. Don't send our household further into debt than it already is because of Shawn's vision and ambition," Consuelo implored. "We'll remember Chris Chrysler and Jonas come reelection time. In a big way. You have my word."

The imposing Jonas removed his shades.

"Hey, these Podesta signs are everywhere, ubiquitous, as they say. Some folks on the street—outside of your Fifteenth Ward—ain't never heard of your husband, no disrespect, but who in the hell is Shawn Petacque? But, ma'am, I want to help and Mister Chrysler wants to help. How 'bout a dozen crews for $5,000?" Jonas responded.

"How about ten crews for two thousand. Cash. Plus, we'll feed 'em," Chemuyil quickly bargained back.

"Miz Gardner, you are a gutsy customer. Lemme call my boss."

Five hours later, ten trucks armed with 10,000 posters, gallons of wheat paste and thousands of staples fanned out throughout Jackson City's African-American community. By Monday morning, a sea of blue-and-yellow "Petacque for PUC" would greet Black voters on every block in every neighborhood. And not a Podesta sign to be found.

*   *   *

Ald. Butchie Kaminski sat in the 6th Ward Democratic Headquarters boiler room, which really was the boiler room. The old coal bin was now Butchie's inner sanctum. He spent the entire weekend perched on a folding chair at a card table, calling Election Day workers and giving them their assignments.

Butchie was in hog heaven when it came time for Election Day assignments. He knew every precinct in the 6th Ward, and most of the precincts in neighboring wards. He knew the capability of nearly every worker in Boss Chizz' patronage empire: who would be drunk by noon, who could run up big numbers in the nursing homes, who could baby-sit, who spoke Spanish or Korean or Polish or Urdu.

Some 200,000 flyers were being distributed door-to-door by veteran precinct captains across Jackson City for the Czyz-Camozzi-Dunne Slate: Burl for Governor, Karmejian for Secretary of State and Kaminski for PUC. Some of the precinct captains knew the parents and grandparents of the residents. They knew who had gotten a waiver on a building permit, whose kid once needed a friendly judge.

Rain was forecast for Tuesday. Low turnout projected by the Elections Board. Kaminski stared at the ward map (which he knew well) and the state map (which he barely knew). If all 200,000 people who get this flyer come out, and they all go for Butchie, he reasoned, he could just win this thing. Imagine. A hockey fan getting elected to the PUC, he mused.

"Hey, Butchie, snap out of it," yelled Mikey Kula. "These Mad Dogs just came in with six hundred, maybe seven hundred Podesta signs!"

"Bonanza!" Butchie cried delightedly, a Mad Dog at heart.

*   *   *

Other than Butchie and Thelma's Great Debate tussle and the Piney Blue incident, the media coverage of the PUC Chair race had been non-existent for nearly a solid year. In the final week, though, the public was being treated to a hot coffee assault, a rapturous levitation, bogus DUI posters and now a plane crash that could have been much worse.

After word of Thelma Barnett's levitation got out, she levitated some in the polls, too. Similar to the polling "bump" she had experienced after the brawl outside the Munich plant a few weeks earlier, Barnett's favorables and unfavorables both increased. She picked up some undecideds in the rural areas, but wasn't making a dent in Blasingame's or Moore's numbers in the suburbs or Jackson City.

Barnett's real bump was with the Crusaders, who were now convinced of her holiness, and other Christian evangelicals who weren't familiar with her candidacy. And some Republicans who said they were supporting anti-abortion activist Phil Driscoll for Attorney General were also now committing to Thelma.

The Crusaders were on the march now. The e-mail and telephone networks were humming. Every Crusader knew when and where to vote, and which candidates Rev. B.J. Crandall wanted them to vote for.

Phil Driscoll could sense the energizing of the state's Evangelical Right and tapped into it. He opened his wallet and Rev. Crandall was a willing conduit to the faithful.

On Sunday, Driscoll spent $250,000 on an automated voice message transmission to 300,000 Republican households in the far suburbs and rural areas Downstate. The 60-second phone message, featuring the voice of Rev. Crandall, urged voters to stand up against the godless forces of immorality and political corruption. Vote for Phil Driscoll and Thelma Barnett. A mechanical voice would then inform the voter of the address of their local precinct polling place.

*   *   *

Pudge Carson didn't have the heart to tell Podesta—flat on his back in the chilly hospital recovery room—that Kevin O'Malley had alas, not come through.

Pudge met the veteran lobbyist to pick up the checks, expecting $150,000 from various utility interests and other O'Malley clients. "Tell the Senator this is the best we could do, Pudge. We wish him well, we really do," a sheepish O'Malley said as he handed over 50 checks totaling $32,000.

"Well, this is a little disappointing. Y'all could end up with this fellah Petacque who's gonna demagogue you guys with no mercy," Pudge said, accepting the envelope.

Of course, O'Malley couldn't tell him about the pressure from the Governor and Jimmy Blake to stiff Podesta. They had clearly made the Mary Moore victory a priority and felt Petacque would be more beatable in November than Podesta. In fact, Blake had already engineered $17,500 in small contributions to the Petacque campaign, without Petacque even realizing it.

Timmy Sullivan was able to put together another $18,000 from the Electricians, Boiler Operators and Carpenters Unions. Podesta would be able to do a final TV buy on Monday, but it would be a fraction of what they felt they needed.

*   *   *

At 2:00 a.m. Monday morning, the Graciela Torres Caravan pulled back into a desolate El Puente.

The trip had been a huge success by any measure. The media coverage was great in smaller markets untouched by Petacque or Kaminski. Graciela spoke convincingly to several thousand likely Democratic voters, from the Michoacan farmers to the West Wheaton Ladies. She had raised $21,000 along the way. Hundreds of Torres posters were plunked into the ground along the Interstate and back roads, too.

Graciela was curled up next to Billy, half-awake as they drove past River's Edge. What a vast and incredible state, she thought. What a strange route from the explosion to the romance to the incredible road trip. She only half-remembered Billy carrying her from the car to her house and tucking in her in.

*   *   *

"DATELINE JJ: Who would have predicted such a wild finish in the PUC Chair contest? Witness Sen. Paul Podesta's plane disaster, Ald. Shawn Petacque's electrifying surge, the nasty trench warfare between Royce Blasingame and Mary Moore.

"*Question: What resonates more, a New Orleans drag queen or a speeding red Mercedes?*

"*Question: Will the Czyz-Dunne-Camozzi sample ballot give the Dems their first-ever nominee named 'Butchie'?*

"*Question: Will the levitating Thelma Barnett return to the Home Planet in time to vote on Tuesday?*"

*　　　　*　　　　*

The battle between Blasingame and Moore could also be viewed as a proxy war between Jimmy Blake and Nicky Pulver, two of the state's sharpest political strategists. Both were faced with similar choices faced by all campaign choreographers in the final inning. TV or field operations? Press the attack or end on a sweet, high note? Go into debt or stay in the black?

Blake argued successfully to continue the incessant "Royce is a Drunk Driver" TV spot until Monday noon and then finish on the Monday night newscasts with the positive Mary Moore bio. Money was no object, as Governor Langley pretty much gave Blake a blank check for Mary.

Nicky Pulver threw the New Orleans attack ad back up on Friday and Saturday, and then switched to a fluffy, positive profile of Royce for Sunday and Monday. Money was no object here, either.

Royce spent Monday pressing the flesh in the suburbs, starting with commuter train stations during the morning rush, zooming over to the Brentwood Mall, doing a live call-in show on the popular "Suburban Scene" cable show and ending up with another round of commuter stations. No sign of the counterfeit Royce DUI signs. Maybe we dodged a bullet, Royce thought.

*　　　　*　　　　*

Mary Moore ended the primary playoff season on stage with the Governor at his Election Eve Luncheon Rally in front of 3,000 Republican patronage workers and precinct volunteers in the Grand

Ballroom of the magnificent LaSalle Hotel. Governor Langley made it crystal clear that he had taken Mary under his wing and he made sure the Party Faithful knew it.

"Four years ago, we gathered at a rally very much like this one, with our terrific ticket," Langley boomed out. "That ticket included my very close personal friend, Calvin Reynolds."

The crowd hushed.

"Ya know, Calvin and I served in Vietnam together, we served the people of our great state together and we served the Republican Party together," Langley said in somber tones. "So, folks, I'd like to ask a moment of silence for our friend and fallen warrior, Calvin Reynolds."

The Party Faithful all bowed their heads and reflected on what might have been. Calvin as Governor. No question. Many reflected on his Cancun caper with Ana Villasenor.

After a moment passed, Langley took the mike in his hand.

"My fellow Republicans, one legacy of a great warrior is to have trained another warrior to pick up his flag should it fall. Calvin Reynolds had a terrific lieutenant in Mary Moore, and that's why Mary Moore is gonna be the Public Utilities Commission Chairperson for a long, long time. Let's hear it for the Pride of Zane Township, a great Republican, Mary Moore!"

The crowd roared, still emotional over Langley's tribute to Reynolds. Steven Page made sure plenty of Moore signs were placed in the front row so they could be waved in full view of the TV cameras. The old Ballroom shook as the crowd stomped its feet and hollered, "Mary! Mary!"

Mary took the podium.

The overhead spotlight shone down on her tiny frame, her blond hair and modest brown business dress bathed in light. She waved to her husband and son in the front row. She looked into the bank of TV cameras.

"Thank you so much, Governor Langley, for those kind words about our good friend—my teacher and mentor and a great Party Leader—Calvin Reynolds."

The crowd erupted again.

"Calvin taught me many things. How to promote state-of-the-art utility service and foster a healthy economy. How to deal with the legislature. How to subsist on the campaign trail diet of rubber chicken and mashed potatoes." The crowd smiled. "The only thing he didn't teach me was how to stay out of trouble in New Orleans!" A good-natured laugh from the crowd.

"Seriously, Calvin Reynolds also taught me about being decent and fair-minded and honorable and that's the legacy of Calvin Reynolds I seek to extend in the Public Utilities Commission."

Mary launched into her final attack.

"Now, I actually have three opponents tomorrow. One candidate who knows only a one-note song—a song of narrow-mindedness and bigotry—and she has this tendency to float from God's Green Earth." Mild laughter.

"And there's another candidate who knows only how to sling mud and tell lies about his irresponsible driving record and spend his grandfather's millions to buy a public office!" The crowd applauded with vigor.

"My other opponent isn't on the ballot. It goes by various names. It's known as lethargy or apathy or complacency. You are on the front lines tomorrow and I need you to help my slay these foes!

"Finally, let me recognize and thank the two men in my life, my patient, long-suffering husband, Randall, and my courageous, wonderful son, Tony!"

Both men stood, bowed and blew a kiss to Mary and faced the crowd in the Ballroom. Tony wasn't sure what the reaction would be to him, considering his mom's Party's record on non-heteros, but he beamed and waved as the standing ovation swept the room.

We're in the home stretch, Mary thought as she waved to the roaring crowd.

*   *   *

Jimmy Juarez had called in every favor, every IOU he'd accumulated over decades of being a major political player in the Hispanic community.

More than a thousand workers—some paid, some volunteers, many patronage workers—would be on the streets Tuesday pumping for Torres.

Jimmy spent the weekend smoking cigars and finalizing precinct assignments. He made sure Sam Roth was monitoring the wise distribution of what few signs they had left and kept bugging Lupe Zarate about the candidate's schedule for the last two days.

Running statewide is a learning experience, he thought as he looked at the state map in the Torres War Room. He never realized how many Hispanics lived out in the "rurals", and was relieved that Graciela and Lupe had identified and worked that constituency hard in the final weeks. He fretted over the enormous sums Graciela was willing to spend on TV, but recognized its value. He even recognized the value of Billy Miller, both as a strategic planner and as the candidate's secret weapon. Miller had put together a respectable Downstate cabal of Podesta-haters and had engineered the whole soccer-mom strategy.

Cruising on only two hours of sleep since the Road Trip, Graciela did the subway station circuit during the Monday morning rush.

While not as electrifying as the Shawn Petacque Subway Sensation, the Torres street heat was still lively and effective. Sam Roth had recruited dozens of "subway shock troops" who would meet Graciela at the subway entrance with banners, bells and brochures. Graciela couldn't shake hands as quickly as Shawn, and her petite hand would invariably be crushed by an overzealous or thoughtless handshake. She would come away from handshaking expeditions rubbing her bruised and sticky right hand, yearning for soap and hot water.

As she and Mariano Vargas pulled up to the 49th Avenue station, the final stop during the morning rush, Sam called the car speakerphone. "Debbie Shane is over at 52nd Avenue station. Go! Go!" Sam barked. "We're shifting a dozen volunteers over there right now to meet you guys. She's got crews!"

"She's on a cruise?" Mariano asked, half-jokingly.

"TV crews! She's got every station there," Sam screamed. "Vamanos!"

"Thanks, Sam," Graciela chirped. "And watch the caffeine there, okay?"

Within three minutes, Mariano zoomed up to the 52nd Avenue subway station, just as a gaggle of Torres volunteers arrived. Graciela hopped out and saw gubernatorial hopeful Debbie Shane shaking hands at Petacque-speed.

"Morning, Senator!" Graciela called out, as every reporter turned towards her.

"Commissioner Torres! What a beautiful day for campaigning!" Shane laughed and motioned for Graciela and the shock troops to join her modest entourage.

Graciela immediately went into handshaking mode, and the Torres volunteers began ringing the bells and chanting "Shane-Torres-Shane-Torres". Graciela glanced at Shane. They had not endorsed one another, but had felt increasingly close during the campaign. Graciela wasn't sure how Shane would take this impromptu merger.

Shane just smiled and the TV crews and newspaper photographers caught the bonding moment between these two charismatic aspirants, these two attractive rising political stars.

*   *   *

Buses rolled into Mohawk Valley all afternoon. Adorned with banners proudly identifying which union local was aboard, the caravans unloaded at the Mohawk Valley town square.

A huge pig roast was underway and cold beer was flowing. The majestic County Courthouse, fresh from a good sandblasting, glistened in the late afternoon sun. The maple trees were starting to turn a blazing orange. A stage was erected between the Civil War cannons on the same spot where Paul Podesta had first placed a stage 35 years earlier in his first run.

Timmy Sullivan had spent the weekend energizing the labor poohbahs. Not every fakir was for Podesta, of course, but Timmy pulled out the stops with the trade unions and any union whose industry dealt with Podesta's Senate Committee on Public Works & Utilities. He figured he had 1,500 precinct volunteers from the various unions, with another few hundred on phonebanks calling union households. Between that and the modest TV buy and whatever the hell Wally Mraz was up to in Jackson City, we should be okay, Sullivan thought.

Pudge Carson had felt pessimistic ever since the disappointing money drop from O'Malley. The TV buy would be too little, too late, Pudge thought. With the candidate banged up, and Mraz off like some loose cannon and Timmy Sullivan—god bless 'im—working like a dog with the labor fakirs but missing other key core constituencies, Pudge reluctantly felt defeat was possible for the first time since Paul first announced.

By sunset, the square was packed, well-fed and slightly ripped. The torches were lit, the Mohawk Valley High School band struck up a few tunes and the pom-pom team did a crowd-pleasing job.

Carpenters Union boss Bill O'Grady emceed the program, which was being covered by several TV stations and aired live on the local radio station. O'Grady told a few jokes, dinged the rich Republicans some, and then introduced the other labor titans, a gaggle of local Democratic politicians and finally Pudge Carson.

Pudge wasn't much of a public speaker, but he proceeded to give a fiery, yet warm, discussion of Podesta the Man. His roots right here in Mohawk Valley. His military service, the dry goods store, his first historic campaign (a victory which he celebrated in this very square!), his splendid legislative record.

The crowd was rapt. Torches crackled and bunting whipped in the pig-roasted breeze.

"Now some candidates in this race have been known to levitate!" Pudge winked to the audience.

"So our good friend Paul Podesta decides he wants to fly! Unfortunately, the plane wasn't cooperating. But, folks, he's okay. 'Cuz ya can't keep a good ole Mohawk boy down! He's our Home Town Hero! He's the next Public Utilities Chairman of this great state! I give you our beloved Senator Paul Podesta!"

The crowd went crazy as Paul, on crutches, was escorted onto the stage by Sullivan and one of the pom-pom girls. He looks so pale, so gaunt and gray, Emily thought. The band struck up "Hail to the Chief" followed by "Battle, O Mohicans", the rousing high school fight song. The spotlights swirled.

Paul was still on painkillers and his foot hurt like hell. He had returned home Monday morning and slept all day. His entire Monday schedule, which had included radio interviews and visits to union halls, had been unplugged, as had, obviously his Sunday schedule after the cornfield brush with death.

The genuine energy of the crowd lifted Paul and Pudge for the first time in two days, though. Union banners waved and the drums continued.

"Please, please, you'll wake the dead!" Paul joked into the mike, not realizing that could be the crowd's intent.

"To my many friends in the labor movement, welcome to beautiful Mohawk Valley!" Boisterous hurrahs. "And to my many neighbors who honor me with your presence tonight, I bow in sincere gratitude."

His voice raspy and wheezing, Paul thanked everyone who had helped, introduced his campaign team, hit a few of his usual stump speech talking points and then paused. This space, this square. Such a personal sacred site, for me, Paul thought. The castle-like Courthouse, the Civil War cannons, the maple trees, the checkerboard tables. The crows.

"When I first decided to run for public office, some 35 years ago, I sat in this very square, right over there on that bench where Joellyn Nell from Laborers Local One-Twelve is perched. Nice to see ya, Joellyn. Hey, somebody wake up Joellyn there!" The crowd laughed warmly.

"A few months after that, in this very Courthouse, I was declared the upset victor, thanks to some of you stalwarts who are in the crowd tonight. Since then I have always tried to do the right thing, the fair thing, what is good for the people of my district and my state.

"I am proud of the path I have traveled since then, in the House, in the Senate, for working people like you all." The crowd cheered and waved flags.

"And it was on the very same bench, almost one year ago, where I decided to apply the values of Mohawk Valley and the values of the labor movement and the values of the Democratic Party of FDR and Hubert Humphrey and..." Paul started coughing and the crowd applauded mightily. He loosened his tie.

"The leaves on these old maples are turnin' colors. Old hands like Pudge Carson and me have watched hundreds of politicians and bureaucrats and taxpayers and criminals come-and-go through those big bronze Courthouse doors. Time marches on..."

His throat closed up and another coughing jag prevented the end of that sentence. Emily then joined him on stage to the uproarious response of the crowd. Pudge grabbed the microphone. "Let's hear it for Emily Podesta, the Senator's Better Half!" Emcee Bill O'Grady handed Paul a bottle of water and took the mike from Pudge. "Less than 24 hours to go, people. Get some sleep and tomorrow let's roll up our sleeves for our friend, Paul Podesta. Go! Go! Go!"

Timmy and the pom-pom girl helped a hacking Paul off stage, and the marching band cranked up "Happy Days Are Here Again" as the crowd promptly headed for the buses.

*   *   *

The "Stand Up for Pride" Rally had been in the works for weeks.

Jimmy LeMans, Benjamin DeForrest of MortPAC, State Sen. Beatrice Madison and the usual crew of clergymen had organized and funded this final push for turnout in the African-American community. Busloads from various community groups, ward organizations and churches rolled up to "Catchin' the Trane", a jazz nightclub whose owner offered the space for free.

"Hello, to all of my beautiful Sisters and Brothers! Welcome to the Trane!" Jimmy LeMans yelled into the mike. Nearly 3,000 folks yelled back. The Ornette Coleman tape was cut off.

"We got a wonderful program! Some more music! Some cold beverages and Jamaican meat pies! Some speeches! Some roof-raisin' on Election Eve! But first! The Elder Stateswoman, the Senior Voice for African-Americans, a Legendary 26th Warder and a Truly Lovely Lady! Senator Beatrice Madison!"

Beatrice slowly strode across the stage, wearing a red silk dress and a diamond necklace. Her silver hair shimmered. How many of these Election Eve rallies have I attended, Beatrice thought. Maybe 30 or 40. The first one was for Adlai Stevenson. 1952 or '56? Dragged there by her Gramps, she recalled. Went to one for Shawn Petacque's Daddy, too, early 1960's. Not too many left in these old bones.

"People. People. I'm Senator Beatrice Madison…" (more cheers from the crowd) "…and you have got to tell everyone, and I mean everyone, you see later tonight or tomorrow to get out to the polls. This is urgent! Urgent! This right, this franchise, is what old folks like Jimmy LeMans and Bishop Robinson here and myself, this is what we fought for in the Fifties and Sixties, so we all can exercise this precious, this sacred right to vote!" (more cheers; Beatrice is pumped.)

"Now we don't have as many of our candidates on the ballot tomorrow as we'd like…" (some boos and hisses; Beatrice milks it like a pro.)

"But, what we lack in quantity, we are very surely making up for it with quality, because we have such great candidates on the ballot tomorrow. Later on we'll hear from my dear friend Judge Sandra Taylor Gibson." (cheers) And while my good friend, Congressman John Brock, is unopposed in tomorrow's primary, we need to stand up for him just like he has consistently stood up for us!" (more cheers)

"And so many years ago, I had the honor of participating in a rally very much like this one for a gentleman who once served in the chamber I now serve in, the State Senate, a great public official, the late Senator Larry

Petacque." (polite applause; not everyone liked the Old Man, and half the audience was in diapers during his reign.)

"And tonight, we are on the brink of victory for another Petacque, Larry's bright and talented son, Alderman Shawn Petacque, the next Chairman—and, I might add, the first Black Man in history to be Chairman—of the state Public Utilities Commission! C'mon up here, young man! Give us a few words now."

John Coltrane's *"Giant Steps"* blasted through the superb sound system as Shawn bounded up the stairs to the stage. He hugged LeMans, avoided a hug from DeForrest, and got a sloppy kiss on the cheek from Madison. "Your Daddy would have been so proud, Shawn," she whispered as they embraced. He motioned for Consuelo and the kids to join him.

Hundreds of blue-and-yellow "Petacque for PUC" signs waved, a hypnotic blur from the stage. The TV crews who were present clicked on their lights, with Channel 14 going live. Coltrane's sax echoed off the smoke-filled ceiling.

Shawn grabbed the mike off the stand, scanned the crowd and deadpanned, "Anybody know where a man can get a cup of hot coffee around here?"

"In your face, Little Brother," somebody yelled over the laughter.

"And I don't even like cream and sugar," Shawn rolled. He put his arm around Monique. "Well, we can laugh about it now, but it was kinda scary at the time, right, honey?"

Monique took the mike and said, "Hi! My name is Monique Sojourner Milagro Petacque and I want you to vote for my daddy on Election Day!" Candidates' kids are guaranteed crowd-pleasers and this audience went crazy for Monique. Consuelo beamed.

"I want to thank Senator Madison for her very kind words," Petacque turned to her. "Madam Senator, you are our inspiration." She bowed to him and the appreciative crowd.

"Well, tomorrow's the big day. Senator Madison eloquently articulated the reasons it is so important that we have a good turnout. And it's not just for Congressman Brock or Judge Gibson or Shawn Petacque running for whatever it is he's running for.

"It's about pride, it's about citizenship and justice, it's about getting an even break from the big gas and electric and phone and cable companies. It's about recognizing and cherishing all those things our parents and grandparents worked so hard for and suffered through, so we could get a better education and maybe afford to buy a home.

"My Daddy was a public servant. We didn't see a lot of him, going to meetings and so forth. But he instilled in his family and friends and supporters a dedication to quality and to public service and to hard work," Shawn paused and lowered his register. "And my Daddy just loved winnin' elections!" (ah, raw meat to the lions; Shawn feels the Mojo Wave.)

"Friends, I'm in a tough race here, make no mistake. My opponents can outspend me and out-TV me and out-endorsement me, but they can't out-hustle me!

"Now, Senator Madison here is too modest to discuss her role at the Democratic Party slatemakin' conclave, but she was utterly fearless and unrelenting when the old-time bosses wanted to have no African Americans on their state ticket. None. Can you believe that? And Beatrice gave 'em H-E-L-L and they turned around like yelpin' little pup-dogs! Let's hear it again for Beatrice Madison!

"Heating bills in the dead of winter. Phone bills. The light bill. This is what the Public Utilities Commission deals with. Anybody here fed up with your utility bills?" (crowd roars; TV cameras run.)

"Well then let's hit the streets, People! First thing tomorrow morning! For Rosa Parks and Doctor King and Beatrice Madison and Congressman Brock and my beautiful daughter and your daughter! Let's go! Let's go! Thank you so very, very much!" (standing ovation; cameras flash; strobes pulsate; Coltrane soars.)

Shawn put his arm around Consuelo, who was sobbing as she waved to the crowd. The kids clinged to his legs. "You're gonna do it, I can feel it," his wife whispered, tears streaming down her cheeks.

"We're gonna do it, cher," he whispered back. "I love you."

*   *   *

"This is Darlene Dawes, live at the 'Stand Up for Pride' Election Eve Rally, where Alderman Shawn Petacque has just wowed the crowd of some three thousand enthusiastic supporters." The undulating wave of Petacque posters crested around her. Onlookers jumped up and down around Dawes.

"Earlier today, similar pre-election rallies in the suddenly red-hot Public Utilities Chairman race took place in rural Mohawk Valley and Jackson City's LaSalle Hotel."

Footage of Governor Langley with his arm around Mary Moore. "The Republicans held a loud lunchtime rally in the Grand Ballroom of the LaSalle Hotel, where Governor Tom Langley invoked the memory of former PUC Chairman, Calvin Reynolds, who was killed a year ago in a Mexican highway accident."

Audio of the Governor: "...the Pride of Zane Township, a great Republican, Mary Moore!"

Cut to footage from Mohawk Valley of Podesta on crutches, looking pale.

Dawes voiceover. "And Democratic front-runner, Senator Paul Podesta, who only yesterday survived a mild plane crash, was helped onto a stage before a large gathering of union workers at an old-fashioned torchlight political rally in the Mohawk Valley town square."

"Finally, another PUC candidate—Commissioner Graciela Torres— joined Democratic gubernatorial candidate, Senator Debra Shane, at the 52nd Street subway station for some old-fashioned hand-shaking."

Footage of Shane and Torres seriously pressing flesh as the Torres Subway Shock Troops chant, "Shane-Torres-Shane-Torres."

"Other candidates include Democratic Alderman George Kaminski, Republicans Royce Blasingame and Thelma Barnett, and Independent candidate Dan Clark. The polls are open at six tomorrow morning, so don't forget to vote. This is Darlene Dawes for Channel 14 News."

* * *

"Whoo!" Sam Roth yelled, pumping his fist in the air in the Torres War Room. "Podesta looks old, Petacque looks Black and you look like a winner!"

"It was only a ten-second clip," Graciela replied, though clearly pleased with the final TV news coverage of the primary. "But, thanks to you, Sam, for making the Shane thing happen this morning. Very resourceful. Quick thinking."

"No sign of Kaminski," Jimmy Juarez observed, always worried about what his friend and rival Boss Johnny Chizz was up to.

"The important thing is that Podesta looks like a wounded duck," Billy Miller said.

"I am so glad you guys did the Road Trip," Lupe Zarate said.

"Me, too," Graciela said silkily, as she took Billy by the arm and urged everyone to go home and get some rest for the Big Day.

* * *

"Randall, you always know my sensitive spots," Mary Moore whispered, her voice shot, her stamina near zero.

As her husband gave her a back rub, she thought of what a year it had been. Calvin's death, River's Edge, the outing of her son by that creepy Thelma Barnett, the New Orleans fiasco, the strange and wonderful campaign trail. Today's rally was one of the most memorable moments of her life, she told Randall.

Only a few more hours, she thought as she drifted off.

* * *

"What's the forecast, Butchie?" Czyz barked out.

"Weather Lady says rain is possible, Boss."

"How many troops we got?"

"Twenny-one hunnert for workin' the polls."

"How 'bout tonight?"

"We got nine truckloads of Mad Dogs leaving right now for the suburbs."

"Okay. Butchie, you just might win this thing. Meet me for breakfast tomorrow. The Danzig. 5:00 a.m."

"'Kay. G'night, Boss."

* * *

Chapter Four

Confluence, Part III

Election Morning. The dawn of a New Day.

The mood of candidates awaking on Election Morning can be akin to nervous newlyweds-to-be on Wedding Day, or maybe John Glenn awaiting countdown in his tiny capsule or Ike on D-Day. The day is just fat and ripe with possibilities.

No more TV or radio ads; the air war is over and the planes are back in the hangars. The final ground assault is beginning in the pre-dawn mist. Tens of thousands of troops flying dozens of different colors, gathered in wet streets across the state, ready for the bloodless war known as Election Day.

The People Yes! are about to speak.

*　　　　*　　　　*

"Daddy, today's Election Day! C'mon!" Monique deliriously yelled as she trampolined on Consuelo and Shawn's mattress in the early morning darkness. Outside, every lightpole, abandoned building and subway station in the African-American community was adorned with the distinctive "Petacque for PUC" posters.

Petacque rubbed his eyes. "Yeah, kinda like Christmas morning, sugar. Did Santa come?"

"Can I come vote with you?"

"Yeah, I need every vote I can get. Did Mommy ever show you how to make coffee?"

"I'm up, I'm up," Consuelo moaned.

*   *   *

Ald. Butchie Kaminski met Boss Chizz at the Danzig for a high-cholesterol breakfast. The fluorescent-lit greasy spoon was already alive at 5:00 a.m.

"We ready?"

"Yeah, Boss. I already heard from Seamus and Camozzi. Everything's in place in their wards. Kula says we're covered in the 6th. The Mad Dogs done real good last night. A few hunnert Podesta signs."

"Rain's gonna help."

"Yeah, but the Weather Lady predicts a sunny afternoon."

"Okay Butchie, finish your pancakes and get back to headquarters and make sure we're covered. And see if you can get a palm card from Trevor O'Brien."

"I thought O'Brien was for Podesta," Butchie said through mouthfuls of pancake.

"He sez he's bumpin' Podesta, leavin' it blank. As a favor for me getting him a few jobs at Port Authority. Ginny Whitehead's gonna do the same in the 30th. She got somebody in her organization in the mix for some high-rankin' post office job."

"We could win this thing, Boss."

"Yeah, well, keep yer eye on the ball here, Butchie." The Boss sounded almost human, Butchie thought.

"Could you pass the maple syrup, Boss?"

*   *   *

Thelma Barnett met Rev. B.J. Crandall for morning prayers. Ever since the rapturous levitation at the Countryway Nuke, Thelma had felt…delivered. She knew that after that mystical experience, her life had new meaning and purpose, and would never be the same.

And Crandall knew that his political life would never be the same after the quarter-million automated phone calls that had been placed over the previous two days, urging a vote for GOP Attorney General aspirant Phil Driscoll and for Thelma. And Driscoll had become so enamored with the technique that he had authorized another $100,000 in automated calls today in rural counties in the state's southeast corner.

Let Moore and Blasingame fight it out in the suburbs, Crandall figured, we're gonna surprise some people in the boonies.

*   *   *

"Showtime, corazon!"

Graciela Torres hadn't slept well until the last hour or so. The drizzle made it good sleeping weather, she thought, as she snuggled closer to Billy. "A few more hours, por favor."

"Yeah, just 14 more hours and it's done. I'll get the coffee going."

"I'd rather get you going," Graciela said mischievously just as the phone rang downstairs. Sam Roth. Just checking in from the Campaign Headquarters with his first hourly report. Jimmy Juarez has it under control in the Hispanic precincts, and Lupe and I have the suburban target precincts covered, he reported proudly.

*   *   *

Despite Nicky Pulver telling him candidates just don't do commuter train stations on Election Day, Royce Blasingame was determined to squeeze in every campaigning opportunity he could. He was up and out before dawn, meeting and greeting suburban voters, some of whom had already voted. Other than one jerk who asked Royce about his red Mercedes, everyone was very polite, and a few even said they had voted for him.

Back at Blasingame Headquarters, Tina Bishop, State Rep. Laura Southampton and ten troubleshooters worked the phones, frantically plugging holes. They had done their homework well, targeting precincts in suburban areas and a few Republican-leaning Jackson City wards where Langley was not popular. They had bought onto the palm cards of several renegade Downstate Republican County Chairmen, but they were already learning of betrayals brokered, no doubt, by Jimmy Blake.

"Well, please put the States' Attorney on. This is State Representative Laura Southampton, that's who…Right, they're handing out Mary Moore brochures right there at the judges' table over in your Precinct 12," Southampton barked into one phone. "Right at the judges' table!"

"This is Jim Davis from the Blasingame campaign. The polls still aren't open in East Jackson, Precinct 39. That's a huge precinct. What the hell's going on over there?"

"You're supposed to have people opening in all twelve precincts over there," Tina yelled. "You have three people for me? What is this bullshit, Angelo? You're coming up very short here, Angelo, very short."

"Whattya mean we're not on the palm card in Ashland County," Nicky screamed into another receiver. "We gave that little asshole three thousand bucks!"

*   *   *

Wally Mraz loved Election mornings, more than just about anything.

"It's like chess and football and life," he once told a magazine interviewer. "All the hard work, the practice, the strategies. All right there. Plus, ya add a few tricks and muscle."

Tricks and muscle.

Wally Mraz was a recognized master of those weapons. In a league with Jimmy Blake and Nicky Pulver as a tactician, Wally brought a first-hand knowledge of Jackson City's political landscape to the Podesta campaign.

He knew that John Czyz was making this a very personal battle. He predicted that the Mad Dogs would raid Mohawk Valley and probably steal the Podesta sign from Podesta's front yard (they did). He figured that

Boss Chizz would force a few palm card betrayals (he did). And he knew that Podesta could probably use a street guy like him if he got elected.

Most of the campaign staffers at Podesta's campaign headquarters were either Mohawk Valleyites or labor whiz kids, none of whom ventured much into Jackson City's African-American community. But Wally did, frequently, and he knew that Petacque had picked up steam recently, rebounding from the goofy "Thelma" tape and deftly using the hot coffee incident for some free press. And these "Back Petacque" signs were everywhere.

Signs are one thing, though, and troops are another. Wally Mraz didn't have the patronage army that Czyz had, but he had a cult-like following of volunteers. And there were six ward bosses who had feuded with Czyz over the years who were discreetly helping Podesta. But with Petacque and Torres both holding firm in their own ethnic bases, Wally knew Podesta would be hard-pressed to do well in Jackson City. Especially since the money had just dried up in the final week.

Too much TV and not enough GOTV in this campaign, Wally thought as he drove to the Podesta Headquarters in the pre-dawn drizzle. And why does it always rain on Election Morning? This weather is good for us though. Keep turnout low. Controlled vote.

As he sat at a red light a few blocks from the Headquarters, he saw a kid, maybe 17, whip out a knife and slash a vinyl Podesta poster Wally had planted in the median strip the night before. Wally calmly pulled up next to the kid, standing in the traffic-less intersection, who looked guiltily at Wally. "Hey," the pimply-faced kid said.

Wally rolled down the window, smiled and motioned for the kid to come over, which he innocently did. Wally quickly reached through his car window, grabbed the kid by the jacket and administered a crushing head-butt. Stunned, the kid froze, dropping his blade.

"Oh, tough guy's got a blade?" Mraz punched the kid once, breaking his nose in a symphony of spraying blood. Satisfied that street justice had been done, Wally released the death grip on the skinny throat and calmly drove off into the pre-dawn darkness, leaving the kid in a bloody heap on the street.

I love Election Day mornings more than just about anything, Wally thought.

*   *   *

Mary Moore awoke before the alarm went off. Randall was snoring, but she could hear the rain.

This is it. One year ago, everyone figured this would be Calvin Reynolds' big day, leaping up to grab the Republican nomination for Governor to replace his old friend Tom Langley. She hadn't really given much thought to succeeding Calvin even under that scenario.

And she certainly never expected the scenario that played out. Reynolds' mysterious Mexican truck collision, River's Edge and the investigation, dealing with characters like Jimmy Blake, Podesta holding up her confirmation, that witch Thelma. What a year.

She looked at Randall. Sawing the wood. So peaceful. He never asked for this. He saw her political activities as a hobby, never thinking it would subject their household to so much personal and financial scrutiny. What a good guy, so patient. We should take a trip, Mary thought, as the wake-up call from Peggy Briscoe jolted the Moore bedroom.

*   *   *

"Morning, this is Senator Mario Camozzi. How you guys lookin' in Six?"

"Senator, we got good coverage here," Mike Kula confidently answered. "Runners and checkers and pollwatchers everywhere. How's it by you?"

"Okay coverage, but one of my guys got beat up by he thinks Wally Mraz. Busted his schnozz at an intersection. Before the polls opened, even."

"Wally's getting' off to an early start," Kula replied. "I'll let Boss Chizz know about this, and we'll take care of business."

"Thanks kid, and hey, good luck to Butchie today. Maybe he gets elected and Kula's the next Alderman, eh?"

"Appreciate that, Senator. Good luck to you today."

* * *

By 5:30 a.m., the approach to every polling place in the state was decorated with dozens of colorful signs. Normally drab grade schools or police stations of VFW halls were transformed into splendid gardens of political slogans and headshots. When the first voters arrived at 6:00 a.m., they ran a gauntlet of pollwatchers after wading through the campaign signs that had sprung up overnight like a thousand blossoms.

The signs and pollwatchers varied by region, even by neighborhood. In most Downstate areas, there were plenty of signs and troops for Moore, Barnett and Podesta. In the Suburbs, Moore, Blasingame and Torres ruled. City precincts varied wildly, but Kaminski, Petacque, Torres and Blasingame had the visibility edge.

There were far fewer Burl for Governor signs than anticipated, thanks to an Election Eve reaming administered by Sen. Beatrice Madison to Chris Chrysler. "Debbie Shane is my colleague. She's for the Black folks," Madison begged. "Don't be helpin' this Burl fellah."

"It's business, Mother Madison," Chrysler replied. "Burl's paying us 20K."

"To do what?"

"Y'know, signs, visibility."

"Well, don't be puttin' those Burl signs up in our community, you got that?"

"You feel better if I send my crews out the to the 'burbs?"

"The farther away the better. Like the next state."

"We'll do what we can, Mother Madison."

And on Election morn, there were no Burl signs to be found in any African-American neighborhoods.

* * *

Each candidate had a unique Get-Out-The-Vote operation.

The Blasingame Campaign had done serious targeting and identified about 400 precincts primarily in Jackson City, plus a few wealthy suburbs and campus communities across the state. Their "Fabulous 400", Tina had dubbed them. Intensive phonebanking and door-to-door contact had identified more than 50,000 "plus" votes, people indicating a preference for Royce. On E-Day, those 50,000 were called at least twice with a reminder to vote. Extra troops and visibility were allocated to those 400 precincts.

Despite losing the exclusive slating by the State Democratic Party, Podesta was relying on the Party Establishment to get the regular Democrats out, at least in Downstate and suburban precincts. His focus was rural areas, communities with high percentages of union households and a few wards in Jackson City whose tribal chieftains hated Chizz or loved Wally Mraz. Timmy Sullivan had compelled the major unions to organize phonebanks by their members to other members. At least 75,000 phonecalls would be made to union households with a pro-Podesta message.

The Petacque strategy was simple: huge turnout in the African-American community. Sound-trucks and hundreds of paid workers going door-to-door were the cornerstones of the plan. No need to persuade the voters who to vote for, just get them to the polls. If the folks come out, Petacque figured, they're mine.

Thelma Barnett became linked at the hip to Attorney General candidate Phil Driscoll. Crandall's Crusaders were notified by e-mail and automated phone message that Driscoll and Barnett were the anointed ones. The location of their local polling place was added to the message. Some households had received four or five messages from Crandall, so the Barnett strategy was comparable to Petacque's: no need to persuade, just make sure the base votes.

Kaminski used the tried-and-true method of GOTV. Incredibly concentrated and patronage-driven, precinct workers belonging to the tribes of Mario Camozzi, Seamus Dunne, Sherman Stumpf, Johnny Czyz and a few other Bosses knew exactly where their votes were and how to get them out.

The palm cards handed out at the polling place by a precinct captain you've known for 20 years are golden to a candidate for a lesser-known office.

Torres employed a multi-tiered strategy. Jimmy Juarez had the Hispanic wards wired. By requiring hourly reports of turnout from every precinct, he was able to shift resources if it looked like key, vote-rich precincts weren't coming out. Billy Miller's "soccer mom strategy" meant targeting about 200 suburban precincts with decent Democratic turnout, and shoveling all of the white, female volunteers who had streamed into Graciela's campaign into those suburban precincts. A dozen phonebanks were set up in the suburbs and calls were made all day. The Downstate strategy was sharply focused on counties were Podesta was not loved, though in these areas, Torres was relying on the kindness of strangers.

* * *

Moore enjoyed the most extensive GOTV effort. By combining the Governor's field operation, exit polls and a sophisticated computer system, Moore had the best dynamic snapshot of what was happening out there on the frontlines throughout Election Day. She had coverage in the greatest number of precincts and, unlike Barnett or Blasingame, had an experienced hierarchy of troops. Her people knew what to do.

Moore was able to know, for example, how many polling places hadn't opened at 6:00 a.m. well before the State Elections Board knew. And since the Moore camp had a good idea of which precincts would be strong for Mary, they protested loudly to the local State's Attorneys in those areas to make the openings of the pro-Moore precincts a top priority.

Moore was able to know how poor the day's turnout would be as early as 6:30 a.m., though the latest weather reports showed a sunny afternoon. Her early exit polls also showed the Republican gubernatorial race between Paul Prentice and Esther Ruelbach to be a dead-heat.

The gubernatorial candidates from both parties did the traditional voting photo opp in the morning, all hoping to make the Noon TV news shows uttering the usual lines about "I can't tell you who I voted for" or

"Oops, I marked the wrong candidate". Democrat Lawrence Burl appeared in public with his wife for the first time in the campaign. She seemed peeved at the whole affair.

The PUC candidates all notified the media of the times and locations for their momentous vote-casting, but other than a few local reporters covering Emily and Paul Podesta in Mohawk Valley, the candidates were forced to exercise their franchise without the media bearing witness.

All of the candidates paused inside the polling booth when they saw their name on the ballot. Petacque brought his daughter Monique into the booth and let her punch his number. Neither Barnett nor Blasingame had ever seen their own name on a ballot before, so they stared at it. Podesta had seen his name on maybe 30 primary and general election ballots, but knew this could be one of the last times. Torres and Moore beamed with pride and a little disbelief that their names were even on the ballot for PUC Chair. Kaminski was extra careful he punched the right hole.

*   *   *

After the early morning voting ritual, each candidate had a distinct itinerary.

Moore went to her office in the Public Utilities Commission, as if today was just like any other day. Business as usual. As the incumbent, she had to maintain the professional veneer. Besides, Jimmy Blake and Steven Page should have things under control in the War Room.

Podesta hopped in the Pudge-mobile (he really didn't feel like flying) and they set off on the three-hour drive to Jackson City, rightly figuring that the major media would be in Jackson City on Election Night. He wanted to get a running start on the General Election. He spent the whole trip on a cellphone, getting reports from bellwether precincts across the state. Turnout was lousy, he told Pudge.

Blasingame went out on the campaign trail to the suburbs, hunting for every last possible vote. He stood at commuter train stations, at grocery stores and at the student union of a community college. This could come down to a handful of votes; he wouldn't want to regret that he hadn't done all he could.

The others—Barnett, Petacque and Torres—all spent the next several hours prodding their bases.

Barnett drove to the makeshift war room in Rev. Crandall's farmhouse and began calling Crusaders across the state with a reminder to vote, a process she would continue until the polls closed. In nine hours, Thelma made more than 500 phonecalls.

Torres was driven by Mariano Vargas on a carefully mapped-out route of the busiest polling places in Hispanic wards. She would say hello to her volunteers, meet the election judges, greet a few voters, plunk another yard sign in the ground and move on.

Petacque kept the street heat going at full burners. His parade was now seven vehicles long, with a marching band on one flatbed truck and Shawn on another. Dozens of the more able-bodied Kiddie Corps members sprinted alongside the entourage with "Back Petacque" signs on sticks. "Bijou" kept the patter going through a bullhorn: "Back Petacque. Today's Votin' Day! A new dawn with Shawn. Meet him, greet him, they cannot defeat him…" Bells and whistles and hip-hop and Sousa.

*   *   *

At 9:00 a.m., the State Elections Board announced the turnout thus far on this rainy Election morning. Downstate counties: 12%. Suburban townships: 14%. Jackson City wards: 9%.

"How do you like those numbers?" Podesta asked Pudge Carson as they zipped along the Interstate.

"Well, you want to get at least a third of your vote by the end of morning rush, right? So I'd say that's not happy news for anyone countin' on big JC numbers."

"Right," Paul said. "And the suburban numbers are probably good for Moore."

"Well, they ain't good for Petacque, that's for sure. But we country folk tend to vote earlier than our busy commuter city cousins."

"Wonder which city wards are comin' in heavy," Paul said as he dialed Mraz for a field update.

*   *   *

In the quiet, tree-lined 39th Ward, Wally Mraz had cut a deal with Alderman Izzy Feldman to put Podesta on his palm cards. Feldman and Czyz had never gotten along, and Izzy thought his City Council colleague, Butchie, was a moron.

Plus, Podesta paid him $5,000.

Wally had assigned a team of Young Democrats to the 39th to do Election Day precinct work for Podesta. About 20 of these freshly-scrubbed young lads with visions of high-paying jobs at the PUC once Podesta got in were stationed at eight different polling places in 39.

The coordination and speed of the eight separate assaults was astonishing.

Around 9:30 a.m., the Podesta volunteers were milling about in front of their assigned polling places, when several carloads of not-so-freshly-scrubbed young men pulled up, jumped out and pummeled anyone with a Podesta button or sign. Deed done, they would calmly pile back into their cars and drive off. Witnesses said they attackers were yelling something like "Mad Dogs" as they sped off. Ten Podesta volunteers required medical treatment, including one with a fractured skull.

*   *   *

"Royce, it's a shell game towards the end," Nicky Pulver was explaining. "You don't really know how much your opponent has in the bank. Hell, you don't even really know how much you've got in the bank. Maybe they have blown it all on TV in the final weekend. Maybe they're holding back an extra $100K for last-minute paid phonebanking."

Actually it was closer to $70,000 for last-minute phonebanking and Jimmy Blake played it perfectly.

The State Elections Board reported unusually high turnout in 20 rural southeast counties known for solid Republican turnout. The counties were also home turf to a respectable number of Crandall's Crusaders. Blake first noticed the spike in turnout figures on the 10:00 a.m. report from the Moore exit pollsters in those counties, who also reported big margins for Thelma Barnett for PUC Chair and Phil Driscoll for Attorney General.

That's where they're focusing their efforts, Jimmy figured. We can't lose anywhere Downstate; that would give Podesta courage for November. Don't concede an inch. Fight back right there, right now.

And so the $70,000 they had held back specifically for Election Day rapid response situations was electronically deposited in the account of a South Carolina firm which immediately transmitted a message from Gov. Tom Langley to 130,000 Republican households in those 20 southeastern counties. Vote today for my good friends Mary Moore for PUC Chair and Aviva Benson for Attorney General.

Any chance Barnett had of sneaking up on Moore was foiled.

*   *   *

The reminder to vote message was being broadcast non-stop to African-American and Hispanic voters on various Jackson City radio stations (although one rock station saw Election Day as the final chance to air "Thelma's a Wicked Bitch" one last time.)

At 11:00 a.m., Chemuyil Gardner sat in the Petacque War Room with one of the Kiddie Corps computer wizards. The turnout figures from Jackson City were much lower than in other parts of the state, and the turnout figures in the African-American wards were even lower than that. The Petacque Parade would need to be really cranked up for afternoon rush, she worried.

Over at Blasingame Headquarters, Tina Bishop and Laura Southampton were learning of new palm card betrayals all morning. The most painful back-stabbing was in their biggest Downstate county, where the Republican Chairman had agreed to put Royce's name on his sample ballot for $6,000.

Royce's name was there alright, directly under Mary Moore's. Nicky Pulver's exit polls showed Blasingame winning in Jackson City, holding his own in the suburbs and coming in third behind a surprisingly strong Thelma Barnett in the rural areas.

Jimmy Juarez and Billy Miller were men on a mission at the Torres War Room. Both men worked the phones like the pro's they were, prodding allies throughout the war zone, shifting around volunteers. Without the benefit of exit polls or a network as extensive as Moore's or Podesta's, the Torres camp had to rely on the painfully slow turnout numbers coming from the State Elections Board and supporters on the ground. The Hispanic precincts were seeing higher-than-usual turnout, possibly due to the intensive coverage of River's Edge in the Spanish-language media recently.

And the high turnout in the suburbs, Billy thought, could only help.

*   *   *

"This is Darlene Dawes, live at the Gaffney School in Jackson City's 39th Ward, where a rash of politically-motivated beatings marred an otherwise peaceful Election morning.

"One man was seriously hurt and another six campaign workers for Senator Paul Podesta were taken to area hospitals for treatment of lacerations and bruises after they were attacked around 9:30 this morning."

Footage of interview with a bloodied Ryan Clayridge, Young Democrat.

"We were just standing there in front of the school, handing out Podesta flyers and this carload of goons pulls up—an old black Buick—and these four guys jump out and didn't say anything. They just started punching and one guy had like a miniature baseball bat and they kept pounding us. Then they just drove away."

Cut to a Police Spokesperson describing the investigation into the six simultaneous attacks and the fact that the State's Attorney has been brought into the probe. No suspects or leads at this time, he reported.

"So, it's old-time politics-as-usual in the mean streets of Jackson City on Election Day. Don't forget, the polls are open until seven tonight. Darlene Dawes for the Channel 14 Noon News."

*   *   *

The drizzle of the early morning hours had subsided by Noon. A bright, sunny September afternoon was predicted.

The State Elections Board released the turnout figures as of 1:00 p.m. Downstate counties: 26%. Suburban townships: 34%. Jackson City wards: 22%.

*   *   *

"These Downstate numbers are flat. What the hell are you guys doing in there?" a limping Podesta yelled at Timmy Sullivan, who was running his War Room. Podesta and Pudge Carson had just arrived from Mohawk Valley and found the Jackson City Headquarters in chaos. The beatings up in the 39th Ward, the lousy Downstate turnout, the fact that the unions weren't coming through as big-time as he needed…

"Senator, the unions have already made 30,000 phone calls. We have every supportive county chairman humpin' out there."

"Can we do more paid phones?"

Sullivan paused, then quietly said, "If we had the money, sure."

"Well?" Paul turned to Pudge.

"Sorry, partner. We're broke. No contingency fund. Spent everything."

Pudge had already told Paul about O'Malley's disappointing gift, but Paul thought there was still an emergency bankroll somewhere.

"Mraz spent whatever was left on walkin' around money and palm cards in JC," Pudge said regretfully.

"Damn. We shoulda muzzled the guy from the get-go. Sorry I barked at ya, Timmy. My leg's hurtin' like a son-of-a-bitch."

"Don't worry about me, Senator. You guys should go get a square meal and then come back here to work the phones, is my suggestion," Sullivan ventured.

"You're a winner, kid. Pudge, let's get a sirloin. We need protein," Paul joshed. "And more Downstate turnout."

*   *   *

"Ma'am, I'll tell you one more time. Writing 'Kaminski' in red magic marker on your arm is considered electioneering, and, as an election judge you should know better," an exasperated State's Attorney lawyer's aide said. "So I'm going to walk out to my car and call my superior and when I return in ten minutes, it better be off, okay? I'm being very patient with you."

As the young legal beagle walked to the polling place door, she turned to look at the grandmotherly judge who was wearing her heart on her sleeve. Grandma was flipping the young woman a major bird, with the word "Kaminski" in bold letters on her frail arm.

*   *   *

At 2:00 p.m., Lupe Zarate received a call from Deanna Drew from the Debra Shane gubernatorial campaign.

The Shane exit polling data showed unusually good turnout in the Jackson City liberal precincts and, more importantly, both Shane and Torres were leading handily in those precincts in their respective races. Deanna also shared the good news that Graciela's soccer mom strategy seemed to be working in the suburbs, with 78 percent of Democratic suburban women saying they voted for Graciela Torres.

After a quick confab with Billy Miler and Jimmy Juarez, Graciela's schedule was changed to have her end the campaign at a subway station in the yuppie Flagstaff neighborhood.

*   *   *

The numbers in Jackson City jumped dramatically when the sun burst through the clouds. All morning, the higher-than-usual turnouts were in the

Bosses' Domains: neighborhoods run methodically by old-timers like John Czyz, Seamus Dunne, Mario Camozzi, Jimmy Juarez and Sherman Stumpf.

But when the sun began to burn off the City's gray dampness, people in other wards started coming out to the polls. The voters who weren't bound to any ward boss. The uncontrollables.

The street-heat of the Petacque operation was getting stoked for one last flare-up. The turnout figures in the African-American wards had been bleak all morning. Now the numbers began to comfort, then enthuse Chemuyil Gardner and the Petacque War Room. The 90%-Black 11th Ward, for example, had 4% turnout at 9:00 a.m. At 3:00 p.m. it was up to 37%. The Petacque Parade began its final noisy tour of Jackson City's African-American community.

The sun was working its solar magic on the suburbs, too.

Jimmy Blake's exit polling showed a spike in the number of senior citizens and stay-at-home moms in the afternoon. Jimmy's data also showed Blasingame holding a modest lead among Jackson City Republicans, Moore enjoying a commanding lead among suburbanites and a three-way dead heat in the Downstate counties. But Jimmy could tell that his last-minute paid phonebanking gamble had stalled Thelma's and Rev. Crandall's move. Who knows? Maybe it helped Aviva Benson, too.

A surge by Sen. Esther Ruelbach in her GOP gubernatorial contest was also seen in the exit polls. Can't hurt, can only help, Blake told Mary Moore, who was still at her office. "Go to the hotel. Have a nice meal. Take a hot bath. Work on your speech," Blake ordered.

"Jimmy, you're starting to sound like your friend, Steven Page," a bemused Moore replied, having never heard Jimmy get so personal or be so warm.

"Need to come out fighting tonight. You'll have a decent TV audience. Hit Podesta as a tool of the big unions, a professional politician who doesn't really get it. Got it?"

"Got it, General. Thanks, Jimmy."

*   *   *

The pace quickened to a frenzy by 5:00 p.m.

Thelma was still dialing every Christian Marcher she could, as the last wave of Driscoll-funded "robo-calls" were being completed.

Blasingame was back at one last suburban commuter station while his War Room coordinated operations in the "Fabulous 400", their highly-targeted top-priority precincts. Thousands of phones and doorbells were being rung at homes of known-Blasingame supporters in each of the "Fabulous 400" precincts, particularly those in Jackson City's high-rise "Poodle Canyon".

Timmy Sullivan and Wally Mraz were feverishly plugging holes in the Podesta closing operation, in which pollwatchers spend the last hour ringing the doorbells of supporters in a last-ditch effort to get them to the polling place, and then stay inside the polls after closing to observe the ballot count.

Torres posted herself and her subway shock troops at the Flagstaff station. Thousands of yuppies poured from the station. Some her staff handed out maps of the area with the locations of polling places clearly marked. "You can go over to the LeMoyne School right now. It's just a five-minute walk on a beautiful day," was a typical rap offered by Torres' youthful volunteers.

Meanwhile, the Torres War Room was in overdrive, with Sam Roth shifting around suburban volunteers, Billy Miller cracking the whip on his Downstate cabal of Podesta-haters and Jimmy Juarez yelling in Spanish while smoking a huge Cuban cigar. Lupe Zarate tried to keep a lid on everything, but the pressure cooker was boiling hot.

The Petacque Parade was sizzling, with hundreds of people running alongside the entourage. It was noisy, it was colorful, it was energizing. But were these folks going to get to the polls in the next two hours, Shawn wondered as he waved to the ecstatic crowds. Chemuyil called him with new unofficial numbers showing good—but not great—numbers in the Black wards. "And Frenchy, we're already at 44 percent in the 15th!" she yelled into a cell phone.

"Home sweet home!" Petacque yelled back as he kept waving.

*   *   *

The State Elections Board released the turnout figures as of 5:00 p.m. Downstate counties: 33%. Suburban townships: 39%. Jackson City wards: 35%. Their projected final statewide turnout: 44%.

*   *   *

"One more hour to go, Mary!" Gov. Langley called with best wishes. "Sounds like the numbers are shaping up fine, too."

"Well, we don't want to take anything for granted, Governor," Moore said. "But the suburban turnout is splendid. What are you hearing?"

"Nervous about Driscoll. Aviva's just not running up big enough numbers in the City to make up for his Downstate surge. Not much we can do about that now."

"You know, this would have been Calvin's big day," Mary mentioned.

"We are both better people for having known him," Langley somberly replied.

"Thank you so much for all of your help, Governor. I really mean that."

"Mary, you've done us proud. Come out swinging in your victory speech tonight. Take a poke at Podesta if you have live TV."

"Good advice, Governor. We'll be checking in."

*   *   *

"This is Darlene Dawes, reporting live from the polling place at Jackson City's Winston Churchill Junior High, where a long line of citizens are awaiting their turn to cast their vote for governor and other important offices. Madam, why are you here, waiting in line on a nice sunny day?"

An elderly African-American woman with thick glasses seemed shocked by the question.

"Why, honey, I'm here because we fought for this precious right and anyone who doesn't get their behind out to vote is a shameful disgrace!"

Several neighborhood kids starting shoving to get the gang-signs on-camera. A few pollwatchers waved blue-and-yellow "Back Petacque" posters. Dawes ignored them all.

"Well, there you have it. One woman's, uh, reason for voting. Just an hour left before the polls close..."

"And furthermore, there's a conspiracy to make Black folks wait in line like this," the senior jumped back in, grabbing Darlene's mike. *"They wait like this in the suburbs?"*

"...an hour left before the polls close. Darlene Dawes, Channel 14 News, Live at Six."

*   *   *

The September sunset blazed as the ground troops of the various tribes gathered for the final battle.

The Blasingame strategy of putting serious resources into just 400 precincts seemed to be working as turnout in nearly all of them was much higher than usual. Hundreds of paid volunteers sporting "Royce is my Choice" buttons were feverishly ringing doorbells and phonebanking their "plus" votes.

After the dustup in the 39th Ward earlier between the Podesta and Kaminski forces, added cops were brought in to patrol larger precincts. The hostilities had raged all day, but with no more injuries, only the tearing down of a few hundred signs.

Kaminski had ample coverage in his target precincts in Jackson City. Petacque had plenty of volunteers in African-American precincts, but not much going on elsewhere. Torres was a little stretched, having dispatched any new volunteers to either the Democratic suburbs or to the liberal Jackson City areas like Flagstaff.

The Moore and Barnett campaigns were polar opposites in terms of their closing operations. Mary's was efficient and extensive; Thelma's was non-existent.

The minutes of the final hour ticked down slowly.

Royce and Graciela were still out there furiously shaking hands at train stations. Shawn was still parading and exhorting passers-by with his rapidly-failing voice to get to the polls. Thelma was still dialing. Butchie and his Aunt Violet were greeting his neighbors in front of his own polling place. Mary and Paul were working on their victory speeches.

Lines at polling places grew as voters went to the polls after work. All across the state, the final ballots were being cast.

Each candidate watched the clock, counting down the minutes. Each candidate knew the end of a remarkable adventure was at hand. They had all put their good names on the line, all had leapt into the arena for whatever reasons and with whatever support. Now it was all ending, so abruptly, each one thought.

No one could believe it was finally over.

*   *   *

Every campaign war room had a similar rhythm.

Once the final polling place assignments were made around 4:30 p.m. and the candidate was all scheduled out, and the last of the paid phonebanking was done, each war room down-shifted for the final half-hour or so. The calm before the insane storm. Everyone assigned to War Room duties knew this would be the political epicenter in a few hours, but now it was eerily serene.

Tina Bishop did some vacuuming in Blasingame's War Room, just to burn off some mindless energy. Wally Mraz and Timmy Sullivan ordered pizza and beer. Chemuyil Gardner, Sam Roth and Jimmy Blake each reviewed their respective precinct data bases one last time. Rev. Crandall and Thelma Barnett knelt in prayer in his farmhouse war room when the clock struck 7:00 p.m. Finally. Peace.

*   *   *

An election day is a snapshot, a freezing of the moment, Billy Miller told Graciela over toast 14 hours earlier. The Body Politic changes minute-by-minute, like those never-ending currents in the human body or a river. Today's election determines who will be the flood and who will become arid and extinct, like Abernathy Creek, he said.

"Mami!" yelled Raisa. "The toilet's overflowing in the basement!"

*   *   *

The counting of the ballots was by no means scientific or uniform. In some of the state's many thousands of polling places, an experienced group of judges could whip through the count in an hour. In places with new judges or judges who slept through training, or where a "helpful" poll-watcher "accidentally" spindles or mutilates ballots, or where an eager precinct worker has brought in dozens of absentee ballots, the numbers wouldn't be known for several hours.

All across the state, in dimly-lit church basements and scruffy bowling alleys and sweaty school gyms, the crystalline snapshot of the Body Politic was being processed. All that was at stake was everything.

*   *   *

The first precinct to be officially reported to the State Elections Board was Jackson City 3rd Ward, Precinct 17. Seamus Dunne territory. Great turnout (84%). The first numbers were posted on the State Elections Board website.

State Public Utilities Commission Chairman
Precincts reporting: 1
Updated: 07:49 p.m.

Republican Primary—55 votes cast
P. Royce Blasingame   32 votes (58%)
Mary Moore   16 votes (29%)
Thelma Barnett   7 votes (13%)

Democratic Primary–392 votes cast
George "Butchie" Kaminski	*297 votes (76%)*
Paul R. Podesta	*42 votes (11%)*
Graciela Perez Torres	*40 votes (10%)*
Shawn L. Petacque	*13 votes (3%)*

In the Kaminski War Room, Mikey Kula was actually viewing the State Elections Board website when the first totals were posted.

"Butchie!" Kula yelled. "First precinct in! You're winning! Mad Dogs Rule!" He printed it out, knowing this lead would last maybe ten minutes. Talk about peaking too soon, he thought.

*   *   *

An hour earlier, every war room was quiet. Now, at 8:00 p.m., the tornado was hitting.

"How many precincts have reported in Farragut County?" "Gimme those numbers again!" "What's Associated Press saying?" "What's happening in the governor's race?" "Whaddya know? Whaddya hear?" Phrases like these were yelled out simultaneously in all sorts of campaign war rooms of all sorts of campaigns across the state.

It was like trying to get a handle on oatmeal, Nicky Pulver told Tina Bishop. No one has a really accurate picture. We try to get totals from our friends around the state and from the media and from our own volunteers who are closing, but ultimately, nobody knows for sure until the State Elections Board declares a victor. Our main challenge, he explained, is to get enough of a handle on the rapidly-incoming numbers to know if it's a win or a loss, a victory speech or a concession.

The Mary Moore War Room was state-of-the-art. Rows of computers and computer operators, precinct maps hanging from every available wall space, dozens of phones and folks to answer them. They had hotlines to other campaigns and news outlets. An efficient system was in place to tabulate totals by precinct and compare them to projections meticulously worked out by Blake.

Located in a suite of rooms in Jackson City's classy old LaSalle Hotel, the victory party would be in one of the ballrooms downstairs. Both Republican gubernatorial hopefuls—Prentice and Ruelbach—were hosting their victory parties in the LaSalle too, so TV crews would be here. Mary continued to work on her speech in a room she and Randall had for the night. Take a poke at Podesta, Blake and Langley had counseled.

*   *   *

The next few dozen precincts were nearly all from Jackson City. Blasingame and Kaminski maintained their leads.

State Public Utilities Commission Chairman
Precincts reporting: 49
Updated: 08:29 p.m.

Republican Primary—2,815 votes cast
P. Royce Blasingame	*1,943 votes (69%)*
Mary Moore	*710 votes (25%)*
Thelma Barnett	*162 votes (6%)*

Democratic Primary—12,864 votes cast
George "Butchie" Kaminski	*6,276 votes (48%)*
Shawn L. Petacque	*2,516 votes (20%)*
Graciela Perez Torres	*2,198 votes (17%)*
Paul R. Podesta	*1,874 votes (15%)*

The hot races, of course, were the gubernatorials, with Sen. Debra Shane enjoying a quick lead of Lawrence Burl on the Dem side, and Republican Sen. Esther Ruelbach jumping out to an early lead over Congressman Paul Prentice. Two women facing one another for Governor? Who would have ever imagined it! Many more precincts to go, though.

*   *   *

"Nicky! Sixty-nine percent! Are we really winning?" Royce asked in his innocent tone.

Pulver looked up from his computer. The numbers were flowing in now, almost faster than they could be inputted and analyzed. Jim Davis and Tina Bishop were both wearing telephone headsets and were typing furiously.

"Well, we've got reports from about 200 precincts. We're ahead of our projections in the Jackson City precincts, although the 'Fabulous 400' counts are sluggish, so far. We're behind our projections in the 'burbs and rurals."

"Yeah? So? Turnout was good in the City, right? Does that mean we're winning?" he beamed.

Pulver looked at the screen, looked at Royce and looked back at the screen.

"No."

*   *   *

By 9:00 p.m., the suburban numbers were arriving in a blur. Those war rooms that were attempting to track the incoming data were getting swamped (except for Moore's). This jigsaw puzzle in time and space was like a calculus problem involving high-speed data and human impulses. Increasingly, each campaign was relying on the media and Elections Board for data.

State Public Utilities Commission Chairman
Precincts reporting: 1,689
Updated: 09:18 p.m.

Republican Primary–136,734 votes cast
Mary Moore   64,181 votes (47%)
P. Royce Blasingame   58,922 votes (43%)
Thelma Barnett   13,631 votes (10%)

Democratic Primary–157,311 votes cast
George "Butchie" Kaminski   43,571 votes (28%)
Graciela Perez Torres   41,737 votes (26%)
Paul R. Podesta   39,070 votes (25%)
Shawn L. Petacque   32,933 votes (21%)

"Not to worry, Frenchy," Chemuyil Gardner assured a nervous Candidate Petacque. "Hardly any Black precincts in, yet."

"We don't know what precincts the State Board has, though."

"Hey, if we don't have the numbers in the African-American wards, they sure as heck don't either. Stay cool."

*   *   *

At 9:35 p.m., Associated Press projected Sen. Debra Shane as the winner of the Democratic gubernatorial.

Despite their basing that projection on only 34 percent of the votes in, it was enough for Lawrence Burl, who called Shane with a gracious congratulations and then went out to meet the media horde at his victory party. After a brief speech endorsing Shane, Burl and his peevish wife left the hall, as did those few Burl supporters who were present.

*   *   *

The Associated Press reporter assigned to the PUC race was unable to make sense of the numbers as they flew in. She was as deluged as Sam Roth or Chem Gardner. Jimmy Blake was only too happy to help.

"Look. We got reports from almost 5,000 precincts. Every corner of the state. There is no place where Royce can make up this deficit," Blake said confidently.

"Okay, gimme your numbers."

"We'd like to have this wrapped up by ten o'clock news time."

"I'm sure you would, Blake, and my job is to make projections based on reality."

"Okay, we got Moore with 315,000, which is 55, 56 percent. We got Blasingame with 203,000, about 36 percent and Thelma with about 41K, maybe seven percent."

"Long way to go, Blake," AP replied dubiously.

"And we don't even have our Zane Township numbers in yet. Absolutely no place Royce can make it up."

"Refresh me in a half-hour."

*   *   *

The African-American and Downstate precincts were flowing the hardest between 9:15 and 9:45 p.m. Kaminski had indeed hit his high-water mark, although he held the lead longer than anyone could have expected. Thelma picked up some ground, as did Podesta and Petacque.

State Public Utilities Commission Chairman
Precincts reporting: 8,216
Updated: 09:54 p.m.

Republican Primary–707,180 votes cast

Mary Moore	*371,082 votes (52%)*
P. Royce Blasingame	*276,118 votes (39%)*
Thelma Barnett	*59,980 votes (9%)*

Democratic Primary–720,074 votes cast

Paul R. Podesta	*203,196 votes (28%)*
Graciela Perez Torres	*196,442 votes (27%)*
Shawn L. Petacque	*183,507 votes (25%)*
George "Butchie" Kaminski	*136,929 votes (19%)*

"Yes!" Sullivan whooped as Podesta moved into first place for the first time in the evening. He called Podesta at his hotel room and gave him the encouraging news. And, as frosting on the cake, Timmy told him, Butchie had plummeted from first to fourth.

*   *   *

The Blasingame War Room knew it was trouble.

Nicky Pulver, Tina Bishop and Laura Southampton knew that the "Fabulous 400" top-priority precincts had nearly all been won by Royce, but by meager margins. With a thousand precincts to go, it didn't look good.

The War Room phone chirped. The secretary said it was Jimmy Blake calling for Nicky Pulver.

"Hey, Nicky, congrats on a good race with a nothing candidate," Blake said in his smarmy way.

"Screw you, Blake. Whaddya got?"

"AP is real close to calling it. We're missing only about 500 precincts. 52 to 40 to 8. No way you can make it up."

"Which precincts?"

"I don't know. All over. C'mon, man. Ten o'clock news is starting. They'll lead with Shane and Burl. Prentice-Ruelbach's too close to call. Maybe then they go to Driscoll beating Benson. You wanna help beat Podesta in November? Have Royce call Mary at the hotel. Right now." Blake was cocky and insistent.

"Lemme get back to you," Nicky said reluctantly. He called Blasingame and relayed Blake's request.

"Where do you think those last 500 precincts are?" Royce asked wistfully.

"If anything, they're Downstate, which has been running 40-30-30 for Moore, or they're Black and Hispanic, which are probably for you, but it's chump change, tiny numbers."

There was a moment of silence. Until the War Room phone chirped again.

"Governor Langley is on line 6. Wants to be patched through to Royce."

Nicky took a deep breath and told Royce to take the call.

Langley was cordial, congratulated Royce on a terrific rookie run and said he knew Royce had a great political future and hoped he could help Royce on whatever his next endeavor might be. Who knows? Maybe Congress? Anyhow, he really hoped Royce would throw in the towel now so Mary could make the 10:00 news broadcasts, so we can beat Podesta.

It was the first time Royce had regarded the PUC race in the past tense. Nice to hear the Governor encouraging his political future. Did he just offer to help with a Congressional bid?

Royce thanked the Governor and called Mary Moore at the LaSalle Hotel to concede.

*   *   *

"This is Ronna Richards, live at the Mary Moore Headquarters, where the candidate has just taken the stage along with Governor Tom Langley. A crowd of maybe two thousand supporters have jammed the LaSalle Hotel Ballroom. Let's listen in…"

At that moment, every TV station went live with Mary's speech.

"…and I received a very gracious call from Royce Blasingame…"

The traditional boos from the crowd followed by the traditional "no, no" protestation by the gracious candidate.

"…and Mr. Blasingame offered to help us in any way to beat the Democrats in November!"

The crowd went crazy.

"And I want to thank Governor Tom Langley for being such a great friend and supporter and the best Governor in our state's history!"

More crowd insanity.

"…and all of you who volunteered in the precincts today and my great staff Jimmy Blake and Steven Page and my loving husband Randall and my courageous son Tony and…"

A few TV crews clicked off their lights after getting the word that their stations were going live with Phil Driscoll's upset victory over Aviva Benson in the GOP Attorney General contest. Mary pushed forward though, acknowledging Calvin Reynolds' mentorship, and advocating tougher utility safety standards and a competitive marketplace. As she was speaking, she debated whether to go after Podesta. She wasn't even sure if he had won, and she thought this was a moment to stay above the partisan fray. She decided to skip the red-meat attack on Podesta. She'd use it tomorrow in interviews.

As she wrapped up her victory speech (which never mentioned Thelma Barnett), Mary felt a little melancholy. This should have been Calvin's big night. Instead it was hers.

*   *   *

Not only was the turnout in both parties much higher than anyone figured, but the "fall-off" between votes cast in the Governor's race and the lower-level races was minimal. Maybe all of the recent publicity of the wild-and-wooly PUC contest had helped, even if the media coverage was for things like smashed windows, hot coffee, plane crashes and levitations.

By 10:30 p.m., the data was slowing to a trickle. With a few hundred precincts still out, Associated Press projected Congressman Paul Prentice the winner of the Republican gubernatorial nomination over Sen. Esther Ruelbach, who gave an eloquent concession speech. The AP would not call the Democratic race for PUC Chair, though. Still too close to call.

A fidgety Shawn Petacque called Chemuyil Gardner at his War Room. "How many of the outstanding precincts are ours?"

"I figure a third. And there are some goodies, too. Your pal Dickerson seems to be holding back maybe a few big precincts. Maybe wants to be the savior, riding in with the margin of victory."

"What a way to win," Shawn groaned.

"Still, Graciela's hanging in there, too. AP is calling it a three-way dead heat."

*   *   *

State Public Utilities Commission Chairman
Precincts reporting: 9,521 (of 9,800)
Updated: 11:28 p.m.

Republican Primary–838,098 votes cast
Mary Moore   *462,143 votes (55%)—WINNER*
P. Royce Blasingame   *311,863 votes (37%)*
Thelma Barnett   *64,092 votes (8%)*

Democratic Primary–843,910 votes cast
Paul R. Podesta   *230,638 votes (27%)*
Graciela Perez Torres   *229,149 votes (27%)*
Shawn L. Petacque   *228,434 votes (27%)*
George "Butchie" Kaminski   *155,677 votes (18%)*

The Torres War Room went nuts as the newest Elections Board numbers were posted. Down by 1,500 votes with less than 300 precincts to go. But Petacque was moving up, too, just 700 behind Torres. Jimmy Juarez made another round of calls to Hispanic pols, Billy Miller feverishly worked the Downstate circuit and Sam Roth was contacting suburban allies. Graciela was taking 95% of the Hispanic vote, winning huge in the suburbs and a surprisingly close second to Podesta Downstate. Across the street from her Headquarters, at the *Restaurante Torreon*, dozens of volunteers and a growing number of reporters gathered, studying the numbers posted on a huge chalkboard and those coming in on TV.

Over at Petacque Headquarters, Chemuyil sat in front of the computer, trying to figure which precincts were still missing and whether or not they would help or hurt Shawn. She decided to call Rep. Seth Dickerson.

"Hey, Representative. Chem Gardner at Shawn Petacque's office. You have a good day there?"

"Okay turnout," the sullen Seth replied. "Your guy did okay here. Is he winnin'?"

"Well, you tell me. We're wondering if everything's been reported from your neck of the woods?"

"Yeah, it's all in. Petacque took it in our ward, with about 82, 83 percent. Torres next with 12."

"Huh. So it's all in?"

"Yeah, all precincts reported. Good luck to you."

"Thanks, Representative. Appreciate your help." At that moment, Chemuyil knew there weren't enough Black precincts left. They couldn't close the gap.

It was all over for Shawn Petacque.

                    *   *   *

All of the TV local news broadcasts signed off by midnight. The big stories—wins by Shane, Prentice and Driscoll—had all been analyzed and punditized. The only unresolved contest was the Democratic race for PUC Chair. Podesta maintained a slim lead over Torres and Petacque, according to Associated Press. At 12:15 a.m., a haggard Podesta greeted his supporters, told everyone it was to close to call, and to go home and get some sleep.

At 12:40 a.m., the State Elections Board announced a canvass of the PUC race, meaning whoever won tonight would be the unofficial victor pending a careful hand counting of the ballots.

With just 52 precincts outstanding at 1:30 a.m., the Associated Press called Petacque for comment. Their numbers showed Shawn moving into second-place. Over Podesta. Petacque was almost too surprised to react.

At 2:00 a.m., the Democrats new standard-bearer, Sen. Debra Shane, called Graciela Torres in the Torres War Room.

"Congratulations, Graciela, or shall I say, Madam Chair," Shane said excitedly.

"Well thanks, Senator and congratulations to you, but we're still not quite sure here…"

"We are! Our people at the Elections Board just called!" Shane was practically screaming. "You won by five hundred votes, pending the canvass! You did it, Graciela! This is so great!"

Graciela was stunned. She quickly thanked Shane and reiterated her congratulations.

She turned to Lupe and bit her lip. Tears welled up. "We won," she whispered.

The War Room exploded in joy. Jimmy Juarez hugged Sam Roth. Soledad Torres hugged her sister. Billy Miller popped the cork on some champagne and began screaming "yee-hah!". The ecstatic crowd of supporters at the restaurant spilled onto the grimy, deserted street.

For a few minutes, this little corner of El Puente, just a few blocks from River's Edge, was the happiest place on earth.

*   *   *

Chapter Five

Flood Stage, Part I

"Sometimes we'd have that whole river all to ourselves for the longest time."
-Mark Twain *(The Adventures of Huckleberry Finn")*

Every candidate treats the morning after in a different way. Many sleep late. Some winners will hit the ground running, using the first morning of the general election campaign as an opportunity to meet and greet voters at a train station or factory gate. All are drained and relieved, some bitter or broke.

Mary Moore, as the incumbent, needed to be at her desk at the Public Utilities Commission office first thing in the morning and she was there, although still dazed. The last week was so brutal, physically and psychologically. Blasingame's final assault was masterful, she had to admit, even though Jimmy Blake gave no credit to Blasingame and total credit to Nicky Pulver for Royce's surge. The size of Blasingame's TV buy was unprecedented for a PUC Chair race, even more than Calvin Reynolds' record-setting buy four years earlier.

Ah, Calvin.

Mary still had a photo of Calvin and her at some conference hanging on the wall. Which conference was that anyhow? She admired his confidence and carriage, grinned at his playful smile. How differently things had turned out. A year ago, most people figured Calvin would be sitting here today, as the Republican nominee for Governor. What a year. She made a note to call Calvin's widow, Moira, later.

Mary took a few congratulatory calls. Governor Langley was as gracious as ever and offered to host another gala fundraiser. Gubernatorial nominee Paul Prentice called to suggest a luncheon for the entire Republican ticket the next day, to which she eagerly agreed; she really didn't know some of her ticket-mates very well. Steven Page called to see how she was holding up. She even took a call from the Alaska PUC Chairman who helped get her in hot water in New Orleans.

Reporters called all morning, mostly for her reaction to the Torres' upset. She said nice things about Graciela and offered congratulations, but stuck to the message suggested by Blake: this job is too important for on-the-job training. That line had worked against Blasingame and she planned to use it to hammer Torres, as well.

She rummaged aimlessly through her in-box, but could not focus on a thing. Peggy Briscoe brought in a stack of clips from the morning newspapers; her victory was not played up nearly as much as Shane's or Driscoll's or Torres', but she got some good ink in the suburban press. She called her son.

"Tony. How's the hangover?"

"Aw, mom. Still hurtin'. Great party, though. I thought Republicans were all stiffs," he said. "I am so proud of you. Really. Congratulations."

"Well, I am so proud of you. I never thought you would get so dragged into this thing and I'm really sorry for that. Your ole Mom's in a dirty rotten business."

"No problem. It'll probably enhance my love life."

"Tony, do me a favor and call the travel agent and your father. Book us a flight to Hawaii, maybe for this Friday. Are you available?"

"Poi oh poi, am I ever! Thanks, Mom, you're the best!"

*　　　*　　　*

Thelma Barnett rose before dawn for morning prayers.

She was amazed that she received as many votes as she did. The whole experience was so strange, so raw. Butchie Kaminski's vicious Debate attack and that obscene rap song would haunt her for several years. She doubted she could forgive or forget.

She called Rev. Crandall at sunrise, knowing he too would be finishing his morning prayers.

"Thelma, you did us all proud," he announced. "Seventy-one thousand citizens of this state can't be wrong."

"Reverend, I can't thank you enough for giving me this opportunity to serve in this fashion."

"You were the Lord's voice, Thelma, His pipeline to the people of this state. Don't be disillusioned."

"I am already preparing for the next mission," Thelma said eagerly.

"Well, I am so happy to hear you say that, Thelma, because your experience was such an inspiration. Our message must continue to be delivered through the electoral process, as seamy and unsavory as it may appear, and I need your help on our next chance to do exactly that…a United States Senate race."

"I'll be there for you, Reverend." Thelma said goodbye and decided to get caught up on her sewing. She was so exhausted.

*   *   *

"It was a great run, honey. You couldn't have done anything differently," Consuelo consoled Shawn Petacque. "You can be proud. Your dad would have been proud, you know that, don't you?"

Still groggy, Shawn aimlessly played with the waffles. "Is it my imagination or did our children grow about five inches since I announced?"

The months on the campaign trail had been much harder than he had expected. He had lost 15 pounds, grown even grayer and barely remembered the precious Sunday morning breakfast rituals with Consuelo and the kids. Would his bruised right hand ever recover from clasping so many thousands of other right hands? But he had learned so much. So many ups-and-downs: the River's Edge hearings, muscling Seth Dickerson and Cassandra Phillips out of the race, Piney Blue's shooting and the wave it sparked, the insane "Thelma's Wicked" fiasco, the hot coffee, the orgasmic final surge.

He still couldn't believe Torres pulled it off. Podesta had cruised the whole race, until the very end, and then it should have been Petacque by a nose. What a crazy business. One thing for sure. Next time he would use Graciela's playbook and campaign statewide, not just in Jackson City. Next time.

*   *   *

At 9:00 a.m., Graciela awoke in Billy's arms.

They had witnessed the sunrise a few hours earlier, and she had broken down in exhaustion and disbelief. She looked at him now, sleeping soundly, still faintly smelling of cigar smoke and champagne and sweat. How this man had changed her life. He had swept into her life, into her imagination, back on the cliffs overlooking the river so many months ago and was the catalyst for her rebirth. Even Roberto and Raisa were warming up to him.

She thought about her late mom, back in Mexico, and wept quietly. Billy would have liked her. They both had a gentle, self-effacing humor. She wasn't sure if Billy would have gotten along with her late husband Bobby, or her brother Ernesto, both gunned down on that awful day in El Puente. What strange twists and turns a life can take, she thought.

"Buenos dias, guapa," Billy whispered. "Or should I say, buenos dias, Madam PUC Chairwoman."

"Hey." Graciela rolled over and faced him, their naked bodies touching blissfully. "You would have liked my mom."

"Why the tears, Babe? You won, remember? Or was there a recount and…it's Butchie!"

She laughed through the tears and wiped her nose on the sheet. "I owe you so much. For the hike to the cliffs, for being such a great organizer, for being so patient. Let's get away."

"Ever been to Miami Beach? We could catch a flight tomorrow. Make it a long weekend," Billy said, hopefully. "I know a great little Art Deco hotel right on the beach. Do some dancing, sleeping, eating, drinking, more sleeping?"

"Oh, Guillermo, let's do it."

"You mean, like 'let's do it'?" Billy said as he kissed her and ran his hands over her slim body.

"Yeah. Right now."

*   *   *

After addressing his supporters on Election Night, Sen. Paul Podesta drove back to Mohawk Valley with Emily and Pudge. No one said much. Once the count was final, he called Torres with congratulations. The next morning he slept in. He knew this was the end of the line. He took a few calls, but his heart wasn't in it.

After breakfast at home with Emily, he drove down to the Mohawk County Courthouse and sat in the town square. The same bench he had sat on when he decided to run, nearly a year earlier, and another 30-odd years before that, too. He set the crutches aside and lit a cigarette. The oaks were aflame with autumn colors. Where did the summer go, he wondered. Where did his lead go?

All he could figure was the unions didn't produce, the Hispanics were in a snit over River's Edge, Kaminski siphoned white ethnic votes and the gender thing. Maybe it was not, as Pudge had told him, a "good fit". Maybe an old-fashioned retail politician can't win a modern air war.

"Hey, Senator Podesta! Really sorry about the election," called out a county employee picking up trash over by the Civil War cannons. "You'll get 'em next time, though. I just know it. Can't keep a good man down!"

"Thanks, buddy. Appreciate it. Next time, for sure," Podesta called back.

But Paul knew there would be no next time for this old warrior, this son of a dry goods salesman, this son of Mohawk Valley. A crowd of crows swirled around the square, darkly crying, *"Loss, loss, loss!"*

Paul stepped on the cigarette, closed his eyes and dozed.

*   *   *

"Butchie! Beer for breakfast?" Helen Kaminski scolded him, affectionately.

"Breakfast of champions, Ma," Butchie said, still painfully hung over.

Butchie knew that he would lose this race almost from the beginning and was doing it for Boss Chizz. He never totally understood Czyz' motivation for putting him up to this. Something to do with protecting PUC patronage, seeking revenge against Mraz and getting dissed by Podesta. Maybe just his Last Hurrah. Who knows with the Boss?

Butchie went through the motions, but had lost his desire in the closing weeks. Mike Kula had kept the campaign going. "Butchie," he said, "Let's win one more for the Boss. Let's kick Wally's big Weasel butt from here to eternity." And Kaminski had picked up enough of the white ethnic vote to deprive Podesta and Mraz of victory.

When he called Torres the night before, she graciously thanked him for being such a great opponent. They both knew that without Kaminski's name on the ballot, Podesta would have won easily. She assured Butchie that she would work with him and Czyz to protect whatever jobs they had at the PUC, and asked for his valuable help in November.

This Graciela is okay people, Butchie thought, sucking down another brew. Wonder what's on ESPN?

*   *   *

Nicky Pulver called Royce Blasingame around noon. "Third, you did great. Get some rest and start planning the next race."

"Nicky, this was the most incredible month of my life," Royce gushed. "Do you think the negative stuff went too far, though?"

"Hey, we had to do it. Had to do it. Look, you jumped from a blip on the radar screen to almost forty percent in a couple of months. This is a rough game, bro."

"I got a call from Jimmy Blake already," Blasingame said. "He wants an endorsement for Moore right away."

Man, what a cold vulture, Nicky thought. "Ahh, screw Blake. Let him stew for awhile. You don't owe them squat. Don't forget the red Mercedes."

"Yeah, okay. Thanks again for everything. Couldn't have done it without you."

"You're any consultant's dream candidate, Royce, I mean that. I only hope for your sake you don't get bitter and quit politics. You've got a great future…if you hire ProAction again," Nicky joked.

"Damn, and I was gonna hire Jimmy Blake for my next run," Blasingame joked back. "Keep in touch, Nicky."

*   *   *

Only one candidate wasn't burnt the morning after.

Having the luxury of avoiding the semi-finals, independent Dan Clark came out fresh and swinging. He started out the day with a visit to the State Capitol, where he held a press conference to blast Moore and Torres as "peas in a pod". Voters in November will have a choice between Tweedle-dee and Tweedle-dum, he said. "A party loyalist is a party loyalist and it doesn't matter which party. Two sides of the same coin."

His attack plan was very evident right out of the box. Mary Moore is a tool of the utility companies and Republican insiders, and Graciela Torres is a tool of the Jackson City Democratic Machine and knows little about these complicated issues.

"Professor Clark," asked one reporter, "If you're elected, how could possibly get anything accomplished without the help of the parties?"

"I'd get much more accomplished, Lillian, because I would take my case to the people directly, unfettered, unbought and unbossed," Dan confidently responded. Liz Chinn had briefed him on the reporters likely to be in attendance, complete with photos, sample clips and bios, so he had done his homework.

JJ Springfield jumped up. "Mr. Clark, with all due respect, do you have any other funding sources besides Petra Dresden?"

"My donor base is huge, JJ. I have hundreds and hundreds of people all across this state. Senior citizens. College students. Small business owners. Everyday consumers. That's who my supporters are, not Big City Bosses or Big Utility Lobbyists."

"Aw, c'mon, Dan," JJ said skeptically. "Dresden gave you more than half of your budget so far plus a bogus research grant, and yet you're saying…"

"JJ, I'm saying it's tough, damned tough, for an independent to get elected in this state. I won't deny Ms. Dresden's generosity, and by the way, that research grant was hardly bogus. It's about time a third voice is heard in the General Election," Dan said. His years in the classroom had given him poise and the ability to think on his feet, a quality he suspected neither Torres nor Moore possessed.

"The bottom line—and the question before the voters of our state—is who will be the most effective watchdog to ensure safe and affordable gas, electric, phone and cable service. I will take my case to the voters in every single county."

With that, he and Liz Chinn zoomed to the tiny Capitol Airport, boarded a single-engine plane leased by Dresden and took his act on the road, visiting nine media markets before sunset. It was an impressive opening act.

*   *   *

There is no chaos quite like the chaos in a campaign headquarters the morning after.

Win or lose, any headquarters will be littered with drooping banners, unused brochures, fried chicken boxes, beer cans, computer printouts, maps, phone message slips and broken chairs. Campaign staffers wander in around noon, moving very slowly. The headquarters and war rooms which housed their dreams and ambitions—and maybe their loves and lusts—must be crated up and shut down.

Some campaign staffers will go back to their less exciting government jobs, people like Chemuyil Gardner or Mike Kula. Some of the rented strangers, the itinerant vagabonds like Tina Bishop or Wally Mraz, will land on their feet with another campaign or cause. Those staffers associated with the victors, the Lupe Zarates or Sam Roths or Steven Pages, begin planning the next phase.

But all have the common bond, a shared experience unique to campaigners, and possibly to actors or soldiers, of having gone through a high-speed condensed version of Heaven and Hell together and surviving, and then abruptly scattering to the winds.

*   *   *

DATELINE JJ: ELECTION SPECIAL…Strong showings by GOP Congressman Paul Prentice over Sen. Esther Ruelbach and by Dem Sen. Debra Shane over gazillionaire Lawrence Burl give these two gubernatorial nominees a running start in the two-month sprint to the November General Election. Neither are well-known; Prentice must be considered the early fave, but don't discount Shane's energy and momentum.

Yesterday's Upset Specials: Biggest shockers were conservative activist Philip Driscoll, who beat prosecutor Aviva Benson for the GOP nomination for Attorney General, and Jackson County Commissioner Graciela Torres, who surged past Sen. Paul Podesta and Jackson City Alderman Shawn Petacque to clinch the Dem nod for PUC Chair. Both Driscoll and Torres face uphill fights and must do much fence-mending.

Question: Can Prentice pull together the Elephants or will lingering animosity over his rough treatment of the venerable Ruelbach doom his chances?

*   *   *

"TORRES!" The screaming headline and subhead of "Hoy!" said it all. "VICTORY FOR US ALL!"

Graciela's victory was viewed not merely as politically historic. It was a momentous milestone in the long journey from the streets of San Juan, the fields of Durango, the death squads of Managua. She became an overnight symbol, even more powerful than the reluctant celebrity status she had been assigned the night of the River's Edge explosion.

It was also viewed as something approximating closure on the River's Edge chapter. Anger at Eaton Gas Company and the Jackson City Housing Authority still simmered, but the Torres win reminded the public of what happened to Eva Vargas and the other victims.

The Hispanic community had voted in unprecedented numbers, and Torres had earned a whopping 95 percent of the Hispanic vote, exceeding even what Shawn Petacque had gotten in the African-American wards. Jimmy Juarez was viewed as a king-maker by the older Hispanic politicians and Billy Miller was regarded with awe by his fellow Downstate rebels. But the margin of victory—539 votes out of some 850,000 votes cast—could not be taken lightly by the Torres team. And they knew it.

*   *   *

Mary Moore sized up the team.

She had met Congressman Prentice several times, and although she endorsed Esther Ruelbach in the primary, Mary felt good about Prentice leading the ticket. His Beltway demeanor, movie star looks and perfect white coif made him appear, well, gubernatorial. Esther's loss may have been a blessing in disguise, Mary speculated.

Incumbent Secretary of State Richard Dobbs was also an impressive figure, although his best years were far behind him. The one-time "Boy Mayor" of a small suburban town, Dobbs was a rising star four decades ago, but had risen as far as possible. This would probably be his last race and it was his to lose.

The only other woman on the Republican ticket was State Treasurer nominee Karen Hogan, who had been engineered onto the slate by Gov. Langley. A member of the state Arts Council, she was the daughter of a veteran Capitol lobbyist, and was no stranger to the state's corridors of power. Quick-witted, outgoing and well-funded, Hogan was clearly a rising star.

Mary had never met Attorney General nominee Phil Driscoll, but knew he had caused Langley trouble in the past. A hard-core abortion foe, he had spent three million dollars on a vicious TV attack on slated candidate Aviva Benson, the pro-choice Jackson County prosecutor who had the endorsement of nearly every newspaper in the state. Driscoll seemed smaller in person, Mary thought, as the group gathered around a huge table for their Thursday morning breakfast. His ads had portrayed him as a masculine, almost macho figure. He seemed somewhat frail and wispy, Mary observed as Prentice tapped his water glass.

"Attention, winners. Attention, winners," Prentice said to the beaming ticket-mates and their key staff.

"First, let me offer my heartfelt congratulations to each of you. The Republican Party has chosen a quality team that is diverse—geographically and philosophically." He glanced at Driscoll with a tight smile.

"We may hail from different backgrounds, but I'm convinced we are all headed in the same direction…towards a Republican sweep in November!"

Mary and Karen Hogan realized this was an applause line, so they clapped politely, and were joined by the rest.

"Since we don't all know one another, I'd like each of you to take a minute or so to introduce yourself, and then we will begin outlining our coordinated campaign plan. We all know and love Secretary of State Dobbs, so I'll ask him to start it up."

As they went around the room, Mary felt awed by the talent among her teammates. So many different paths to power, so many strokes of luck, strokes of genius. Why was she here instead of Calvin? Her turn to speak came.

"I'm Mary Moore and I still can't believe I'm in this room with such a high-powered and good-looking group," she said to warm smiles.

"Just one year ago, my mentor, Calvin Reynolds, was killed in a tragic accident. Calvin taught me everything about the Public Utilities Commission and about statewide politics, and I plan to dedicate myself to honoring his legacy in this campaign," she said to mild applause.

"I was weaned in the rough-and-tumble world of Zane Township Republican politics, starting with Barry Goldwater's race in '64. I have an MBA in utility economics and a decade at the Public Utilities Commission, and am honored to have a very patient husband and a very strong son," she paused, measuring the reaction to the mention of Tony. Driscoll didn't blink. "I am so eager to roll up my sleeves and hit the ground running, so let's go!"

"Bravo, Mary!" Prentice practically shouted. This guy's a cheerleader, she thought. We could sure do worse.

After breakfast, Prentice turned it over to Republican State Chair Gretchen Hanson, who announced that the coordinated campaign would be headed by one of Gov. Langley's favorite organizers, Jimmy Blake. Mary's jaw dropped. This was the first she knew of it. Her relationship with Blake had soured in the waning months of the primary, and his animosity to Steven Page had intensified. Why did Langley let this happen?

Almost on cue, Blake walked into the dining room, carrying an armful of charts and files. He glanced a hello to Mary, but quickly began outlining the battle plan for the upcoming two months. The coordinated campaign budget would be $10 million, with each candidate expected to raise assigned amounts. The candidates for State Treasurer and PUC Chair, he calmly stated, would need to each raise a million. Mary and Karen Hogan swapped glances. Blake briskly marched through the plan, which included TV, direct mail and an unprecedented paid phonebank effort.

"Great plan, Jimmy, especially on such short notice. Very comprehensive," Prentice gushed. "Any questions?"

Karen raised her hand. "Jimmy, is there a fundraising component to your plan, or are we all going to be calling the same people asking for cash?"

Blake smirked, the greasy, cocky, smug smirk that Mary had come to loathe.

"You're each on your own. We can expect some support from the Republican National Committee in the form of polling and message development, and Governor Langley will assist in his own way," Jimmy said, looking directly at Mary. "But, this is the price of admission, you all know that."

Philip Driscoll, who hadn't said much, cleared his throat. "Uh, Mr.Blake, does your plan include a coordinated strategy on key issues, abortion, for example?"

"Look. Secretary Dobbs can talk about his terrific record on literacy. Karen Hogan can discuss rates-of-return on state tax dollars. Mary Moore can emphasize her superior grasp of utility economics. If you want to discuss abortion, that's your call," Blake said impatiently. The group all looked at Prentice.

"I think Jimmy's right on that one, Phil. You really can't expect Karen or Mary to be out there campaigning on the choice issue," Prentice gently explained.

"The life issue, Congressman," Driscoll shot back.

"Well, we each need to craft our individual campaigns within the larger framework of the coordinated effort. Let's raise some cash first and issues later," Prentice said jokingly.

"I'd think it would be the other way around, Congressman," Driscoll said. Blake dramatically rolled his eyes.

This could be a long two months, Mary thought.

*   *   *

Democratic Party State Chairman Niles Flint scheduled a conference call for the entire ticket on the afternoon after the election. While Flint had at one time hoped to be a candidate himself on this ticket, it never materialized, so he had to be content with the behind-the-scenes role he had played for six years as Chairman.

The conference call was somewhat awkward, with gubernatorial nomi-nee Debra Shane on a car phone and incumbent Attorney General Lou Calcagno—the only Democratic incumbent on the ticket—calling in from a phone booth in the Bahamas. But the good feelings and sense of cooperation was strong, perhaps the strongest in years, with Langley on his way out and a Republican ticket that seemed fractured.

Flint opened the call with congratulations all around and asked Shane to run the meeting.

"Well, Niles, we have a terrific ticket, and I have my broom ready, because I smell sweep!" Shane was just as much a cheerleader as Prentice. "I want to say how excited I am to be going into battle alongside Attorney General Calcagno, are you there Lou?"

"I am, Senator," Calcagno yelled through static from a Nassau pay phone.

"…and our great candidate for Secretary of State—the Giant Killer himself—Bill Karmejian, and the next State Treasurer, the pride of Hubbs, Representative Tom Cummings, and the first Latina ever on a statewide ticket, Graciela Torres. What a great team."

Several voices chimed in simultaneously, causing Niles Flint to ask for a cease-fire of all this goodwill in order to get down to business.

"People, Senator Shane and I have discussed a general plan of action. Now I know that Lou is in Nassau until next week, Karmejian is going to his piney retreat to, uh, chop wood for a few days and Graciela is off to sunny Florida tomorrow for a long weekend, so let's get together a week from today. Meanwhile, our staffs can meet in my office tomorrow—if their hangovers have cleared—to sketch out a statewide bus tour, a basic fundraising plan, a coordinated scheduling system and so forth. How does that sound to everyone?"

Everyone squawked their assent and the conference call was termi-nated. Graciela called Lupe and asked her to plan on attending the meet-ing in Flint's office with Sam Roth and Jimmy Juarez. She then called her sister, Dolores, to make sure everything was okay for Raisa and 'Berto to stay at her place. She really needed this trip.

*   *   *

"So did Thelma's outing me hurt you politically?" Tony Moore asked his mom as they broiled in the Maui sun. His dad, Randall, was napping nearby.

"No. Maybe helped, actually. Sort of marginalized Thelma as a bigot. There was some unexpected support for me in the gay community because of it. Maybe some gay voters would've gone with Royce."

"Crazy business," Tony said, applying more sunscreen.

"A rotten business. Did it hurt you? Personally, psychologically?"

"Naw. Pissed me off, but that was more for the repercussions on your campaign. The fallout. How'd she get it anyhow?"

Mary had wondered the same. Thelma couldn't afford to do opposition research and probably didn't have ties to the G&L community. She probably had the info fed to her from either the Blasingame or Podesta campaigns, Mary figured. Jimmy Blake said it had Nicky Pulver's fingerprints on it, but Steven Page rightly suspected it came from Podesta's research during the Senate confirmation hearings.

"Either Podesta or Blasingame. Either way it was a real crossing of the line and I felt so bad for you, honey."

"Don't worry about it. I'm the only guy at Club 520 whose mom's a big-shot."

"Well, be careful."

"I will, Mom. You too. Need some sunscreen?"

"No, but another pina colada works. Join me?"

*   *   *

"A bus trip?"

Jimmy Juarez was skeptical already of the "coordinated" campaign. As he, Lupe Zarate and Sam Roth sat at the huge conference room table in

State Democratic Headquarters, representatives from each of the statewide candidates arrived and sized each other up.

It was an odd mix. Debra Shane's energetic Deputy Campaign Manager, Deanna Drew, was there. A team of slick young lawyers represented Attorney General Calcagno and the brother of Secretary of State candidate Bill Karmejian was present. State Treasurer hopeful Rep. Tom Cummings represented himself.

With Chairman Niles Flint presiding, there were introductions and a few election day anecdotes shared. Flint set the agenda.

"First off, we've done a quick-and-dirty analysis of Tuesday. We'll pass these around. I think it shows the need for us to shore up what bases we have Downstate. Our two Downstate candidates, Senator Shane and Representative Cummings here, will no doubt help on that score. We need to keep the Hispanic vote high—thank you very much, Mister Juarez and company—and figure out why the African-American turnout was a little flat.

"We can do certain things more efficiently as a coordinated campaign. The Shane campaign has a terrific scheduling system in place, very state-of-the-art. I'd like to suggest that we funnel information about any and all events through Deanna at Shane's headquarters. A coordinated schedule can help us avoid duplication of our candidates' precious time.

"We can share our polling data. In fact, the state AFL-CIO will pop for the first poll. They'll be in the field next week. You will all get the results, including crosstabs and a walk-through by the pollster."

Anthony Karmejian raised his hand. "Mister Chairman, the Karmejian campaign already has a pollster. On contract."

"Well, you can't have too many snapshots. Information is power, Anthony."

"Niles, will this poll have all of our races listed?" asked one of Calcagno's young suits.

"Yep. Both a head-to-head question—Calcagno versus Driscoll—as well as a blind horserace, y'know, 'Would you vote for an incumbent AG with courtroom experience who fights for seniors or for an inexperienced millionaire who is a right-wing nutcase?' Something like that. Plus the usual issue preference stuff to help us put together a coordinated message.

"Okay, next. The State Party has hired Anna Bloom who's on leave from the Democratic National Committee to set up a coordinated budget and fundraising plan. She's very good. A preliminary report will be ready for the meeting with all the candidates next week. Each of you will of course have your own fundraising operations, but the State Party's plan will complement your own.

"Finally," Flint said pointing to the huge map of the state on the wall behind. "The Bus Tour."

"I just love bus trips," Deanna Drew said somewhat sarcastically.

"I hate 'em," Jimmy Juarez growled.

"Well, the important thing is—besides that Jimmy Juarez doesn't have to go—is that with only 59 days to go, the bus trip is a way to get the ticket out there to every little media market in the Downstate counties. Meet some of our County Chairs and local activists to get 'em fired up. Plus, the ticket can get better acquainted, get on the same page."

"Attorney General Calcagno has a pretty tough schedule when he returns from Nassau, Mr. Chairman," offered one of the slick lawyers.

"It will be a week-long tour, about 50 stops. The Attorney General doesn't have to camp out with us every night, but we are asking each candidate to spend as much time on this project as possible. The State Party and Shane campaign will coordinate advance and media. Each candidate is asked to provide at least one staffer and a vehicle for the caravan. Fun?"

"Fun, Mister Chairman," everyone groaned in unison.

*   *   *

"DATELINE JJ: Item. Disingenuous Dan. Despite claims to this reporter that he isn't reliant on the generosity of one single donor, Independent candidate for PUC Chair Dan Clark has a very thin donor base beyond Petra Dresden and DresPAC. Still, the glib and brainy Clark

will shake up the equation in the PUC contest, and is expected to keep issues like utility campaign contributions, the cost of nuclear power and gas pipeline safety on the front-burners.

"Question. Will Disingenuous Dan get any traction outside of college campuses and editorial writers' cubicles?"

*　　　　*　　　　*

Billy Miller had become an ardent South Beach devotee over the past few years. After his divorce, he had discovered the charms of Art Deco, wide beaches and endless nightlife. Graciela had never been to Florida and was especially interested in visiting the Cuban Calle Ocho neighborhood. Mostly, she was interested in relaxing for the first time in a year or so. Especially with Mr. Billy Miller.

They flew into Fort Lauderdale, rented a car and drove into Miami. It's so green and lush, she thought, so different than Monterrey or El Puente. She hadn't seen palm trees in years and had only seen the Atlantic Ocean once before. They checked into "The Pescador", a run-down, orange-creamsicle Art Deco hotel right on the beach.

"The Pescador has always been might favorite hideaway," Billy said as they pulled up. "Hope it's not too grungy for a statewide candidate."

"The Fisherman. It's perfect," she whispered, leaning over to him a putting her tongue in his ear. The room had a great view, a dank refrigerator and a huge bed. He had arranged for a bottle of champagne and a tray of chilled shrimp and lobster, which they devoured hungrily, licking the cocktail sauce off each other's fingers. Slightly tipsy and still drained from the election, Graciela took a long shower and was joined by Billy. They soaped each other and then made furious love, starting in the shower, continuing on the balcony overlooking the beach and ending in the large lumpy bed.

"Billy."

"Oh, guapa," Billy said, winded from their passion.

"It's been years since I've said this."

"Said what?"

She leaned close to him. "Te amo, corazon," Graciela whispered.

Billy couldn't recall such joy. "I love you, too, Grac."

              *   *   *

Chapter Five

Flood Stage, Part II

The fatal heart attack hit Boss Johnny Czyz out of the blue.

As one might expect, Chizz croaked as he sat at his usual greasy booth in the rear of the dimly-lit Danzig Café. The Warrior went as he came. At the fatal moment, Chizz was engaged in a post-mortem (a pre-mortem post-mortem, it turns out) about the primary results with fellow Ward Poohbahs Jimmy Juarez, Mario Camozzi and Seamus Dunne.

Dunne, the hulking 3rd Ward powerhouse, had initially supported—then ceremoniously dumped—Podesta in the primary. Dunne always sported sunglasses, never wore a necktie and spoke in clipped, cryptic bursts.

Over a cholesterol-packed breakfast plate, Dunne was congratulating Jimmy Juarez on Torres' upset. "This Grashella…evvywhere…even the rurals. Nice, Jimmy."

"Aw, Seamus, thanks a lot," Juarez replied. "Yeh, Forty percent in the boonies. Graciela's a comer, I'm tellin' ya. Easy on these old eyes, too."

On that note, Czyz clutched his chest, turned blue instantly and dove headfirst into a plate of potato pancakes sprinkled with powdered sugar, his favorite.

The maneuvering to replace Czyz as 6ᵗʰ Ward Committeeman (who could replace an institution, a tribal chieftain?) commenced almost before his ancient noggin crashed into the plate.

Of course, Butchie Kaminski was in the succession mix, but his foray into a larger arena was an embarrassment to many locals and he had lost his zeal. Mike Kula knew every inch of the Ward and every precinct captain, but the Piney Blue caper would haunt him. Stan Plucharski, the young attorney at the Public Utilities Commission once considered as a possible successor to Kaminski by Boss Chizz, was the right ethnic and a bright fellow, but unknown outside of his own precinct.

About a dozen veteran precinct captains floated their own names, but Czyz' death was so unexpected that no one was really prepared or positioned for this mortal inevitability. The Mayor's people and a few neighboring ward leaders were taking inventory of Czyz' vast patronage army and sharpening their knives. The pie would certainly be cut up.

*   *   *

The wake was a classic, right out of *"The Last Hurrah"*. Everyone was there. Governor Langley. Mayor Townshend. Four Congressmen. Gubernatorial nominees Prentice and Shane. Hundreds of neighbors, patronage workers and those Johnny had helped out over the past six decades or so. A large 25-year old photo depicted a suave and dapper gentleman. A dirge by Paderewski played over scratchy speakers.

Fresh from Miami Beach, a tanned and relaxed Graciela Torres was escorted by Jimmy Juarez, both resplendent in their mourning attire. As they worked their way up to Czyz' coffin, Torres was struck by the crowd's size and ethnic diversity. She knelt at the coffin. She had met Czyz a few times and always thought he was sort of crabby, not a very nice man. But she appreciated that he was a friend and occasional ally of Jimmy Juarez, and she respected his status and reputation.

She gazed through her mantilla at Czyz' pale, shriveled hands, entwined in a black rosary. A whole lifetime in the rough-and-tumble of politics, shaking thousands of hands and engaged in bare-knuckle brawls with guys like Wally Mraz, and yet his fingers are so tiny and feminine. His fingernails were like those of an infant.

As she crossed herself and rose from the kneeler, Graciela saw that every pol in the room was eyeing her. Seamus Dunne, Alderman Florian LeClerq, State Senator Mario Camozzi, Committeeman Sherm Stumpf, even Butchie Kaminski and Jimmy Juarez couldn't take their eyes off of this petite woman in black who was so obviously a rising star.

She walked directly to Butchie in the back of the parlor. "Alderman, I am so sorry for your loss."

At first, Butchie thought she was referring to the election, which Graciela immediately sensed, adding, "I know how close you were to John."

"Well thanks, Graciela, I 'preciate your comin' tonight," Butchie stammered, his head still spinning over his mentor's unexpected passing. "He taught me a real lot."

Dunne, sans sunglasses, stepped over.

"Commissioner Torres. Before he left, John told us. Rally behind Torres." Dunne draped his huge arm around Graciela's shoulder, as the other chieftains gathered in a circle. "The Party," Seamus intoned, "Takes care of its own, Grashella. Takes care of its young. Solidarity. Lech Walesa. What he stood for."

Hmm, Graciela thought. Is this a pitch for patronage, a sincere pledge of support or just a chance for this old goat to touch my shoulder? But then Juarez locked the boys in. "One of Johnny's last wishes was that we hang together. Fellahs, Graciela is one of us."

*   *   *

Upon her return from Hawaii, a well-rested Mary Moore hit the ground running.

She tore into the work that had piled up at the Public Utilities Commission (being an incumbent is a double-edged sword, Mary thought as she scanned updates on pending water rate cases.) She tackled the growing list of thank-you notes to key donors and volunteers. She reviewed Steven Page's analysis of the Election (major problems in Jackson City, he felt) and scanned the dozens of resumes for campaign jobs sitting in her in-box.

She had lunch with Gov. Langley, who wrote her a check for $150,000 from his own campaign fund. "Hell, I was kinda savin' this for Calvin. I'll never have a need for it," he told her. He also handed her the resume of a possible new campaign manager. Damen Maxwell, some high-powered wiz-kid from Delaware.

"So, Governor, Jimmy Blake will be on the state coordinated campaign payroll?"

"Right. Prentice needs somebody with statewide experience, and somebody who can stand up to Driscoll. Blake'll be looking out for you though. Doctor's orders," Langley smiled.

"How about Steven?"

"Well, we were thinking of bringing him back to the Governor's office, but if you want to keep him on board with you in some capacity that's fine. You should look at this Damen Maxwell kid, though. A real nuts-and-bolts guy. Rising star, I'm told."

Message received, Mary thought.

                    *   *   *

The first meeting of the entire Democratic slate was rocky.

With all candidates and their staff present, Anna Bloom presented her proposed budget. Two million for polling, TV, direct mail and some Election Day operations. Shane, Calcagno and Karmejian would each kick in $150,000 immediately and another $150K each on October 1. Cummings and Torres would get a pass until October 1; then they'd both kick in $100,000. The balance would come from joint fundraising activities, the DNC and the unions.

The first to gripe was Karmejian. First off, he already had a pollster. Secondly, he felt he should be in the second tier with Torres and

Cummings, since Calcagno was the incumbent and Shane was the standard bearer.

Calcagno questioned the viability of joint TV. Jimmy Juarez wanted specifics about the Election Day funds. Cummings said he really needed help with opposition research on Karen Hogan and asked if he could wait until mid-October to ante up. Deanna Drew of the Shane camp asked for a full-time staffer to help her with the coordinated scheduling system and and another full-timer to do advance for events like the bus tour.

"Look, people," Flint pleaded. "We hear on the grapevine the elephants have a ten million dollar budget. Anna's put together a very workable document here. Let me try and address each of your concerns.

"Lou, TV is the way to go here. The Democratic message can help all of us, plus Anna thinks we can get funding from National.

"Jimmy, I know you're a nuts-and-bolts Election Day guy. We'll work very closely with you and other GOTV veterans like…"

He almost said Johnny Czyz, but stopped just in time. "…Camozzi and Seamus Dunne and so-forth to make sure we have a well-oiled Get-Out-The-Vote operation, with plenty of troops.

"Representative Cummings, I don't know what to tell you about the oppo; my hunch is you're on your own there. Does anyone else need oppo?"

Graciela gingerly raised her hand, as did Calcagno.

"I was really expecting to be up against Aviva Benson," Calcagno said.

"And I really wasn't expecting to be here," quipped Graciela to laughter.

"Okay, we'll look into it, but this is really not the kind of thing a coordinated campaign does," Flint said. "We can make some referrals and some suggestions, though.

"And in terms of your delaying your payment until mid-October, I would say this is a carefully crafted budget without much wiggle room. Printers and TV stations need their dough upfront from politicians, you all know that. We'll probably need yours by October 1, Tom. I'm sorry. Better crank up the money machine."

Cummings said nothing.

Flint looked at Karmejian. "And the same would go for your concern, Bill, although an argument can be made for a middle-tier. Let me discuss it with Anna and the Shane and Calcagno brain trusts.

"Okay, and to the suggestion that we put a coordinated campaign funded staffer or two in the Shane scheduling and advance operation, I would say yes, assuming we find someone for under five or six thousand for the next two months."

"Fifty-three days, Mister Chairman," Deanna offered.

"Right. Just fifty-three more days of donkey bliss. Okay, let's discuss the Magical Mystery Bus Tour. First stop, a kick-off rally in Jackson City hosted by Mayor Townshend. Then we saddle up and drive 150 miles to beautiful Merrimac, home of the next Governor, for an old-fashioned pig-roast..."

*   *   *

Damen Maxwell had an impressive resume for someone just 27 years old.

The Delaware native had managed an unsuccessful U.S. Senate race in Idaho and a successful long-shot U.S. House race in Alaska. He had maneuvered into the inner circle of a nearly-successful vice-presidential bid. He was the banking industry's lead lobbyist on their effort to rescind the Community Reinvestment Act. He was working on his Master's Degree in his spare time and jogged ten miles daily.

Wiry, intense and tight-lipped, Maxwell had met Gov. Langley at the Conference of Governors last year and the two hit it off. Langley thought he would be perfect for Mary's race. Not as confrontational and contentious as Blake, yet with a better, big-picture grasp of campaigning than Page.

Maxwell's resume showed his experience with fundraising, polling, direct mail, TV, issues, field operations and GOTV. He was named "Rookie of the Year" by *"Modern Campaigns"* magazine after the Alaska race. He had been an all-conference cross-country runner at Princeton, where he graduated cum laude.

"I need $10,000 a month, plus moving expenses and a place to stay. I need a car, a cell phone and a laptop. I need two personal staff, one administrative and one political. I do all hiring and firing," Maxwell cooly informed a flabbergasted Mary Moore and Steven Page.

"Well, Damen," Mary slowly replied. "You certainly have an impressive background, but $10,000 a month is, uh, a little out of my range."

"Fine. You lose. I happen to know that Governor Langley has very recently infused your kitty. You can't afford not to bring me in. Time's a-wastin'."

Steven had an immediate dislike for this brash punk. Was I this cocky when I was 27, he wondered. "We're not a U.S. Senate campaign..." Steven started to say.

"And you never will be if you think small," Maxwell cut in. "Although I know the Govenor has high hopes for you, Mary, in two years."

"...and our budget is maybe $800,000..."

"I can make sure your budget is double that," Maxwell asserted confidently. "So let me say it again, slowly. Ten thousand a month, moving expenses, apartment. Car, cell, laptop..."

"Damen, let me talk it over with a few of my people and call you tomorrow," Mary interrupted.

"I'm booked on a 7:30 p.m. flight back to Dover tonight. Here's my pager number. Let me know in three hours or just forget it." He smiled, gathered his materials and walked out.

"Patronizing jerk," Steven murmured.

"I agree," Mary said. "But the Governor is so very high on him."

"Almost makes Blake seem personable." The two had a good laugh.

*   *   *

The Torres team needed some expansion and fine-tuning, too.

Graciela's loyalty to Sam, Jimmy and Lupe was unwavering. They got her here. But the team was moving into a larger, tougher arena. The

National Hispanic Women's Alliance had offered to pay for a campaign manager. By agreeing to their offer, Graciela would lock in their commitment to her race. But would her inner circle feel slighted? Would a new person run roughshod over her loyal friends who had sacrificed so much?

When Sandra Siquieros flew in for an interview, it was love at first sight. For everyone.

Siquieros didn't have the pedigree or electoral experience that Damen Maxwell brought to the Moore campaign, but she had been around the block. About the same age as Graciela, Sandra's family was from Saltillo, Mexico, not far from the Torres family roots. She came up through the ranks doing voter registration in Texas, union organizing in California and electoral politics in New Mexico. She was a rising star in national Hispanic politics and had earned a reputation as a diligent, 100-hour a week worker.

She met first with Graciela and Lupe, and they hit it off famously. Then Jimmy, Sam and Billy broke bread with Sandra, who assured Jimmy she would not step on his toes on field operations, and the deal was done. She would start in three days.

With a projected budget of a half-million, Graciela knew she needed to hire a fundraiser. Lupe would continue to oversee scheduling and media. Sam would run the suburban field operation and the issues team. Billy and Jimmy would be responsible for the Downstate and Jackson City field ops, respectively, and both would continue to liaison with the Party establishment.

With Sandra's union credentials, her first order of business would be to set up getting-to-know-you meetings for Graciela with all of the major unions. She would run an aggressive voter registration drive and supervise the growing staff in Headquarters.

This team was going to be just fine, Graciela thought.

*   *   *

Since he had no primary contest, Dan Clark was well-rested and ready. He was still sitting on a pile of Petra Dresden's cash and had a bankroll of

$60,000. He had earned rave reviews for his fly-around. His first poll would be done in a week.

Liz Chinn was doing a masterful job of volunteer recruitment. Her campus outreach effort was successful beyond expectations, and she set up an intern program with 40 college and high school students who brought energy and zeal to the Headquarters. Her Dresden network was operating at full throttle, and veterans of Petra's many projects and causes were volunteering for field, issues and fundraising activities.

The lights burned late into the night at Clark's storefront Headquarters in the hip Flagstaff neighborhood. Dozens of volunteers and $10 donations came in every day via his website, which immediately exceeded the lackluster efforts by Moore and Torres to take their campaigns cyber.

Clark realized he wasn't as battle-tested as Torres nor as scrutinized as Moore, but he was confident in his superior grasp of the issues and in his strategy. He would go after Moore first, battering her as a tool of the utilities and blaming her beloved mentor Calvin Reynolds for the River's Edge tragedy. He would establish himself as the consumer advocate, then turn his guns on Torres as an inexperienced party loyalist.

"You know it's gonna be tricky getting into River's Edge without invoking the image of Saint Graciela de El Puente," Manny Ruiz cautioned Dan.

But Clark felt he could keep the focus on Eaton Gas and the Republicans' cozy relationship with the industry. He hijacked material from the old Shawn Petacque website, inheriting many of the wacky conspiracy theorists who lived in Shawn's site. He knew he only had about seven weeks to re-heat the issue, ride it, and then go after Saint Graciela.

*   *   *

Things were gradually returning to normal in Ald. Shawn Petacque's Ward Office.

After a week of sleeping, mourning, analyzing and feeling inadequate, Shawn returned to his aldermanic rhythm and Chemuyil resumed her

Chief of-Staff duties. They were back to handling constituent complaints about broken sidewalks and unleashed dogs in the park. They both missed the excitement of the campaign trail—the zeal of the Kiddie Corps, the intensity of the street heat—and were a little jealous of all the fun Graciela and Lupe and the rest of her team must be having now.

Chemuyil was eating a bowl of soup at her Ward Office desk when the receptionist buzzed her to announce a visitor. "A Mister Arnold Wiser to see you."

"Roz, I'm having lunch. He doesn't have an appointment and I don't recognize the name. Take a message, please, or ask him to come back later."

Roz buzzed back. "He apologizes for not making an appointment. He says you may know him as 'Mountain Referee'. Does that make sense?"

*   *   *

Mayor Townshend's rally to launch the Democrats' statewide bus tour was a rain-soaked bust. Gale-like winds and poor planning by the Mayor's people resulted in an embarrassing kick-off of their Victory Tour. The TV coverage would not be kind tonight.

Then the ventilation on the bus malfunctioned and part of the eight-vehicle caravan got lost in traffic leaving Jackson City. Attorney General Lou Calcagno was angry with Chairman Niles Flint over something and was a no-show. Flooding slowed their trip to Bill Karmejian's suburban Headquarters for another disastrous rally. They were already an hour behind and the planned six-day trip was only three hours old.

As the bus left exurbia heading for Shane's hometown in Downstate Merrimac, the rain subsided and the sun suddenly burst through the clouds. "A good omen," Sen. Debra Shane yelled out to her ticket-mates on the bus. "The sun always shines on Democrats," Karmejian yelled back. The tension of the morning gradually eased and the team began to get better acquainted.

"So, how do you like campaigning Downstate?" Shane asked, as she sat down between Graciela and Sandra Siquieros, who was on her second day as the Torres Campaign Manager.

"It's a big state. I really had no idea," Graciela laughed. "Pig roasts, fish boils, county fairs, deer. Nothing like this in Jackson County."

"This area reminds me of California's vegetable fields," Sandra said, as they zoomed through the harvested cornfields. "Flat. Endless horizons."

"Oh, you'll like our politics here, Sandra," Debra said. "Very complex, very diverse. A real cast of characters, some of whom you can see already on this bus tour."

"Some of whom I've already seen in Graciela's campaign," Sandra smiled.

"So, tell me about your team, Graciela," Shane settled in and offered the women some popcorn.

"Well, you know Jimmy Juarez, of course. He's been my mentor and teacher, my patron saint really, ever since my husband and brother were murdered."

"I am so sorry," Shane said.

"Oh, thank you, but that was a long time ago. Anyhow, Jimmy knows the Hispanic political landscape as well as anyone. Got me onto the County Board. Watches my back. He's our GOTV expert, too.

"And Lupe Zarate. What a gem! She was a reporter on the Spanish-language TV station, and then joined my staff at County. Knows the media, is a great writer. We're still learning how to do high-tech scheduling and advance."

"That's an art and a science," Siquieros jumped in.

"Definitely. And Sam Roth, our Boy Genius. Ran the suburban outreach effort, set up our computer system, does all of our issues stuff, questionnaires and so forth. His dad is my biggest donor and a real sweetheart, too. He was the employer of Mariano Vargas, who lost his wife and two daughters at River's Edge."

"Oh, right, I remember reading about him," Debra said, offering more popcorn. "And Mariano is a volunteer on your campaign, too?"

"Yep, in fact he's driving right behind us in one of the caravan vehicles."

"Hope he like's a good pig roast," Shane said. "And speaking of Downstate, what about this secret weapon of yours? My colleague on the State Central Committee? The Sauk County Democratic Chairman?" Shane grinned.

Graciela blushed. "He was a real find." Over the noisy ventilation fans, she described to Shane and Siquieros how she wrote personal notes to every Downstate Party Chairman who wasn't on board with Podesta. The successful visit to Sauk County. The epiphany trek to the bluffs overlooking the river.

"He has this poetic, yet down-home way of explaining things, of analyzing politics. And he came up with the soccer-mom strategy that is the reason I'm sitting here instead of Paul Podesta."

"My Senate colleague who would not have been a fun guy on a week-long bus trip," Shane explained to Siquieros. She turned back to Graciela. "So, I hear you and Chairman Miller are..." She winked.

"Why, Governor Shane! Mixing politics with pleasure? Me? I am so shocked!"

The three women had a good laugh and ate more popcorn.

*   *   *

Once the housing, car and cell phone issues were worked out, Damen Maxwell moved to Jackson City and began a thorough shake-up of Moore's entire operation. He fired all of her field staff and gave her fundraising staff a week to turn things around. He personally took over the media operation and managed to immediately annoy every political reporter in town.

One of Damen Maxwell's first phonecalls was to Royce Blasingame, who had just returned from a week in the Virgin Islands.

"The reason I'm calling is that Mary Moore needs your explicit and enthusiastic endorsement, Royce. Explicit and enthusiastic."

"What happened to Jimmy Blake?"

"He's at Coordinated Campaign. Steven Page is going back to the Governor's staff. I'm in charge here. So, how 'bout it, Blasingame. Can we count on you?"

"Well, I'm not sure I'm quite ready for a formal announcement of my support..."

"I had breakfast with Governor Langley yesterday," Maxwell casually mentioned. "He said you ran a terrific race and might be looking at a Congressional seat."

"Well, that was very kind of Governor Lang..."

"Yeah, well, you can forget it if you don't come out for Mary Moore. ASAP. Explicit and enthusiastic. I'll call back in two days." Maxwell abruptly hung up.

What a jerk, Royce thought. Worse than Blake, if that's possible.

Royce called Nicky Pulver at ProAction and shared the Maxwell threat.

Within two hours, the complete opposition report on Mary Moore was hand-delivered to Sam Roth at the Torres Headquarters.

*   *   *

"DATELINE JJ: Day Three of the Democrats Statewide Lollapalooza. No homicides or defections to report yet. After a sloppy start Monday in Jackson City, the tour has regrouped and is now wowing large crowds in small towns across the state.

"Question: Where is Attorney General Lou Calcagno? Rift rumors are rife.

"Question: Can anyone name the youthful campaign operative who is well-known to political insiders as the arrogant kid whose hardball tactics probably cost his boss a U.S. Senate seat in Idaho? Answer: Damen Maxwell, who just took over the Mary Moore PUC campaign. Expect the worse."

*   *   *

"Damen, this is not the kind of press we were hoping to get with the announcement of your hiring," Mary told an impatient Maxwell.

"Hey, this guy Springfield is a small-timer. Strictly second-rate. I really wouldn't worry about it, Mary."

"Well you wouldn't because you're headed back to Delaware when the Election's over. Some of us have to stay here and deal with JJ," Mary gently explained. "Besides, he's regarded as an institution."

"So's Playboy Magazine. Doesn't mean we should all buy it. Look, my style can rub people wrong, but you want results? I'll get them for you. We've already raised more than $50,000 from out-of-state sources—all of them my personal contacts—that your previous team couldn't touch. I'm talking with a friend of mine at *"Modern Campaigns"* magazine about a profile of your primary victory. We'll get you past the finish line without stepping on too many toes...of people that matter."

Mary was already missing Steven Page and even Blake.

*   *   *

Billy Miller connected with the Dems Bus Tour as it swung through his area, although he skipped the rally graciously organized by Podesta in the Mohawk Valley town square, site of so many Podesta events.

The ticketmates (except Calcagno) had become one big happy family on the bus trip. The advance work being done from Shane's office was superb, with enthusiastic crowds holding each of the candidates' signs (except Calcagno's). And after giving the same stump speech ten times each day, not only were the candidates' oratorical skills improving greatly, but they all knew the punchlines of each other's stock jokes and everyone's closing lines.

As Graciela and Billy held each other in her room at the Dakota Lake Holiday Inn, he told her about the unsolicited gift from Blasingame and Pulver. Sam had already briefed him on new details about the Moore fundraising apparatus, her taxpayer-funded graduate education, juicy details on a few junkets and her husband's shady stock dealings.

Several pages about her son Tony's nightclub habits were graphically described, too.

"Well, I don't think we want to go there," Graciela said about Tony. "How about the husband's stock?"

"I think that's fair game. They have a beautiful house with a lagoon-sized swimming pool out in Zane Township. Did that come from his ill-gotten gains? Besides, who knows what they're digging up on you as we speak," Billy joshed. "All your dark secrets…"

"Don't! You're scaring me. Making me all paranoid!" Graciela said as she playfully put her head under the covers and began biting Billy's chest.

*   *   *

Chemuyil Gardner connected Arnold Wiser with Darlene Dawes at Channel 14 TV. After all, Dawes was the first reporter on the scene at River's Edge and had inadvertently propelled the blast and Graciela Torres into national consciousness, even if for only a few days. Chem recognized that Wiser's willingness to blow the whistle on Eaton was an act of courage, one that carried significant political consequences.

Many people had felt that responsibility for the River's Edge tragedy was never really assigned. The various investigations pointed fingers and everyone knew that Eaton Gas may have been negligent, but proof and punishment never came.

Until Arnold Wiser tucked his little girl in bed one night and decided to go public with his secrets.

When he approached Chemuyil Gardner with his intentions, she saw this as an opportunity for Graciela to re-ignite the issue during the final month of the campaign. Chem contacted Lupe Zarate, who agreed to find Arnold an engineering job in the Jackson County Harbor Authority.

Darlene Dawes knew this was a potential bombshell and the station began promoting it a few days before it aired. The interview was dramatic. With his face in silhouette and his voice digitally altered, Arnold told all in a 90-minute interview with Darlene. It was edited into three ten-minute segments, one of which was picked up by network TV.

Wiser mentioned for the first time the fact that Eaton's "Go-Team" had jumped immediately into the smoking chamber he had just been pulled from and that he assumed they had confiscated the valve. Eaton steadfastly held that the valve was destroyed in the explosion. Vaporized.

He described the intense pressure placed on him to fudge his story by Eaton's attorneys, investigators and even Vice-President Stan Flanders in the days after the blast. He detailed the well-known codeine dependency problem of Inspector Qualls and the little-known role Qualls played in another blast caused by an improperly sealed valve.

He explained the company's procedures for tracking minute traces of gas leakage and provided logs he had surreptitiously copied showing that Eaton had the data showing a leak at River's Edge, but had ignored it. And Eaton's corporate attitude about its many Spanish-speaking customers bordered on racism, Wiser alleged.

But the most dramatic moment came when Darlene Dawes asked Wiser point blank, "What did Eaton management know and when did they know it?"

Wiser slowly, almost reluctantly, pulled from his briefcase several 8x10 photos of a mangled device of some sort.

"This is the missing valve, the only tangible proof of Eaton's negligence. Despite Eaton's claims that this valve was destroyed in the blast, here it is. It can be found in the Eaton Gas Headquarters in a storage closet next to the office of Vice-President Stan Flanders."

Wiser paused.

"What did he—Vice-President Stan Flanders—know? Everything. When did he know it? From the very start, I believe. He quarterbacked it."

The suggestion that the cover-up began immediately after the blast was huge news. Every paper in the state ran the story, as did some national media. *Newsweek* re-ran the classic photograph of Graciela and

Paco Rivera. The U.S. Attorney hinted at a new probe. Eaton refused comment.

*   *   *

The Eaton Gas cover-up continued to be front-page news for a solid week, and while Torres' dramatic photo was burned into the public consciousness, Dan Clark clearly had the best grasp of what exactly went wrong.

Clark used the League of Women Voters Candidates' Forum as an opportunity to launch into Moore. While not covered by TV, every print reporter jotted down Clark's unrelenting attacks.

"Calvin Reynolds? Mary Moore's self-described mentor? Either he was asleep at the switch or just plain looking the other way while his golfing buddies like Eaton Vice-President for Cover-ups Stan Flanders let River's Edge happen!"

And, "Mary Moore has accepted tens of thousands of dollars in campaign cash from the big utility companies. Maybe even more. Not just the electric company or the water company or the phone company, but from Eaton Gas Company. Then, she presided over an inept investigation into the River's Edge explosion that basically let Eaton off the hook. This is blood money dripping from your hands, Chairperson Moore!"

And, "The industry she is supposed to regulate has sent Mary Moore on fancy junkets and has paid her thousands of dollars in fake honorarium. The fox is not only watching the chicken coop, but the chickens are payin' for it!"

Mary was so unprepared for the incessant attack that she failed to hit back and suddenly the front-runner was on the run.

*   *   *

The crew at Clark Headquarters went crazy when they read JJ Springfield's morning update.

"DATELINE JJ: The first post-primary tracking poll in the PUC race shows strong moves being made by Independent Dan Clark. Following the bombshell revelations by an Eaton Gas whistleblower that Eaton big-wigs knew all along, and Clark's ferocious attacks on incumbent Mary Moore at the Leaky Women Voters' forum, the numbers show serious volatility. (Source: Argo Dispatch, Margin-of-error +/-4%.)

Mary Moore	*31%*
Graciela Torres	*26%*
Dan Clark	*10%*
Undecided	*33%*

"Question: Can 'Disingenuous Dan' cripple Moore enough to allow Torres to waltz in?

"Question: Will internal friction within both Democratic and Republican statewide tickets have any damaging fall-out on their respective PUC candidates?"

*   *   *

Gov. Langley knew the tension between Congressman Paul Prentice and Phil Driscoll had indeed escalated, and was becoming increasingly public.

The GOP's nominees for Governor and Attorney General had spatted since Day One, and Jimmy Blake's take-no-prisoners approach had been only exacerbating matters. It wasn't even about issues, although their strife became most evident during policy discussions. It was more a matter of style, with Prentice having played the cautious, Beltway insider game his entire career and Driscoll having been an outsider, an agitator for his entire career.

Part of the problem was Driscoll's decision to shun the coordinated campaign battle plan Blake put forward. He didn't need the Party's money; he had his own. He certainly had his own issues agenda which was much further in right field than the rest of the ticket. And since he was running against the only Democratic incumbent—Atty. Gen. Lou Calcagno—he felt he faced more of an uphill battle, so an unorthodox approach was needed.

Bringing Rev. B.J. Crandall into the Driscoll campaign brain trust didn't exactly endear him to Mary Moore, either.

*   *   *

"Welcome to Sunday Morning Roundtable. This is Ronna Richards. Today, we'll hear from the two candidates for State Treasurer and the three candidates for Chairperson of the State Public Utilities Commission, and I say three candidates, because we have an Independent candidate who will join the Republican and Democratic candidates on the November ballot. After a quick break, we'll hear first from the Public Utilities candidates."

Moore, Torres and Clark sat awkwardly on oversized sofas in the faux living room. A round oak table and potted plants gave the studio a homey feel. Richards shuffled through some notes and sipped water from a coffee mug. No one spoke for sixty seconds.

"We're back on the Sunday Morning Roundtable with three candidates who hope to oversee the regulation of the state's phone, electric, cable, gas and water systems. We have Jackson County Board member Graciela Torres, of Jackson City's El Puerto neighborhood…"

"El Puente," Graciela gently corrected.

"El Puente, excuse me. And we have the incumbent Chairperson, Mary Moore of suburban Zane Terrace and Professor Daniel Clark, who teaches at Flagstaff Community College here in Jackson City. Welcome all. Let me ask each of you to share your single most important priority as head of the Public Utilities Commission, also known as the 'PUC'. And please, since we have only twelve minutes in this segment, give it to us in a single sentence. Chairperson Moore?"

"One single sentence. Whew!" laughed Moore.

"Is that your one sentence, Mary?" Clark joshed.

"Oh, no, Professor." Damen Maxwell had prepped Mary to address Clark as "professor" at every opportunity. How can an egghead run a huge state agency?

"Well, Ronna, in my many years of experience at the Public Utilities Commission, I'd say my priority has been to provide safe, reliable and affordable utility service to every resident of our state," Mary said earnestly.

"Okay, safe, reliable and affordable service. Sounds pretty good, doesn't it Commissioner Torres?" Host Ronna Richards clearly wanted to move this along at a brisk pace.

"Well, Ronna, who on earth could argue with that? But let's think about the thousands of people who had their heat shut off last winter, or the senior citizen who can no longer afford phone service. Or…"

Richards jumped in. "So you would make a higher priority of guaranteeing utility service to everyone? Agree with that Mister Clark?"

"This all sounds real nice, but until the big utilities and the big political machines are curbed, they'll continue to call the shots. An independent voice cannot be heard," Clark said. He had terrific camera presence considering he was the only non-politician. Then he zinged in with, "The PUC chairperson should accept no campaign cash from utility companies, like my opponent, Mary Moore, who has taken tens of thousands of dollars, maybe more…"

Damen had counseled Mary to hit back and not sit there "like a punching bag" as she did at the League of Women Voters' forum. She reached over and put her hand on Clark's knee. "Well as long as we're on the topic, Professor, what is your source of funding? Doesn't more than half of your campaign war chest come from one single millionaire?"

Richards called truce. "Okay, okay. Hold your fire. It's Sunday morning. Let me ask each of you this. What prepares you for this important job? What regulatory or utility experience do each of you have?"

Moore outlined her years at the PUC and her Master's Degree in the economics of utility deregulation. Clark described his fight for safer electric transmission lines. Torres touted her grasp of water reclamation and delivery systems.

"The thing is, Ronna, utility technology is increasingly sophisticated. And with all due respect to Miss Torres, nuclear technology is just not the same as making sure the sewers are flowing," Moore sniped.

Graciela understood the jibe. "Well I beg your pardon, but I am self-taught in the very complex field of water reclamation. I didn't go to graduate school at taxpayer expense like Mrs. Moore here." She finally had a chance to use some of the oppo research material ProAction had dug up.

Clark, enjoying the feisty exchange, jumped in. "Ronna, it's not so much the level of formal education the voters are looking for, it's the character, the background. The fact is that one of my opponents is a tool of Big Utilities, and the other is a tool of a Big City Machine. I will be a tool of the consumers, the People."

"And I am a tool of commercial TV," Richards cut in. "So, let's take a break, and we'll be right back on Sunday Morning Roundtable with our candidates for Public Utilities Commission Chairperson."

After everyone sat stone-silent for another 60 seconds, Ronna Richards resumed. "The big utility story, of course, is the tragedy at River's Edge. Your thoughts?"

Clark spoke first. "You could blame the overcrowding and faulty sprinklers on the Housing Authority or you could point the finger at the gas company for the lack of Spanish-speaking operators and the mysterious valve, but the real blame is much deeper, more profound. The current rotten system of..."

Moore interrupted him. "Professor, it must be easy to sit in a classroom and spin your little theories, but we at the Public Utilities Commission conducted a thorough probe, brought in experts, asked some tough questions..."

Torres interrupted her. "Your investigation let the gas company off the hook! Eaton Gas was clearly to blame and they were extremely uncooperative to the Mayor's Blue Ribbon Commission, of which I was a member.

Now, Alderman Shawn Petacque has proof that Eaton was aware of the leaking valve 36 hours before…"

Clark interrupted her. "Miss Torres, your Blue Ribbon investigation went nowhere and the same goes for the PUC investigation headed by the incumbent here. Window dressing. Nothing substantial came out of either probe. Because this current rotten system of…"

Richards interrupted him. "Okay, Professor, I'm told we are just about out of time here. One last quickie question for each of you—sort of a personal question—and no sniping please. How much do you pay in utility bills in your household? Say in the month of August. Commissioner Torres?"

"Whoa. Excellent question, Ronna. Let's see. Maybe $125 for electric, I have a teenager and a pre-teen who let the AC run while they play video games. Another $30 for gas, much higher in winter, of course. The phone bills are killing us. Maybe $150, $175 for phones. Another $30 for water. We don't have cable. I know. It's barbaric. Total in the Torres household, $350, maybe $400 total."

"Okay. That's a good breakdown. Professor Clark?"

"Well, I live alone, no kids, no cable. Maybe $150 a month. Total. Which is still way too much."

"Ah, the advantages of living alone. Chairperson Moore? Your household?"

"Well, our water bills are much, much higher in the suburbs. And my home does have cable; my husband loves MSNBC. I'd say about $400 a month."

"Okay, that sounds about right. In the Richards household, we spend about $300 a month on utilities, which I'm told is pretty close to the statewide average.

"Well, since we're talking about money, let's take a commercial break and then we'll hear from the candidates for State Treasurer, State Representative Tom Cummings and Arts Council member Karen Hogan. And let me thank our candidates for the Public Utilities Commission— Democrat Graciela Torres, Independent Dan Clark and Republican Mary

Moore—for this lively Sunday Morning Roundtable discussion. We'll be right back."

Petra Dresden smiled as she watched the show on a portable TV in her gazebo. Clark held his own, made his points. Time to write another check, she thought.

*   *   *

While the Clark campaign did indeed rely heavily on DresPAC, the fundraising efforts for both the Moore and Torres campaigns were more diversified and had picked up considerably.

Despite all his bluster and arrogance (or maybe because of it), Damen Maxwell did produce. His national connections were impressive, and Moore raised $60,000 in just one trip to New York City. Pro-industry PAC money poured into her coffers. The old Calvin Reynolds fundraising donor base proved lucrative.

In the Torres camp, Sandra Siquieros recruited a savvy fundraising expert she knew from New Mexico who tapped into a national network of big money Hispanic leaders in a way Lupe and Sam could only dream of. Big Labor was starting to write Big Checks. And after *Newsweek* ran the River's Edge photo again with a thumbnail analysis of the race, contributions from Democratic women flowed in from around the country.

A month before E-Day, the State Elections Board made public the latest campaign disclosure reports on its website:

"State Public Utilities Commission Chairperson:

Candidate/Party	Raised/Loans	Spent	Cash-on-Hand (Sept. 20)
Moore–R	$1,601,724	$1,181,656	$472,113
Torres–D	$ 630,803	$ 333,052	$317,983
Clark–I	$ 302,110	$ 217,090	$ 85,020

Serious air wars were about to begin.

*   *   *

Chapter Five

Flood Stage, Part III

Dan Clark was in the campaign headquarters "war room" with Manny Ruiz discussing the encouraging poll results they had just received when the receptionist up front rang him. "Mister Candidate. Line three. It's your friend, Shelly."

"Uh, I don't know anyone named Shelly. Can you take a message?"

"She said it's very important. You know her from the big snowstorm, she says."

Still not sure who was on the line, Dan picked up.

"Hey, Professor, this is Shelly Baldini. Remember me?" Clark hated when people played games like that. Her voice was familiar, though. Maybe a former student?

"I'm going pretty crazy on the campaign trail here, uh, Shelly. Refresh my memory, if you would."

"Our happy snowstorm. You and me and Manny and my roomie. You were so good that night. My feelings were hurt that you never called me again."

Dan stopped dead in his tracks. The coke-and-rum party girl. He had actually thought about calling her, but the campaign had kicked in soon after their night of screaming ecstasy, and he had forgotten about it and her.

"Shelly. Wow. How are you? Geez, I, uh, meant to call. We had such a great time." It was rare for Dan to be at a loss for words. Manny looked up from the computer. He knew immediately.

"Well, it doesn't matter, besides I started dating someone my own age, anyhow."

Ouch, that hurts, Dan thought. Why is she calling?

"Oh, well that's great, Shelly. Great. Hope it's working out okay."

"Whatever," she said, sounding very young to Dan. "Hey, I see you on TV a lot these days. That millionaire lady must really like you. Anyhow, I was actually calling 'cuz Donna and I were a little upset that you and your homie Manny stiffed us on those little packets of white stuff."

He was silent. He had totally forgotten that he and Manny had agreed to pay them the balance due on the coke. Let her make the next move. Is this conversation being taped?

"So now the price has gone up a little due to 'late payment fees'," Shelly said. "Five thousand bucks."

"What! Are you crazy? That's extortion!" Dan screamed.

"Whatever. Anyhow, I'm in a jam here and need some cash and I just know you don't want me blabbing to reporters about our little party. Right? How's your friend Manny, anyhow? Maybe he can meet me tomorrow night back at the bar where we met in Flagstaff and started up our memorable romance," Shelly oozed innocence and evil simultaneously.

"And tell him to bring me something."

*   *   *

"The thing about extortion is that it's never over and done with," Manny said. "They'll keep on coming back for more."

"Just like snorting coke," Dan said ruefully.

"Right. So we could pay her the full amount and hope she doesn't come back, pay her something and hope she's satisfied, call her bluff or just kill her."

"Great options there, Ruiz. First, where the hell can I rustle up $5K? Not an option. Second, if I call her bluff and she blabs, not only is the campaign over, but maybe Manny and Danny go to the canny.

"So let's just 'off' her?" Manny joked.

"Man, why didn't we just blow them off in the bar? Damn, damn, damn." Clark pounded his fist against his head.

"Cuz we were horny and buzzed, and they were hot and ripe?" Manny offered. "How would you explain this to Petra and Liz, and all the Clark Crew?"

"Lemme agonize on this tonight," Dan said. "You're available to meet her at the bar tomorrow?"

"Yeah, maybe I'll see if she wants to go back to her place to par-tay."

"Damn. Thanks, Man."

*   *   *

Every TV station in the state led with the story.

"In a stunning political development, Dan Clark, the independent candidate for state Public Utilities Commission Chairman, has dropped out of the race, just days before the deadline for doing so," blared Phoebe Jacobsen on Channel Six. "Professor Clark had been surging in the polls recently and was trying to become the first independent statewide elected officer in our state's history."

Tape of Clark at his press conference. "I have decided, after much consideration, to remove my name from the ballot. This campaign was intended to make the point that ballot signature requirements are unfair to independent candidates in this state and that the big utility companies have an inordinate voice in the electoral process. We believe we have made those points loud and clear.

"That is why I will endorse Jackson County Commissioner Graciela Torres for this position and will do everything in my power to help a dedicated consumer advocate like Ms. Torres get elected."

Photo of Torres. Voiceover by Jacobsen. "Most of Clark's hundreds of student volunteers are expected to help the Torres campaign, Clark said today. No reaction yet from Republican candidate, incumbent Mary Moore."

       *   *   *

"Doesn't mean much," Damen Maxwell assured Moore. "I had the professor pegged at four, maybe six points tops. Hell, half his base is stoned-out college kids who wouldn't remember to come out anyhow."

"Still, Damen, we need to go after whatever base he had. The liberals in Jackson City. Young people. Maybe we should do a college campus tour," Mary said nervously.

"If it makes you feel better, then go, but I'd rather see you dialing for dollars than campaigning for scholars," Maxwell said, always pleased when he could make a point and a rhyme at the same time. Mary hung up and immediately asked her scheduling staff to put together a quick tour of the state's major schools.

       *   *   *

When Manny met with Shelly Baldini, it was not cordial as their first encounter.

First, he tried to talk her out of the whole thing. Shelly explained that she had run up some gambling debts and needed the $5,000 or else. Manny tried some hardball, declaring their intent to call her a coke-snorting liar who was trying to extort a highly-regarded academic. She called his bluff, but quickly came down in her demands to $2,500. The conversation went nowhere. Manny excused himself and called Clark, who authorized the Bail-out Solution. Pay her $1,000 and then Dan would drop out to prevent embarrassment of Petra, which Manny then did.

Petra slapped Dan in the face when he explained it to her. She had already sunk more than $100,000 into the race and had given up Liz Chinn for several months. Manny tried to spin it the way that Dan would at his press conference: we made the points we had set out to, and, if we can't win, we don't want to cost Torres the election. Petra agreed to keep the reasons for his bailing out quiet, even from Liz.

*   *   *

Prior to the press conference, Manny drove to the Torres campaign headquarters and met with Torres, Sandra Siquieros and Jimmy Juarez. He explained that their polling showed no chance for Clark and that Dan didn't want to hurt Graciela.

"Professor Clark is willing to drop out, but has a few conditions," Manny told the group.

"Yeah? Like what conditions?" Juarez asked, puffing heartily on a foot-long stogie. He had doubts about this. Like Damen Maxwell, he had never figured Clark for more than five points.

"First, he'd be very interested in helping your administration with a possible position as special investigator at the PUC."

"Well, Professor Clark certainly has the credentials. I'd give him a fair shot at a job like that, but I just can't give you an outright 'yes' right now," Graciela said.

"A fair shot is all he'd want," Manny soft-pedaled. "Second, we have a modest campaign debt, maybe $13,000 in the hole. Any help towards retiring that debt would be appreciated."

"We can give you $5,000," Juarez said without hesitation. Manny thought he should have asked for more. "How about five now and another five after you win?"

"Done." Graciela said. She appreciated Jimmy Juarez' no-nonsense negotiating stance, but wanted this thing wrapped up. "What else, Mister Ruiz?"

"Well, we have quite a few very capable people in our campaign who could really help your administration," Manny said.

Juarez roared. "No fuckin' way. Nobody tells us who to hire. No deal."

"Jimmy, Jimmy," Graciela touched Juarez on the arm.

She knew Juarez had every intention of being the Patronage Chieftain of the Public Utilities Commission and didn't want to be jammed one single inch. She also felt, as she touched his arm, a subtle shift in the balance of power between the two of them. Jimmy, after all, had rescued her when she was a young widow and nurtured her through the political wars. For the first time, she would be in a position to repay him for his benevolence, but she worried that his territoriality could sour this essential and unexpected deal.

"Look Manny, you get us resumes and, like I said before, we can give a fair shot to your people," Graciela said, as Juarez simmered.

Siquieros jumped in. "Maybe some of your key people can join the Torres campaign in this final month so we can see what they're made of, see how they perform." Nicely done, Graciela thought, everyone's face is saved.

"Deal. Good luck, Commissioner, I really mean that."

*   *   *

Damen Maxwell seemed happy with the new 30-second TV spot.

Graciela's head superimposed on an overweight puppet's body danced under the strings of a leering, cigar-puffing puppeteer.

"A product of the Big City Democratic Machine, Graciela Torres has held one patronage job after another.

"As an administrator in the Jackson City Water Department, Graciela Torres ignored the growing pollution problem in Jackson Harbor. Now, fish caught there are contaminated and inedible." (slow-motion video of a scummy, trash-filled harbor inlet, reminiscent of Dukakis' Boston Harbor.)

"As a member of the County Board, another patronage job, Graciela Torres voted for a whopping 13 percent property tax hike." (blow-up of mock property tax bill.)

"Now, despite no formal education in the utility field, Graciela Torres wants yet another government job.

"Harbor pollution, higher property taxes, a history of patronage. The stakes are too high for on-the-job training. On November 7, say no to the puppetmasters

and tax-hikers. Paid for by Committee to Elect Mary Moore Chairperson of the Public Utilities Commission."

"The photo of her is too nice. We need more cheesy make-up or more weight," Maxwell observed. "Maybe go back to the puppetmaster image at the end."

"Hey, she doesn't take a bad pic. Want to play up the more personal stuff?" asked Norm Fiddler, Maxwell's newly-hired Deputy Campaign Manager. He thumbed trough the preliminary opposition research report. "No college degree, husband was a drug dealer…"

"Late husband, right?"

"Yeah. Bobby Perez. Shotgun blast in a drive-by along with her brother, also a gang-banging druggie. Nothing too heavy, though…reefer, speed. Let's see. We have her defaulting on car payments six years ago. Almost repo time. Her son, Roberto, was arrested for spray-painting graffiti on playground equipment. Campaign contributions from some guy who's now doing time for fleecing the County. And her guy Jimmy Juarez was charged but cleared in some petition forgery stuff a few years back. Plus, we hear she's screwing some Downstate county chairman."

Maxwell flashed his tight, terse smile. "Hold off on that stuff for now, Norm. Maybe use it in other ways. Roll the bio spot."

Images flash by of Mary Moore teaching in a classroom, presiding over a meeting, listening to senior citizens.

"A leader in the classroom. A leader in the Board room. When Mary Moore was called upon unexpectedly to take the reins of power at the state Public Utilities Commission, she was uniquely qualified.

"A Master's Degree in utility regulation. Years of service at the Public Utilities Commission. Learning first-hand how to protect taxpayers and consumers.

Cut to a robust, beaming Gov. Langley standing in front of the Capitol.

"I'm Governor Tom Langley. One of the great pleasures of public service is to work with people who are committed to excellence. I appointed Mary Moore to succeed my good friend, Calvin Reynolds, and Mary has surpassed all expectations.

"This is no time for on-the-job training. On November 7, elect a superb public official, Mary Moore."

"Paid for by Committee to Elect Mary Moore Chairperson of the Public Utilities Commission."

"Not bad. Education. Experience. Langley. Need more Mary and Mister Mary. Maybe more white folks," Maxwell said. "Okay, let's work on the radio spots."

* * *

Channel 14 devoted three minutes during its lead segment to the local Emmy Awards Presentation.

"And Channel 14's own Darlene Dawes was a big winner tonight at the local Emmy awards for television excellence. Darlene brought home two awards for her coverage of the tragic gas explosion at the River's Edge housing complex last year." (clips of a glamorous Darlene in a shimmering gown accepting the Emmy)

"Darlene and Channel 14 won the Emmy's for 'Best Spot Coverage of a Breaking News Story' and for 'On-going Investigation' of the horrific explosion which cost 19 lives."

* * *

"Now I know that some of you might not have voted for my friend Graciela Torres in the primary…"

Nervous laughter from the crowd of 1,500 jammed into the church.

"…and that's okay. It really is. But friends, she won fair and square, and she's a terrific candidate—honest and dedicated—and that is why I am proudly gonna cast my vote on November 7 for Graciela Torres and I hope you all do, too." Ald. Shawn Petacque was in good form this Sunday morning.

The fence-mending that Torres needed to do she had done. She had personally called Sen. Paul Podesta, Ald. Butchie Kaminski, Ald. Shawn

Petacque and even Royce Blasingame on a weekly basis following the primary.

Podesta had been civil, but she could tell he was still hurting and bitter; her romance with Billy didn't help things. Kaminski was appreciative of Graciela's attendance at Czyz' wake and funeral, and agreed to serve as an informal pipeline to the "etnics"; she could sense his depression, though, and knew his heart wasn't in it. Other ethnic leaders such as Sen. Mario Camozzi and Seamus Dunne played a much greater role as liaisons. Blasingame had to maintain a partisan distance and Graciela never let on that she knew he was the source of the free oppo; still he quietly funneled contributions to her war chest as his way of dinging the Moore team.

Petacque obviously had an eye on the future. He was eager to be Torres' link to the African-American community and took her under his wing on the Sunday morning church circuit. They even did a few subway stations together, his specialty. He continued to beat the drum about Eaton Gas' cover-up at River's Edge and Moore's money connections to the industry. He and Graciela hit it off personally, and after one long night on the campaign trail, Shawn, Consuelo, Chemuyil, Graciela, Sandra Siquieros and Billy Miller enjoyed a laughter-filled bonding over dinner and drinks.

Graciela recognized how crucial the Black vote was and what a rising star Shawn Petacque had become because of this election. With no African-American on the statewide ticket and no real contests at the Congressional or state legislative levels, turnout would be a problem.

Petacque threw himself into the Torres effort. So far the Moore campaign had made only token efforts as wooing the African-American community. Petacque made it his obsession that Moore should receive less than 10% of the Black vote, an objective made somewhat more challenging by the fact that "Moore" sounded vaguely Black, while "Torres" definitely did not.

But Shawn introduced Graciela to players like Jimmy LeMans and Benjamin DeForrest. MortPAC agreed to do a fundraiser. Both Chemuyil and Consuelo got involved in the Torres effort and soon many of the

Petacque "Kiddie Corps" were recruited. Subway station street heat became an automatic on Graciela's schedule every weekday morning.

The remnants of another vanquished army soon arrived.

Liz Chinn brought in fresh troops and new lists from the disastrous Clark campaign. While Petra Dresden didn't dabble in candidacies that weren't third-party, independent or quirky, this race had sunk its hooks into her. She and Liz invited Graciela and Sandra Siquieros out to the estate for a gazebo brunch. A rare synergy was felt by all four and Petra's commitment increased measurably. She cut a check to Torres for $10,000 and offered Liz' services for the final month. Siquieros quickly suggested that Chinn be named Deputy Campaign Manager and it was done.

*   *   *

"Who are all these people?" a delighted Mary Moore asked Peggy Briscoe as she walked into to her bustling campaign headquarters.

The place had grown from a sleepy three-room second-floor base of operations on a quiet suburban street a year ago, to a full-fledged army camp. The campaign had since taken over the entire building, and now had more than a dozen staffers along with 20 volunteers and student interns crowded into cubicles and around folding tables.

Maps of every county and every suburban township adorned the walls, along with blown-up news clippings and Moore posters. Three large TV's hung from the ceiling. A graphic of a huge thermometer showing the amount of cash raised was painted red every morning and now stood at $1.98 million, ready to burst the $2 million bubble.

Posters on a wall in Field Central displayed a county-by-county breakdown of election day volunteers, the number of yard signs distributed and the number of absentee ballot applications. Over in the Scheduling Room, Mary's daily and weekly movements were outlined on huge "dry erase" boards.

The Communications Department was always humming. Peggy Briscoe and Del Zink had both taken unpaid leaves from the Public

Utilities Commission; Del would draft well-researched press releases and position papers, and Peggy would methodically work the dozens of political reporters she knew across the state. Volunteers kept the fax machine and e-mails humming.

Campaign volunteer Amy Harris took it all in. A petite and articulate college senior, Amy had been volunteering every afternoon for three weeks and had demonstrated great poise in every task given her. She was assigned to the headquarters front desk where she answered phones, faxed press releases, steered volunteers, handled walk-ins and ordered pizzas. Even the hard-to-impress Damen Maxwell took a special liking to her. Amy quickly became a star volunteer.

And every night Amy would go home, call the Torres headquarters and report to her former college apartment mate, Sam Roth, about her day in the enemy camp.

*   *   *

DATELINE JJ: Watch for Dem Chair Niles Flint to appoint Congressman Ziggy Prybyl as Acting Committeeman of the 6th Ward, replacing the legendary Boss John Czyz. The move represents an olive branch to Prybyl, whose beak was bent by Party pooh-bahs when he was passed over for statewide slating. It also is a bit of a rebuff to Ald. Butchie Kaminski, whose unsuccessful bid for PUC Chair was a joke and probably cost Sen. Paul Podesta the nomination.

Chinn music: We hear that Dresden operative Liz Chinn, fresh from the ill-fated Dan Clark campaign, has assumed a high-ranking post with Graciela Torres' campaign staff. The savvy and likeable Chinn is viewed as a rising star by many. Good luck, Liz!

Agitated AG's: What is it about running for Attorney General that angries up the blood so? Both Party standard-bearers—Dem incumbent Lou Calcagno and GOP gadfly Phil Driscoll—have shunned their respective coordinated campaign efforts, refused to appear with their ticket-mates and basically thumbed their noses at their party leaders. Should make Inauguration Day real interesting…

*   *   *

Sandra Siquieros lived up to her billing as one who could cobble together labor support. During the primary, most of the old-time trades were firmly for Podesta. A handful of unions went with Kaminski or Petacque, and Torres had earned the endorsement of the Needleworkers' and Janitors' unions. But Sandra locked everyone in for Graciela in the General Election.

And it was worth its weight in gold.

Troops and cash flowed in, and not just from their state. Sandra used her connections to bus in dozens of volunteers from Texas to go door-to-door. The AFL-CIO sent slick mailings to every union household calling Graciela's candidacy the "…most crucial race for working people in years." Even Timmy Sullivan appeared one day at the Torres Headquarters, offering to do "…whatever was needed." He was assigned to sit with the candidate a few hours every morning to make fundraising calls to union locals across the state.

During the Democrats bus tour, Graciela learned just how vital the unions were to the equation in Downstate communities. In some tiny, rural towns, the Democratic Party and the local locals were one and the same. Economically depressed old river towns—ghost towns, almost—were sustained politically by handfuls of committed tradesmen. Billy had explained to Graciela how ingrained the union spirit was in places like Risserville, site of a bloody coal miners' strike in the 1930's.

Sullivan taught her how to "talk the talk" with rural union bosses, and Sandra gave Graciela a crash course in the history and agendas of unions affected by the industry. Electrical workers, telecommunications workers, drillers, pipeliners, boilermakers, drill press operators. Trades she didn't even realize existed. This complex state just kept getting more complex as she traveled further up the river.

*   *   *

The Moore campaign wasn't having as much luck in reaching out to the vanquished. After Maxwell's pugnacious threat to Blasingame, calls to

Royce went unreturned. And Rev. Crandall was on board the high-speed Driscoll Express, so he could care less about helping Mary shore things up with the Christian Marchers.

Mary was doing fine, though, in establishing herself with the Republican Party Establishment.

Her ties to Calvin Reynolds and Gov. Langley were golden in most Republican enclaves of the state. She was articulate, classy, attractive and not too dogmatic; a perfect candidate in the eyes of many. She parlayed her Zane Township Party Leader status into that of being a statewide GOP honcho.

Damen Maxwell escorted a parade of national Republican big-wigs into the state to campaign with her. The Republican National Committee kicked in $20,000. Maxwell's authoritarian style made him a feared and hated figure in the campaign headquarters, but he tightened up Mary's scheduling operation and insisted on at least four solid hours of fundraising "call time" every day. He even convinced a very reluctant Mary to call Moira Reynolds—Calvin's widow—and ask for some of the million bucks which Moira had converted from his campaign fund. Moira was gracious and agreed to transfer $25,000 (much less than Damen had hoped for.)

River's Edge would not go away, though. And Mary began to regret accepting so many contributions from utility employees. She had little doubt that Torres would hit her just as hard as Blasingame did in the primary on that issue. She blamed Blake for this, although at the time, she needed the cash.

Mary was also a little nervous about the potential for backlash on her negative Torres TV spot. She wondered if they should tone down the education/"on-the-job training" aspect of it. Maybe sounds too snooty and elitist, she told Damen. And she was convinced there were white ethnics who she could snatch away from Torres, but the "Machine Puppet" tactic could backfire with them.

Maxwell was unconvinced and unconcerned, and the first TV attack ads ran in mid-October.

*   *   *

Crafted by Lupe Zarate and Liz Chinn, the Torres response to the TV attack ads was rapid, hard-hitting and specific.

The Jackson Harbor had been in trouble for years, Torres' press statement claimed. In fact, Graciela had been part of a delegation that met two years ago with Gov. Langley himself to promote a regional, long-range solution for dredging the Harbor. She clearly couldn't be blamed for the pollution that was caused by many of the big industries that had given campaign cash to Langley for years, some of which was since funneled to the Moore campaign.

And the property tax hike Graciela had supported, along with every other Democrat on the County Board, was earmarked for construction of a new County Jail to relieve overcrowding at the century-old County Pen. If Mary Moore wants criminals running loose, well, let's ship them all to Zane Township.

And the bit about Torres learning on the job, well, Graciela is a self-taught expert on water reclamation and other issues affected by the PUC. Mary Moore has a "one-dimensional perspective" on utility regulation; Graciela Torres has a "bigger picture, one that appreciates the needs of consumers." And besides, taxpayers picked up at least $20,000 of the tuition tab for Moore's Master's Degree.

Time to go after Randall, Graciela's Brain Trust agreed.

*   *   *

"Insider stock deal allows Mary Moore to live large."
The postcard direct mail piece was sent initially to every lower-income rural household, and then rolled out to every middle-income household in the state, regardless of party affiliation. A color photo spread of the "Randall and Mary Moore Mansion" included the pool, the Cadillac and BMW parked in the garage, and the tennis court. Sam Roth knew how to use a zoom lens and Sandra Siquieros knew how to use Blasingame's oppo.

"As an investment analyst for a big Wall Street firm, Randall Moore made more than $400,000 on one single stock trade, a deal the SEC called 'suspicious'.

The Moore household income last year was $1.18 million. Not including the $200,000 that the utility companies pumped into Mary Moore's campaign for PUC Chair. Or the $25,000 "honorarium" Mary Moore received from a pro-utility think tank for a speaking engagement in New Orleans…a trip funded by the taxpayers!

"Who wants to Elect a Millionaire? Do you think Mary Moore really understands how tough it can be to pay these skyrocketing electric bills and gas bills and phone bills and cable bills and water bills?

"On November 7, elect a Public Utilities Commission Chair who knows how tough it is. Elect Graciela Torres."

*   *   *

An outrageous invasion of privacy, Moore's press statement responded. The $400,000 stock deal in question was totally legitimate and the $200,000 that went into the Moore campaign fund was not intended for personal use, nor was it used for anything but political purposes. A cheap shot.

High-fives all around at the Torres Headquarters. "Don't want to discuss River's Edge? Okay, let's talk stock deals and utility cash! I love it," Sam yipped.

"Nice photos, Sam. The place looks palatial," Sandra Siquieros said. "And let's offer a toast to Royce Blasingame and Nicky Pulver and their oppo team for these tasty tidbits!"

"Class warfare!" Billy Miller howled. "Get the pitchforks, people!"

"Nice swimmin' pool," Jimmy Juarez growled.

"She's gonna come back hard, though," Sam warned. "I figure a push poll…"

*   *   *

The phonecalls seemed innocent enough at first. The caller (always a female voice) identified herself as being from "Insight Market Research Associates" and asked a few questions about the gubernatorial race.

Then the respondent would be asked about the Public Utilities Commission race.

The cheerful and professional-sounding interviewer inquired, "Are you familiar with one of the candidates, Graciela Perez Torres?"

If the respondent said yes, the next three questions were: "Would you be more or less likely to vote for Perez Torres to run this 230-person agency if you knew she had defaulted on her automobile payments and was threatened with repossession? Would you be more or less likely to vote for Perez Torres if you knew her husband and brother were both known drug dealers and gang-bangers? Would you be more or less likely to vote for Perez Torres if you knew that one of her chief contributors was doing five years in prison for a bogus county contract?"

Nearly 40,000 of these calls were made to Democratic and independent voters in suburban and rural communities in just three days. Damen Maxwell smiled his tight little grin as he watched Torres' negatives creep up in his tracking polls. You want to talk about swimming pools? Fine, Senora Perez Torres, let's talk about your gang-banger past, he mused.

*　　　　*　　　　*

The Torres camp first got wind of the push poll, strangely enough, through Pudge Carson, Paul Podesta's old pal. A neighbor of Carson's had gotten the call one night and quickly wrote down the questions. She passed it on to Carson who passed it on to Podesta who, in his one magnanimous moment of the post-primary campaign, passed it on to Billy Miller.

The Torres Brain Trust convened an emergency session, including Miller, Sandra Siquieros, Liz Chinn, Jimmy Juarez, Sam Roth, Lupe Zarate and Shawn Petacque. The candidate herself was specifically not invited.

"I'd say we ignore the specifics and blast Moore for her sleazeball tactics," Sandra opened. "Push polls are the worst form of negative campaigning and…"

"And they work. Quite effectively," Billy jumped in. "We have to address the allegations being made and turn it to our advantage."

"Hey, so, a very long time ago her bro and hubby were druggies and gang-bangers," Lupe said. "That doesn't mean she is."

"Okay, okay. First things first. What was the deal with the car repo? True?" Liz asked.

Nobody knew the answer to that one. They couldn't afford a serious opposition research effort on their opponent, let alone do one on their own candidate, an increasingly common practice.

"Hey, she was a young widow, a struggling single mom, a working mom. People might cut her some slack," Juarez said.

"Maybe. I still say we ignore that one," Sandra slipped in. "What about the contributor who's in jail?"

"Ah, some asshole who doled it out to everybody on the County Board," Jimmy said, drawing on his cigar. "We shoulda fuckin' known better…"

"How much was it?" Liz asked.

"I dunno. Maybe five, six grand total over three years."

Petacque spoke for the first time. "Maybe we use it as an opportunity to address the whole issue of campaign financing, how tough it is, how Moore is taking much larger sums from industries she's actually regulating. The conflict-of-interest angle…"

"Okay, that's a start," Liz said, becoming the unofficial scribe. "Maybe we mention the $200,000 Moore took from utilities again and cite specific Eaton Gas donors."

"And the gang-banger issue?" Sandra looked at Billy, wondering how touchy a subject this was, especially for her paramour.

Billy and Graciela had actually never discussed her late-husband. Billy had once asked her about her brother as an indirect way to raise the subject, but she seemed reticent, so he dropped it. They had talked a few times about Billy's ex-wife, but the Miller-Torres romance was always on the fly, defined by her campaign schedules and strategies and experiences. Their respective pasts were never in the forefront.

Lupe jumped in. "Look. Lots of young adults in lower-income or immigrant communities get involved with gangs. It's as much of the American Dream as the Statue of Liberty. It's almost a racist thing for this suburban gringa to be raising it…"

"Yeah, 'specially in this chicken-shit poll," Juarez said.

"Right, Jimmy. Plus, the poll doesn't mention that her husband and brother were both murdered, plus it was a decade ago," Lupe continued. "We can play it as racist, play it for sympathy…"

"Yeah, young widow, single mom…" Jimmy was smoking like a chimney now.

"Bootstraps, hard-worker, no rich husband with a shady stock deal," Sam offered.

"Okay, we got our message," Liz said. "How to play it?"

"Well, we could go directly to the Moore camp, make them denounce it…" Sandra said, thinking out loud.

"Maybe have Graciela call Moore herself? Then we do a certified letter blasting the push poll technique, send it to the media?" Petacque suggested.

"We could call the Moore camp, but they'd say it was a 'legitimate polling function' and blow it off," Sam said. "I say we go right to the media."

"The editorial boards," Liz said. "Most haven't announced their endorsements yet. Her use of push polls is a charcater issue. Convince them this sucks…"

"Yeah, pointy-heads hate this kinda bullshit," Jimmy said.

Sandra and Billy both grinned. They were definitely warming up to Jimmy.

So a working group of Lupe, Liz and Sam was convened to draft a statement and prepare an editorial board package to be distributed the next morning.

*   *   *

Mary was sitting in the back room at Moore Headquarters with Peggy Briscoe and Damen Maxwell, exhaling for the first time at the end of a 14-hour day when the receptionist buzzed her. "It's your husband. Says it's urgent."

What now, she wondered.

Randall sounded agitated, choked up. "Honey, it's about Tony. The Jackson City Police just called. He was attacked on the street near his place. Beat up. Cops say maybe a hate crime…"

"Omigod! Did they say what happened?"

"No details. He's going into surgery now."

Mary sat stunned. Street violence had never touched their lives before. Ever. "Surgery? What hospital?"

"Our Lady of Hope. I'm headed there now."

"I'll meet you there," Mary said, not even sure where that hospital was. Tears began to stream down her cheeks as she thought of the horror of the incident. Poor kid. And she'd been meaning to call him for several days now. Always too busy. Damn.

Mary related the phonecall to her shocked staff and Peggy offered to drive her to Lady of Hope. Maxwell had no genuine response, although what he was thinking was "great, another distraction".

*   *   *

The surgeon introduced himself to Randall and Mary in the waiting room. The surgery went well, he reported, and the patient will be fine. Tony had suffered a concussion, a broken arm, a fractured jaw and a chipped front tooth. He needed 30 stitches in his face. The attackers had used a blunt object, the doctor reported, maybe a baseball bat.

A Jackson City detective arrived, and said a witness provided a description of the incident, the attackers and the vehicle.

"Your son was apparently returning to his apartment with a bag of groceries, when a carload of punks—maybe 'skinheads'—slowed down, had words with him and someone threw a brick at him. Two of them got out of the vehicle—a blue, late-model SUV—and began hitting him with a pipe or baseball bat. He put up a brief fight, but it was all over with within seconds. Sorry to ask this folks, but, uh, do you have any idea who might want to do this? Did your son have any enemies, scorned lovers, problems at work, gambling debts?"

Tears were still rolling down Mary's face, but she was summoning the control she knew was required of her. "Not that we know of, officer. He's such a sweet kid..."

"Well, here's my card. If you think of anyone, call me. Anytime. There have been other hate crimes in your son's neighborhood, so it's possible it's a random act. The witness, unfortunately, couldn't get a license plate number. We'll keep on it, though."

Mary and Randall then began an all-night vigil in the waiting room. She took a few calls on her cell phone from Maxwell and Briscoe, and then the word got out about Tony's attack. A few reporters called, as did Governor Langley, Congressman Prentice, Mayor Townshend and even a very sympathetic Graciela Torres.

"When things like this happen, it reminds us how fragile we are, how important our families and loved ones are, how trivial the game of politics is," Graciela offered. "Please accept my good wishes."

"Thank you so much, Commissioner," Mary replied. "Your call means so very much to my husband and me."

When Tony regained consciousness a few hours later, Mary told him about the various calls, including Graciela's.

"Was nice of her," he mumbled through his wired jaw. "You're in a crazy business, Mom."

*   *   *

"So, should we suspend campaigning? Out of respect for the kid?" Siquieros asked those still gathered in the Torres headquarters.

"Hell, no," Jimmy Juarez barked. "Por que?"

"It does look a little tasteless," Lupe said. "Maybe we suspend our public campaign schedule for a day or so…"

"Yeah, use the time to fundraise," Siquieros said. "She hasn't been on the phones enough lately."

"What about our edit board package on the push poll?" Sam Roth asked, having just spent several intense hours pulling it together.

Sandra glanced at Jimmy and Billy, then turned to Sam. "Do it," she ordered.

*　　　　*　　　　*

Tony Moore's vicious beating received scant notice in the major media, but it was front page news in the *InterOcean* and other newspapers in the gay/lesbian community. Tony had achieved some celebrity status a few months earlier when Thelma Barnett "outed" him in the infamous candidates' forum. His mom's compassionate defense of her son's choices endeared her to many in the usually Democratic G&L community.

When Tony left the hospital with Randall and Mary the afternoon after the attack, he was greeted by more than 40 well-wishers who carried banners protesting hate crimes and "genocide". Since his jaw was wired shut, Mary took a few moments to thank the group for coming and to pose for photos.

*　　　　*　　　　*

All day, Sam and Lupe had worked the phones to every editorial board editor in the state, decrying the ugliness of the Moore push poll. While many newspapers had already decided their endorsements, a few had not and the Torres counter-offensive probably swayed some.

Lupe, however, was the bearer of bad news after hearing from an old friend who worked at the copy desk of the *Jackson City Review*, the state's largest paper. An advance copy of the next day's editorial was e-mailed over. Lupe and Sandra Siquieros got on the speakerphone in Sandra's office, called Graciela on her cellphone and read her the bad news.

"Our picks: Prentice, Dobbs, Moore, Cummings"

"The state's voters have some excellent candidates to choose from in the fast-approaching statewide election. While State Senator Debra Shane has terrific energy and a bright future, we must endorse Congressman Paul Prentice for his experience and moderate approach."

"Okay, fast forward," Graciela said.

"Okay, they went with Dobbs, skipped the AG race, endorsed Cummings by a hair," Lupe read. "Here's us."

"The Public Utilities Commission Chairmanship is a tough call. We gave Mary Moore a strong nod in the primary, but have been disappointed in her handling of the River's Edge tragedy and the excessive amounts of campaign contributions from the utility lobby. However, Moore's grasp of the highly technical issues facing utility consumers gives her a slight edge over County Board Commissioner Graciela Torres, who we admire as a County Board member—especially for her role in the harbor dredging battle—but has run a lackluster campaign."

"Lackluster, huh. Well, at least it's not a ringing endorsement for Moore," Graciela said, clearly disappointed.

"Right. River's Edge. Utility cash. They're disappointed, blah, blah, blah. She won't be reproducing this for her mail," Sandra optimistically offered.

"Yeah, well, she'll still add it to her list of supporters. Have we heard from any other endorsements?" Graciela asked.

"The *Orbit* down at the state university. The Sandburg chain..."

"Oh, that's a good one," Graciela said.

"A few others. Most will come out this weekend."

"Any word on Mary's son?"

"Surgery went well last night. He was released from the hospital today. The cops have no suspects, but the gay community is playing it like the hate crime of the century," Lupe reported.

"Ladies, let us not belittle street crime. Could happen to any of us," Graciela sharply said. "And for this to happen to a candidate less than two weeks out is incredible to think about. She's a human being, a player, just like us."

"Got it, Boss-Lady."

"Anthing else?"

"Yeah, Sam seems to think Moore will spend most of her final week campaigning in Jackson City. That her suburban base is strong, and the push polls and organizational support will sustain her in rural areas," Sandra said.

"Well, Sam's been right on target in reading her moves lately," Graciela said. "Does that argue for our spending our final week outside of the City?"

"Well, if your 'etnic' buddies like Dunne and Camozzi come through, and Black turnout is as good as Petacque thinks it could be, I'd say hit the road, Chica," Lupe suggested.

"I agree," Siquieros chimed in. "Grab your corazon Billy and go!"

"Let me think about it. Thanks for the *Jackson City Review* update."

*   *   *

Chapter Six

Waterspout, Part I

"Thy summer voice, Musketaquit,
Repeats the music of the rain;
But sweeter rivers pulsing flit
Through thee, as thou through Concord Plain."

"Thou in thy narrow banks art pent:
The stream I love unbounded goes
Through flood and sea and firmament;
Through light, through life, it forward flows.

"I see the inundation sweet,
I hear the spending of the stream
Through years, through men, through Nature fleet,
Through love and thought, through power and dream..."

-Ralph Waldo Emerson *("Two Rivers")*

A week before E-Day, the State Elections Board made public the latest campaign disclosure reports on its website:

"State Public Utilities Commission Chairperson:

Candidate/Party	Raised/Loans	Spent	Cash-on-Hand (October 15)
Moore–R	$1,927,185	$1,661,090	$318,140
Torres–D	$1,010,484	$ 708,365	$332,351

The two obvious stories were that Moore had outspent Torres by nearly a million bucks and that Torres had actually raised a million bucks, and that, for the first time, Torres had nosed into the lead in the all-important "cash-on-hand" category. That could change overnight, however, with a few calls from Gov. Langley.

This category was less crucial for Moore, of course, since her name ID was high and had been since the primary. Torres was still unknown to many, particularly those outside of Jackson City. And both candidates' negatives had inched up ever since both campaigns had gone on the attack.

Different polls revealed different angles. The *Argo Dispatch* was the first to survey on the impact of Dan Clark's exit. Of the 11% who said they favored Clark or an "Independent" in the three-way, 39% said they now leaned to Torres, 8% leaned to Moore and 53% were undecided.

The Moore tracking polls showed their TV spot and push poll were connecting. More than half of the Downstaters and suburbanites polled said they would be less likely to vote for a candidate who was a "puppet of a Big City Machine", and 42% of them identified Torres as such a puppet. And 56% of suburbanites polled considered Torres to be a "big tax-and-spender".

The gang-banger connection seemed to be resonating, as well. Damen Maxwell wasn't quite sure how to address the white ethnics; the polling found them soft on the entire statewide Democratic ticket, but history showed only rare instances of ticket-splitting. He was holding what he called the "Perez Torres" race card, but hadn't decided how to play it.

The Torres polling revealed that Moore's negatives were soaring in rural areas, thanks to their attack mail. "We rural folks don't cotton much to

BMW's, insider stock deals and fancy backyard swimmin' pools," deadpanned Billy. They had rolled the piece out to blue-collar and middle-income households in suburbia, part of Sandra Siquieros' new "forget-the-soccer-moms-go-after-the-workers" suburban strategy, which Billy was not enthralled with. The African-American community seemed solid for Graciela; the only question was turnout. Petacque urged the Torres Brain Trust to bring in the Chrysler Crew for some serious visibility during the final week.

Early indications suggested that once again Sam Roth's instincts were accurate; Moore seemed to be focusing on Jackson City for her final lap, especially in the gay/lesbian neighborhoods and moderate Republican areas where Blasingame had done well. Moore scheduled several highly-publicized rallies in Jackson City locations and increased her Jackson City TV buy while letting her smaller market buys shrivel on the vine.

Moore and Torres strategists were all confronted with the perennial Get-Out-The-Vote question: go wide or go deep? Focus on generating huge turnout in your base or try to persuade the undecideds in "swing" areas?

Both candidates displayed reluctance about their endgame strategies. Moore felt she needed one more fly-around, a notion endorsed by Steven Page, but vetoed by Damen Maxwell. Torres wasn't confident about the Black turnout or white ethnics, but Shawn Petacque, Seamus Dunne, Mario Camozzi and even Ziggy Prybyl (what a crew, she thought) all assured her the base was fine. Billy Miller continued to whisper sweet nothings about finishing Downstate.

So both campaigns decided to roll the dice on a similar tack: go wide, not deep.

*   *   *

One week before the election, the *Jackson City Review* released the results of its polling of all statewide candidates.

Governor
42%   Paul Prentice (R)
39%   Debra Shane (D)
19%   Undecided

Attorney General
44%   Lou Calcagno (D)
37%   Philip Driscoll (R)
19%   Undecided

Secretary of State
48%   Richard Dobbs (R)
31%   Bill Karmejian (D)
21%   Undecided

State Treasurer
33%   Karen Hogan (R)
32%   Tom Cummings (D)
35%   Undecided

Public Utilities Commission Chair
34%   Mary Moore (R)
32%   Graciela Torres (D)
34%   Undecided

*   *   *

Governor Langley convened one final conclave in the "Dungeon".

As the candidates or their surrogates filed into the storied basement meeting room in the Governor's Mansion, Langley demonstrated one last time why he was the consummate schmoozer: boisterously rubbing a shoulder here, quietly commenting on a gossip tidbit there, and adroitly serving as bartender, chief strategist and Big Daddy.

Some of the attendees, like Mary Moore and Karen Hogan, had never been in the Dungeon before, and were bemused by the mirthful photos and free-flowing bar. Others like Jimmy Blake and State Republican Party Chair Gretchen Hanson knew exactly which chairs were comfy and which had lumps. Some, like Phil Driscoll seemed uncomfortable and ready to exit.

"Congressman Prentice, since you'll soon be living here, can I show you the secret bourbon stash?" Langley joked.

"Governor, I'm strictly a white wine and dark beer man, but I'll need that secret stash to lobby the legislature," Prentice quipped back. "What my grandchildren need to know is how to play the Space Invaders game without quarters."

"Well, our man Jimmy Blake can provide an in-service on that," Langley replied, clearly in a buoyant mood. "Okay, folks. Unless anyone else needs a beverage or a refill, let's get down to business. The *JC Review* poll looked pretty promising. Let me turn it over to Space Invaders champ Jimmy Blake for deeper analysis."

Blake shuffled through a file of papers and computer printouts, and slowly rose with a scotch-and-soda in hand.

"Alright, our internal polling shows the same as the *JC Review's*: at least one of five likely voters don't know what the hell to do in nearly every race," Blake said, as he distributed copies of the Republican Coordinated Campaign's tracking poll.

"Congressman Prentice and Secretary Dobbs, you are both in pretty good shape. Your support is solid; we just need to get the base vote out. And Congressman, tell your grandchildren the key to free Space Invaders is a sharp whack on the left side."

"Jimmy, a sharp whack on the left side is precisely what the lower end of our ticket plans to administer on election day," Langley joshed.

"Well, Governor, both Karen Hogan and Mary Moore can do very well in traditionally Democratic bastions, our genius pollsters tell us. Karen's artsy-fartsy background—if you'll pardon me—should give her traction in Jackson City, as should Mary's recent inroads into the gay and lesbian community. And, uh, Commissioner, I'm sure everyone here has your son in their prayers," Blake hurriedly mumbled. Driscoll only glared.

Blake glared back at Driscoll. "Fortunately, the Democratic ticket has even more discord than we do, what with Attorney General Calcagno pissed at Shane and Flint and everyone else."

"And that presents us with an opportunity—right Jimmy?—to exploit their divisiveness by hitting them from left-to-right, from inner city to farm towns in the final inning," Langley said. "Is that what I'm hearing?"

"Absolutely, Governor. We need Driscoll to energize the right, Moore and Hogan to reach out to the left, and Prentice and Dobbs to turn out the Great Center," Blake said, sitting down in his favorite recliner chair and sipping his drink.

"It will be a challenge to energize the right—my 'base' as you put it, General Blake—while pandering to the gays and the so-called artists and the Jackson City welfare moms," Driscoll acerbically shot in.

"Just as tough as it is for us to be talking to moderates with some mean-spirited Neanderthal strapped to our shoulders," Karen Hogan shot back. "But I guess that's what politics is all about. Addition, not division."

"I always thought it was about principles and beliefs," Driscoll practically shouted.

"Well, your radical extremism sure doesn't help us with the thiry or forty percent of the voters—the swing voters—who consider themselves moderates or independents or pragmatists," Hogan yelled back.

"Whoa, team. How about we all calm down. Truce. Anybody need a refill?" Langley offered. "No? Okay. Look. Phil. We need some better numbers in Jackson City. Prentice, Moore, Hogan, even you. And, Karen, for crying out loud. Reality check, please. Cummings is coming at you from the right on some issues. You—more than anyone—need the pro-lifers and gun-lovers. Mary, too. So, let's all just swallow our pride, place our ideologies on the back-burner and think like a team, okay? Is that possible? For just one goddamn friggin' week or so?" He dramatically slammed his glass on the table.

Few in the Dungeon had ever heard Governor Langley raise his voice and only Jimmy Blake had heard him cuss, so the dramatic impact was not lost. Everyone nodded their head and mumbled solidarity.

"Fine. Now, let's discuss the coordinated campaign TV budget and the fly-around for the final weekend. Jimmy?"

$$*\qquad\qquad *\qquad\qquad *$$

A similar session was taking place at the State Democratic Headquarters.

All of the candidates and their top staff were present (except for Attorney General Calcagno, who sent a junior staffer), along with key State Central Committee leaders including Sen. Beatrice Madison, Cong. Ziggy Prybyl and Mayor Townshend's floor leader, Mary Ikeda.

"People, let's get settled here," Niles Flint urged. "Welcome to the newest member of the Committee, Congressman Ziggy Prybyl."

"Glad to be here, Niles." Prybyl always looked so pink, Graciela thought. And his skin was like butter.

"Okay, our internal numbers are pretty close to the *Jackson City Review* numbers, except we show Undecideds breaking heavily our way. Which is very good news for Senator Shane, Commissioner Torres and Representative Cummings."

"I'll be glad to pick up a few of those Undecideds, too, Mister Chairman," Bill Karmejian gamely said.

"And, of course, good news for Mayor Karmejian," Niles quickly recovered. "I will note that your opponent's numbers are very soft in Jackson City, Bill. Very soft."

"Any crosstabs on those Undecideds, Niles?" Shane asked.

"Well, Senator, it varies by race. In your race, the white male, age 35 to 49, hasn't made up his mind. In the SOS contest, it's mostly Black and Hispanic voters. Further down the ticket, for Cummings and Torres, it's more the soccer-moms and pink-collar workers in the 'burbs."

"Mister Chairman?"

"Yes, Senator Madison."

Madison still hadn't forgotten her biting exchange with Flint at the slatemaking. "Lacking any African-American candidates on the state ticket, it will be daunting for us to generate much excitement out there on the street, y'know, but with the proper allocation of state party resources we shall not only hold our own, but put the entire ticket over the top."

"Okay, Senator. I will remind you that the slatemakers did find Alderman Petacque as 'qualified' for the PUC job, but you are absolutely right. What sort of resources are we talking about here?"

Madison pulled a proposed Get-Out-The-Vote budget from her bulging briefcase.

"We are talking about a massive blitz on Black radio, extensive street heat—rallies, sound trucks, parades and so forth—a GOTV mailer, automated phones, sign crews and walkin' around money," Madison said, passing copies of the budget around the table.

"Three-quarter mil! Aw, Beatrice, c'mon," Flint practically shouted. "You'll break us."

"Time to pay for past sins, Mister Chairman," Madison grinned.

"Anna, how much in the bank?" Flint asked his finance director.

"About $1.2 million," Bloom replied. "About half of that is already committed. TV, direct mail, staff, pollsters. We expect some soft money from the DNC, maybe another $30,000 from various unions. And some of the candidates still haven't kicked in their share, yet." Bloom glanced at Torres and Karmejian.

"Ours is coming, Mister Chairman," Sandra Siquieros promised.

"Time to pay for past sins, Mister Chairman," Beatrice was getting giddy.

"Yeah, I heard you, Senator. Look, it's already too late to do any new direct mail. Everyone agree?"

No one spoke around the table. Let Flint sink or swim here.

"But, geez, $150,000 just for Black radio? That's like one spot every five minutes!"

"You're doing TV in the rural areas, Mister Chairman. And Black folk don't need to be persuaded to vote Democratic, just nudged to the polls," Madison knew she had him.

"Okay, I like doing sign crews, I'm with you there—I assume we're talking about Chris Chrysler?—and we're already planning on paid phones, but $50,000 for walkin' around money? That's a whole lot of walkin', Senator," Niles was getting his second wind. "Let's hear from the candidates. Senator Shane?"

Shane shook her head slowly. "Well, we need huge turnout in the African-American community, Niles. There aren't any hot local races to boost turnout, which wasn't too hot in the primary anyhow." Madison had already lobbied her Senate colleague on her proposal.

Karmejian jumped in. "It really helps the whole ticket, Niles."

"My opponent is spending buckets of cash on Jackson City advertising. Weekly newspapers, organizational newsletters, billboards. I need something in the City, Niles," Cummings pleaded.

Graciela piled on. "I've had the pleasure of Alderman Petacque's involvement in my campaign for the past month. He's done a great job crunching the numbers. The Black vote could be as much as eighteen, maybe twenty percent of the entire statewide vote. And we're looking at ninety percent Democratic, the Alderman tells me."

"And I know that Mayor Townshend supports any and all efforts to boost turnout in the City," Ikeda volunteered.

"Okay, I get it. Senator Madison, could you and Anna and maybe Alderman Petacque revise this budget, maybe get it below three hundred K? Drop the mail and paid phones, trim the radio and walkin' around money, get more specific on the rallies and street heat and viz, and we should have a winner," Flint suggested.

"Thank you, Mister Chairman," Madison sweetly replied.

*   *   *

"Sam, I think they may be on to me," Amy Harris nervously whispered over the phone.

"Why are you whispering. You're at home, right?"

"What if my phone is tapped?"

"Aw, Amy, I really doubt that." Sam was genuinely concerned about her well-being, though, and even more concerned that the cover on his little espionage mission might be blown. That would not be cool. "Why do you think that?"

"Just the way Damen Maxwell looks at me. He is such an asshole, Sam."

"Yeah, well, maybe he's horny. It's a long way from Delaware."

"Yeah, right. He's incapable of horniness. I hear he had some big blow-out with the coordinated campaign. That they want to do a statewide fly-around, but Maxwell wants to keep Moore close to home. Mister Compassionate says it's because of her son, but I think that's a crock."

"When's the Republican flyaround scheduled?"

"The Saturday and Sunday before the election."

"You know the itinerary?"

"I can get it tomorrow. Sam, I'm getting really nervous about this whole thing."

"You're fine. You're doing great. Tell you what, get the flyaround schedule tomorrow, do whatever snooping you can, y'know, see if there are any surprises up their sleeves and then tell them you need a few days off for some big exams at school. Then, I'll treat you to a big steak dinner and red wine."

"But, Sam, they need me!"

"Amy!"

*　　　　　　*　　　　　　*

The Dems African-American Outreach budget was quickly retooled by Sen. Madison, Ald. Petacque and Finance Director Anna Bloom. Shane's people and Mary Ikeda from the Mayor's cabal signed off on it, leaving Flint little choice.

The big ticket item was radio. Two spots would be taped the next day, one featuring Madison sweetly endorsing her State Senate colleague, Debra Shane, and the other featuring Petacque and philanthropist James LeMans pushing the whole Democratic slate. Price tag for production and a non-stop buy on seven stations: $65,000. LeMans pledged to raise $20,000 and the Democratic National Committee kicked in another $10,000 for this effort.

The Chrysler Crew was retained to blitz the entire city and low-income suburbs with 100,000 new posters at a cost of $50,000 for printing and labor. Another $30,000 was allocated for 100,000 door hangers and 150,000 palm cards.

The Election Day "walkin' around money" was turned into "volunteer expenses": $32,000 to be disbursed by eight different Ward Committeemen (including Petacque and Madison). At their discretion.

Despite Flint's protestations about paid phonebanking already being "covered", the team went ahead and ordered 100,000 automated phonecalls to occur the Sunday before the election. Again, Senator Madison's sweet motherly voice would be used. The cost: $40,000.

Four sound trucks at $500 each and a big "Pride" Rally with a $25,000 tab brought the new budget to just under a quarter-million.

"Well, this should just about do it," a triumphant Sen. Madison told a nervous Anna Bloom.

*　　　*　　　*

The hastily-organized Wednesday night Get-Out-The-Vote rally hosted by leaders of Jackson City's gay/lesbian establishment was a huge success. Trying to demonstrate a bipartisan spirit, they invited all candidates from both parties, but only Debra Shane, Bill Karmejian, Karen Hogan and Mary Moore showed.

As a crowd of 600 and three TV crews jammed into the tiny Biloxi Lounge, activists and politicians paraded onto the stage. But it was Mary Moore's appearance with her son Tony that brought the house down.

"My son has had to put up with a lot in his short life," Mary said. "Growing up gay in a conservative suburb with a dubious father…" (Many in the crowd smiled and exchanged knowing looks.) "…and having to put up with a mom in politics. But I cannot imagine anyone being beaten with a baseball bat purely because of her or his sexual orientation! I just cannot imagine it! It sickens me!"

The crowd roared and the TV crews lights went on. A bandaged and bruised Tony gamely waved.

"Now I know that some of you may have come to Jackson City from smaller towns, less tolerant places…"

"I came from Straightsville, Mary!" yelled someone in the crowd.

"So did I, my friend," Mary quipped back. "But now, we are here in a community that practices tolerance, even teaches the rest of us tolerance, and you are to be honored for that!"

"Ma-ry! Ma-ry! Ma-ry!" the crowd began chanting. Moore glanced down the stage at a beaming Karen Hogan and an unsmiling Debra Shane.

"I have learned so much, so very much, from my son Tony. He is my teacher. And let me announce to you right here, right now, that I intend to sign a domestic partnership rule at the state Public Utilities Commission, the first of its kind in the state! It's the right thing to do!"

The crowd roared approval and continued to chant. Mary's triumph was featured on TV that evening and in a full-color photo in the *Jackson City Review* on Thursday morning.

*   *   *

Jimmy Juarez, of course, downplayed the value of Moore's moves in the gay community, but others in the Torres Brain Trust were nervous.

"Do you think I should scratch the final swing Downstate? Stay closer to home?" Graciela asked the group Thursday morning.

Sandra seemed to be most nervous about sending the candidate on the road. "I've always believed you should finish strong in your base," Sandra said. "Plus, we still need you on the phones dialing for dollars."

"Ah, the base is fine," Juarez scoffed. "The Black turnout's gonna be great, Camozzi and Dunne and the Boys'll be getting' out the 'etnics'. Don't worry about a coupla tootie-frooties."

"Oh, Jimmy." Graciela rolled her eyes.

Similar to her triumphant pre-election tour in the Primary, an aggressive "drive-around" had been organized by Billy and Lupe. Once again, some 50 stops and a thousand miles in a three-day period, including return visits to the West Wheaton VFW, the field where they met had with the farmers from Michoacan and Billy's home town in Sauk County, where the romance was first kindled.

Sam piped in. "Well, rumor has it Moore has abandoned her earlier plan to stay close to home the final weekend. The gay thing last night was it for her. The whole Republican ticket, except for Driscoll, will be doing a flyaround. Wheels up Saturday morning. Six stops Saturday, overnight in the Capital, six more stops Sunday. I'd say Jackson City is safe for us to leave to the powers that be. Go wide, not deep."

"How'd you hear about their flyaround?" Sandra asked. This kid is amazing, she thought.

"Oh, y'know. Word on the street," Sam quietly replied.

"Well, that's very useful intelligence, Sam. I think you're right," Graciela said. "It's safe to leave the City. I hope we can turn out those ladies in West Wheaton again."

*　　　　*　　　　*

The cracks in the Torres base, though, began appearing Thursday.

Seamus Dunne heard that Graciela had been bumped from the Election Day palm card in a few Irish-American wards, most notably the

30th Ward, whose Democratic Committeeman, Harry Griffin, enjoyed a serious patronage pipeline through lobbyist Kevin O'Malley. While the patronage of most Ward Bosses was on public payrolls, some like Harry had his troops placed in the private sector (and usually making better money.) O'Malley had given Griffin dozens of jobs at Eaton Gas Company and with other clients. It was payback time.

And Sen. Mario Camozzi was surreptitiously notified by his favorite print shop that two suburban township Dem chieftains had also dumped Graciela. Something about "favors" owed to Governor Langley, was the rumor.

Even a few low-level Hispanic politicians were making noises, although Juarez pounced on them like the Big Dog he is and threatened to yank every patronage job they ever had or ever will have unless they produced "at least 95 percent" for Torres.

The Jackson City liberals were also flirting with Moore, partly because of her growing appeal in the gay community, but mostly because they just hadn't connected enough with Torres. Many of the old-type lefties saw her as Jimmy Juarez' puppet, thanks partly to Moore's TV.

So Sandra increased the TV buy in Jackson City and trotted out the gorgeous "American Dream" spot Graciela had used in the primary. The plan to leave town was still in motion.

*   *   *

"So you're okay with this?"

"Reverend, I'm fine with this," Phil Driscoll replied. "My reaction to Miss Moore's trip to this gay nightclub and her shocking pronouncements is exactly the same reaction as yours and your followers and my supporters."

"A write-in campaign takes some educating," Crandall said.

"Well, it's all part of the political education process you began a year ago with the Marchers. Furthermore, it holds Mary Moore accountable, sends her a message. Plus it helps my campaign with turnout. And who knows what impact it can have two years from now in the U.S. Senate race. I think this is precisely the right thing, Reverend."

"Then we'll launch the missiles tonight, Phil. May the Lord Jesus Christ be with us Tuesday."

"I have no doubt about that, Reverend. God bless you."

And with that, 20,000 e-mails and 30,000 automated phone messages were dispatched urging the Christian Marchers to march to the polls on Tuesday and cast a write-in vote for Thelma Barnett for Chairman of the Public Utilities Commission.

*   *   *

Graciela's final press conference in Jackson City Friday morning, just prior to her road trip, was not as well-attended by the media as Lupe had hoped.

Featuring the still-grieving Mariano Vargas, whistleblower Arnold Wiser and former Mayor Pinky Banks, the Torres campaign intended to inject River's Edge back into the public's consciousness one last time. The media, though, was either sick of the topic or more focused on the tight gubernatorial contest and increasingly wild-and-wooly Attorney General's race.

Still, Darlene Dawes from Channel 14 was there (and, in a clear breach of journalistic ethics, gave Graciela a hug afterwards), as well as several radio and newspaper reporters, plus an Associated Press photographer.

Mariano provided poignant first-hand testimony of the tragedy and how much he missed his wife and daughters. Arnold ripped his former employers at Eaton Gas for their ineptitude and subsequent cover-up. Mayor Banks rambled about his Blue Ribbon Investigation and praised Graciela's tenacity on his Panel.

Graciela became emotional at the podium as she described her first impressions when she arrived at the scene of the disaster. "Such carnage I have never imagined. The screams. The smells of gas and smoke and burning bodies." She paused and bit her lower lip.

"And for us to know it was due to a utility company that did not care. That hired codeine addicts to check their valves. That refused to have adequate Spanish-speaking operators on duty. That covered up this evil which instantaneously took the lives of Mariano Vargas' beautiful young wife and his two children and the many others who perished at River's Edge.

"This company, which has continued to stonewall on this case, refusing to make good with the victims, refusing to hire more Spanish-speaking staff. This company which donated tens of thousands of dollars in campaign cash to my opponent, who is supposed to be regulating them.

"It is this kind of attitude which compelled me to run for this office more than one year ago. It's people like Mariano Vargas and Arnold Wiser, whose strength and courage have pushed me, encouraged me, when I seemed down or hopeless. These two men have inspired me. I salute you and thank you both so much."

Graciela hugged Wiser and Vargas and even the awkward-looking Mayor Banks. Channel 14 led with the story Friday night and the AP photo of a lip-biting Graciela showed up in many of the state's newspapers the next morning. By then the final Torres Road Trip was well under way.

*   *   *

DATELINE JJ: Shane, Driscoll surging. Our tracking polls show amazing surges by Sen. Debra Shane in her gubernatorial bid and Phil Driscoll in his effort to oust incumbent AG Lou Calcagno. Undecided suburban white males have broken for Shane while undecided seniors statewide seem willing to dump Calcagno.

Our polls further show Secretary of State Richard Dobbs could take a vacation to Tahiti right now and still not be caught by Dem hopeful Mayor Bill Karmejian. There is something to be said for having your name on every driver's license in the state.

The lower-ticket races are in the too-close-to-call column, with Republicans Karen Hogan and Mary Moore both holding single-digit leads.

Some troubles in Paradise, though for both PUC Chair candidates. A JJ Double-Scoop: a write-in campaign is underway for Thelma Barnett (who was thoroughly thumped by Moore in the primary.) This could siphon a few thousand votes from Moore in the Bible Zone. And a few Dem Bosses have dumped Graciela Torres from their palm cards, including 30th Ward Committeeman Harry Griffin and East Bentonville Mayor Vanessa Martin. Both Martin and Griffin have pranced with pachyderms in the past.

*   * *   *   *

"Griffin? Seamus Dunne. How ya lookin' for Tuesday?"

Harry Griffin had never liked Dunne. Never understood him. Dunne was a little too enigmatic, too cerebral for Harry, who played politics the old-fashioned way. They were both gut-punching tribal leaders; Seamus had gotten much further in Party politics than Harry, while Harry controlled more patronage. Something about those weird tinted glasses Dunne always wore and his strange, choppy way of speaking.

"We're okay in Thirty, Seamus. Plenty of troops. Every precinct covered deep. How you lookin'?"

"Covered. Fine. Karmejian's DOA; rest is fine."

"So, Seamus, ya callin' just to wish me well?"

"Hearin' things, Harry. Goin' south on the ticket, I hear."

"Aw, c'mon, Dunne. I got a few precincts, ya know, they never voted fer a colored and they ain't voting fer no messican. So she's off a few goddamm palm cards. Ain't gonna hurt her none. Probably help Shane and Cummings even more."

"Gotta keep it together, Griffin. A fragile web. Hate to see you break just for a few stinkin' meter reader jobs." Dunne was getting hot. "How many precincts?"

"I dunno," Griffin lied. "I was gonna put Moore on about a dozen, leave the rest blank."

"How 'bout all blank?"

"So what's in it for me?" Griffin heard a long Dunne sigh.

"Moore's on a single palm card in the 30th and no Harry Griffin-sponsored judicial candidate ever, ever, ever gets elected. Ever. Clear?"

"Hey, fuck you, Dunne. Mind your own business," Griffin said as he slammed the phone down.

Griffin promptly called the printer and cancelled the palm cards with Moore listed, leaving the PUC slot blank for his 35,000 Democratic loyalists.

*　　　*　　　*

The "Rally for Pride" event quickly became the official State Democratic Party's Get-Out-The-Vote event. Instead of being held in the heart of the African-American community, it was scheduled for Monday at Noon in the heart of Jackson City's downtown commercial district. While Sen. Beatrice Madison and a few other African-American players grumbled at first that their event had been hijacked, everyone appreciated the value of having one big shindig Downtown.

As City employees tore open their paycheck envelopes Friday, they found a flyer inviting them to a "nonpartisan" election rally. The City's Senior Outreach phonetrees were activated to invite every senior citizen to the event and arrange for transportation. Every City Council member was allocated 50-100 "VIP" tickets and given a quota to bring anywhere from one to ten busloads of party faithful from their neighborhood. A portion of the massive radio buy on African-American stations was changed to get the word out.

Mayor Townshend felt the need for redemption. His Downtown Rally to launch the infamous bus tour following the primary election had been a disaster. Torrential rains, poor planning and bruised egos suppressed turnout. Since then, the State Democratic Party leadership was in flux, with Czyz' death and Podesta on the wane and the Blacks sniping at Flint. Townshend wanted to put Mary Ikeda into play as the next State Party Vice-Chair; a good turnout for the ticket was crucial on Tuesday, and this rally could help.

*　　　*　　　*

Senior aides Steven Page and Jimmy Blake were both asked by Gov. Langley to participate in an emergency meeting at Mary Moore's Headquarters on the Thelma Barnett write-in rumor. Joining Mary were the Governor's top election lawyer—Dickie Kyle—and Mary's senior staff (Damen Maxwell, Peggy Briscoe and Del Zink).

As the group settled in and picked at the cheese and veggie tray in the conference room, Mary was relieved to see Page and even Blake. What a strange trip this had been, starting with the awful phone call from Steven more than a year ago relaying the information about Calvin's Yucatan tragedy. She smiled recalling the meeting in the Governor's office the following morning when Blake and Page—such an Odd Couple—angelically awaited Langley's instructions. She regretted that Steven hadn't been around lately and even that Blake had been reassigned to run the Coordinated Campaign. Maxwell was a royal pain and the staffers who had taken a leave from the PUC to work on the campaign were hard-working and well-meaning, but just not politically-savvy.

"So, do we have a copy of the e-mail itself?" Kyle asked. He was a no-nonsense litigator and Mary was delighted to see him there.

"Yessir. We planted a few names onto the Christian Marchers' e-mail list during the primary. The message was sent from Reverend Crandall last night, 9:21 p.m. Our person immediately sent it here," Zink reported.

"Subject: Election Day Alert. Attention all Christian Marchers! Tuesday is Election Day and we have exciting news! Our very own Thelma Barnett, who so capably coordinated our 'Amen, Now!' drive last year and who ran a noble race for state Public Utilities Chairperson earlier this year, has agreed to allow her name to be placed in contention as a write-in candidate for that spot.

"Thelma narrowly lost in the September primary election to the incumbent, Mary Moore, who recently was seen on TV pandering to the gay/lesbian/transvestite community in Jackson City. Moore has vowed to give the homosexuals in the Public Utilities Commission full marriage benefits!

"It's time to send Mary Moore and her kind a message! When you vote on Tuesday, punch "write-in" on the ballot card next to Public Utilities

Commission Chairperson. Then, on the ballot punchcard envelope, there is a spot that says 'Write-in Candidates'.

"That's where you can PRINT—LEGIBLY-Thelma Barnett. (Two "T's" in "Barnett")

"If you do not know where your polling place is, contact your local county clerk or e-mail us at the Christian Marchers. And don't forget to vote for Philip Driscoll for Attorney General. Sincerely Yours in Christ, Rev. B.J. Crandall"

"So, does that meet state write-in requirements, Mister Kyle?" Mary asked.

Kyle pulled at his silver goatee. Like Steven Page, he was a veteran of Gov. Langley's very first race and had been around ever since. Most of his election law experience dealt with petition challenges and an occasional electioneering charge. Write-in candidacies were pretty rare and write-in candidacies that made any difference were rarer.

"I see one possible omission in the instructions. The voter must identify on the ballot punchcard envelope the name of the office their write-in choice is seeking. The ballot envelope does state the need for the office to be written in, but it's in tiny print."

"So, Dickie, does that mean we could challenge all write-ins for Thelma, even if the voter punched the 'write-in' hole next to PUC Chair and there were no other write-ins on the ballot?" Blake asked.

"It's a hazy area and I'd have to check precedent on that, but I believe we could, yes."

Maxwell jumped in. "Can we just challenge every single ballot that has any write-in?"

"Well, legally yes; politically, I wouldn't," Kyle replied. "Most of those Thelma write-ins, frankly, are probably going with Prentice for guv, Dobbs for SOS…"

"Those are drops in the bucket for Prentice and Dobbs, but could be huge for us," Maxwell said.

"Hey, Damen, some of us do care about the rest of the ticket, ya know," Blake said.

"Hey, Blake, I'm here to do one thing. Get Mary Moore elected PUC Chair. Sorry, but I really don't give a rat's ass about the rest of your ticket."

"Right, you're on the next flight back to Vermont…"

"Delaware," Maxwell corrected him.

"…Vermont or wherever, with your batting average intact. If we start a wholesale challenge of these twenty or thirty thousand write-ins, maybe we win for Mary—who is my very good friend—but lose the Governor's Mansion," Blake snarled. "And you're okay with that?"

"You do what you gotta do, Blake," Maxwell blithely retorted. "Like you dragging my candidate out of Jackson City for another tour of Tiny Towns when she could be making inroads with the libs here."

"Fellas, c'mon. It's probably gonna be a tiny, insignificant number of write-in ballots," Kyle said. "I'd be more concerned about the Donkeys stealing this thing at nursing homes than I am about a few write-ins for Jesus."

"Dickie's right," Steven Page said. "Let's make sure we have enough volunteer lawyers on hand Tuesday and enough pollwatchers to prevent monkey-business."

"Yeah, we'll have 'em," Maxwell proclaimed.

"Okay, what else can be done with this?" Mary asked. "Any media strategies, Peggy?"

"Well, between Saturday morning and Monday evening, our 60-second spot is on fifty Downstate radio stations, about 1,500 occurrences. We could up that some."

"How much would that run us?" Mary asked, knowing the money would be there.

Briscoe pulled out a calculator. "We could get a nice package at most of the stations, assuming they still have space available, maybe, uh, another 500 occurrences for about $45,000, maybe fifty?"

"I say do it," Blake quickly said.

"For once we agree," Maxwell shot in. "Place the buy, Peggy."

"Here's a wild thought," Kyle grinned. "Didn't Crandall have a few Black preachers helping him during the primary? Maybe we get the word out to them about this write-in campaign, they preach it to their congregations from the pulpit this weekend, we can nibble at Torres' city base some."

"I love it," Zink said. "I have a list, actually, of a dozen or so preachers who endorsed Thelma. We can send the e-mail or even call them about it today."

"Without fingerprints?" Blake asked.

"No fingerprints," Zink replied.

"That is devilishly clever, Counsel," Mary smiled. "But, Del, no fingerprints."

"Here's something else. I assume you know which precincts Thelma did well in during the primary," Kyle said. "Maybe you throw more resources into those precincts. More phonebanking, more door hangers, etcetera."

Maxwell rummaged through a file. "Let's see. Barnett won just 58 precincts statewide—almost all in Crandall's home county—and got at least 48 percent in another 150 precincts or so…"

"More robo-calls," Blake said. "Call every single voting household in all of those couple hundred precincts. Maybe even roll it out to any precinct where Thelma got 40 percent or more. Won't cost more than a few thousand bucks. And pay volunteers if we have to in those precincts."

"So, the question remains: what instructions do we give to our poll-watchers on the challenging of write-ins Tuesday night?" Maxwell asked, munching on a carrot. "Knock off every write-in and worry about the consequences later?"

"I'd say we challenge only those Barnett write-ins with obvious problems, like a misspelled name or a missing office on the ballot envelope," Kyle said.

"I have to agree, Damen," Mary said, her exhaustion growing more apparent.

"Let the record show. I warned you." Maxwell said.

*   *   *

"Sam, they had a big meeting today about the Thelma write-ins. They are totally freaked."

"Who was there?" Roth asked Amy Harris.

"They brought in a bunch of the Governor's guys, Jimmy Blake, Steven Page, some smoothie lawyer named Kyle. I heard shouting between Maxwell and I think Blake. Plus, I hear on the grapevine here Maxwell threatened to quit the campaign. With just five days left! Can you believe it?"

"Not really, but I'm glad to hear they're squabbling."

"Big time," Amy said. "That is not a happy place."

"Well, here at Torres Central, we are one big happy familia."

"She's ready for the drive-around?"

"Yep. Leaves before dawn tomorrow. Billy, Liz Chinn and—get this— Dan Clark in the tail car, and the candidate, her sister Soledad and Mariano Vargas in the war wagon. Although there could be some vehicle-hopping, I suspect."

"Tell Professor Clark to stay away from snowstorms," Amy laughed, knowing—as many where beginning to learn—the real reason he had dropped out of the race.

"Right. You're the best. Talk to you tomorrow."

*   *   *

Chapter Six

Waterspout, Part II

All night long, the "devisibility crews" returned from their assignments to the drab 6th Ward Democratic Headquarters.

As in the primary cycle, many of the crews had been dispatched far outside of the 6th Ward to do their dirty work. The bounty for tearing down and bringing in posters for any Republican candidates was still 25 cents per sign. And the customary grand prize—a case of booze, scotch this time—was again offered, along with dinner for four at Bongi's, a local steakhouse.

But it just wasn't the same without Boss Chizz.

His absence was noticed more that night than at any time since his fatal dive into a stack of potato pancakes at the Danzig Café. Congressman Ziggy Prybyl had taken over as 6th Ward Committeeman, and Mike Kula had rebounded from his brush with the law, and even Butchie Kaminski seemed re-ignited about politics, but the spirit was not the same.

In the old days, a playful slap on the cheek from the gruff Czyz would send a young Mad Dog into Seventh Heaven. John's ability to teach and inspire the newly-arrived Pakistani, Serbian and Palestinian members of his tribe showed what a genuine and rare leader he was.

Oh, the crews performed. One group brought in a 10-foot wooden "Prentice for Governor" sign and another team had snatched more than 200 Mary Moore yard signs from Mary Moore's home precinct, but their hearts just weren't in it.

*　　*　　*

"Oh, candidata! Time for a road trip," Billy whispered in Graciela's ear. She looked so lovely, so tiny, he thought. Her silky dark hair fell across her pink nightgown. He rubbed her shoulders and she came to.

"Do we have to? I was dreaming. I was in a maze."

"It's no dream. This state is a maze and the ladies of West Wheaton await you."

Graciela yawned and stretched. "It's too dark. What time is it?"

"5:45. Boat leaves at 6:30. The polls open in, uh, just 72 hours."

Graciela took Billy's unshaven face in her hands and gave him a long, sweet kiss. She rolled out of bed and trotted to the shower. "Can you get the coffee going? I need about a gallon."

Billy smiled, laid back in the bed. What a woman. What a romance, the most intense and exhilirating he had experienced since the early days of courtship with his ex-wife, so long ago.

"I'll start the coffee only if I can join you in the shower," Billy called out.

"No deal. The polls open in 72 hours," she dreamily sang out over the running water.

Billy pulled on his jeans and a sweater and went downstairs. Graciela's son, Roberto, was already up and had started the coffee.

"Hey, 'Berto. Up so soon?"

"Yeah, figured you guys would need coffee. I think it's gonna be very strong."

"Aw, you're a good man. Your mom has a big weekend ahead of her. Your tia—Soledad—is goin' with us, too."

Roberto nodded his head and watched the coffee drip.

"I hear you're gonna meet my grandfather."

"Yeah, but probably not until Election Night. Should be a pretty amazing day. Any advice on meeting him?"

Roberto stretched. For the first time, Billy noticed a hint of facial hair on the kid. "You gonna ask him for permission to marry my mom?"

Billy was startled by the question. He hadn't really thought about it. "Pretty heavy question before coffee, hombre." Billy had never discussed the romance with Roberto and had certainly never talked to the kid about Graciela's late-husband, for whom Roberto was named.

"I am so crazy about your mom, ya know. She and I have really...connected. I've never known a woman quite like her," Billy stammered.

Roberto stared at him, almost through him. "Well, I think she feels the same way 'bout you. My sister and I and my aunts all see the change in her, a good change. She seems very happy, more alive. I hope this isn't just about politics...or sex."

"Man, those are two heavy items, 'Berto. I dunno," Billy filled up his cup. "You know the rock-and-roller, Iggy Pop?"

"Hearda him," Roberto shrugged.

"He has this one song where he talks about 'love in the middle of a firefight'. Sometimes I think about that. During political campaigns, your emotions are raw, you're vulnerable, you need shelter from the incoming bombs, the insanity. It's not normal. But I think our romance is real and deep. I think it will survive Election Day, win or lose."

"Maybe even survive meeting my grandfather," Roberto grinned.

"Hello? Anybody? Café! Quiero caffeine ahora!" Graciela yelled from upstairs.

The phone rang. Mariano Vargas and Liz Chinn were already at the Headquarters, and wanted to know if they should pick up doughnuts.

*   *   *

"I can't believe it," Randall Moore told his wife as he brought the morning paper in from the front lawn. "You won't believe it."

Mary was brewing tea and looking over the schedule for the flyaround. "Believe what?"

"They took every single yard sign on the block. Stripped clean to the bones."

Mary could only grin and shake her head. *What low-life thugs I'm up against. Graciela Torres seems nice enough—her phonecall wishing Tony well after the beating was classy—but her supporters are goons.*

"Well, if we don't get every vote on the block, it's probably because you burned the hot dogs at last summer's block party," she smiled. She reviewed the day's schedule. *What a killer.*

8:00 a.m.	*Candidate to be picked up by Del Zink and driven to Jackson City Airport.*
8:45 a.m.	*Press conference at Airport. Will be joined by Cong. Prentice, Sec. of State Dobbs, Karen Hogan.*
9:15 a.m.	*Wheels up. Live phone interview from plane with WIQM-AM re: overview of the race. Possible call-ins.*
9:50 a.m.	*Arrive Peshtigo Airport. Driven to Library by local volunteer.*
10:00 a.m.	*Press Conference at Peshtigo Public Library. Return to Airport.*
10:45 a.m.	*Wheels up.*
11:20 a.m.	*Arrive Fargo County Airport. Driven to College by Mayor Taylor.*
11:30 a.m.	*Rally at Fargo Community College. Expect 1,000 attendees. Return to Airport. Meet with Fargo Republican leaders during ride.*
12:10 p.m.	*Wheels up.*
12:45 p.m.	*Arrive Fox County Air Center. Meet with Republican Chairman Tug Blaney. Rally at Air Center.*
1:30 p.m.	*Wheels up. In-flight meeting with State GOP Chair Gretchen Hanson re: GOTV plans.*
2:20 p.m.	*Arrive Belmont Park Airport. Driven to State Building by PUC employee Sheila Fonda.*
2:45 p.m.	*Press Conference with Gov. Langley and Moira Reynolds at the newly-renamed "Calvin Reynolds State Office Building".*

3:45 p.m.	*Wheels up. Gov. Langley to join the flyaround.*
4:45 p.m.	*Arrive Capital City Airport. Governor's Security Van to take group to Capitol.*
5:00 p.m.	*Press Conference with Gov. Langley at Capitol.*
6:00 p.m.	*Reception for local party activists at State Republican Party Headquarters.*
7:00 p.m.	*Check-in at Parker Hotel. Freshen up if necessary.*
8:00 p.m.	*Fundraising Gala in Grand Ballroom of Parker Hotel. Black tie. Expect 500 attendees.*
10:00 p.m.	*Overnight—Parker Hotel.*

And then we do it all over again Sunday. Well, home stretch. Hope Tug Blaney doesn't try to pin me down on PUC patronage, Mary thought. And that event in Calvin's hometown with Moira should be a gut-check.

"Honey, Tony's on the line. Just wants to say bon voyage," Randall called out.

Mary picked the phone. "Hey, sweetie. How are the bruises?"

"Aw, fine, mom. I'm almost healed," Tony assured her. "And good news. Cops called last night. Have a suspect. They want me to look at some photos this afternoon."

"That's great news! The best news I've heard in a long time. Let's get these creeps off the streets," Mary said emphatically.

"Hey, thanks again for your speech at the Biloxi. It caused major buzz in the community. Everybody's got your signs up. Thanks for standing up for me, too."

"What any mother would do…if she had such a great son."

"Okay, good luck with the trip, Mom. I love you."

"Love you too, kiddo."

*   *   *

"So, Hermana, how's the romance doing?" Soledad Torres asked her sister as they sped through rain-soaked cornfields. Driver Mariano Vargas kept his eyes on the road and smiled.

Graciela was stretched out in the back seat of the "War Wagon", a lumbering SUV the campaign had rented for the final month. Billy, Liz Chinn and one-time candidate Dan Clark drove behind them in the tail car.

"Well, it's still pretty hot. Miami Beach was fantastico," Graciela said. "We had our first spat a few days ago. Over some stupid thing. But, he is really something. I think I'm in love."

"Ready for him to meet Father?"

"Not looking forward to that. He is. I'm not."

She knew that Tuesday would be another emotional roller coaster: not only the election, but seeing her father for the first time in more than a year, plus having Billy meet her father for the first time. Her father and her late-husband Bobby Perez never got along; Bobby was too fast, too street, too American. Her father always blamed Bobby for the murder of Graciela's brother, Ernesto, Jr., an incident that left Ernesto, Sr., bitter for years. Graciela wasn't sure how her father would handle her romance with Miller.

"How do you think Father will feel about Billy?" Graciela asked her sister.

"Besides the fact that he's a gringo and speaks no Spanish? As long as Father is convinced Billy is good for you and won't harm his precious daughter, everything should be okay, I guess," Soledad said.

Mariano chimed in. "As long as your Father senses the love—which I think he will—he should be proud. He'll be proud anyhow when you win this election."

"Ah, Mariano, you don't know our Father," Soledad laughed. "Tough old guy. Much pride."

"Well, Billy's pretty charming. Pretty smart guy. He'll probably be drinking shots and laughing with Father before the night is over," Graciela said wistfully.

A quarter-mile behind them, a similar dialogue was occurring. Liz Chinn, at the wheel, had been welcomed into the Torres inner circle ever since the

Dan Clark campaign had imploded. She could see the warmth in the campaign, the diversity (Sam Roth and Jimmy Juarez were odd teammates), the passion for success. The romance between Miller and Torres was very evident and sort of cute, in a teenaged puppy love sort of way, Liz mused.

"So, Billy, how did you and Graciela first meet anyhow?"

Billy related the curious handwritten note Graciela had sent early in the primary and his invitation to the Sauk County event. "And after the event, she and I and Sam and Lupe climbed to the bluffs overlooking the river—one of my favorite places on this earth—and I started waxing poetic about politics and rivers and we just clicked," Billy said. "The four of us polished off two bottles of wine as we watched an incredible sunset—it was really magical—and that night…"

"Say no more," Clark said from the back seat.

"Say more! More!" Chinn giggled.

"Anyhow, I never liked Podesta, and even before our little hike up the bluffs I was planning on maneuvering into Graciela's campaign as sort of a, y'know, red-neck liaison. I thought she had very little chance, to be honest. Hell, it was Podesta's to lose with Petacque coming in a strong second, was my guess. But I figured she'd be a good vehicle for me to ding Podesta and make in-roads with some of the city folks like Jimmy Juarez."

"And that strategy worked," Clark said.

"Yeah, I think so. Podesta was deprived of a majority at the slatemaking; I'll take some credit for that. And the key Dem players in Jackson City got to know me a little. I definitely understand Jackson City politics better. It's pretty wild and wooly," Billy said. "Pretty raw."

"So, more on the romance, please," Liz implored.

"Well, it got hot and heavy pretty quickly. I'd been divorced for a long time and Graciela's husband had been killed in a drive-by in El Puente a long time before. Neither of us had been in any serious relationships for awhile. Both of us were ready for something, I guess."

"Has the campaign placed any additional stress on things?" Liz asked.

"Well, we had our first quarrel last week. Minor stuff. She was right and I was wrong. And sometimes, she's frazzled, just exhausted. Plus, she's trying to raise two kids in an inner city environment while being a County Board member. But overall, she's incredible."

"Future possibilities, if I may ask?" Dan said.

"Maybe, maybe. Anything's possible. We had a terrific trip to Miami Beach after the primary and the romance only got better. We're planning on a trip to the Florida Keys after the election," Billy said. "And I'm meeting her dad for the first time. He's coming up from Mexico for Election Day."

"Whoa. That's big. How's your espanol?" Clark asked.

"Muy mal. But the old man speaks some English. Sounds like a decent guy. The family's had a hard life. The mother died in Mexico, the murders here, eking out a living in the cold, hard winters of Jackson City. He must be a man of great character. I could think of better circumstances for our first meeting, though.

"Ah, the life of a politico. High-speed roller coaster rides through peaks and valleys," Liz said. The car phone rang. Mariano wanted to know which exit to take to get to the rally in Hubbs.

*　　　*　　　*

The first of the four sound trucks edged into Jackson City traffic. Each was festooned with posters urging a vote for the Democrats and equipped with a booming sound system. A closed loop 30-second message from Sen. Beatrice Madison, with her distinctive schoolteacher voice, urged people to get to the polls Tuesday and vote for "my beautiful colleague, Debra Shane, for Governor" and the other fine Democrats.

The trucks followed carefully designed routes in African-American communities, driving down busy commercial strips and through high-density neighborhoods. Each truck had a microphone so the driver could issue live messages a la The Blues Brothers: "*You there. In the purple hat. Don't forget. Tuesday's votin' day!*"

Sometimes the truck would linger wherever a crowd may be. One such location was outside of the New Jerusalem Baptist Church as a crowd exited from a Saturday morning "prayer council".

"People! This is Senator Beatrice Madison urging you to be proud and be loud! Vote on Tuesday for my beautiful State Senate colleague, Debra Shane, as our next Governor. Debra Shane stands for equality and justice. Debra Shane truly cares about our community. Let's make history! Vote for the whole Democratic Party ticket. Democrats, the Party of the People. The Party that Cares! People! This is Senator Beatrice Madison..."

"What about that, Pastor Lee? I've always voted Democratic," one of the faithful asked the aging man-of-the-cloth.

Pastor Lee had just called upon the 150 or so attendees who jammed into the tiny storefront church to write-in "Thelma Barnett" for Chairperson for the state Public Utilities Commission. He had described the "unfortunate, sinful pandering" to gays by incumbent Mary Moore and had described the "power of prayer" that Thelma Barnett would bring to the PUC.

"Miss Carter, there are some good Democrats and some good Republicans. But, not all of them are as God-fearing as you and me," Pastor Lee replied gently. "I have met this Thelma Barnett and I am so convinced that she will bring the power of prayer into the highest levels of government. The highest levels."

"Pastor, your word is always good by me, you know that. But, my son works for the City, you know, and he's even an assistant precinct captain for the Democrats in our Ward. I'd hate to do anything that might jeopardize his duty."

"I totally respect your dilemma, Miss Carter. One write-in vote, though, will certainly not jeopardize your hard-working son's status, though, and it could go a long, long way to enhancing the morals and the values in our state government," the kindly Pastor placed his arm around her shoulder as Sen. Madison's endless loop rang out.

"...The Party that Cares! People!..."

*   *   *

Mary Moore was still a little rattled from the WIQM radio interview. After a successful press conference at the Jackson City Airport with Congressman Prentice, the Republican ticket (except for Attorney General nominee Philip Driscoll) jetted north towards Peshtigo, a conservative, blue-collar town that was gradually becoming a Republican bastion. En route, Mary did a live interview on WIQM, a popular radio station in Shannon Valley.

The interview was going well—the usual questions about the cost of utility service, a few specific customer complaints, nothing, fortunately on River's Edge. Mary handled each question effortlessly.

"Okay, time for one more question for Public Utilities Chairperson Mary Moore, who's flying directly over Shannon Valley as we speak. Caller from, uh, East Ashford, you're on the air with a question about your cable bill," DJ Lefty Kavanaugh practically yelled.

"Yeah, Miss Moore. Actually, I'm more interested in knowing how you can justify, in the eyes of the Lord, appearing before a whole group of perverted gay transvestites the other night, and why you said you'd be for gay marriage and why won't you disavow your own son, your own flesh-and-blood, who sleeps with other men, even though the Bible clearly states..."

Lefty cut off East Ashford. "Well, we thought East Ashford was interested in your views on cable TV, but, uh, that's the risk we take here with live radio, Miss Moore. We do apologize, but, uh, would you care to respond at all?"

Mary was taken aback, not sure how to respond to this maniac. She started slowly.

"Well, Lefty, I think most of your listeners really are more concerned about their cable bills than my son's love life. And the Public Utilities Commission has taken strong steps to rein in spiraling cable bills and shady cable TV installation practices..."

"Right, right," Lefty said.

"But let me say this, Lefty. I know you have a well-informed, intelligent listenership. And any intelligent person knows that bigotry is a stain on our entire community. It's not a matter of one person's interpretation of the Bible. We have a Constitution and a political culture that demands equal justice under the law. That's why I'm willing to provide equal benefits—and not authorize gay marriages, as the, uh, listener from East Ashford just suggested—to employees at the Public Utilities Commission..."

"Right, right..."

"And, Lefty, let me say one more thing. My son Tony was beaten up, brutally, the other night, by the forces of bigotry. The forces of evil. That's not what any truly Christian person can condone." Mary was getting really warmed up now.

"Well, Madam Chairperson, we are all glad to hear that your son is recovering and wish him well and we appreciate your candor and, uh, wish you well on Tuesday!"

"Thanks, Lefty. Always a pleasure."

"Next up on WIQM, the best way to insulate your roof before those winter winds start a-blowin'. This is Lefty Kavanaugh. Back after this."

Maybe that was a little heavy-duty for a Saturday morning audience, Mary thought as she hung up and stared out the window of the tiny jet. A vast, endless checkerboard of harvested fields extended for miles. Can any families down there really be more concerned about equal benefits for a few gay state employees than about the cost of their cable TV? And how can anyone who reads the Bible be so upset and downright venomous about the personal life of another?

"Mary! You okay? You look a little pale," Karen Hogan shouted from across the aisle. Mary smiled and gave a thumbs-up. The plane hit some turbulence and the pilot switched on the seatbelt sign. She reached down to the airsickness bag and threw-up.

*   *   *

State Treasurer candidate Rep. Tom Cummings was, like Graciela, clearly on the fast-track, a no-doubt-about-it rising star in statewide politics. He and Graciela had seen a great deal of each other on the campaign trail during the primary and had become friendly. Cummings appreciated her help in getting his materials translated into Spanish, and distributed in El Puente and other Hispanic neighborhoods.

The Democratic Party organization in rural Hubbs was near extinction until Cummings was elected to the Legislature a decade earlier and revitalized it. He now had hundreds of hard-core volunteers and they all turned out for his Election Weekend Rally and Fish Boil. Graciela and Secretary of State candidate Bill Karmejian were invited to speak to the huge crowd in the village square. The old courthouse and an eroding bronze World War I statue flanked the makeshift stage.

"Friends," Cummings said, the wind blowing his Kennedy-esque hair, "Sometimes out there on the campaign trail, you find a special kind of person. A gem. That's who I found as I campaigned during this past year. Graciela Torres has the relentless heart of a fighter, but it's a big, compassionate heart, as well. Graciela Torres will stand up to the big utility companies and their high-priced lobbyists. She'll stand up for the little guy! She'll stand up from the mean streets of Jackson City to the quiet streets of Hubbs! Our next PUC Chair, my very good friend, Graciela Torres!"

The crowd roared as Graciela leapt onstage, thanked and lauded Cummings, and went into her stump speech for the thousandth time.

At the back of the crowd, Dan Clark and Billy Miller chatted.

"She's very impressive. She'll do well," Clark said. "I hope I can be of some assistance in her administration."

Billy knew about Clark's request for a high-level position and Jimmy Juarez' reluctance to commit. Graciela could definitely use someone who understood the whole utility regulatory business; Clark knew his stuff. "I'm sure," Billy replied, noncommittally. "She'll need all the help she can get. Lots of technical, complicated stuff. So, how'd you like being on the campaign trail? A little different than academia?"

"Oh, yeah. I loved it. It gives you a glimpse that few get. A perspective of how people live, work, think. Too bad it takes so much dough," Clark said. "If it wasn't for Petra Dresden…"

"Yeah, that part sucks. But, you're right about the campaign experience. Nothin' like it in the world," Billy said. "You really grow as a person."

The crowd was laughing and applauding at something Graciela had just said. Karmejian and Cummings were both cracking up.

"She's really developed as a public speaker, too," Billy said. "More confident. Better timing, body language."

"She's less rigid, too. I remember her at that first candidate's forum. Seemed sort of programmed, over-coached. Now, she's very easy-going, but persuasive. A very engaging style," Dan observed.

"Yeah, she's got a gift. She's an artist in her own unique way. And she's put together a solid team. And we sure appreciate Liz Chinn being a part of our campaign. Your loss was our gain on that," Billy said. "She really filled a void."

"Liz is great. Savvy, a great motivator. She kept me on track, that's for sure," Clark said. "And I know she really enjoys your whole group."

The crowd was roaring as Graciela waved and gave Tom Cummings a hug.

"On to West Wheaton," Billy said, worried that they were already a half-hour behind schedule and it was still early in the drive-around.

*　　　　　*　　　　　*

At Moore Headquarters, dozens of volunteers were feverishly looking up phone numbers, using every internet connection and phone book available. Damen Maxwell had identified 350 precincts where Thelma Barnett had gotten at least 40% of the primary vote. The campaign's high-priced voter file, unfortunately, had very few phone matches, so nearly 20,000 phone numbers needed to be looked up by Sunday morning so the "robo-calls" could be placed.

Maxwell was acting like a bull in a china shop, screaming, whining, throwing papers. Peggy Briscoe tried to tell him how well the fly-around was going and he swore at her. Several volunteers said they couldn't stand it and would come back later.

Amy Harris watched it all and called her pal, Sam Roth. "It's a nuthouse here," she whispered. "But I hear her flyaround's going well."

"Okay, keep your eyes open. And can you get us the list of the 350 precincts they're targeting? And try not to get in Maxwell's path."

        *   *   *

"Now, Miz Moore, we got a great organization here. I know ya may have some well-founded doubts after that whole caucus thing, but we fixed all that," Tug Blaney was making his pitch to a wan and disinterested Mary Moore at the Fox County Air Center. The rally was poorly-attended and Mary just wanted to get back on the plane.

Blaney, an old Republican Party warhorse, had been slipping lately. His organization was a shadow of it's former self and his patronage was diminishing due to early retirements and corruption. All he had going was a recipe cookbook published each year by the Women's Auxiliary, always a big seller.

"Tug, I'm just trying to get through the next three days. I really haven't made any decisions about staff changes. Calvin Reynolds had a great team…"

"Oh, I know. He surely did…" Tug said, his huge unlit cigar dripping saliva.

"…including several fine members of the Fox County Republican organization. We'll keep those people safe, as long as we get a day's work for a day's pay…"

"Oh, you will. Good people, all solid people."

"But, I can't give any assurances about any new hires. I'm trying to be straight with you here, Tug. And we need a good turnout on Tuesday here in Fox. Okay?"

"Ah understand completely, ma'am. A good turnout we will have."

Cong. Prentice touched Mary's arm and said, "Tug, we gotta zoom. Really appreciate your help here today. Need a good turnout Tuesday, Tug."

"You're gonna make us proud as our next Governor. I can feel it," Blaney gushed.

"Well, let's get to work, Tug. Thanks again," Prentice said as he steered Mary to the jet idling on the tarmac. "Ole Tug's really over the hill. We'll need to think about a successor right after Tuesday," he said into Mary's ear.

Wow, Mary thought. He's already assuming the role of state party honcho. Well, I guess he needs to. Within minutes, they were in the clouds and on their way to the Belmont Park ceremony honoring Calvin Reynolds.

$$*\qquad\qquad *\qquad\qquad *$$

"So, you guys having a pleasant drive in the country?" Sandra Siquieros asked Graciela on the car phone.

Back in the Torres Jackson City Headquarters, 30 volunteers—under the supervision of Jimmy Juarez, Sam Roth and Lupe Zarate—were calling hundreds of other volunteers across the state to give them their Election Day assignments. While many would be working in the polls in their home precincts, some would be operating out of centralized phonebanks, mostly in union halls. Others would be floaters, who would be moved around on Election Day depending on turnout. Sam's plan was to move some of these folks into the 350 precincts targeted by the Moore camp for extra effort based on Barnett's primary showing, wherever geographically possible.

"Great! Cummings had an excellent rally, maybe a thousand people, TV cameras. The West Wheaton event wasn't as great as in September, but still pretty good," Graciela said. "Even raised some dinero."

"Well, that's good, Graciela, because that's why I'm calling," Siquieros said slowly. "I've crunched some numbers—financial numbers—and I'm afraid we are barely running on fumes. We've raised about eighty-five of the 100-K the State Party asked of us; I spoke with Anna Bloom and Niles

Flint and they still expect to see that $15,000 balance before Tuesday. Our last TV buy ended up costing nearly $200,000. The printer needed $30,000 for the final mailer. And between staff salaries, rent and walkin' around money for Jimmy Juarez' guys, we're looking at a $40,000 deficit."

"A deficit? Damn. I thought we were right on track," Graciela said as Mariano hit 85 mph on the Interstate. They were getting desperately late for the AFL-CIO rally in Fontana Falls.

"Yeah, well, I've been urging more call time all week," Sandra said.

"I know, I know. Things get so crazy."

"Uh-huh. Whatever," said an unimpressed Siquieros. "Well, I gave Liz Chinn some call sheets, just in case you had some downtime. Is she in the car with you or is she in the tailer?"

"She's here. I'll get going."

"Forty thou or staff doesn't get paid or you dip into 'Berto and Raisa's college funds, not to pressure you or anything," Sandra said. "And you've got until Monday to raise it. Piece of cake."

"You're a motivational genius, Sandra. Thanks."

Graciela turned to Liz. "You've got call sheets?"

Liz, who knew Sandra would be calling with this "emergency" appeal, smiled sweetly. "Would you like me to start dialing, Madam Commissioner?"

"I really hate this," Graciela grumbled as she shifted gears into fundraiser mode.

*   *   *

As Mary expected, the ceremony in Belmont Park was gut-wrenching. The half-century old State Government Building had received a tuck-pointing rehab and a new parking lot, and was re-named the "Calvin Reynolds State Office Building", a fact proclaimed by a large bronze plaque in the lobby and a 10' sign by the parking lot. Several hundred local residents and every TV station in the state were on hand to see Gov. Langley cut the ribbon. Gray clouds threatened. Langley warmed up the crowd with a few Calvin anecdotes and introduced Prentice, Dobbs, Moore and Hogan.

"Now, I knew Calvin back in his Vietnam days," Langley told the crowd. "He was a no-nonsense fellow even then. And he always believed in the maxim: Stand up, Speak up and then Shut up! So, let me be brief and then be gone.

"Very few public servants in our State achieved so much for so many so quickly as Calvin Reynolds. His legacy lives far beyond the bricks and mortar of this spectacular State Office Building. So, we were honored to have the friendship of Calvin and of his lovely wife, Moira, who is here today. Moira, give me a hand here."

Moira Reynolds, still wearing black and still appearing exhausted, walked to the Governor and gave him a hug. She took the oversized scissors used only for ceremonial ribbon-cuttings and did the deed. Langley asked her to pose for the TV cameras and newspaper photographers.

She took the mike. "I want to thank the Governor for this gracious gesture and thank the Republican ticket for making this trip so close to the election. I'm sure you are all so very busy, so this means a lot to us. Calvin always loved this building. He would come here often, early in his political career, to do research or make friends. And if you look through the desks of many of the employees working here even today, you'll probably find some 'Reynolds is My Man' nail files."

The crowd laughed warmly. A cold drizzle began to fall.

"Anyone in public life knows the toll it takes on your family and loved ones. It's not easy being a political spouse or the child of a politician. So many nights and weekends alone. Such turmoil, especially at election time. But, the benefits or public service are extensive and worth the sacrifices.

"So, Governor Langley: you and Calvin went through so many battles together, from Saigon to the State Capitol. He admired you so. I am truly humbled by this honor and know that Calvin would have appreciated it. Thank you all so much."

To a standing ovation, Moira bowed to the crowd and hugged everyone on stage. "You're doing such a great job, Mary. I know you'll do fine on Tuesday," she whispered to Moore. Mary could see the tears welling in Moira's dark eyes.

"I had a great teacher. The best," Mary replied, as tears began to stream down her own face. Twenty minutes later, she and the Governor and the GOP ticket were back on the jet, headed to the Capital.

*   *   *

"So, how's progress?" Amy Harris asked one of the volunteers. The search for phone numbers had become all-consuming in the Moore Headquarters. Volunteers were seated at long tables, armed with raggedy phone books from across the state. Damen Maxwell had declared it the top priority of the campaign to find the phone numbers in the 350 precincts, which he had characterized as the "Thelma Precincts".

"Slow. There's got to be a better way," replied a sweet, blue-haired senior with a magnifying glass.

"Now, Mrs. Adams, what precinct are you working on?" Amy quietly asked.

"Well, honey, I've got all the targets in Wells County. That'd be Precincts 3, 9, 16 and 52," Mrs. Adams replied loudly.

"Well, keep up the great work." Volunteer by volunteer, Amy continued to discretely compile the list of "Thelma Precincts", a list only Maxwell had. She didn't want Maxwell to know she was pulling this list together. She wasn't even sure why it was so important for Sam Roth to have it, but she was on a mission.

*   *   *

After chatting with Debra Shane at the huge, muscular labor rally in Fontana Falls, the Torres campaign itinerary was altered. Deanna Drew, from Shane's staff, came up with the plan for Shane and Torres to ambush the Republican ticket in Capital City. "Gotta think opportunistically," she said. "Gotta seize the moment." After a quick Brain Trust conference call, Graciela agreed. The caravan regretfully cancelled a coffee and press conference in Peshtigo and headed for the Capital.

As they drove, Graciela dutifully continued dialing for dollars while Liz Chinn provided her with the call sheets and recorded the result on each one. "Pledged $250" or "I'll think about it" or "Sorry, I'm tapped out" would be scrawled across each page. In just two hours, Graciela had solid commitments of more than $13,000, including a $2,000 check that could be picked up in Jackson City immediately. She reported her success to Sandra back at Headquarters, who administered a mild pat on the back, but reminded Graciela that she still had at least $27,000 to go.

Nearing the Capitol, Graciela got a call from Deanna Drew with the plan. Graciela and Shane would appear outside of the State Capitol press room about halfway through the GOP ticket's press conference. As the media exited, Shane and Torres would conduct their own "Democratic response" press event.

As Graciela walked into the Capitol building rotunda with Billy, Mariano, Soledad and Liz (Dan Clark agreed to remain invisible), she looked up at the historic dome. She smiled at Billy. "Remember the trip to the bluffs?" she whispered, taking his arm. "How could I forget? The cosmic milkshake. And you're a flood, not Abernathy Creek," Billy whispered back, kissing her neck. "Showtime."

They met up with Shane's entourage and strolled past the aging murals of long-forgotten battles to the press room, which featured a state-of-the-art press conference facility. Several of the Republican staffers in the hallway were stunned to see the army of Democrats approach and one scurried into the Republicans press conference in progress to report on the unwelcomed visitors.

"What's our message here? Party line?" Graciela asked Deanna.

"Well, Senator Shane will blast Prentice for being out of-touch after his many years in Washington, probably go after him on education funding, maybe his crime package," Drew said. "Maybe you can blast Moore on taking utility campaign contributions, pipeline safety and River's Edge, the usual stuff."

Suddenly the press room door swung open and Governor Langley was standing there. "Greetings, Ladies. Would you care to join us?" He smiled, gesturing into the press room. Several reporters scrambled out to catch this moment.

Shane smiled back. "Wouldn't want to crash your party, Governor. Commissioner Torres and I will sit patiently out here until you're done. Thank you, though for your hospitality."

"Well, actually, we are done. Just teasing. Good luck to you both on Tuesday," Langley said, ever the gentleman.

And just as suddenly Graciela was face-to-face with Mary Moore.

"Commissioner Torres. What a pleasant surprise," Moore politely said. The two women shook hands and Graciela intentionally held the pose for a few seconds as photographers snapped and TV crews rolled.

"Well, Commissioner Moore, we're in the home stretch. Quite a state, isn't it?"

"A wonderful state. Today we've been in Peshtigo, Fargo, Fox County, Belmont Park…"

"Well, we're traveling by car," Graciela shot in, "So we're not covering quite as much ground, but we've had huge rallies in Hubbs, West Wheaton, Fontana Falls…"

"Well, good luck to you on Tuesday, Graciela," Moore said sweetly.

"You, too, Mary. You've been a classy opponent. Hope your son is doing well."

And just as quickly, the Republican ticket was on the move and out the door, save for two GOP spinmeisters who remained behind to respond to the Dems' response.

The Shane and Torres press conference itself was uneventful; the real news was the face-to-face between Langley and Shane, and between Moore and Torres, images that flashed on TV screens across the state that evening.

*　　　　*　　　　*

"Well, I was able to pull together a list of about 200 of the 'Thelma Precincts'. I think Maxwell was on to me, though," Amy told Sam over breakfast on Sunday morning. "They're scattered all over the state. None in Jackson City, very few in the suburbs."

"Yeah, Thelma's appeal was purely Bible Zone. Agent Harris, you have earned your stripes as Campaign Spy Extraordinaire," Sam said through mouthfuls of waffle.

"So, now that I risked my life, can you tell me what do you plan to do with them?"

"Well, a couple of things. First is we do our own paid phoning into these precincts. Mostly reminder calls to Democratic households and yes, we do already have their phone numbers. Second is we get the local Democratic organizations to focus on those precincts with their own local GOTV operations. This is our secret weapon in some of these rural areas, the only way we can inch up on Moore in a few of these counties."

"Huh. Sounds kind of convoluted to me," Amy said. "But, hey, I'm just a little college kid who's risking her life for you."

"Knowledge is power. This will make all the difference. People will be talking about this for years," Sam said.

Amy wasn't sure if he was kidding or not. "You still owe me a steak and red wine, buster."

*   *   *

The automated phonecalls started Sunday morning, escalating the air war in a new milieu.

Every statewide candidate used some form of "robo-call". Some called only their base, with a simple reminder-to-vote message. Some called the so-called "swing" voters with a message designed to persuade. Sometimes the candidates had their own voice on the message; some used a celebrity, such as retitred Navy Admiral Charles Alexis plugging for Phil Driscoll or Governor Langley plugging the whole Republican ticket. State Treasurer candidate Karen Hogan had a humorous soundtrack on her message, complete with a brass band and a barking dog. Some, like Atty. Gen. Lou Calcagno's, were amateurish and embarrassingly stiff.

The calls burned up the state's phonelines all day long. Some highly-targeted households received as many as seven or eight different messages; voters became numb.

Sunday was also the biggest day for TV and radio ads to air. Non-stop, incessant messages leapt from TV screens and radios, ripping the opponent one last time. Even some judicial and state legislative candidates were on the airwaves, most with their one and only spot.

Shane and Prentice had the largest buys, with Driscoll and Dobbs close behind. Moore and Torres both had respectable closing buys, with both using their positive "bio" spots. No more dancing puppets, no more smoldering River's Edge images.

The free media on Sunday focused on a Shane rally in her hometown and a minor gaffe by Prentice, with cameras catching him saying that there is "nothing wrong" with more minorities being on Death Row, because they "were found guilty so they deserve to be executed." Shane and leaders of Hispanic and African-American civil rights groups were all over him, citing cases of prosecutorial misconduct and judicial corruption, and he was forced to back-pedal some.

Every newspaper in the state reiterated their endorsements and the *Jackson City Review*, like many other papers, printed their sample ballot on the front page.

Day Two of the Republican flyaround went smoothly (except for Prentice's slip-of-the-lip) and they basked in the $650,000 that was raised the night before at the Gala Fundraiser in Capital City. Much of that cash would go for election day operations in suburban and rural precincts.

Mary's performance at each of the four press conferences was masterful, prompting Karen Hogan to ask Mary what she put on her Wheaties at breakfast. Even the taciturn Richard Dobbs said Mary was "at the top of her game, peaking at the perfect time." She felt unusually connected with the audiences, with the media, with herself.

The Torres drive-around continued to lag behind schedule throughout the day Sunday, but Graciela assiduously worked the phones and raised another $18,000. Her appearance at Shane's huge rally in Merrimac was well-received, although the TV crews were there only for Shane. A labor rally in Risserville was poorly-attended and a press conference at the state university drew only one reporter. Torres was starting to question this final trip.

The Torres caravan limped into Jackson City just past midnight with Graciela falling asleep on Billy's shoulder and Liz Chinn falling asleep on Dan Clark's. Less than 30 hours until the polls open, Billy thought to himself as they rolled into El Puente.

                    *   *   *

Chapter Six

Waterspout, Part III

The Monday morning *Jackson City Review* had it on the front page, with a photo of Tony.

"Police Charge Two with Attack on State Official's Son"
"Jackson City Police last night charged two 'skinheads' with the baseball bat beating of Tony Moore, son of state Public Utilities Commission Chairperson Mary Moore.

"Mr. Moore, 24, was attacked near his Jackson City apartment last week in an apparent 'hate crime', suffering a concussion, broken arm and fractured jaw. Police charged Dwight Herscher, 28, and Thomas Annarelli, 27, both of Jackson City, with felony assault. The States' Attorney is investigating the possibility of charging both men with a hate crime, based on comments made to the victim just prior to the attack. Herscher was recently released from the state penitentiary after serving 14 months for a similar attack on a Filipino tourist three years ago.

"The victim's mother, who is in a tough campaign for retain the Chairmanship of the Public Utilities Commission in tomorrow's election, expressed gratitude for the many cards and e-mails she and her son have received. She also praised the Jackson City Police Department's Special Hate

Crimes Unit for '...their prompt and effective action in resolving this vicious and cowardly crime.'"

*   *   *

The leather-lunged Bijou belted out his refrain to bemused subway commuters at the busy 52ⁿᵈ Street station. "Shane-Torres...The Perfect Team...Shane-Torres...Ain't No Dream! Meet 'em-Greet 'em...They cannot defeat 'em!" Volunteers handed out coffee and sweet rolls. Alderman Shawn Petacque and his crew, led by Chemuyil Gardner, had a sea of Shane and Torres posters undulating.

"Need your help tomorrow...thank you so much...don't forget to vote...Tuesday's the big day...need your help," Graciela said over and over. She and Shane had a perfect location at the entrance, a pinchpoint requiring thousands of early morning commuters to shake their bruised hands. Two TV crews were on hand.

Graciela recalled that it was at this same subway station during the waning days of the primary where she crashed Shane's street heat, and a bond between the two was formed. That bond—that genuine friendship—had only gotten stronger during the general election campaign, she thought. Others on the ticket had been cordial—well, except Lou Calcagno—but Graciela knew that, no matter what happened tomorrow, she and Shane would remain close allies and buddies because of this experience.

"Prentice-Moore-Prentice-Moore!" A chubby twenty-something commuter began yelling after eating two of the candidates' sweet rolls. He and Bijou began competing, but the kid was no match for Bijou's eloquence and decibel level. The kid snatched one more sweet roll and hopped on the next subway train.

"So, Alderman, no hot coffee facials today," Shane yelled to Petacque over the subway's metallic shrieks.

"Right, just some pimple-faced punk eating your pastries," Petacque yelled back.

Shawn had earned a reputation as a master of subway platform street heat, due partly to Chemuyil's stylish choreography of noisy sign-wavers. More importantly, Petacque had situated himself as the African-American rising star in statewide politics. His respectable primary race and subsequent role in the Democratic coordinated campaign put him on the fast-track, much sooner than even he had anticipated. He was delighted to be welcomed into the Torres campaign, along with remnants of other vanquished armies, like Liz Chinn. He had new respect for Graciela for welcoming new blood into the Inner Circle, the sign of a confident leader, he thought. And between Jimmy Juarez bringing in characters like Seamus Dunne and Mario Camozzi, and Billy Miller locking in rural Democrats, the Torres camp was uniquely poised for a broad victory, Shawn figured.

"Alderman, after we win this thing, you and I need to talk, okay?" Shane yelled into his ear.

"Definitely, Senator. I'll look forward to it," Shawn replied. "And you are gonna win this thing."

* * *

The Moore campaign also had a sea of sign-wavers at a suburban commuter rail station.

As Mary stood in the cold rain, she could feel the raspy tickle of a sore throat and regretted having this very Republican stop on the schedule. She did agree with the arrogant Damen Maxwell that she needed to close in the city, especially with the liberal-moderates. She was angry with herself for not reaching out more to Royce Blasingame and his Jackson City ally, Rep. Laura Southampton; they really could have helped in these final days.

"We're with you, Mary," one young commuter yelled out as she dashed for her train, clutching her briefcase, cell phone and coffee mug.

"Thank you so much," Mary shouted. "Spread the word. Tomorrow's the election." Her throat was feeling worse. She had gotten only a few hours of sleep after the flyaround to "Tiny Towns", as Maxwell had put it,

and had been at the station for about a half-hour when several Torres supporters waving hand-made "Remember River's Edge" posters appeared.

"I am not in the mood for this," Mary uttered to the volunteer serving
as her "body person". "How did they know I was even going to be here? It
wasn't on the published schedule."

Back at Moore Headquarters, Secret Agent Amy Harris hurriedly jotted
down the rest of Mary's Monday-Tuesday schedule before leaving the
office for the last time.

*   *   *

"Good morning Jackson City! Freddy Fritz here on WJAW-AM, your
place for good talk.

"This morning's guest on 'Jawboning with Freddy' is Arnold Wiser, the
one-time college football star who blew the whistle on Eaton Gas
Company for its role and cover-up in the tragic, horrible River's Edge
explosion. Mister Wiser, whose honesty cost him his job at Eaton Gas, was
one of the first investigators on the scene of the explosion and helped
reveal how Eaton higher-ups actually concealed the faulty valve in their
office. We'll hear from Arnold and take your calls right after this…"

Lupe Zarate smiled. She had been pitching Freddy Fritz, a self-styled
muckraker with a top-ranked morning radio talk show, for weeks about
Arnold Wiser's story. After Graciela's press conference on Friday, Fritz'
producer called and Arnold was booked. The morning before the election.
Drive-time. Does it get any better, Lupe thought.

*   *   *

"So, Damen, how are we looking for troops tomorrow?"

"Fine. We've got about 400 paid all-day workers at $150 each, mostly
assigned to targeted suburban precincts. We've got another 800 unpaid
volunteers who will be available for part of the day, mostly the last two or
three hours, closing," Maxwell impatiently informed Moore.

"Where are we sending them?"

"Well, we still need to make the assignments and calls, and we're a little light on volunteers here. I'm not sure where Amy Harris is. She was supposed to coordinate that whole thing. Anyhow, I'm torn between sending the 800 volunteers into the 'Thelma Precincts' to boost our closing numbers and challenge the write-ins…"

"Which Jimmy Blake is firmly against, as you know," Mary interjected.

"…uh-huh, or putting them into some of the precincts where your other primary opponent, Mister Blasingame, did well."

"I like that. And I agree with you that I should spend most of my final hours in Jackson City."

"Well, finally, the candidate agrees with her Campaign Manager."

"Damen, you don't have to get snotty here. Just make sure scheduling has me finishing in the City, okay?"

Maxwell hung up without saying goodbye. What a jerk, Mary thought, as she headed to the Jackson County Republican Women's luncheon rally.

*   *   *

School buses lined up for several blocks in each direction approaching the Civic Center. The pre-dawn rain had headed east and sunshine gingerly poked through the clouds. All weekend, the Mayor's political operatives had worked the phones, threatening, cajoling, begging. Hundreds of city employees were either involved in getting troops on buses parked outside of their local ward organization headquarters or helping set up at the Civic Center. Thousands of senior citizens were plucked from the City's Senior Centers for a "field trip" and free lunch.

Each Alderman had been given VIP tickets, with instructions to have those seats filled no later than 11:00 a.m. for the Noon rally. One of Mayor Townshend's operatives had the sole task of determining how many bodies each Alderman had lined up. Good records were kept.

For three days, radio spots on African-American and Spanish-language stations touted the event. A free "Taste of Jackson City" would be held afterwards, with the city's major restaurants all contributing culinary treats. Several prominent sports stars were on the agenda. A raffle of trips to warm and sunny places would also be held, with every attendee eligible.

*   *   *

After the subway street heat at 52nd Street with Debra Shane, the Torres campaign took to the streets. One of the sound trucks that had been cruising in the African-American neighborhoods was peeled off for Graciela to use in Hispanic neighborhoods. She sat in the front seat with the live microphone, her petite voice booming in Spanish and English as the truck motored through commercial strips in one community after another. She could see that the "Chrysler Crew" had done their work well the night before; "Vote Democratic" posters and "Shane-Calcagno-Karmejian-Cummings-Torres" signs were plastered on every available lightpost.

As she waved to thousands of mid-morning shoppers, Graciela wished her campaign had done more voter registration. How many of these people can actually vote? Pequeno Barragan and other leaders of the Spanish media had done a great job of boosting her name ID to unbelievable levels. The daily newspaper "Hoy!" found an excuse to put her on the front page nearly every day the past week, including a huge color photo today.

The sound truck drove up to the 33rd Ward Democratic Headquarters. Jimmy Juarez had done his duty and then some: 10 school buses were packed to capacity and another 20 cars and pickup trucks—all adorned with "Torres" banners and red, green and white balloons—lined up behind them. They would noisily parade down to the Civic Center Rally.

Graciela took the mike in the sound truck and her voice boomed out, "Jimmy! Jimmy Juarez! Stop goofing around and get some work done!"

Juarez stood at the curb and beamed. He knew that Graciela's success was due to her own intellect and style, but also knew she wouldn't be at the edge of victory without him. He felt like a proud papa whose child was about to make history or a baseball scout whose prospect was stepping up to the plate in the World Series.

"Hey, guapa! Heard you had a nice weekend drive in the country!"

The sound truck parked and she bounded out, giving Juarez a kiss on the cheek and a huge hug for the hundreds of members of his 33rd Ward organization to see. "Oh, Jimmy, it was great. We had great turnout at the rallies, good media and I even raised some money."

"Hopefully enough to pay for these buses," Jimmy smiled.

Graciela did a double-take.

"Hey, just kiddin'. We're okay here. Hope the other ward guys do as well."

Lupe Zarate walked up. "Welcome home. Good trip?"

"Yeah, I was just telling Jimmy we had great media coverage and I had a little-face-to-face with Mary Moore…"

"Yeah, we saw it on TV here Saturday night," Lupe said. "And did you hear? We had Arnold Wiser on Freddy Fritz' show this morning. He was great! One full hour during A.M. Drive of River's Edge and Eaton Gas and valves and cover-ups. Lots of callers, even some we didn't plant ourselves."

"Fantastic!" Graciela felt things were breaking her way. "We could actually win this thing!"

"Ay! What do you think we've been saying?" Lupe laughed. Juarez continued to beam. The first school bus honked its horn and the caravan headed downtown.

*   *   *

"So, Nicky. What should I do here?"

Nicky Pulver hadn't heard much from Royce Blasingame since the primary election. Royce went back to the Steel & Coil business, while licking his wounds and plotting his next bid for elective office. Nicky had his hands full with *ProAction* clients in other states, including the wild presidential race in Panama and an intense "tier one" U.S. Senate race in Oregon. This was an interesting development, though.

Moore's Communications Director, Peggy Briscoe, had just called Royce inviting him to join Mary for some Election Eve campaigning that afternoon and evening, and to please bring along his pal, Rep. Laura

Southampton. They would appear together at a subway station, outside of a major shopping mall and at a busy restaurant in the heart of the gay/lesbian community. TV coverage would be likely.

"Well, it might score you some points with the elephants. And no offense, good buddy, but they're probably just as interested in Southampton as they are you," Pulver said. "How does she feel about it?"

"Southampton? I haven't called her yet. She'd probably say okay. I'm a little annoyed that they waited until the day before the election to reach out to me, y'know. Other than those jerks Blake and Maxwell trying to hardball me on an endorsement."

"Right. Well, their tracking probably shows lots of undecideds and persuadables in JC. They've been riding the kid's hate crime attack and I hear they've muscled Torres off of a few palm cards," Pulver said. Even though he was focused on Oregon and Panama, he still had his ear to the ground in Jackson City. Plus he read JJ Springfield devoutly.

"Any downside to me doing it?"

"Downside is it diminishes your image as an independent, makes you appear like some typical party stalwart. I dunno. If they had called you a few weeks ago, it might've been different. Look, they're not gonna help you in whatever race you make next and Southampton has always been persona non grata with these people," Pulver said. "My gut is to plead a scheduling conflict, but wish her well."

"Yeah, and I trust your gut, Nicky. Speaking of which, let's work out at the Club next and then do lunch at *Harbor* some day next week. And good luck in Wyoming."

"Oregon. Thanks buddy. We'll do lunch. *Harbor*."

*　　　　*　　　　*

"How did it go with the Jackson County Ladies?" Peggy Briscoe asked her candidate as Mary zoomed to the next event, a seniors bingo in the City's southeast side.

"Great! More than a thousand happy ladies. Prentice was charming, Hogan was funnier than usual, and Dobbs and Driscoll were no-shows. We recruited everybody for election day and signed up 15 volunteers for street heat this evening," Mary bubbled. "What did Blasingame say?"

"Well, Commissioner, we have bad news, bad news, and some good news."

"Okay. Blasingame first," Mary sighed.

"He was noncommittal initially, then called back with some scheduling conflict. Wished you well and said he'd messenger over $500."

"We'd rather have his body, but we'll take the cash. What else?"

"Well, we had a little ruckus here at Headquarters. Damen and Del went at it. One of the volunteers had to break it up."

"Went at it like, uh, fisticuffs?"

"Yep. A real battle of the titans, bantam division."

"Oh, for pete's sake. What prompted this?"

"Well, turns out nobody has contacted the volunteers for tomorrow yet with their assignments. Amy Harris was supposed to coordinate, but she's MIA. Nobody can figure out the lists, so Maxwell asked Del to do it and Del said he was working on your speech for tomorrow, and then Damen said Del was just an impotent wonk and couldn't organize a two-car funeral, and Del called Damen an arrogant, selfish mercenary, and…"

"Okay, I get the picture. Nobody knows where Amy is? She's been so reliable."

"Nope. I know she had some big test or something. So anyhow, Del calmed down and started supervising volunteers to make the election day worker calls."

"Great. What's the good news?"

"Besides that Maxwell is locked in his office packing his stuff into boxes? Well, Dickie Kyle called and said the write-in rules are a little hazy, but there is some precedent that the voter must write the name of the office their written-in candidate is seeking on the ballot envelope. And Kyle figures that should knock out about half of Thelma's write-in votes."

"Well, we need to get that word out to the Republican Party Chairs across the state. I know you're crunched with media stuff, but can you..."

"No problem. Can I take just one swing at Maxwell though? I know I can hit harder than Del."

"Go for it, Buiser. But, really Peggy, let's try to keep the headquarters homicide-free for just one more day."

*   *   *

Noon rallies never start at Noon, but this one unusually slow in getting ignited. One reason was the massive traffic jam of chartered buses disgorging the party faithful. The Mayor's people had done all they could and it showed. A crowd of more than 50,000 packed into the Civic Center, shoehorned between the City Hall on one side and the lagoon on the other. Banners proclaiming their allegiances were proudly unfurled: "Plumbers, Local 1933", "Jackson County Indo-American Democratic Club", "Gay 49th Warders for Shane".

The VIP seating was totally jammed by 11:30 and the senior citizens filled in the next 50 rows of folding chairs. A scaffold riser for the media loomed over the gathering and a dozen TV crews, photographers and others jockeyed for position. By 12:30, Mayor Townshend gave the green light and the Navy Reserve Band played the national Anthem. The sun was shining brightly.

Townshend served as emcee and if it was redemption he was seeking, it was redemption he got. The crowd was loud and appreciative. Townshend introduced the athlete VIP's, raffled off a trip to Cozumel, and then recognized half the City Council and a good part of the Legislature.

He turned the mike over to Mary Ikeda, who recognized State Party honchos and introduced Party Chairman Niles Flint. Flint brought up onto the stage some of the unsuccessful statewide primary hopefuls: Lawrence Burl, Paul Podesta, Butchie Kaminski and Shawn Petacque. Due to the crowd-building that had taken place during the weekend, Kaminski and Petacque both received thunderous applause.

Then Flint described the "Dream Team", and had the statewide ticket dramatically come onto the stage. Tom Cummings, looking like a young Bobby Kennedy. Graciela, who heard Jimmy Juarez' boys chanting "Torres! Torres!". Bill Karmejian, who may have been the only person in the crowd who still believed he could win. Even the elusive Attorney General Lou Calcagno joined the ticket for the first time in a long time. And when Debra Shane vivaciously leapt onto the stage, 50,000 voices roared as one.

Each candidate was given three minutes to speak, except for Shane, who could speak as long as she wished. Cummings gave a very brief thank you, I am so humbled speech. Calcagno had the look of Death about him and rambled. Karmejian was up next and was a little too animated. The crowd seemed a little restless. Then Torres took the podium.

She had never spoken before any crowd larger than maybe 4,000. She had to adjust the mike, which screeched feedback. Seniors cringed. Graciela looked out at this sea of people. She had never seen so big a crowd in the Civic Center before, and so diverse. She glimpsed a banner reading "Free Zimbabwean Poets Now".

"Amigos y amigas! My friends!"

Her words echoed off City Hall and bounced around the square in a swirling, circular, sonic motion. I can't believe I'm doing this, she thought. She saw her sister, Dolores, with 'Berto and Raisa in the front row of the VIP section and smiled in their direction.

"My friends, when I first decided to run for statewide office, I never realized how many wonderful people there are out there. Compassionate people, intelligent people, hard-working people. And we call these people…Democrats!"

A red-meat crowd pleaser. Laughter and applause boomeranged across the plaza. Graciela had never experienced the transmission of her voice in this manner. Could they really hear her way in the back? Is a rock concert like this? Workers in adjacent high-rise buildings watched through tinted windows.

"Not many people know what the Public Utilities Commission does. All it's supposed to do is guarantee public safety, and consider rate hikes to the electric companies and gas companies and phone companies and cable companies. But, all it has done recently, this so-called 'public' utilities commission, is to grant huge, outrageous rate hikes to these utilities and look the other way when a tragedy like River's Edge happens!"

As if on cue, lusty boos from the crowd. One reporter commented to another, "Oh, yeah. She sure can wave the bloody shirt."

"When elected Chairperson of this Commission, I will have the guts to say 'no' to the utility company lobbyists and say 'yes' to the consumers, to the little children in places like River's Edge!"

"But I need your help tomorrow. This whole Dream Team needs your help tomorrow. Will we get it?"

"Yeah!" the crowd yelled.

"I can't hear you, my friends. Can we count on your help tomorrow, from before dawn until after the votes are counted?"

"Yes! Yes!" the crowd screamed. Graciela smiled.

"Well, I hope so. You know, all across this state, there are Democratic rallies like this taking place today. In farm towns, in suburbs. And while it may not seem like we have a lot in common with the good Democrats in, for example, the tiny village of Hubbs, which is the hometown of my wonderful Dream Teammate, Representative Tom Cummings, we have much in common. Democrats believe in the People! Democrats fight for the little guy! And together, united, like a tidal wave crashing through the doors of the State Capitol, we will make our state a better place! Thank you so much! Muchas gracias! I love you all!"

She waved to the crowd, blew a kiss to her children and saw Billy off-stage with tears in his eyes.

The applause was so deafening that some people in nearby buildings thought a plane had crashed and the geese in the lagoon began flying south.

*   *   *

"DATELINE JJ: A final tracking poll shows too-close-to-call races for Governor, State Treasurer and PUC Czar. And even Phil Driscoll has been sneaking up on incumbent AG Lou Calcagno. Plenty of undecideds in every contest, except for the runaway train we call Secretary of State Dobbs. (Source: Argo Dispatch, Margin-of-error +/-5%) Turnout expected to be slightly above normal, though Mother Nature may have some input on that."

"Question: Will today's mega-rally organized by Jackson City Mayor Townshend mean anything?

"Question: Is it true that Campaign Managers for both Calcagno and PUC Chair Mary Moore are already packing their bags?"

*   *   *

"What the hell happened there with Maxwell?" Gov. Langley asked Jimmy Blake.

"He and the candidate never clicked, maybe he wasn't ready for a state this complicated, there was not enough of a second echelon on staff and most of the staff hated him," Blake replied as the two warriors sat in the Governor's inner office.

"Should we be worried about Mary?" Langley asked as he poured himself a shot of bourbon. He gestured to Blake to join him.

"No, thanks. I've always been worried about Mary. The Thelma write-in thing could hurt in the Bible Zone. Suburban soccer moms are way too undecided in our tracking. And, other than in a few gay areas, Mary never got any traction in the City; Torres' people did a nice job of consolidating. And River's Edge always hung like a cloud. Even this morning, that whistleblower guy from Eaton was on Freddy Fritz' gabfest."

"Well, Maxwell taking a hike at the twelfth hour doesn't help. Maybe we should have kept Page in there. Keep an eye on it, wouldja?"

"Definitely. And I'm keeping an eye on Driscoll, too. We could get the AG's office back."

"So to speak. Well, Driscoll'd be a pain, but at least he'd be hiring lots of Republican lawyers."

"Maybe I will have that drink, Governor," Blake said.

*   *   *

9:00 p.m. As the Moore caravan pulled up to the Jade Paradise, the City's busiest gay/lesbian restaurant/hangout, they were blocked by a huge crowd on the sidewalk that spilled onto the street. Now what, Mary thought.

"Here she is," someone called out as a raucous cheer greeted Mary and her entourage. Instantaneously, dozens of "Moore" posters were being waved and the chanting began.

"I sure didn't expect this," a puzzled candidate said to her volunteer driver. "I thought we were doing a simple meet-and-greet in the restaurant." As she emerged from the car, she was mobbed by hundreds of well-wishers who escorted her to a small riser set up in front of the Jade.

There, in a wheelchair with his arm in a sling, sat Tony, triumphant.

"Hey, Mom. How's it goin'? I asked a few of my pals to come out and say hello."

Mary hugged Tony gingerly and couldn't hold back the tears. "You are some kind of kid," she whispered.

"Well, you're some kind of mom. So, I wanted to make your final campaign stop something really special," he said. Just then a brilliant fireworks display was launched from the roof of the restaurant, huge speakers started blasting Ella Fitzgerald (Mary's favorite), her husband Randall appeared and hundreds of Tony's friends roared their support.

*   *   *

"I wish you were staying here," Graciela told Billy as he walked to his truck.

"Me, too, but the Sauk County Democratic Chairman must be with the Sauk County Democrats. We need to run up some big numbers in Sauk," he joshed.

"Yeah, right." They embraced and after a lingering kiss, he got in the pickup.

"You did great today, Babe. The speech of a lifetime. Really amazing."

"You like the part about the tidal wave crashing through the Capitol doors? That was for you."

"Yeah, I caught that. Thanks. Get some rest. Daddy's coming," Billy said and drove off into the night.

*   *   *

Election morning. Fat with possibilities. The bloodless revolution. But unlike primaries, when thousands of troops representing hundreds of tribes take to the battlefield, the General Election is more like a single heavyweight boxing match, with just two principals brawling all across the huge state.

As usual, the drama is played out in crummy weather. A freezing rain in Jackson City turns into sleet in the suburbs and slushy snow Downstate. A high of 39 degrees is predicted. Must have been a tough night for the sign crews, Graciela thought as she hit the snooze button. She wished Billy was here instead of down in Sauk County. She drifted for a few minutes until the doorbell rang. She heard the voice downstairs of her father, Ernesto.

After his retirement from the garment factory four years ago, Ernesto moved back to Mexico. His daughters were all grown up now and he could finally escape the brutal winters. He never liked driving in the snow. The El Puente neighborhood brought back a rush of difficult memories; he never really recovered from the murder of his only son. His siblings were all in Monterrey, so he went back to Mexico and helped out at the bookstore/botanica his youngest sister owned. He shared a modest house with a distant cousin.

Ernesto was proud of Graciela's success, though he never understood what exactly she did as a County Board member. He was a little hazy too on the PUC, but decided to fly back for her Big Day. He had arrived last night and this morning was proudly escorting his famous daughter to campaign at the garment factory that put the bread on the Torres table for so many years.

"Hija!" My daughter, he cried out, his raincoat drenched.

His perfectly-trimmed mustache was showing signs of gray and his broad smile seemed to flash more gold, but Graciela saw that he was in great shape, maybe better than when he left El Puente. The long days at the garment factory, coming home with bloodshot eyes and bloodied fingers had taken their toll on this proud son of Mexico. The bleak winters and challenges of single-parenthood in the inner city must have been so rough on him, Graciela thought as the three generations gathered for an unusual pre-dawn meal.

After a quick breakfast, Graciela, her father, her sisters and her two children were picked up by Mariano Vargas in the campaign van and brought to the entrance of the Wicker Embroidering Company. TV crews were already there as the 6:00 a.m. shift arrived.

As the cold rain pelted the entourage, the whole Torres tribe greeted the 500 or so workers who filed into the plant. It was old home week for Ernesto, who saw many of his former co-workers and friends, all of whom he introduced with great pride and gusto to Graciela. One elderly, weeping woman gave a blushing Ernesto a sloppy kiss on the lips and then gave Graciela an endless *abrazo* captured on TV, a tender, hugging image that would air on the morning news shows.

The entourage visited another factory gate and a subway station. By 8:30 a.m., her voice was shot, and her right hand bruised and bloodied. Ernesto still couldn't believe it. "Hija! You're a star, a superstar!" he kept exclaiming.

*　　　　　*　　　　　*

"That was quite a party last night. Quite a surprise which, I assume, you had a part in," a slightly hungover Mary said to Randall after the alarm went off.

"Tony's idea. He pulled it together. Hopefully you get some votes out of the deal," Randall said. "He told me he raised about $5,000, as well."

"Great kid. Hope he's not hung over."

"Probably still on the codeine. Ready for showtime?"

"Not much more we can do. I never told about my Campaign Manager. He flew the coop yesterday. Hope he didn't sense the Titanic about to hit the iceberg."

"These hired guns. Probably should have stuck with Steven Page. You really liked him, right?"

"Got overruled on that one. Governor's orders. Hope it doesn't backfire too much. Now we have Del and Peggy running the show, but they've never done this type of thing before. I better get rolling."

"I'll brew up some tea."

"Honey, you are so patient. What a great guy to put up with all this."

"I just want to know one thing from my political expert wife. Why does it always rain on Election Day?"

*   *   *

Bosses Seamus Dunne and Mario Camozzi had gathered all the intelligence they needed by 7:30 a.m. None of the possible renegades among Jackson City's "etnics" had dumped Graciela for Moore. Even Harry Griffin put Torres' name on palm cards in a few precincts (and made sure Dunne saw it.)

Seamus called Jimmy Juarez with the good news.

"Everybody held okay, Jimmy. Even Griffin has her on a few palms. Your Grashella looks good, very strong," the cryptic Dunne reported.

"Aw, Seamus, you're a pal. 'Specially on that whole Griffin thing. Whatcha hearin' on turnout?"

"Decent where we need to be. Six, maybe eight percent over. Considerin' the weather, Camozzi 'n me, we're pleased."

Six to ten percent over the normal turnout by 7:30 a.m. was just fine with Juarez. It meant fewer reminder calls and less door-knocking later in the morning.

"Well, they got crappola weather in the 'burbs and rurals, so that should help us plenty, Seamus."

"Sun here, snow there, Grashella wins. We'll keep in touch."

*　　　　*　　　　*

At Moore Headquarters, the initial pre-dawn panic experienced by Zink and Briscoe had turned into frenzy. They were getting dozens of calls from the paid workers across the state reporting duplicate assignments or that they never received their worker kits and pollwatcher credentials or that they were promised their cash upfront. Since the still-MIA Amy Harris and the Delaware-bound Damen Maxwell had lined up most of these folks, Del and Peggy weren't sure how to handle the rapidly-growing mountain of crises.

When Jimmy Blake called the Moore Headquarters at 5:45 a.m. and was put on hold for 10 minutes, he knew the operation was not moving smoothly. When he finally got through to Zink and learned of the frenzy, he called Gov. Langley.

"Governor, Mary needs an A.P. Hill," Blake reported, referring to the hard-charging Civil War general. Langley understood and quickly dispatched Steven Page to ride to the rescue.

Turnout reports in the suburbs were decent, according to numbers being gathered in the GOP War Room, but the snow was suppressing the rural numbers. Blake ordered another round of 85,000 robo-calls to "soft" Republican households, that is homes with voters who don't vote regularly, but when they do, they vote Republican.

Blake was increasingly concerned that the Moore Get-Out-The-Vote operation was not where it needed to be. In fact, he felt she had a more sophisticated operation in the primary. He and Langley had probably relied too heavily on Damen Maxwell. Can't worry about that now, Blake thought. Just push.

*   *   *

It began at 8:00 a.m. and continued through the day.

"People! This is Senator Beatrice Madison urging you to be proud and be loud! Vote today for my beautiful State Senate colleague, Debra Shane, as our next Governor. Let's make history! Vote today for the whole Democratic ticket! Shane! Calcagno! Karmejian! Cummings! Torres! Today! Democrats, the Party of the People! Our People! The Polls are open until seven! Vote Early! People! This is Senator Beatrice Madison..."

The sound trucks cruised down every street in every African-American neighborhood. No city block was untouched by Senator Madison's sweet street heat.

*   *   *

At 8:20 a.m., Mary and Randall greeted the pollwatchers and election judges as they walked into the dimly-lit church basement where their polling place was located. Two reporters were standing by.

"So, Loretta, how's turnout?" Mary asked the first judge.

"Well, Mary, it's sort of light. It's this cold rain. Let's see. You're the 39th and 40th voters out of, uh, 582 registereds. So a little under ten percent," the judge sweetly replied.

More like six or seven percent, Randall quickly calculated. Not a good sign.

*   *   *

In rural Wells County, an elderly voter emerged from the voting booth and approached the judges' table.

"Sweetie, am I doing this right? I'm trying to cast a write-in vote. Is this right?"

The judges glanced at one another. "Uh, ma'am, we're really not allowed to assist you with that. Here's a manual, if you'd like to look through it."

After a few frustrating minutes of thumbing through the manual, the voter placed her punch card ballot in the envelope and dropped it into the box.

*   *   *

In Jackson City's 6th Ward, the polling place at the huge Kingsbridge Nursing Home was hopping.

The line of elderly voters extended from the cafeteria all the way into the hall. Wheelchair gridlock. By 8:45 a.m., nearly 50% of the 712 registered voters had cast their ballots. To help ease the logjam, helpful poll-watchers from the 6th Ward Democrats were on hand. "Got another visually-impaired voter here," Eddie Czyz called out to the judges, all of whom had been recruited by his late Uncle John years ago.

"Okay. Visually-impaired voter requires assistance. Booth number six," the top judge called back.

"Okay, gramps, lemme help ya with that. Boy, these punch holes sure are tiny," Eddie said.

*   *   *

At 9:00 a.m., the State Elections Board announced the turnout thus far. Downstate counties: 13%. Suburban townships: 18%. Jackson City wards: 26%. The snow in the rural precincts and larger-than-usual numbers in Jackson City did not bode well for the Republicans. Blake ordered more robo-calls.

*   *   *

Labor whiz-kid Timmy Sullivan saw the same numbers as Blake.

Sitting in the Democratic State Party War Room with Niles Flint, Sullivan began calling union leaders across the state, urging them to make yet another round of reminder calls to their members. Some unions, like the Federation of Teachers, had high-tech automated calling systems capable of calling 5,000 members simultaneously. Most others used old-fashioned member-to-member phonebanks set up in union halls amidst card files and cold-cuts. Within an hour, Sullivan had lined up pledges of 40,000 calls to be made to union households before 2:00 p.m.

Flint was feverishly working the phones, too.

He and his Republican counterpart, Jimmy Blake, probably had the best perceptions of this ever-changing kaleidoscope of voter turnout. Weaving together turnout reports from County Chairmen and Ward Committeemen and the State Elections Board, plus some exit polls, plus his own instincts, Flint had a pretty good grasp of what was happening out there. The City seemed fine. Huge—possibly record-setting—turnouts in the white "etnic" and African-American wards. The sound trucks and Black radio buy seemed to be paying off. Thank you, Senator Madison, he smiled. And there were reports of above average turnout in the yuppie and Hispanic areas.

The Downstate counties were puzzling; sort of a mixed bag. Low turnout in both Republican and Democratic counties. Blake and the Republicans had more troops out there, but the snow was killing them, Flint figured. The battleground, at least for Shane, would be in the suburbs.

"You doin' more robos?" Sullivan asked Flint.

"Yeah. Hundred thousand. Soft Dems and independents in the 'burbs."

And so, for the next three or four hours, the pugilistic battle became stealthy, nearly invisible, as automated phonecalls generated from computer centers in other time zones rang in the living rooms and kitchens of "soft" voters across the state.

*　　　　*　　　　*

"So, did you remember to vote today, Mister Sauk County Chairman?" Graciela coyly asked Billy when she finally had a chance to call.

"Oh, shoot! Was that today? I knew I was forgetting something!"

"How's turnout down yonder?"

"Lousy," Billy replied seriously. "Four inches of snow since last night. I had a miserable drive back. How's your dad?"

"Whew. We had a great time at his old sweatshop. He must have been quite a ladies man when he worked there. I think he's going back there after his nap this afternoon to meet up with one of his sweeties. He looks great, though. Lost weight, has good color. And, oh boy, he's getting an earful about you."

"What?" Billy feigned indignance. "From who?"

"Oh, everybody. The kids. My blabbermouth sisters. Even Lupe told him about our little hike up to the bluffs."

"Great. Did you tell him you were going to crash through the Capitol doors like a tidal wave?"

"Naw. We haven't gotten that far. I'll let you explain it to him tonight."

"How's turnout in the ciudad?"

"Great in the Black wards. And Camozzi and Dunne say we're getting huge numbers in their neck of the woods. Hispanic turnout's okay; wish it were more in places other than the 33rd, though. Jimmy's guys are working like men possessed."

"Yeah, possessed with keeping their jobs. Well, whatever it takes. Can you take a little nap yourself?"

"I would if you were here, lover. We could cuddle a little," Graciela flirted.

"Hey. Gotta save your strength for the victory speech. Any thoughts on that?"

"Sam and Lupe are both doing talking points, for both speeches. We'll see what happens."

"Well, just speak from the heart and you'll do just fine, corazon."

"I wish you were here, now," Graciela cooed. "But, I know. You've got to get some turnout or Niles Flint will be mad at you."

"Don't want that. I'll call you later. Te amo," Billy said softly.

*   *   *

Steven Page had arrived to a scene of mayhem in the Moore Headquarters.

Volunteers were waiting in line to get their credentials and worker kits, and a few were grumbling about not getting paid yet. Del Zink looked suicidal. The phones were ringing unanswered. The copier was jammed. A delivery man waited patiently for someone to pay for a dozen pizzas.

First things first, Steven thought. He put the pizzas on his own credit card, informed the paid "volunteers" that they would have to wait until after the polls close to get their cash, recruited two of the senior citizens who were reading newspapers to become receptionists and cleared the copier jam.

"Del, find Peggy and I'll find some cokes and let's have some pizza and sort things out here," Steve quietly ordered. He walked into what had been Damen Maxwell's inner sanctum, to find it totally cleaned out. Drawers empty, maps off the walls. A stack of newspapers in the corner and an overflowing trashcan. It appeared that Maxwell had even swiped the laptop.

"Oh, Steven! Are we glad to see you," Peggy Briscoe exclaimed as she entered what would have been their Election Night War Room.

"Cuz I popped for the pizzas?" Page always liked Briscoe. "What the hell happened here?"

"Well, we had this Mister Know-it-all asshole running things," Zink said, rolling his eyes. "He bailed on us last night. Back to Delaware. Said he was finished here. Had done all he could."

"Guys, let me tell you how badly the Governor feels about this. He realizes he sort of forced Maxwell down Mary's throat. The guy came with great references, had a good track record. Maybe he was just having some personal problems," Page said.

"Yeah. Asshole-itis," Peggy said. "And on top of that, we had this super-volunteer, Amy, and she was sort of in charge of election day worker assignments and she flew the coop, too. So Del and I have been flying in the dark for the past two days. We've never done this kind of thing before..."

"And you guys have both done a superb job under the circumstances," Page said, rolling up his sleeves. "Now we just need to figure out where we're at, where the workers are, what holes we have in target precincts and we can salvage this thing. And, by the way, Blake ordered another 100,000 robo-calls just for Mary, so don't worry. We're gonna be okay."

Just then a volunteer stuck his head through the door. "Hey, do you guys have any more yard signs to give out?"

*   *   *

Snow continued to fall Downstate, along with wintry winds, causing wicked drifting in some places. The sleet and rain that drenched the metropolitan area subsided, however, and the temperature hovered around 33 degrees.

The State Elections Board released the 1:00 p.m. turnout figures. Downstate counties: 23%. Suburban townships: 31%. Jackson City wards: 39%.

*   *   *

The robo-calls being made by the Republicans and the Democrats and the unions weren't the only contacts being made.

Tens of thousands of Christian Marchers had been sent an e-mail on Monday and given a reminder phonecall on Tuesday morning. And this time the message said not only to write in Thelma Barnett's name, but also to legibly write in the name of the office she was seeking: Public Utilities Commission Chairperson.

Rev. BJ Crandall had lawyers, too.

*   *   *

"Hi, Lupe, this is Darlene Dawes, Channel 14. Any monkey business going on out there?"

"Very quiet, Darlene. Maybe too quiet, eh?"

"Boy, during the primary, we had signs ripped down and beatings and electioneering. Maybe General Elections are different?"

"That's true. More macro, maybe. Less of the local tribal warfare passions. Anyhow, if I hear of anything juicy, I'll give you a buzz. And don't forget our victory party tonight. The Hotel Cardenas in the heart of beautiful El Puente."

"Ah. None of these fancy downtown hotel ballrooms for the Torres campaign," Dawes laughed. "So, how's la candidata holding up?"

"Real good. Her dad's in from Mexico and we did some street campaigning with him this morning at his old factory and a subway station, so that's kind of sweet. She's tired, but feeling pretty confident," Lupe said. "Our Downstate drive-around went very well."

"Well, I thought she was superb at Townshend's rally yesterday. Peaking at the right time. I can't help but think of the very first time I met her, in the middle of the burning rubble at River's Edge. What an incredible year for her. Hey, how's the romance? Off the record."

"Well, seems pretty hot to me. Billy's a good guy. We'll see if it lasts."

"They're a cute couple. Okay, keep me informed if you hear anything, Lupe. Good luck tonight."

* * *

One reason there were fewer beatings or other monkey business on the streets was that Wally Mraz, Podesta's Bad Boy, was sidelined during the General Election. And the local tribal passions were slightly reduced. But that didn't mean there weren't a few posters torn down or instances of minor electioneering. And the boys in the 6th Ward and other wards like it were quietly running up unprecedented numbers in the nursing homes. "Voter assistance", they called it.

The only arrest was made in tiny Grove County, where two election judges began slapping one another over a dispute regarding write-ins.

* * *

"Congressman Prentice on the line for Mary Moore," the official sounding operator intoned. And of course, when Mary picked up the line,

Prentice was not there. But, when he finally got connected, he did not sound like a happy camper.

"Mary, I heard Steven Page has ridden to the rescue. Sorry to hear about your former Campaign Manager."

Boy, he cuts right to the chase, Mary thought. "Well, you know this business better than I, Congressman. Ups and downs. We've had a rough couple of days here, but I'm sure Steven will salvage things. He's very methodical. How's it looking out there?"

"Not good, I'm afraid. The weather is not helping us. The sun is shining brightly on Jackson City, though."

Well, Mary thought, maybe we should have allocated more time and money there. Maxwell made the right call on that one.

"Congressman, we still have a few hours. There are plenty of these robo-calls being made and I have confidence in my fellow suburban township committeepersons. The vote will come out heavily when our people get home from work. All of those commuters will go right from the train stations to their polling places. That's how it works in the suburban townships. Don't you fret, now," she gently assured him.

"Ah, your words are just the tonic I needed. Well, let's keep in touch here and I'll see you at the victory party. You've been running a great race, Mary. A great race. You were masterful during the flyaround."

"Thanks, Congressman, you too. And get your broom ready; we're going to have a clean sweep tonight!"

After hanging up, Mary thought how differently Prentice operated than Langley. Maybe Langley was just more seasoned. Prentice was certainly a smooth operator, but it was Washington D.C. Beltway smooth. Maybe Langley was just a better listener, more of a student of the human condition. That's really where the art of politics comes in, she thought. It's not just having the right sound-bites or being able to rattle off your three-point plan on this or that. It's being able to look people in the eye and hear their concern, genuinely hear their story, connect. It's all about connecting, she thought, the same as great art.

She glanced at the clock. 3:00 p.m. She agreed to meet Karen Hogan at the main commuter train station at 4:00 p.m. for one last push. She wished Calvin were here to experience this.

*   *   *

If the art of politics is the ability to listen and connect, the science of politics is the ability to know where your votes are and turn them out. And nobody did it better than the old-timers in Jackson City.

More than 85% turnout was expected in wards run by Dunne, Camozzi, Juarez, Harry Griffin, Izzy Feldman and Sherm Stumpf. In tribute to the fallen hero, John Czyz' 6th Ward was looking at 90%. Who knows? Maybe they could even exceed 100%? It's just science. Methods.

In the "etnic" wards, the city-employed precinct captains and their army of lieutenants knew every voter in every household. They had visited them at least once during the prior week with a sample ballot and an absentee ballot application, along with a casual mention of the time they got that alley light installed or when they manufactured that jury duty excuse. And if the precinct captain noticed you hadn't voted by Noon, another visit was paid. Then phone calls. Then they would camp out on your front porch until you relented. Baby-sitting? A ride to the polls? No problem!

That's science. Pure.

*   *   *

"People! This is Senator Beatrice Madison urging you to be proud and be loud! Vote today for my beautiful State Senate colleague, Debra Shane, as our next Governor. Let's make history! Vote today for the whole Democratic ticket! Shane! Calcagno! Karmejian! Cummings! Torres! Today! Democrats, the Party of the People! Our People! The Polls are open until seven! Vote Early! People! This is Senator Beatrice Madison…"

*   *   *

Steven Page had turned chaos into order.

The holes in Moore's target precincts had been plugged, every volunteer had received their assignment, instructions and pollwatcher credentials, and a makeshift War Room was established. He was in constant touch with Jimmy Blake, Gretchen Hanson and others in the Republican Party's coordinated campaign War Room, and knew where the turnout was flat.

He didn't have too many volunteers to spare, that was for sure. But the fact that Blake had ordered another 100,000 robo-calls eased his concerns. And he was glad that Mary was off to do the commuter train station with Karen Hogan. The two had become friends on the campaign trail, and, frankly, Hogan's connections in Jackson City couldn't hurt. That was a good location for Mary to close. Every remaining volunteer and what few posters were left in the Headquarters were dispatched to the commuter station. One last blast of heat.

Page thought about that day, more than one year ago, when he and Blake and Moore sat in the Governor's office, discussing Calvin Reynolds' accident. Going through Calvin's stuff, the nail files, the utility donor list that Mary acted so innocent about. Was she really that naïve? Well, she certainly blossomed in the past few months, and, win-or-lose, would be a player far beyond today's tally, Page thought.

The 4:30 p.m. turnout figures released by the State Elections Board showed modest gains by the suburbs, but the snowstorm Downstate was taking its toll on the voice of the people: Downstate counties: 39%. Suburban townships: 51%. Jackson City wards: 61%. Page knew the conventional wisdom held that suburban commuters often vote in the final hour. He hoped conventional wisdom would prove true today.

*   *   *

One last subway station for Torres. Ald. Petacque had suggested the busiest station in downtown Jackson City, just beneath the Civic Center, site of Graciela's roof-raising yesterday. For the afternoon rush, this was the one, Petacque urged.

So Graciela, her dad, Petacque and his crew (including the leather-lunged Bijou), and Liz Chinn took one final walk down the grungy, gum-bespeckled stairs.

Once again Ernesto, Sr., (who indeed had lined up a hot date for the victory party with one of his old co-workers) was mystified by the spectacle. The waving signs, the chanting, the response to his daughter, her ability to greet so many people and shake so many hands. Her right hand was covered with bruises and every nail was broken, so, at Petacque's suggestion, she started using a two-hand style.

Bijou couldn't think of anything that rhymed with "Graciela" or "Torres", so he stuck with "Torres is your candidate…Vote today and don't be late!" It was a stretch, but seemed to work. With Petacque and Chinn there, they had an effective rainbow thing going, too. Shawn would catch the eyes of the African-American commuters and steer them to Graciela, while Liz would do the same with Asian-Americans.

Graciela was amazed at how many commuters told her they had already voted today…for her! Some said they had been in the crowd at the rally yesterday and loved her speech. A few commented on her TV or radio spots and one fellow said he didn't like the fact that Mary Moore had a backyard swimming pool. "Well, don't forget to vote then," Torres cheerfully shouted as another subway creaked into the station. A TV crew from Channel 8 arrived.

Petacque was right, she thought, this station is incredible. She kept shaking hands and Bijou kept chanting and the signs kept waving and the crowds just kept on coming and the levels of heat and noise seemed to increase. Until Petacque tapped her on the shoulder and held up his wrist. His wristwatch said it all. 7:00 p.m. Graciela hugged Petacque, then her dad, then everyone in the entourage and even a few friendly subway riders. The polls are closed.

It's over.

* * *

Mary and Karen Hogan had also gotten terrific responses at the commuter train station just a few blocks from where Graciela's subway heat
was happening.

In more of a hurry than subway commuters, many of the workers dashing for their scheduled trains took a few seconds to stop and offer encouraging words to Mary and Karen. The crowds at the commuter station had
tapered off, though, and by 6:30, Moore and Hogan congratulated one
another, hugged and parted ways. Mary was in her car gridlocked in
downtown Jackson City traffic with another faceless, nameless volunteer
driver when the clock struck 7:00. The polls are closed, she realized.

It's over.

*   *   *

As in the primary, each campaign's War Room enjoyed a weird calm
before the storm.

Since Miller was out in Sauk County and Juarez was over in his 33rd
Ward office, Sandra Siquieros and Sam Roth were staffing the Torres War
Room, and would be soon joined by Chinn and Zarate. They both quietly
sat before computers, looking at turnout projections as well as the projections of what they figured they needed, their so-called "50+1 plan". Sam
ate an apple. Neither spoke.

The hastily-established Moore War Room consisted of a few desks, two
TV's, three computers and six phones, one of which would be a dedicated
direct line to the State Republican Party's War Room. Page, Zink and
Briscoe would staff the operation. More pizza was ordered and Page
offered to pay for a beer-run.

But, it was neither quiet nor calm in the thousands of polling places
across the state, as election judges carefully followed the procedures
spelled out in the judge's manual. By 7:10 p.m., 9,800 large metal boxes
were opened, and the will of the people spilled out onto tables in school
gyms, barber shops and firehouses across the state.

*   *   *

The first sign of trouble came in the rolling hills of Ellsworth County. Precinct 6.

Almost as soon as the first ballots spilled from the box and the election judges sorted out those ballot envelopes with write-ins scrawled across the front, the Republican pollwatcher began challenging.

"This ballot envelope has a candidate's name written in, but is lacking the office that candidate seeks," the pollwatcher announced. "I therefore challenge it." The ballot was put aside.

During the next hour, the same exchange occurred hundreds of times (9,588 times, to be exact) across the state, mostly in rural precincts. The Bible Zone. The Thelma Precincts.

*   *   *

The first precinct to be officially reported to the State Elections Board was Jackson City 3ʳᵈ Ward, Precinct 31. Once again, Seamus Dunne was the first in. The precinct, mostly working-class Irish families and some Puerto Rican, enjoyed 82% turnout. The numbers were posted on the State Elections Board website.

State Public Utilities Commission Chairperson
Precincts reporting: 1
Votes cast: 562
Updated: 07:58 p.m.

Mary Moore (R)	70	*(12%)*
Graciela Perez Torres (D)	487	*(87%)*
Other/none	5	*(1%)*

"Yow! Siquieros! Check it out!" Roth yelled. "Crazy old Seamus is a man of few words, but great deeds."

Sandra smiled. If the rest of Jackson City holds for us in the 80's, we can get the bubbly out real soon.

*   *   *

The challenges to the Thelma Barnett write-in effort had slowed down the counts in hundreds of Downstate precincts. Election judges, who had been up since before dawn, were cranky. Republican pollwatchers, who had been given this assignment only yesterday, were unsure of the rules themselves. And Democratic pollwatchers didn't know exactly what was happening, but were grinning. States' attorneys and election lawyers were hastily dispatched to problem precincts, often a serious drive through snow-drifted rural roads from the county seat.

Could be a long night in the Bible Zone.

*   *   *

Exit polls are not delayed by write-ins or slow counts, and, since media organizations pay good money to conduct them, projected results from exit polls are touted early in the night, sometimes eclipsing the need for a campaign War Room.

That was the case in the Secretary of State's contest. While only one precinct had officially reported (which was won handily by Bill Karmejian), Channel 14 gave the race to incumbent Richard Dobbs at 8:03 p.m. And just 20 minutes later, the first shocker of the night was projected by Channel 12, when it gave the Attorney General's race to challenger Philip Driscoll over incumbent Lou Calcagno.

Republicans began to think sweep. The coordinated campaign War Room was sky-high, despite these projected victories coming from exit polls rather than real vote counts. Nevertheless, Gov. Langley put in congratulatory calls to both Dobbs and Driscoll. Karmejian issued a concession statement; Calcagno preferred to wait.

By 8:45 p.m., the suburban numbers were starting to roll in, and the early leads enjoyed by Shane, Cummings and Torres began to melt. It was just so difficult to track the data that poured in from different sources: reporters, volunteers who had just closed their precinct, local party leaders, local election boards, the State Board. The jigsaw puzzle in time and space. Getting a handle on oatmeal. At one point, Shane was at 71% and then, minutes later, was at 44%. The Torres numbers were experiencing similar swings, though she had never dropped below 54%.

The mood in the Moore War Room began to improve, though, when the State Elections Board updated their website at 9:00 p.m.

State Public Utilities Commission Chairperson
Precincts reporting: 1,438
Votes cast: 578,688
Updated: 08:57 p.m.

Mary Moore (R)	*272,080*	*(47%)*
Graciela Perez Torres (D)	*300,901*	*(52%)*
Other/none	*5,707*	*(1%)*

Both the Moore and Torres War Rooms were feverishly trying to plug what numbers they had into their computer spreadsheets to compare with the projections of their respective 50+1 plans. The State Board numbers were useful and they were large, but where were they coming from? Both War Rooms were flying in the dark and could only assume most numbers represented Jackson City and the suburbs.

*　　　　*　　　　*

"How's it lookin' up there?" Miller said, still miles away in his Sauk County Democratic Headquarters.

"Big numbers in the City. Black Wards are huge, like 70 percent turnout and 90 percent for us. Same with the white ethnics. No real handle on the burbs or Downstate," Sam reported. "What's happening out there?"

"Well, here in tiny Sauk County, we've got about 52 percent turnout, and in the 21 precincts reporting so far, we got Torres up with…68 percent!"

"Hey hey! The rurals are comin' out for Torres! With a little help from her sweetie."

"Seriously, though, Sam. I hear the Thelma write-in thing has got some of my rural brethren in a snit. Lots of challenges. Lots of grief. Hopefully it doesn't keep us up all night," Billy said. "How's the candidate?"

"She ended strong in the Civic Center subway station with Petacque and her dad. She's at dinner now with la familia, then they're headed to the suite at the Hotel Cardenas."

"Okay, Roth. Helluva job. Keep me posted."

*   *   *

Jimmy Blake and Gretchen Hanson had a team of computer operators and a massive phonebank in the Republican coordinated campaign War Room. No one in the state—not the media, not the State Elections Board, not Niles Flint—no one had a better way of processing the flood of information. With his extensive network of ground troops, Blake knew of Driscoll's upset victory even before Channel 12.

The suburban numbers were really starting to flow in, and Blake thought sweep for awhile. But Shane, Cummings and even Torres were doing slightly better in the Downstate precincts than he had projected. And only Hogan was holding her own against his projections for Jackson City; Moore and Prentice were both in trouble, both single-digits in some African-American wards. And this stupid Thelma write-in thing was really slowing down the count in what should be strong Republican precincts. I hate uncertainty, Blake thought.

*   *   *

The Wells County States' Attorney—a Democrat—issued her order at 9:20 p.m.

The challenged write-in ballots shall be counted for all races in Wells County precincts. Further, if a voter has punched "write-in" on the punchcard under the Public Utilities Commission Chairperson list of candidates, but neglected to write the specific office their write-in candidate seeks, that voter's intent is clear, and that write-in shall be deemed valid.

Other States' Attorneys began to issue similar orders and the counting proceeded.

*   *   *

The 10:00 p.m. news broadcasts all reported on Driscoll's stunning upset of Calcagno, whose concession speech was aired live at 10:10 on every station. Then, Dobbs gave a gracious speech, vowing four more years of efficient drivers' license service. Most stations then cut to Driscoll's victory party, which resembled the winning side of a revolution, which is quite possibly what it was.

Several stations reported on the delayed counts due to the Barnett write-in effort and every media outlet continued to characterize the races for Governor, State Treasurer and PUC Chair as too close to call.

Every War Room was now operating at insanity level, juggling calls from their ground troops, the media and anxious candidates, while trying to crunch what numbers they had as TV's and radios blared.

Debra Shane put a call into both Tom Cummings and Graciela Torres, partly to troll for data and partly to encourage them to hang in there. Gov. Langley did likewise with Hogan and Moore.

At 11:00 p.m. the State Board updated is website again. It showed Prentice, Torres and Hogan with tiny leads. The Downstate numbers were now flooding in.

*   *   *

"Steven, where are we at?" Mary was cool and collected.

"We think that once all of these Downstate precincts are in we'll be okay. The City was a toughie; you got crunched big-time. And our suburban numbers could have been a little better. I think a few of the state legislative races in the 'burbs boosted Dem turnout some," Page succinctly reported.

"What about this Barnett write-in thing?"

"We're figuring she may pick up one or two percent, tops. And then, if it's close, we could challenge. The problem is, of course, that the votes have already been cast and they probably took much more from you than from Torres. Nothing we can do about that now."

Mary was silent.

"So, keep your powder dry. We're in constant touch with Blake, and he's got the best system in the state. Hang in there. Don't worry."

"Okay. Thanks for everything, Steven. You're a gem," Mary said.

*   *   *

The Downstate precincts were now reporting quickly. At 11:20 p.m., the Associated Press called the State Treasurer's race for Karen Hogan, with a 52% to 48% margin over Tom Cummings. The young Kennedy looka-like called Hogan to concede and then addressed a boisterous crowd in the snowy Hubbs village square. Hogan's extra efforts in Jackson City had clearly paid off.

The State Elections Board posted new numbers at 11:30 p.m. showing Shane with a 9,100-vote margin with fewer than 200 precincts out. The Torres edge was about twice that.

State Public Utilities Commission Chairperson
Precincts reporting: 9,613
Votes cast: 3,066,852
Updated: 11:27 p.m.

Mary Moore (R)	*1,504,751*	*(49%)*
Graciela Perez Torres (D)	*1,531,769*	*(50%)*
Other/none	*30,332*	*(1%)*

*   *   *

The Torres War Room was now packed like a sardine can. Sandra Siquieros, Lupe Zarate and Liz Chinn were all handling media calls, sometimes giving statements and sometimes swapping data. Jimmy Juarez, Shawn Petacque and Dan Clark were working the phones with tribal chietains. Sam Roth and Amy Harris (fresh from her espionage assignment) pecked at the computers. Billy Miller was driving in from Sauk County, but was working the Downstate County Chairmen from his pickup truck. The outer office of the Headquarters was a mob scene, especially after Graciela and her family showed up.

"It all depends on where these last 200 or so precincts are, and we just don't know," Sandra was telling one reporter. "The margin is, what, less than a hundred votes per precinct. If those are mostly high-turnout Republican precincts, we're in trouble."

*　　　*　　　*

Peggy Briscoe's spin over at Moore Headquarters was almost identical, though a mirror image. "Sure, we can make up that difference. We believe most of the City precincts are in, and the Downstate precincts—especially those Republican precincts where the Barnett write-in thing was going on—those probably comprise the lion's share of those still outstanding," she told one reporter. "Sure, we can make it up. Absolutely."

Their Headquarters was also jammed with supporters, although many had gone to the LaSalle Hotel for Hogan's victory speech. Mary put a congratulatory call in to Karen, but the din was too great at Hogan's place for any conversation. She'll be a great State Treasurer, Mary thought. She knows the art of connecting with people.

*　　　*　　　*

Precinct reports dribbled in, but at too slow a pace to discern any patterns. Governor Langley, meanwhile, had strolled over to the Republican coordinated campaign War Room. Tonight would be his final night at the helm, and he needed to be hands-on, especially if it was a sweep, what with Dobbs, Driscoll and Hogan already in. Three for three. Amazing. He was especially happy for Karen Hogan, and thought back to that night in the Governor's Mansion "Dungeon" when her name was first floated as a statewide candidate. What a terrific future for her, he surmised.

When he walked in, though, the look on Blake's face spoke volumes.

"Prentice is toast."

"Can't make it up? Where are those last 200 precincts?"

"Well, our count is more like 120 precincts, and Shane's lead is at twelve or thirteen thou," Blake said, gazing at the maps on the wall. "And way too many of those are in the City. I think Camozzi's holdin' back a couple dozen precincts. Big precincts."

"Damn. So it's over for Mary, too?"

Blake stared at his computer. "Unless she cut some weird deal with Camozzi."

*   *   *

"Hey, shut up!" Jimmy Juarez bellowed. "Would everybody just goddamn! Shut! Up!"

The Torres War Room quieted. Even the outer office festivities stopped.

"Ya got what now, Mario?" he spoke into a tiny cell phone.

"Camozzi?" Graciela whispered to Sandra, who nodded her head.

Juarez dramatically hung up the phone, a grave look on his craggy brown face. He pulled a foot-long cigar from his jacket.

"Well?" Sandra asked, breaking the silence.

"Mario's been holdin' back. He got 25 precincts not reported. A fifty-two hunnert vote margin. She can't catch us. We're in."

Juarez cracked up laughing and hugged Graciela, who screamed triumphantly. The place went crazy, with dozens of volunteer shrieking and applauding. "Does that mean you won, hija? You won?" her father asked, tears flowing. 'Berto and Raisa did a victory dance they had created for the occasion. Sam Roth stood on a desk and sprayed a bottle of champagne. Juarez passed out cigars. Associated Press called it for Torres ten minutes later.

* * *

Mary took it like a trooper. She first found out from Gov. Langley, which she thought was appropriate, as he was the one who put her in the position in the first place. The Associated Press reporter called a few minutes later.

Mary gathered the staff and supporters in her Headquarters, and told them it was over. Peggy and Del and others were crying. Steven Page offered a brief speech on what a superb public servant and candidate she was, and that she can be proud.

Mary then went into the tiny War Room, and with only her husband and son present, called the Torres Headquarters. She could hear the victory celebration already underway, but after being on hold for a few minutes, heard Graciela say, "Hello, Chairperson Moore?"

"Well, let me be the first to call you Chairperson Torres. Congratulations, Graciela, you ran a spirited race. I know you'll do just fine."

"Mary, you are so kind to call me. You are a very classy person, and a great public servant, and I am just so awed at this moment."

"Well, go and meet with your supporters, and get some rest and when you're ready, let me buy you lunch and we'll chat about the transition, okay?"

"Thank you so much, Mary, thank you."

Moore hung up and turned to Randall. "Well, that's that. Let's go address the crowd at the Hotel."

* * *

Pandemonium reigned at Torres Headquarters. Reporters were calling for comment. Debra Shane, Tom Cummings, Mayor Townshend and Seamus Dunne called. Even Paul Podesta and Gov. Langley called. Graciela felt like she was bouncing from one congratulatory call to another. "I need to talk to Billy," she whispered into Lupe's ear. Lupe smiled and steered Graciela into a supply room and shut the door. "Use my cell phone, Madame Chairperson," Lupe grinned, "And I'll stand guard outside. A girl needs a little privacy now and then."

As she dialed Billy's car phone, she was sorry he wasn't with her at this very moment, this most incredible moment that he played such a crucial role in, politically, lyrically, romantically.

"Hey, Loverboy," she said when he answered, barely able to contain herself. "This is the tidal wave crashing through the Capitol!"

"Don't tell me. Are you sure? Yee-hah!" Billy shouted and began honking the horn on his old pickup. "Yee-hah!"

"Yep. Associated Press called it and Moore just conceded and we had a very nice chat. Why aren't you here, right now? I need you."

"I'm just 25 miles away. Had to count all those Sauk County precincts. That's what put you over the top, ya know," Billy laughed. "Yee-hah!"

"Well, Camozzi may have some dispute with that, but I'll tell you everything when I see you. I love you so much. Hurry up!"

"Okay. Hey, I just heard on the radio that AP called it for Shane. Whew. What a crazy business, eh? Lots of streams and creeks."

"Yep. Just need to know how to navigate. Meet us at the party. Hotel Cardenas. Hurry!"

*   *   *

"The people have spoken. A little while ago, I called Graciela Torres and offered my very sincere congratulations on her victory. I offered to buy her lunch and chat about the transition. The Public Utilities Commission is a very complicated agency with a full agenda, so I vowed to do everything possible to facilitate an orderly transition."

Mary was addressing a near-empty ballroom. The Hogan victory party had come and gone, and the news of Prentice's defeat had sent most supporters home. But she was addressing the folks in their living rooms around the state as six TV cameras rolled.

"I want to thank Governor Langley for his confidence and inspiration. He taught me the art of politics, the value of making a connection with people. I want to thank my wonderful staff and all my campaign volunteers. What a team. I want to thank my mentor, the late Calvin Reynolds who taught me more than I can possibly express right now.

"I want to thank the one-and-a-half million voters who showed their confidence in me today. And, finally, let me thank my husband Randall and my son Tony and the rest of my family who have put up with so much out of consideration for my career."

Mary paused, finally realizing it really was over.

"The Public Utilities Commission has provided me with an opportunity to serve the public for many years. That public trust is something I value, cherish. I only hope I have lived up to that public trust. Thank you and God bless."

There was a smattering of applause from the 100 or so people in the room and then the TV lights abruptly—almost cruelly—shut off.

And with that, the public career of Mary Moore was over.

*   *   *

If the Phil Driscoll victory party seemed like an ideological revolution, the Torres party seemed like a genuine people's revolution.

Fireworks and honking horns disrupted the night in El Puente. No one from the neighborhood had ever achieved this kind of political victory. It was a triumph not just for this one politician, but for everyone whose ancestors had crossed the Rio Grande or the Gulf of Mexico or the Caribbean to end up here. It was, for many residents of El Puente, the first night they felt a genuine pride in their citizenship.

As the noisy caravan of cars, trucks and bicycles moved through the streets to the Hotel Cardenas, Graciela continued to accept congratulatory calls from various public figures. But suddenly Jimmy Juarez pulled her out onto the flatbed of one of the pickup trucks and she began waving to the hundreds of people gathering on the curbs. Some weren't even sure what was happening, what was all this commotion? But the word quickly spread and the chanting of "Torres! Torres!" echoed through the night.

A line of TV trucks with their "eyes in the sky" towers were parked in front of the Cardenas, a once-ornate hotel that had seen better days. There hadn't been this many TV crews in El Puente since River's Edge, Graciela thought, scanning the crowd for Mariano Vargas. He should be with me now, too, she thought, as she looked for Billy's pickup.

Channel 14's Darlene Dawes rushed up to her. "I am so happy for you. This is great. We want to go live in five minutes, if that works for you."

"Fine. We'll do it," Graciela said, as a mob of supporters practically lifted her off her feet and escorted her into the old ballroom. Ten TV crews had been waiting patiently for several hours. Their producers all told Lupe they wanted Graciela's speech fairly quickly on live TV, and then Prentice would concede and then Shane would deliver her victory speech to wrap up Election Night.

The chanting continued as Graciela walked onto the stage with her father, her children and her sisters. It took a few minutes to calm down the crowd, but when the TV lights went on and Darlene Dawes gave her a panicky gesture to move it along, Graciela began her speech.

"More than one year ago, just a few blocks from this hotel, the tragedy at River's Edge shook our lives. Some people lost their loved ones or their homes. Some people lost their jobs or their innocence. I was fortunate, though. The tragedy helped me understand how fragile and precious this life is, and how important government and agencies like the Public Utilities Commission are."

The crowd was hushed.

"So I dedicated the past year of my life to the memory of those who suffered because of River's Edge, campaigning all over this great state, telling people how important it is to get involved. How important government is in protecting us. And that message, apparently, has gotten through to people."

She saw Billy walk in the back of the room and smiled.

"And today those people have spoken!"

Like a floodgate, the crowd erupted and the chanting re-ignited. Graciela motioned for the crowd to calm down again.

"I received a very gracious call just a few minutes ago from my opponent, Mary Moore. She is very classy and she offered her congratulations and her gracious help in an orderly transition…to the Torres Administration!"

The crowd was now banging fists on chairs and feet on the floor. The ancient crystal chandelier seemed to quiver.

"So, let me thank all of you who were out there on those cold and wet streets today and all of my wonderful volunteers and generous donors and my great campaign team, Sandra Siquieros and Lupe Zarate and Sam Roth and Mariano Vargas and Liz Chinn, and my mentor Jimmy Juarez…"

The crowd went especially crazy at the mention of Jimmy Juarez.

"And let me especially thank my great family, my father, Ernesto, who came all the way from Mexico to be here today, and my crazy hermanas, Dolores y Soledad, and my beautiful, wonderful kids, Roberto Junior and Raisa." Roberto shyly hugged his mom as Raisa waved.

"…And someone who has taught me so much about politics and rivers and our complicated state, mi corazon, Billy Miller!"

The crowd was now weeping and laughing and roaring lustily for Graciela's corazon and her family and her victory and their victory and la raza and la lucha and the People, Yes! The balloon drop began.

"And congratulations to my good friend Debra Shane, who is our new Governor! Thank you! Everybody party!" Graciela yelled, and it was over. The crowd was as insanely jubilant as a crowd can be, the TV lights shut off, the mariachi band struck up *La Negra* and Billy bounded onto the stage. Graciela hugged him and he whispered, "You are my river."

*   *   *

Chapter Seven

The Afterward: Ebb and Flow

"Is that what you mean? That the river is everywhere at the same time, at the source and at the mouth, at the waterfall and at the ferry, at the current, in the ocean and in the mountains, everywhere, and that the present only exists for it, not the shadow of the past, nor the shadow of the future?"

-Herman Hesse *("Siddhartha")*

On January 20, Graciela Torres was sworn in as the first Hispanic statewide elected official. As the only Democrats to hold statewide office, Torres and Governor Debra Shane quickly built upon the strong alliance and friendship they developed on the campaign trail.

Mary Moore insisted on a cordial and cooperative transition of power to the Torres Administration. She agreed to put Lupe Zarate and Sam Roth on her PUC payroll during the interregnum to assist with that goal. In exchange, Torres agreed to avoid wholesale layoffs of Moore's staff (despite Jimmy Juarez' misgivings) and promoted Del Zink to Deputy Commissioner for Policy. Zink played a crucial role in the transition, enabling the Torres Administration to get off to a running start.

Moore continued as Zane Township Republican Committeewoman, went on to a lucrative job in a management consulting firm and retired to Tucson with Randall three years later. Her son, Tony, fully recovered from his attack and moved to Boston for grad school.

Sen. Paul Podesta was embittered by the campaign. He served out the final two years in his State Senate term, but had lost his zeal for war. He continued as Chairman of the Senate Public Works & Utilities Committee, but the wind had been knocked from his sails. He began drinking heavily and left party politics. He and Emily moved permanently to their Florida vacation home, where he fished daily and was elected Secretary of the condo board.

Ald. Butchie Kaminski was more embittered about being passed over for Boss Chizz' Committeeman's job than losing the PUC race. He declined to seek re-election to the City Council and endorsed aide Mike Kula, who narrowly won a four-way civil war. Butchie stayed on the Jackson City Department of Electricity payroll, until his freakish death soon after in a bleacher collapse at the hockey stadium.

Royce Blasingame went back to Steel & Coil, but was so energized by the experience that he immediately began planning a Congressional race. He was still a little embarrassed by the negative tone of his PUC campaign and vowed to put his next candidacy on a higher ground. He placed ProAction on retainer to help build institutional support and keep his name in the news. Mayor Townshend appointed him to the Jackson City Humanities Council.

Thelma Barnett didn't miss a beat after the election, despite her mental breakdown and levitation. She continued her crusade for school prayer and even testified before a Congressional Subcommittee on the subject. She continued to assist Reverend B.J. Crandall with his plans for the upcoming U.S. Senate race.

Dan Clark went back to teaching at Flagstaff Community College and wrote a book (never published) about the campaign experience. He and Liz Chinn began dating shortly after the General Election and later married. Chinn was hired as Government Affairs Director in the Torres administration.

Ald. Shawn Petacque became the state's best-known African-American public official as a result of the PUC race, and he began planning for another statewide race, possibly another shot at PUC Chair if Torres moved on in four years. He turned down an offer to work with the Shane Administration, as it would require heavy commuting between the Capital and Jackson City, opting instead to stay close to home with his family and further consolidate his power within the African-American community.

Graciela Torres' romance with Billy Miller continued to blossom and her name was already being floated as a candidate for U.S. Senate.

*   *   *

"O Captain! my Captain! our fearful trip is done!
The ship has weathered every rack, the prize we sought is won…"

-Walt Whitman *("O Captain! My Captain!")*

-fin-

About the Author

Born in 1952, Claude Walker has spent a lifetime in the rough-and-tumble of Illinois politics.

Walker has served as a senior campaign advisor to U.S. Senator Carol Moseley-Braun, Washington State Insurance Commissioner Deborah Senn and Illinois State Treasurer Pat Quinn. He also worked on the campaigns of U.S. Sen. Paul Simon and Chicago Mayor Harold Washington.

A fourth-generation "pol", Walker has done it all, from running successful statewide political campaigns to running Election Day votes in his Chicago precinct. A veteran of more than 45 campaigns and a dozen election night war rooms, Walker has been a grassroots organizer, spin doctor, dirt-digger, body-person, strategist, campaign spy, street heat maestro, advance man, direct mail specialist, legislative candidate, lobbyist, actor in TV campaign ads and Lincoln impersonator.

Walker was Special Assistant to the Illinois State Treasurer, lobbyist for the Citizens Utility Board ("CUB"—one of the nation's largest consumer groups) and twice-elected State Chairman of Common Cause-Illinois. A graduate of Loyola University of Chicago, Walker has worked in municipal, county and state government.

Walker has published essays on Asian baseball and wandering in Mexico. He and his wife, Ngoan Lê, live in Chicago with their fox terrier, Perro.